JAN 16

SKINNER
LUCE

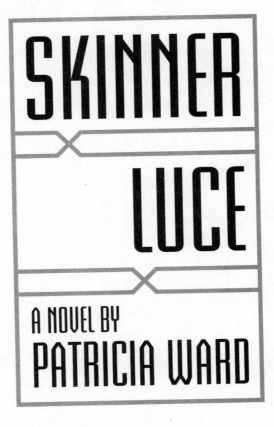

SKINNER LUCE

A NOVEL BY PATRICIA WARD

Talos Press
New York

Talos Press books may be purchased in bulk at special discounts for sales promotion, corporate gifts, fund-raising, or educational purposes. Special editions can also be created to specifications. For details, contact the Special Sales Department, Talos Press, 307 West 36th Street, 11th Floor, New York, NY 10018 or info@skyhorsepublishing.com.

Talos Press® is a registered trademark of Skyhorse Publishing, Inc. ®, a Delaware corporation.

Visit our website at www.talospress.com.

10 9 8 7 6 5 4 3 2 1

Library of Congress Control Number: 2015937875

Cover illustration by Anna Dittmann
Jacket design by Claudia Noble

Print ISBN: 978-1-940456-35-5
Ebook ISBN: 978-1-940456-46-1

Printed in the United States of America

for Tamer

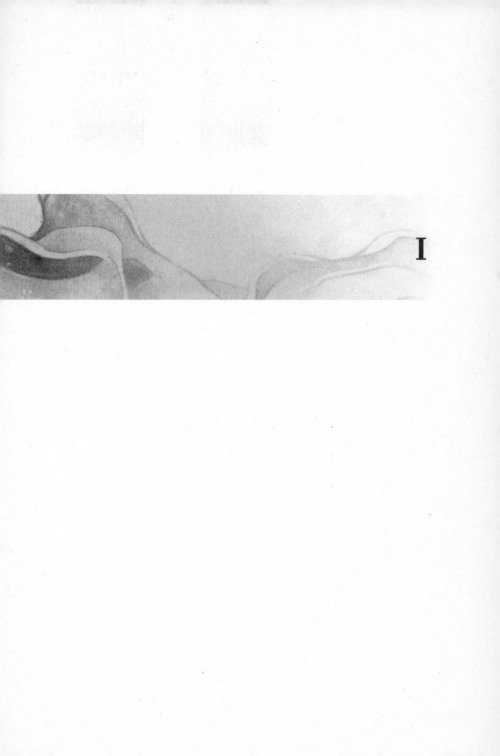

I

BERNIE'S SPENT SO MANY years in that wooden chair ruling his shit little kingdom, the carpet's worn threadbare from the wheels rolling back and forth. He burps, and Lucy catches his eye, delivers disgust in her stare. He lets out a theatrical sigh. His sausage fingers deal another hand of solitaire. The cards are old and stained and look soggy. The barred window over his desk gives onto the main hallway, where Bernie's expended the effort to set up a crappy plastic Christmas tree with blinking lights, as if he's actually vested in running this dump. To the right of Bernie's window hang all the keys to Hotel Paradise. About half the keys are gone, due to the upcoming holidays, everyone with a little extra to spend and a need for philandering.

The stroller is parked in the corner with the brakes on. Lucy's stashed her small suitcase in the storage basket below the seat, that way she doesn't have to push one and pull the other at the same time. The arrival is about eleven or twelve. He's in an adult diaper and a threadbare Spiderman tee shirt that clings to his sweaty skin, his temperature still near boiling point. His mouth hangs slack, drooling. He was walloped into la-la land the instant he came into this world, and the only sign of life is in the crazy blue of his half-open eyes. Even in their drugged state they're startling against the white freckled skin and dripping black hair.

He shifts abruptly, one skinny arm twitching. Lucy feels dread looking at the knobby knees poking the blanket, the rigid little fingers. She can practically feel the bruises already. This one looks really scrawny and weak, though, a thin, bony lump in the too-small stroller.

She looks away. Bernie shakes his head in resignation. For all his grossness, he's got a vat of pity and sorrow inside him; don't they all. He says, "Nothing you can do, Lucy."

She stares him down, sickened by the powerlessness they share. He shrugs, goes back to his card game. The pipes clank deep in the basement, and the vent gushes lukewarm air into the room, heating up the odors of Bernie's crap dinner of chicken, potato chips and beer, and of his sagging sweating body, and underneath it all pot smoke and vomit, pervasive throughout the hotel.

"He better show up soon," Bernie warns.

Lucy lifts an eyebrow at this. "Or what?"

"I can distribute to anyone I please," Bernie whines, but he's already retreating from his dumb remark. He gathers up the cards and shuffles, sighing with impatience, as if what, as if he has better things to do? This is it, this is his life, ever since the Gate handed down notice that he'd be this district's overseer. He'll be processing arrivals and mediating petty bunk conflicts till he drops dead.

Bernie shifts his bulk, settles deeper into the chair. Lucy imagines him fusing with it, sitting there getting fatter and fatter like some kind of Jabba the Hut, his thick lips splattering chip crumbs all over his greasy cards. His letting himself go like this is deliberate, it proclaims his freedom as an overseer: no regular serv could ever get away with it. She can't stand looking at him, but she can't stop, either. It's like she needs the hate she feels and pours all over him in this dead silence. She drags her eyes away. On the wall over the antediluvian plaid couch hangs a poster of a snowy, mountainous vista, Switzerland, maybe. When he's alone shooting up, Lucy supposes, Bernie sits and stares at that scene, dreaming himself out of his existence here. It's the number one dream of every serv, to get the hell away.

Whatever. No one ever does. Servs get tagged with a titanium anklet on arrival, GPS encoded, setting off alarms at the slightest damage. Even if you get around that obstacle, you still have to watch over your shoulder the rest of your life. Snitches get paid with reduced Services, coveted above all else in this world: hence the old joke about the serv who got away, but was so dumb he snitched on himself.

The reality is there's hardly a corner on earth a serv can escape to, except maybe the deep hot heart of the Amazon jungle or some sweltering African or Indian village. But that kind of heat's as intolerable to servs as it is to the Nafikh. You might as well just kill yourself.

Barring that, the only way to get out of Service is to make quota, then you're wiped off the roster. Lucy could make her 303 quota in about eight years: she's down to 127 remaining, putting her survival rate at over 50%. She'll be thirty-seven if she makes it out, which used to feel like light years away. Maybe she's the one moving to Switzerland, she fantasizes with vindictive pleasure. She'll learn to ski, fly down icy mountains with the wind on her cheeks. She'll have a chalet with those big wooden chairs and a chandelier made from antlers. When the Nafikh come, she'll hunker down indoors, drinking cocktails and shooting pool in her spacious game room.

She's only seen such opulent places, of course, because of Service. But that's a serv's life right there: a string of sick ironies.

The buzzer goes off, making her jump. Bernie plants one fat finger on the button without consulting the grainy black and white screen, the image further obscured by the blowing snowstorm. Lucy makes out a figure standing on the stoop, then it vanishes. The noise of a hard-slammed door reverberates down the corridor, sending a shudder through the walls. Julian thumps past the Christmas tree. Lucy's Source spikes new slivers of pain, though she barely notices, she's already in agony just being near the arrival. She takes a few deep breaths, which does little to control the searing nugget within her chest. The Source burns hard and mean for the duration of a serv's existence, like a battery indicating life. At some point, the Source goes on the fritz and the serv weakens, gets sick, and then drops dead. It could be today, tomorrow, or in a decade.

One of many reasons not to bother making friends.

The pain is generally tolerable, gets aggravated in the proximity of other servs, is way worse near an arrival, and is mind-blowing in the presence of the Nafikh. Bernie's status earns him a sweet painkiller regimen handed down from on high. Then there are the likes of Julian, able to afford his own cocktail, while Lucy, bottom-feeder that she is, has to make do with White Label, or Jack as the case may be, which latest bottle is currently stashed in her suitcase.

Julian comes into the office, closing the door behind him. The fresh scent of wet snow fills up the room. He pulls his hat off, spiking up his black hair. He's got a narrow, bony face and green wolf-eyes, always suspicious, like the world's out to screw him and he's ready to fight back. Once upon a time, Lucy was crazy in love with him.

He addresses Bernie: "How long's he been under?"

"Not even an hour," Bernie replies, a little smug about his promptness.

Julian couldn't give a fuck. "Come on," he commands Lucy.

She grasps the stroller handles, struggles to release the brake. The arrival's body jostles, and his left arm slides off his belly and dangles. Lucy lifts it by the wrist, the bones like two hot pebbles between her fingers. Julian counts out the bills under Bernie's greedy, nervous gaze. Now that everything's moving along, Bernie just wants it done. Overseers aren't supposed to sell. They're supposed to set up every arrival with a bunk, an ID, and some crap job scrubbing toilets or serving burgers to help foot the bill of their existence. Once newcomers are adjusted, insomuch as that's possible, they get greenlighted for Service and the merry-go-round begins. Overseers who risk selling on the side do so intermittently, so as not to attract attention. They make the deal, then log the arrival as deceased. No one ever checks, especially if it's a kid. The Gate doesn't get involved in details, so long as there are enough servs for calls.

Bernie folds up the bills and stuffs them into his pocket. The buzzer rings, startling them.

"Come on, chop-chop," Julian snaps.

"It's been busier than usual," Bernie mutters, handing over the room key. "You see what I mean?" he adds, as the buzzer goes off again. He slams his palm down on the button. Lucy grabs a blanket and drapes it over the arrival. No human would think he's anything other than a normal sleeping kid, albeit way too old for a stroller. But then, they'd assume him to be helpless in some way, autistic or something. People see what's put in front of them and nothing more. That's how servs get by every day undetected.

Too late, Lucy takes note of the hurt sparking anew inside her chest. Julian tenses, on alert. The serv who enters the office is wearing a long camel coat and no hat, her snow-flecked black hair pulled back, accentuating her angular features.

This is followed by the shock of recognition: Margot. They bunked together years ago. By the narrowing of her eyes, Margot recognizes her, too, but makes no comment. Instead, she nods at the stroller. "I'm not too late, then?"

"Indeed you are," Julian says. "You can get going."

"Just who's in charge here?"

"You didn't get notification," Bernie tells her.

"I get dibs on kids, and I'm down two. That's two empty beds, Bernie. He should go with me."

"Are you joking?" Julian scoffs.

Are you joking is right—Margot running a kid bunk, who would've thought? Lucy's amazed, and a little envious. Bunk bosses get a fat stipend, and they hardly ever Serve, hence her fancy duds and superior air. Though that, she always had.

"I am not joking," she informs Julian coldly. "What do you want with him? Look at him. Skin and bones. Let me take him."

Julian's not used to being defied. "Everyone gets a turn. That's how it works."

"I have funds."

"I don't need your funds."

Margot leans around him to address Bernie. "I can double whatever he paid."

The idea lights Bernie up for a second before reason prevails. He waves his fat hands in protest. "You better head on out now. You'll get the next one, I promise. Settle down," he warns, but Julian grips Margot's arm, pushes her backwards out the door.

"I can't stand your type," he says. "You're so goddamn *righteous*." He makes the word sound like a sickness. "Get the fuck out before I smack you."

"Get off me!" Margot cries, twisting her arm free.

Julian's hand clenches into a fist.

"Go, Margot," Lucy blurts. "Just go."

"You *know* this bitch?" Julian exclaims.

Margot turns on her. "I can't believe this is how you ended up!"

Shame fills Lucy, but also resentment. Margot always did think herself so much better.

"He's just a boy," Margot hammers on. "How will you use him, running drugs? Whoring? What's the matter with you? How can you do this?"

Julian whips his hand up within an inch of her face, silencing her. "The distribution's done. Leave."

Margot hesitates a second longer, pink-cheeked and furious. She slaps Lucy with one last look, then turns and strides out. They listen to her fast, angry steps, the creak of the front door swinging open. The noise of the storm howls down the hallway, then the door slams shut. Lucy lets go her breath.

"You have got to be fucking *kidding* me," Julian starts.

"Give it," Lucy says, snatching the key out of his hand. She pushes the stroller past him, turns left down the hallway towards the elevator. Margot's accusations smart awfully. She wishes she'd fought back, said something. But what? She had no case to make, is the reality, which compounds her shit feeling.

"If she's going to be a problem, tell me now, Lucy," Julian threatens, hovering close. "We don't need some friend of yours digging around, do you understand?"

"I don't have friends."

"Well, there's a surprise."

"Look, I haven't seen her in years, O.K.?"

"Oh, really?"

Lucy keeps her focus straight ahead. She parks the stroller and hits the button to call the elevator. There's a ding from way up in the building. Once Julian starts, he never can stop. His anger is like a wire running off its spool.

"I am finding it hard to believe you haven't seen her till now, till right now, when she shows up here. That's bullshit."

"Now you're being paranoid."

"Watch your tongue."

Lucy grips the stroller handle, her knuckles whitening. "Listen. I can't even remember the last time I ran into her. It was years ago."

He considers this, appears somewhat mollified. "Will she come looking for you? Ask around?"

"We barely knew each other."

"Huh," Julian nods. "I can see why. Holier-than-thou."

The elevator arrives with a whoosh and a thump. The door clunks open. They step inside. Julian lights a cigarette. The smoke blows out in a fine steady stream, filling up the small space at once. "I can't believe she talked back like that. What the fuck," he marvels.

Lucy can't believe it either. Margot used to be such a priss in her patterned dresses and pink lipstick. They're all older now, she supposes. Everyone changes.

Julian doesn't say anything more, but he's got that anxious look about him, foot tapping, cigarette clenched in his fist. He's never been good with blips in plans. She used to joke he had Asperger's, that the Nafikh screwed up making him. He's turning this incident over in his mind, sharpening it, and no doubt he'll come at her again.

Whatever. She's got the hell of the next few days she needs to focus on. Deep under her ribs the Source flares knives of hot pain. If she could afford it, she'd buy high-end stuff from Julian to get through these jobs. But she can't waste the money, and he'll never offer it for free. She hunches her shoulders, sucking breaths, aware he's watching her struggle. Bastard.

TOP FLOOR, FAR WEST corner, number 1215: one of a handful of rooms used for processing arrivals in Hotel Paradise. Bernie will keep the rest of the floor vacant from now till it's over, but still, they go down the hall fast, and Julian's got the door open and closed in a matter of seconds. Not that anyone who patronizes Hotel Paradise would give two shits, but there's never any telling when an arrival will wake up, what it might say or do.

They shrug off their coats and hang them in the closet. The economy bulbs take forever to brighten, so the dismal rooms come into view with the slowness of a scene opening on stage. It's a two-room suite, though that's a generous-sounding description. The South End's been on the up and up over the last several years with art galleries and swank restaurants opening all over the place, but the hotel's not in one of those hip zones, and the Gate's hardly going to sink funds into renovation, anyway. The whole building is crumbling to pieces with rot and roaches in the walls, decaying furnishings, and the cloying odor of room freshener seeping from plug-ins. This suite is no different, decked out in faded puke-green and pink vine patterns with a tired painting of a house on a river nailed to the wall, like someone might care to steal such a masterpiece.

Lucy flips the switch in the bathroom, checks for enough towels and a first aid kit. The front room has a double bed with a striped comforter, and a wooden chair tucked under a writing desk. The attached smaller room has a fridge bar, a TV, and a sleeper sofa. The crate's in the corner next to the sofa, already stocked with a clean mat, a fresh stack nearby for when she needs them. There are also diapers, garbage bags, and cleaning supplies. On top of the pile lies the signature blue-tinted baggie of narcotics the Gate delivers with every arrival.

Julian stubs out his cigarette in an ashtray, leaving a spray of smoldering flecks and a thin stream of smoke snaking towards the ceiling. Lucy gathers up the arrival's legs, waits for Julian to lift him by the armpits. They carry him across the room with crab-like steps, uncoordinated, Julian cursing under his breath.

"Leave him," Lucy says impatiently. "I can do it alone."

Julian's only too happy to comply. He crosses the room and pops open the window, does the same in the bedroom. Arrivals can't take heat, not at first, so that's part of the reason; but this one's also already stinking up the room with his sweat stench, to be followed soon enough by shit and vomit. Julian parks himself at the desk near the cool air pouring into the room. He lights another cigarette.

The arrival starts moaning, utters a cry, his face twisted up in pain. His leg jerks, kicks out, nailing her in the chin. Julian looks away, exhaling smoke. The pain of arriving is monumental, Lucy's been told. She must have endured it, too, but the Nafikh made her an infant, and she has no memories of that time.

She swiftly unwraps a syringe, inserts it into the tiny vial marked with the numeral one. The minuscule doses seem ridiculous, but if she popped one into her own vein she'd be dead in seconds, which isn't to say the notion hasn't crossed her mind. But arrivals are possessed of a phenomenal constitution, and the dose will serve; at this stage, he's still in in the throes of creation, though it's finishing up fast.

"*Anesh ay?*"

The thin cry is pitiful, and shocking to the arrival himself, who gapes at her. *Where am I:* the first thing usually out of their mouths.

"*Alee,*" Lucy says. "*Alee. Alee.*"

It's O.K., one of her rudimentary stock of Nafikh phrases. It's pointless, of course. He's going into a panic. Lucy grabs his arms, pinning him, but this makes it worse. "*Alee!*" She barks, and the arrival flails harder.

"*Nafikh ay? Nafikh ay?*" the arrival wails. *Where are the Nafikh?*

"*Osh Nafikh,*" she utters through clenched teeth, her strength consumed by keeping him still. *No Nafikh.*

Julian crosses the room to help, pinning the legs down. She grabs the syringe, taps up the air bubbles and makes the jab. The arrival goes rigid, then slackens. His face looks tiny, dominated by the limpid, uncomprehending blue eyes brimming with tears. He stares up at her, lost.

"*Alee,*" Lucy mutters.

She hates doing this job. She has to process three or four arrivals a season. The older ones present challenges, being way stronger and prone to fits of rage, but she'll take that any day over this pitiful, teary-eyed kid. She can't help thinking if he'd gone with Margot, he'd be in a clean bed, transported by cutting-edge narcotics that speed compression. When he woke, he'd be taught to speak. He'd learn basic reading and writing, how to ride the T from here to there, how to use cutlery. From what she's heard of kid bunks, he might even see a playground now and then, in between Services, if he made it.

"You got a problem, Luce?"

"No, I do not."

She drags the arrival into the crate, arranges him on his side in case he throws up. She draws the latch, gets to her feet, trying to keep her expression neutral, but no such luck Julian will drop it.

"You wish he'd gone with her," he accuses. "Isn't that right? Maybe he'd make quota, get himself a nice little real-people life, go to school with his happy people friends?"

"Julian, come on."

"Ridiculous, isn't it."

She clamps her mouth shut. She throws her suitcase onto the stand and unzips it.

"Thing is," he says, "those kid-bunks aren't all that. Even with cut quotas they barely get a 1.5% starting rate, and that's being generous."

"It's still better than the regular kid rate."

He shrugs that off. "You know what those numbers mean on the ground. You really think that twig would make it?"

She can't help glancing at the crate: no meat on him, no muscle. Why did the Nafikh even bother creating him? "I heard their quotas can be cut up to half."

"So what? They still hardly ever get out."

"I wasn't the one bringing this up," she snaps.

"And you better not."

He slouches down in his chair with an air of having scored, what she doesn't know, but at least he's finally finished with the topic. She lays her suitcase on the rack and unzips it. She's brought food, coffee, whiskey, cigarettes, a sleeping bag, which is an extravagance she indulged in so she doesn't have to sleep on the hotel bedding. She gets two shot glasses from the bar and fills them with whiskey, per their routine, though all she wants is for Julian to leave now. She chugs hers right away, desperate to dull the pain in her chest. It'll take a lot more than that, but she doesn't want to keep sharing with him. She waits at the opposite end of the table while he drinks and smokes, scrolling through emails on his phone, punching out replies.

A memory flits up of her bedroom in Charlestown, the sheets tangled around their legs. Open window, pale blue sky with wisps of cloud. Springtime, years ago, when everything was just beginning.

He looks up, says, "There's one thing you have to remember, that's all."

"What's that," she obliges.

"At least what Theo does, it doesn't hurt. They just arrive, they float around a bit, then it's over."

"Sure," she nods. "I know."

"So quit torturing yourself." His cigarette makes a hiss when it falls into the shot glass. He shrugs his coat back on. At the door, he turns to warn, "Don't screw up the recording again."

Then he's gone. Without him, the room feels wide and empty. Except for the creature breathing heavily in the crate.

LUCY PILES THE FEW clothes she brought in a drawer, then lays out her toiletries on the tiny bathroom counter, rinsing out the cup before putting in her toothbrush and toothpaste. She rezips the suitcase and stashes it in the closet. She checks the burner Julian left on the table, makes sure it's on in case he feels the need to harass her about some detail. She digs through her purse, pulls out her personal cell. No messages, which is a relief. If the temp agency calls, she'll have to turn down whatever they offer, because there's no way she can leave this room even for a few hours. It sucks, because every time she says no, which happens a lot during Service season, it's a black mark against her. But she's got no choice. At least the Service cell won't ring, as Bernie's got her blocked. It's the only positive of having to do this awful job.

She makes sure the digital recorder is working, sets it on the desk, and directs the microphone towards the crate. The arrival's sound asleep now, and will stay this way for a few hours at least, but she starts recording anyway, because last time she didn't and her pay got docked.

The Source feels like a smoldering ember revolving in place, shedding hot razors through her body. She pours another shot, downs it. Her temperature is way up—nowhere near what it must have been when her screaming infant self dropped into this world, but still, it feels like being boiled alive. She leans out the window into the frigid air, jams her fists hard against her ribs, taking deep breaths. She remains in this pose for several moments until the pain starts to abate. All servs are used to the subtle tugs alerting them to each other's presence, but an arrival is a whole other ball game; it's almost as bad as being near the Nafikh Themselves.

She sinks down at the desk. Her body sags with exhaustion. She's been coiled with tension ever since Julian's call earlier in the evening. She should take this chance to nap: the next two days will be brutal. The moaning, the nonsensical begging, the weeping. The ferocious violence turned against the naked, helpless body. For all the grief she's ever gotten for having arrived an infant, she's still glad she can't remember what it was like. She gets enough of a taste during these jobs.

She drinks methodically, one shot after another. Her bleary gaze falls on the notepad under the brass lamp, emblazoned with the words *HOTEL PARADISE*. It's a relic from another era. Early on, she used to record falling temps on these pads, then phone in. These days, she just texts the readings as she takes them.

His temp is 137, coming down a touch faster than usual. She uses the burner to text the three digits to yet another burner that Julian, or someone, is monitoring. Even though the Gate will never check, Theo has a system everyone has to follow. The reply comes in: *O.K.* When the number hovers around 120, that's when they'll get interested.

She stares at the boy's curled-up form, the arms flopped over each other, hands slack and open. His skin looks so soft, sprinkled with freckles. His chest moves up and down rapidly, the breaths still coming fast.

She won't sleep, she knows it. She sits shivering in the bitter cold breeze blowing through the open window, staring out at the dawn sky, listening to the traffic starting up.

A THUMPING SOUND. OVER and over. And something else. A voice.

Darkness. The ache in her shoulder.

She becomes aware, so slowly, of her cheek mashed on the table, drool seeping from her mouth. Her first attempt to sit up results in pain shooting down her back, so she tenses, breathing. She registers that it's still dark out, though the snowstorm's abated. The bedside clock informs her that she's slept more than an hour, with her back to the arrival, completely vulnerable. Her breaths turn harsh with anxiety. She whips around in her chair, hands up in self-defense.

There is no one there.

He's still locked up, she realizes, awash in relief. Last season, one of them got out. Nothing she wants to see happen ever again.

The insistent thumping that woke her resumes.

"Oh, Christ," she mutters. She grabs the ziplock bag and creeps forward, each step tense, slow, toe to heel. Stands rooted, aghast.

I can't deal with this, an inner voice wails. *I can't I can't I can't.*

The arrival's backed up against the crate bars, shoving at the bunched-up comforter with his feet, over and over. That's the noise that woke her, his heels thumping the plastic crate pan. She has no idea why he's freaking out about the comforter. He's ravaged himself. Blood speckles his white skin, his mouth is a wet red gash. His crazy eyes flick-flick-flick constantly. There's a ragged wound in his thigh. He chewed it, she understands, making the connection with his stained mouth. Like an animal trying to free itself from a trap.

He opens his mouth wide, lets out a high-pitched wail.

There's the pain of arriving, and then of the body being hurt for the first time: it is an absolute shock. His hands hover over the ugly wound, the blue eyes stricken.

"*Alee, alee!*" she says. She averts her eyes from the contorted face, unpacking the syringe. "This will help," she continues in English, her Nafikh too limited. "You must try and control yourself. Don't do this again."

She talks even though he can't understand. Her voice has a soothing effect. She unlocks the crate, murmuring softly, mindful of the rage that might whip up and smash into her. He squirms and jerks, lets out a howl. His body goes rigid, a bony, scrawny plank, the abdomen sucked all the way in so every rib stands up. Lucy stabs him with the needle, backs away on her knees. He's fading fast. Stilled by the drugs, he's no more than a sad little boy again, black hair falling over his heart-breaker deep blue eyes, the lids heavy, almost closing then darting open as he tries to focus on her. Misery leaches from his gaze, reaching towards her in mute appeal.

"*Alee,*" she tells him.

He passes out. His breaths shorten, then he exhales a deep sigh.

If he'd gone with Margot—

She shuts off the thought, gets up off the floor, her knees aching from crouching for so long. So what if Margot had taken him. He'd still have to Serve. And if he fell afoul of her bunk's rules, he'd end up on the street, shunted around, preyed upon, sold as a dupe or prostitute. She's seen it. She'd never wish it on him, on any of them.

The truth is, no one wants to deal with the kids. Even do-gooders like Margot, even with their fat stipend, they can crack and give up. *We arrive perfectly made*, is how the saying goes, and kids fuss and whine, they blubber and freak out. They just can't cope.

It's a gift, what Theo does. Painless and fast. That's the reality she has to hang onto, whenever this shit job feels like too much to bear.

She slides the pocket door almost shut, sits at the desk and pours herself another drink. She checks the recorder. In a few hours, the arrival will be able to talk.

SHE CROUCHES IN FRONT of him with the recorder. *"Safreen am ay?"* What do you remember?

His eyes flick. Strands of dried spit hang between his slack lips. There's a gurgle in his throat, then he coughs, his small frame racked violently. She hurries to the bathroom, fills the small paper cup, comes back and holds it to his lips. He slobbers and drinks, eyes wide with surprise at this first, pathetic pleasure.

"Safreen am ay?" she repeats loudly, to make sure Theo hears her putting in the effort.

He's got his hands on his mouth, like he's looking for the water he just swallowed. He looks like a little bird perched inside a bird cage. She closes her eyes.

"Dabaar," he whispers. *"Dabaar."*

Ice.

One down, two to go. Why Theo imagines he'll ever hear anything more than *ice, endless,* and *dark,* she'll never know, other than he's a relentless son of a bitch, and even after the umpteen years he's been at this, he won't give up looking for details about Before. He believes servs were once Nafikh, that they've been condemned to this mortal existence. So he wants to hear why, he wants to hear how.

But as far as Lucy can tell, he can keep asking till every arrival drops dead and he'll never hear anything more than this. If servs were indeed once Nafikh, then that's all their memories boil down to and all that remains: the abiding sensation that all servs share, deep inside, of an empty, eternal, freezing darkness.

Given the evidence, it could be argued this world is better. Maybe that's why They come here all the time.

"*Safreen am ay?*" she repeats, checking the recorder.

The arrival holds himself, a tightly meshed mess of knobby arms and legs. Tears pop out his giant eyes and he begs, "*Nafikh ay?*"

Lucy draws in her breath, forcing patience. It's going to take hours till the meds wear off and he gets sucked back into the maelstrom of pain. In that time, he'll eat, probably vomit, defecate, urinate, and beg for the Nafikh again and again. He'll also eventually answer her question with *endless* and *dark*. And then finally, he'll crack, get a massive dose, and she'll get some sleep.

She drags herself backwards, leans against the wall. His sobbing fills the room. She lifts the bottle to her lips, takes an obliteratingly deep drink.

"*Safreen am ay?*" she asks again, during a lull.

LUCY'S HEART IS BEATING so hard it feels like her ribs will explode. She gasps for air, fighting the tunnel that sucks her straight back in a whoosh to her own infantile cries, Aah, aah, aah, drenched in sweat, crushed by a boiling heat that threatens to make her mind explode—

She wakes. She's on the bed, in the hotel, the sleeping bag rumpled around her legs. It was the nightmare, she has it all the time.

She focuses on her short, harsh breaths in the dark, trying to calm herself. The nightmare's always so real, so immediate, she can't help thinking it's not just a dream. She feels it in her body, that acute, physical rush of recovered memory, the sensation of being trapped within a tiny blob of skin and fat, crooned at and swaddled and stroked, and the stench of her diaper, the putrid taste of the bottled milk, the body's hideous, cloying need—it has to be real. Though like a dream, it's already receding, fading out of body and mind, wisps of nothing.

Gone.

She turns onto her side, chewing on her knuckles, staring into the dark. She can't hear the arrival. She should check on him, but she's so damn exhausted. She presses backwards in her mind, striving to remember. She's heard the stories so many times it's like she does. She screamed and did not stop screaming, and her adoptive parents Frank and Eva bobbed their baby girl on their forearms, bouncing and humming, all their efforts doomed. The overseer who left her in the Children's Hospital parking lot must have been out of his mind: how the hell were humans supposed to care for an infant serv? Lucy screamed until she vomited, then screamed again, and her clueless parents bounced and cooed to no avail.

You were a colicky baby, Eva likes to reminisce.

Lucy grew into an introverted, awkward kid who didn't fit in no matter what. She did try, she really did. But she was who she was. Blurting out weird stuff, driving everyone away. Skinny, pale, tall, wispy-haired freak, scurrying along the walls like a cockroach, trailed by mean laughter. Ghost-girl, they called her, because she was so pale. Eva's nephew Sean, technically Lucy's cousin, ended up in detention for getting in scrapes over her: Family sticks together, he said.

And there was the pain: the steady, boiling hurt inside her chest. Her temperature always hovering around 100, no matter what. It hurts, she wept to Eva. The doctors listened to her heart, they administered EKGs, they tested her for every disease they could think of to explain the temperature. They found nothing. Stress, they said, and so began the parade of shrinks and meds that did nothing to help. At night Lucy curled up tight, she dug her nails into the hurting place, she wept.

The day she learned the truth of what she was, she was skipping pebbles on the unfrozen part of an inlet out in Hull, where she grew up. She was nine years old. Her chest seized, she felt like she was choking. A decrepit grizzled guy in a tweed coat and rubber boots crossed the ice-encrusted beach, peering at her hard.

Well, lookey what I found! he said, gripping her chin and turning her face this way and that. You're the Hennessey girl, ain't that right?

Get away from me!

This amused him greatly: he chortled, the noise carrying on the still winter air. Lucy wished Sean was with her. She looked around frantically, but their only company was some seagulls standing on the ice formed from the frozen wavelets. To her horror, the old guy grabbed her by the arm, bent down, and started pulling at her jeans.

Aaah! she screamed, emitting just a puff of air, she was so terrified.

But all he did was push up the jeans past her ankle, then he let her go. I'll be damned, he said in amazement. You ain't been tagged.

If you do anything my da will kill you! she blurted.

Oh, yeah? Frank Hennessey up and left this past summer, I heard. Probably all because of you.

This was about as close to the truth as a stranger could get. Lucy's eyes smarted and she blinked fiercely, ready to fight with all her strength, the way Sean had taught her: fists like windmills.

Do you even know what you are? You're not one of them real people. You're a serv.

I'm gonna tell my ma about you, Lucy threatened.

He guffawed. Ain't no serv ever had a ma!

I do so have a ma!

You're a serv, you twit. You can't have family. You can't be loved: it ain't your lot.

Those words flew into her like bullets. They exploded inside her, leaving black jagged wounds that never healed.

Drunk Pete was all twisted up and rotten in the heart, no different than many of the old-timer servs she's worked with since. If you survive so far as to make quota, it's surely not on qualities of kindness and empathy. He got so hung up on her not being tagged that he called in an overseer from Boston. She had to make the appointment, he told her, or she'd be killed.

Lucy doesn't know how she managed to ride her bike all the way down to the parking lot at Nantasket Beach, she was so scared. The wind whipped frigid spray onto her cheeks, and she huddled in the lee of the boarded-up refreshment stand, waiting for ages. She expected a sleek black limo, a guy in a shiny suit and dark glasses. Instead, a rented Corolla pulled up, and a middle-aged guy with a briefcase stepped out, gazing around like he'd just landed in Timbuktu. Her chest hurt awfully now that he was here, and she stood there panting with her fists pushing her ribs.

You really are clueless, huh, he said. You shouldn't be drawing attention like that. Straighten up. Get your hands down.

It hurts, she stammered.

Damn right it does. But it's how we know each other. Otherwise, how could we tell? We look just like them.

Them: meaning her ma and da. Sean. Everyone at school. It still sounded nuts to her, but deep inside, she was starting to understand it was all true.

He told her to get in the car, to get out of the wind. Lucy felt awkward, like they were up to something wrong, but she obeyed so he wouldn't kill her. All he did was ask for whatever details she knew, which were meager at best: she'd been found in the parking lot at Children's Hospital on December 2, 1983, assessed to be no more than a week old. The date helped narrow things down. He dug through a huge binder, opening file after file, his annoyance visible—how overseers coped in the pre-computer era, Lucy has no idea.

Finally, he concluded she'd never been officially logged. He explained there actually weren't baby servs anymore; in fact, the last on record was the year prior to her own arrival. Lucy had been a mistake, and most likely, no one had wanted to deal with her.

She blinked and tears blobbed down her cheeks.

No reason to cry, he admonished. It's a miracle you were dropped off at a hospital like that. The way things used to be, babies were usually, well—he paused to look at her sideways from under his brows. Let's just say, you're a very lucky little serv.

Lucy saw in her mind her small dark house, the air thick with her ma's grieving and shame, the rooms empty of her da's bluster and projects. She didn't feel lucky at all.

There might be a record at the Gate, the overseer continued, but it's not likely to be found. No one would bother. There's always the next one to process.

What's the Gate?

It's where the Nafikh come through. All the places in this world that the Nafikh like to visit, there's a Gate.

Lucy pictured a gate with a door swinging open onto the heavens. She couldn't fathom how records were kept there.

It doesn't matter, he waved away her questions. You don't need to know about all that. I've made my decision: you just stay here and have a normal life.

She was aghast. She'd wanted him to say, Come on, we're going to your real home. Instead, he listed rules she had to follow. The number one rule was: never divulge. She couldn't ever, *ever* tell anyone what she was. She could be hurt, experimented on. There were stories of people hunting down and killing servs, thinking they were ridding the world of demons. Did she want to bring that on herself and the rest of her kind? No. So she had best keep her mouth shut, at all costs.

Also, she couldn't complain about her Source, so as not to draw attention. And she had to stay away from Boston, in case she ran into other servs. If you do come across one of us, he warned, you just keep right on walking. Don't talk, don't engage, or you'll get hauled in and tagged, and trust me, you don't want that. Don't ever forget how lucky you are.

Then he let her out and drove away.

Even after all these years, even knowing what a gift he made her that day, she can still call up the desolation she felt watching his car go off in the distance.

Drunk Pete didn't take this development well. He couldn't bear her getting off scott free, just like that. She deserved to suffer, he said. Still, no matter how mean he was, she sought him out: he was all she had.

Tell me about the Gate, she begged. How does it work?

Who the fuck knows? Ain't no regular serv knows anything about the Gates.

But how do people not see them?

They're inside buildings, stupid.

The closest Gate was in a Chelsea warehouse, as it so happened, nondescript, no attention drawn, which was the way the serv world liked it. Every Gate was protected by two servs called Qadir who were made just for that, and who ran the show. Only a special class of servs, the sentries, got to interact with the Qadir: Ain't no regular serv ever met one that came back to tell the tale, Drunk Pete said, but in her fantasies, she was brought to the Gate and the Qadir were kind and took care of her. They waved magic wands and the hurt in her chest vanished.

Drunk Pete found this hilarious. You are one dumb skinner, he mocked.

Skinner was what servs called each other. It was because they were fake, their skins a disguise. She wasn't a person like her ma or Sean or any of the kids in school. She wasn't even really a serv, because she was here, living among people. She was nothing, a dumb skinner that everyone teased, and she'd never fit in, not ever. She didn't even have God to talk to anymore. She was made by the Nafikh, and Drunk Pete told her servs didn't have no god other than Them, and They would smite a whining little skinner like her dead.

One day when she was ten, she incised cuts into her chest, to try and let out the hurting, just scratches really, but enough to send Eva into a panic. Things progressed from there into years of ambulance calls, shrinks, pills of all shapes and sizes. By the time Lucy turned fourteen, she refused to go to school;

most days she wouldn't get out of bed. Even Sean couldn't coax her out of her dark room. She curled up in a ball under the sheet, hands over her eyes.

The state stepped in, alerted by her truancy. Eva was unfit, they said. Lucy needed special care. Eva should give her up, for everyone's sake.

You never let yourself be ours, Eva blubbered in a shocking display of emotion, snot pouring out her nose. You never let us love you.

They were in a conference room in the courthouse, with social workers and a cop. Lucy looked across at this woman who had dressed her and fed her and, she now realized, tried so hard, and she felt a huge sadness engulf her. She tried to speak. She tried to say no, she'd be good, that she wanted to go back to the ramshackle house on the bay, to the shed with all the ratty old lobster traps and the boat growing barnacles because there was no money to fix it. She wanted to beg them all, Let me go home.

Instead, she built up all her courage and said what was truer than all that: I don't belong with you.

Eva shook her head in sorrow. She kissed Lucy on the forehead, gathered up her stuff, and went out the door.

Lucy spent her teenage years in a string of foster homes, with spells at McLean Hospital for her tendency to self-harm. Maybe what sorted her out was living with so many kids who were fundamentally more fucked up than she ever could be—sure, she was a serv stranded in the human world with a boiling hurt inside her chest, but she was used to that. She'd never been beaten unconscious, or abused by an uncle, or been forced to live on the street. She'd grown up poor, but always had enough clothes and food and toys, and she was smart, could read and write no problem. Above all, she had a ma who stayed in touch. All the other kids envied that. Eva sent pretty cards with a few dollars tucked inside and news about the cats and what she'd cooked for dinner. Sometimes she called. During those calls, Lucy stayed mostly quiet. Eva's persistence weighed heavy, sucked the breath out of her so she couldn't speak. She wasn't supposed to have a ma or be loved, just like Drunk Pete had said. She'd never be able to live up to Eva's faith in her.

She kept trying, though. At seventeen she was placed in a group home where she buckled down and passed her GED. Eva was over the moon: she sent a whopping twenty-dollar bill tucked into a pink, gushing card: *You're a one-of-a-kind daughter.* The card both pleased and embarrassed her, and made her housemates jealous. She slipped it into the rubber-banded pile she kept in the back of her drawer. She filled out an application to Bunker Hill Community College, put in for loans, took a job as a barista. She visited Eva in Hull, bringing specialty coffees in fancy tins. Eva kept the tins in a row on the mantelpiece, like trophies.

In those days she hardly ever ran into her kind, the home being in Quincy, far outside the radius of serv activity. But she had some run-ins in town. One time going across the park headed for the T, she felt the slow hot creep of pain radiating from her chest. Before she knew it, the other serv was on her. Hey, you, when did you get here? she demanded. What bunk you in?

I'm not, Lucy said without thinking.

What do you mean, you're not? The serv edged in close, her grip hard as a rock. Bloodshot eyes, swollen bruised cheek. I haven't seen you around. Who's your boss?

Lucy wrenched her arm free. Fuck off, she snapped. She ducked the furious serv's grasping hands and ran. For days she replayed the incident in her head, her adrenaline pumping anew. She wondered what a bunk was, if it was a boss that had socked that lunatic bitch. The few other times she ran into servs, they were always like that, pissed off and run-down, hungry for trouble.

That overseer had been right, she had to stay away.

So that's what she did. She rented a cupboard-sized room near the college, sharing with three other students. To her barista job she added regular stints as a Kelly girl, stuffing envelopes and filing. Eva insisted on taking out a home equity loan to help with college tuition and all her expenses: My Lucy Belle is a freshman in college! she announced to anyone who would listen, per Sean's reports from home. Lucy was proud of herself, too. She relished the crisp new notebooks and sets of pens in blue, black, and red; the textbooks so carefully selected from the second-hand section in the bookstore; the reading assignments, the schedule, the grades. She sat in the front row taking notes and asking questions, brimming with the thrill of all her plans for the future.

And then, along came Julian.

He walked through the coffee shop doors and the Source burst its pain, sending fiery tendrils through her flesh. Panic flared: she couldn't just duck out, she had to work. She zeroed in on the serv, a guy in jeans and a button-down approaching the counter. He looked different from the others she'd run into: clean-cut, at ease. He smiled crookedly with all kinds of knowing in his eyes as she tried to remain aloof, parked behind the espresso machine. He gestured that she meet him at the end of the counter. She pretended not to see, but he just stood there with no shame, waiting for her to comply. Her workmate giggled, elbowed her. Lucy had no choice.

Well, well, well, he leaned on the counter, looking her up and down. She felt herself blushing like an idiot. He asked, When did *you* arrive?

She was so used to dodging questions and taking off at a run, she had no ready answer. A few years ago, she fumbled.

He raised an eyebrow, bemused. You don't sound too sure.

I really have to get back to work.

What is there to hide? What bunk are you in?

I'm not, O.K.? she blurted.

Not in a bunk, he marveled, sliding a little closer on his elbows, gazing at her as if she were the most fascinating creature he'd ever seen. I wonder how you're pulling that off, you sly, pretty thing.

In the pause, any number of meanings tumbled out of this remark, all of them ugly. I'm not—I don't—get out of here, O.K.?

She never stood a chance. He had her sussed out right away, like he'd reached in and closed his fist around the lonely girl who used to pedal down to the shore in tears, stare at the Boston skyline because she yearned so badly to live among her kind. How she'd longed for this, exactly this: him waiting outside when she got off her shift, falling in step, dogged in his pursuit. The first time he came over to her place, she gazed in mute anguish at his cruelly scarred chest, where he must have tried to stab out the Source when he arrived, she knew without having to be told. They did not speak. She was acutely aware of their silence. Of their profound communion, impossible in the real-people world. He reached out and slipped his wiry, powerful fingers into her hair and dragged her close. When he discovered she'd never been tagged, she told her story, all the years of confusion and loneliness tumbling out.

You won't turn me in, will you? she whispered.

I will not, he said. His thumb stroked the razor scars on her wrist. He kissed one. But you'll never be one of them, he told her. Do you understand? No one suffers like us, even you. You can't run away from it.

I don't want to run away, she whispered.

Lucy heard his breaths and her own, and felt the Source throbbing hurt, but now she craved it, because it meant he was near. He mesmerized her. The sharp slant of his cheekbones, his broken nose. His scarred hands spanning the taut, pale width of her stomach. Her housemates thought he was hot. Little did they know how much he disdained them. They've got no idea there are gods right in front of them, he sneered.

It's greatly embarrassing now, but Lucy enjoyed thinking of herself as a fallen immortal, her true identity hidden from oblivious passersby. It became a thrill just to walk down the street. They tromped through the apartment, smug with their secret, and closed the door on her silly housemates. After making love, they lay on her bed, sweat drying on their bare bodies. He lit a cigarette, dragged a book off her bedside table, flipped through the pages, saying, All this reading you do, it's of no use to us. It's a complete waste of time.

Until the instant Julian disparaged them, Lucy had been so proud of her books, evidence of her status as a bona fide college student. She shrugged and said, It's required.

You need to get out of here.

Why would I go? she teased. I like my pad.

You really think you belong here, palling around with people, going to classes?

Yeah, maybe I'll go to law school, too.

Law school, he chuckled. You are too much.

She bristled at his mockery, but he said she was missing the point. The laws she fancied herself studying had no meaning. Servs inhabited a whole other world she couldn't begin to grasp, with a whole other set of rules. She was the one who complained that no matter what, she couldn't shake the deep-down feeling of not belonging. And yet here she was, still trying to stuff the square peg of herself into the round hole of life among people.

You just don't get it, he concluded, which infuriated her.

So show me! All you do is tell me I don't get this and I don't get that!

What, you wanna get tagged? He barked a laugh. Don't even go there. You *really* don't get it.

She could have socked him in the face, she was so pissed. First he goaded her for being so stupid about serv existence, then balked at bringing her into it. Not that she should be so eager to go. He had cigarette burns up and down his arms, and his left hand was crooked from an encounter with a steel-toed boot, as he joked. Those injuries were just from the time after arrival, when he ended up in a really bad bunk. The broken nose, the faded scars, the slight blindness in his left eye, that was all from Service to the Nafikh.

About Them, she had a curiosity she couldn't settle. What are They like? she asked. Why are They so cruel?

You can't see it that way. You have to think of Them as gods. They can do whatever They want. They come and go, They make us, They break us.

But there has to be a reason. Everything has a reason.

Not with Them. A Nafikh would just as soon break your arm as have an ice cream and watch the traffic go by.

Then how does anyone get through, if it's so unpredictable?

He tapped his forehead. It takes brains, and guts. You figure out, eventually, how to work Them. Most of the time. The rest, anything could happen.

He told her about the Faithful, who ran towards Service like lemmings. They were crazy as shit, they believed if they just did their best, like trained dogs, they would one day all be Returned, meaning the Nafikh might take them back to the home world. How they carried on believing when there was zero evidence it would ever happen just proved how loony they were.

Lucy, though, could kind of understand. There wasn't much difference between that and hoping to be swept up to heaven by Jesus, which she'd always assumed would one day happen, right up until Drunk Pete told her she wasn't God's child.

Julian made it through several seasons, then he met Theo, which changed his life. He'd been with him going on five years now. Talk about brains, he said admiringly. Theo had arrived in St. Petersburg. He started out on the bottom in a drug bunk, and within a handful of years, he'd stuck a knife in the bunk boss's neck and taken over. Then he made a fortune in the arms trade, bought himself out, and set sail for America. Theo Elander wasn't his slave name, as he called it: that would never be uttered again. Theo was a visionary, a rebel. He'd bought Julian out from Service, given him his freedom. Those who worked for Theo, that was just one of the perks. He'd created a world within a world, Julian said, a space where servs could live free and strong, and no one could take that away. The lowliest grunts in his bunks might not get bought out or even duped up, but they were paid for their work, and every one of them got three square meals and a roof over his head.

Lucy wanted to meet Theo, but Julian said she had to be patient. Theo knew about her, and now she'd just have to wait for an invitation.

It got under her skin, to be treated like that. He kept going off to meet Theo, but she had to stay behind. He'd cancel dates at the last minute, because Theo needed him. And then one morning, he told her to wait at the bottom of a hill on the Common and trudged up towards a lone figure standing in the sun. It was spring, the air heavy with the smells of wet bark and earth and grass, and children's cries carried across the open spaces. Lucy grew increasingly furious at being left standing there. Her anger boiled into her legs and before she knew it, she was marching up the hill, hands jammed in her pockets, chin up in defiance.

Julian was about ready to have a cow. Theo just looked her up and down, said, So this is the famous Lucy.

She shrugged and said yes, pretending nothing could faze her, though truth be told, she was jittery inside and regretting her bold move. It wasn't anything about how he looked; in fact, he wasn't what she'd imagined. He was short and stocky with thick black hair combed to the side, a round pale face, eyes so dark the pupils disappeared. Dressed in jeans and a loose cotton sweater, he could've been anybody just out for a stroll. Except he wasn't: he'd knifed his boss through the neck with those same hands now tapping a smoke out of a pack and offering it to her. She accepted, grateful for something to do, though her fingers shook a little, to her embarrassment.

He lit her up with a gold Zippo. He said, Julian tells me you were dropped.

That meant dropped out of the system, as in, not tagged. She nodded, not daring to even look Julian's way, he was so irate.

So you cannot possibly appreciate the meaning of spring, Theo said, examining her.

She was taken off balance. What do you mean?

This is the time of year servs look forward to the most, he said, because it is the end of the Service season. It means they have lived. It means they have survived. What does it mean to you?

Lucy took a drag off her cigarette, scrambling for something adequate. But of course, there was nothing that she could say. Light sweater weather, was what Eva called it.

Julian took her arm. Let's go.

It's all right, Theo said, and Julian's hand fell away. I'm curious, now that she's in front of me. You were dropped as an infant. So you remember nothing of arrival.

Sometimes it comes back. It was horrible.

Julian says there was no one to help you. You were alone in the world.

My mother took care of me. It was harder on her, I think.

That was the wrong thing to say. Theo's eyebrows lifted in Julian's direction. Julian opened his hands, shrugging as if to say he'd tried.

My mother, Theo repeated, tilting a smile at her. I don't think I've ever heard a serv say those two words in my life.

Julian chuckled at this.

So what is your plan, Lucy? You will, what, live with your people, but love our Julian? Go to your people-school by day, but come dine with us at night?

Is that an invitation?

The cocky retort was out before she could stop it. To her relief, it seemed to amuse him. She's a firecracker, he told Julian. When you think she's ready, bring her. And now, perhaps we can have our meeting.

Lucy blushed at the dismissal, but she backed off a little ways, out of earshot. They talked a while, smoked a few cigarettes. Lucy wondered if they discussed her at all. They stood so easily together, heads bent in conversation, to all appearances just friends hanging out on a raw spring morning. A couple with a dog strolled past, nodding hello at the two men, oblivious to the truth about them. And about her. She was attached to Julian and Theo, in a secret bubble with them, and the feeling of that was thrilling.

Julian wasn't as mad as she'd expected. He seemed more preoccupied than anything, turning stuff over in his head, working things out. When she prodded him, asking what Theo meant by *ready*, he said, Look, you heard him. You can't go back and forth. It's one or the other.

O.K., then. I'm ready.

No, he cautioned. You are not.

But he was the one who didn't get it now. It was like she'd been coasting along, and suddenly her wheel nicked a rock and sent her careening off a cliff. It had been bad enough with Julian pointing out her ignorance all the time, but that encounter with Theo peeled off the last layer of defense. She felt stuck on the outside of everything: outside of the serv world, outside of the one she lived in. It became torture to lug her backpack into class, into that cacophony of girls chattering about their dates, boys slouching in loose jeans, hungover and bored and mumbling into phones, the professor shouting at everyone to settle down and turn to such-and-such page. All those bodies, all the crossed legs and tapping pencils and hushed exchanges and travel mugs of coffee spiraling steam up all around, it had given her pleasure before, a sense of purpose and yes, even belonging.

But it was all an illusion, a farce. She wasn't one of them and never would be. The game was up, rendered meaningless by the nights with Julian, his scarred body pressed to hers, the stories he told in the dark. By that chilly spring morning with the muddy grass and birds chirping, that inquiry in the urbane Russian accent: What is your plan, Lucy?

Of course she hadn't forgotten the warden's caution all those years ago. But the truth was, there was no way to steer clear. Every time she stepped out of her house, she was in danger of getting picked up by some serv, even a sentry, and who knew where she might end up. Her safest option was to go back to Hull and hide out, but what kind of life would that be—the mental adoptee who screwed up Eva Hennessey's life and then moved back in? And what would she do, work in a gift shop? No, thank you.

It's my only choice, she argued to Julian. You keep telling me, don't go down that street, don't go here or there. I'm gonna be picked up at some point. So shouldn't it be by you? At least then I'll be safe.

When she said that, he went quiet, his mouth clamped hard like he was trying to hold in a torrent. Not of protest, but of love. It spilled from him in silence, in his stare, and then he grabbed her, crushed her close. O.K., he spoke into her hair. O.K. You'll be fine. We'll take care of you.

The day he took her to get tagged, he was electric with a kind of nervous, adoring delight, her hand held tightly in his. They wound through the maze of streets towards the North End, where the closest overseer was located. It felt exciting, all new and brilliant and special, as if they were on their way to get married, which they kind of were, she supposes now, seeing as he probably couldn't love her, not truly, until she was one of them.

Meaning, until she'd been hurt like them.

Back then the overseer in the North End was lodged in an office behind a pawn shop. This is where we're going? she asked Julian, disappointed. She'd expected mahogany furniture, a plush rug. The overseer was a stern old bitch in a crappy navy blue pantsuit. She got up from the couch, dislodging a fat Bichon Frise who growled at Lucy, baring a row of tiny teeth. There was a nametag pinned to the overseer's lapel: Ms. R. Olnov. She looked Lucy up and down, uttered something in Nafikh. She doesn't understand, Julian said, and then explained Lucy's situation: arrived as an infant, never taught a word of Nafikh, never been tagged.

No tag? Ms. R. Olnov was amazed. How he get you? Bad luck, heh. Well, no serv get by so long like you. First I've heard. Dropped servs less than one percent, and they always get snatched up right away. Crazy how long you went. How you want the finder's fee?

Cash is good, Julian said.

Olnov withdrew a couple hundred from a drawer, handed it over to Julian.

You get paid? Lucy asked in confusion.

Here, Julian tucked the cash into Lucy's jeans pocket. You keep it.

Oh my God, the overseer shook her head. You a volunteer for this shit? You the dumbest skinner I ever saw.

Julian said something sharp to her in Nafikh, which earned an indifferent shrug. The overseer's words pricked Lucy with dread. She wanted to say maybe she should think things over. But Julian was squeezing her shoulders, nuzzling her ear with his lips. It'll be fine, he whispered. I'll take care of you, don't worry.

Olnov dug around in a drawer and withdrew a metal box. Inside, razor-thin anklets of various sizes lay on a cloth. Lucy lowered herself onto the indicated stool, and the overseer tried several tags, criticizing the thinness of Lucy's bony white ankle, before settling on the right size. She clicked the locking mechanism to, drew herself upright, then announced a 300 quota.

Julian snapped something in Nafikh. Olnov snapped back.

What's going on? Lucy asked.

You been living high life, Olnov told her. Now you get penalty.

Forget it, Julian said. You'll never have to do them anyway.

The overseer rolled her eyes at this. She smacked her adding machine until the numbers flickered on. Lucy watched in confusion as she tapped out equations. The calculator spewed a chit that the overseer thrust at Lucy, egging her to take it already.

The bottom line read: 0.22229219984.

That's your starting rate, Olnov said. It means you have that percentage chance of surviving your quota.

What? Lucy stared uncomprehendingly at the string of numbers.

It goes up with every Service. Jesus, haven't you explained anything to this bimbo? Olnov demanded of Julian. You got options he can go over with you later. You can dupe, she counted on her fingers, you can aim for a boost, but that's high-risk, or you can hunker down and do the bare minimum, which is my advice to you.

She heaved a binder off a shelf. Julian said, Put her in Joe Brynn's bunk.

All the same to me, she said, flipping to a page lined with columns of names, many of them crossed out. She wrote in slow cursive, *Lucy Belle Hennessey*, followed by the date. Then she booted up the computer on her desk and laboriously entered Lucy's profile while they waited. The room felt close, dark. The Bichon Frise kept its beady, malevolent gaze on Lucy the entire time.

The swivel chair creaked as Olnov turned back to face them. You get two meals a day, she told Lucy, but you need to work if you want more, and you also gotta pay flat bunk fee, unless loverboy here is footing that?

Julian shook his head.

I have two jobs, Lucy said. I'm a barista, and I'm also a Kelly girl.

Huh. That won't fly in season. You need to find cleaning, delivery, messenger, kitchen, waitressing, catering, etcetera. Jobs where no one looks or gives a shit if you don't show up. You gotta think like Mexican just come through the fence, you hear? You don't make fee, you start compounding interest.

But I already have my mom's loan, Lucy said.

Your mom? Is this some kinda joke?

Julian hustled Lucy outside. You know you can't mention that, he said. Now, stop worrying, it'll all be fine. That bunk's a resort compared to what I was in.

What about this? Lucy held up the chit. Twenty-two percent, that's nothing—you didn't tell me!

If you're gonna be a serv, he laughed, you need to brush up on your math.

He explained that a serv's life was all about making calculations. Knowing your rate and everyone else's, so as to gauge choices during Service. If you can fork out for a dupe, and whether you ought to. She had the whole summer to learn all that. As for the 22% she was worried about, it meant nothing. It was calculated off a quota that was moot, because Theo would buy her out soon enough.

But it doesn't make sense, she said, lost.

He pulled a quarter from his pocket and balanced it on his thumb. He said, Think of it like tossing for heads or tails. There's a 50% chance you'll get heads if you throw once. But what if you have to throw 300 times? You're bound to get a lot of tails. So that 50% chance goes down the more times you're gonna throw. So, the survival rate for each individual service is 99.5%, but you've got a 300 quota. That's where the 22% comes from.

All this was confusing and frightening, but he said it was what servs dealt with every day, it was completely normal. She had it good, he reminded her, because Theo would buy her out. All she had to do was take Services one at a time, focus on the 99.5% rate, and she'd be fine.

Things could have been way, way worse, was what she reminded herself when she got upset about the numbers. She could have been randomly picked up, forced into a bunk with strangers. She was beyond lucky she'd met Julian, and now here they were on a train riding out to Ayer to dine with Theo. The train raced along, clackety-clack, past green fields and pretty towns. Theo kept a low profile, Julian explained. The Nafikh weren't brought to the smaller towns out here, so there was no serv presence. Never draw attention, Julian reminded her. Number one rule is—

Never divulge, she interrupted. I know.

Theo was also building a complex way up north in Maine. She might live there one day, if she played her cards right. He described the meadow, the vast views of mountains, the river coursing through acres of forest. Theo called it Eden: a paradise where servs he had freed could live in seclusion, on their own terms.

This vision seemed to fire Julian up, so she made an effort to be enthusiastic. She'd be able to come and go, she supposed, so it didn't matter if home base was in the middle of nowhere. As for Theo's current house, it was a modest Cape on the edge of a field. A brown horse nickered and bobbed its head at the fence. There weren't any other houses nearby, just fields, a farm across the way. The door opened as they approached, and there Theo stood in a pair of jeans and a rumpled white button-down. His feet were bare. They had to take off their shoes in the entryway, as it turned out. Lucy did so, growing ever more self-conscious. She had holes in her socks. Her cheeks heated up under Theo's gaze.

Congratulations, Lucy, he said. There is only one true bond, and you have recognized it at last. He touched his fingertip to her chest where the Source stirred beneath. You are with your true family, now.

She followed them down the hallway, slouching with her hands stuffed in her pockets, trying to appear uninterested and cool while her insides fluttered with excitement. All her life she'd felt adrift, no matter how much she worked not to. Walking into that house felt like coming home at last.

They led her into the kitchen, where a pine table was laid with white linens, a few bottles of open wine, a vase of lilies. Pots steamed on the iron stove. There were other servs there. Ernesto was the closest in age and tucked up to her right off the bat, peppering her with questions about her life among people. The other two were Alita and Soren, a couple who spent most of their time in Maine overseeing the contractors. Highway robbers, Theo shook his head, cursing the industry as a whole, and Lucy found it funny that someone like him was subject to such petty frustrations.

When they sat down to eat, Theo raised his glass and said, To survival. The rest of them murmured the same, and Lucy felt a thickness in her throat, a welling up of emotion for being included in this special circle. The wine flowed, conversation was lively, and Lucy's head spun with the hot arguments that melted into laughter, the raunchy jokes, the sudden drops into grave discussion about the nature of their existence.

Is it always like this? she whispered to her new best friend Ernesto.

It helps if you're wasted, he hissed back, and refilled her glass.

He took her out the French doors onto the back porch where they shared a joint and gazed out into the darkness. The sky filled with stars. Lucy had never been so happy in all her life. One day, she would be here all the time, she reveled drunkenly. She'd be on this porch, curled up on a chaise lounge, watching the deer slip by in the mist, and this happiness would go on forever.

The next day, she broke her lease to move into the bunk, get going on her obligations. Service season wouldn't start for several months, but in the meantime she was to earn a salary running errands for Theo, and he didn't want her living with people anymore.

Eva parked herself on the landing at home, unleashing a relentless barrage of criticism as Lucy carried boxes to the attic. You'll never go back to school if you quit now! You listen to your mother, you hear me? You're going to ruin your life!

I'm keeping the books, aren't I? Lucy fired back. It's just for a little while!

Julian was waiting in the car, but Eva blocked the front door. She was more robust back then, and Lucy had to push hard. They stood there, locked in a wordless huffing battle, until at last, Eva yielded, mad with disappointment and frustration.

It'll be fine, I swear, Lucy insisted. She felt guilty, but how could she possibly explain the importance of what she was doing? She gave Eva a last hug, then ran down the steps two at a time towards Julian, towards her new life.

SHE STARTS AWAKE WITH her head slamming, mouth dried up and foul. She's on the bed, on top of the sleeping bag, she realizes. And it's fucking freezing. A blurry memory comes of shifting the thermostat lever all the way left, a gesture for the arrival, drunken pity. She pushes herself up off the bed and pads clumsily to the wall, readjusts the heat. Leans there, gasping, her stomach sloshing acid and pumping it up her throat.

"Anghhh!" the arrival cries pitifully. The sound that woke her.

"Just a minute," she calls.

The heat comes on, ticking through the metal baseboard vents. She didn't eat, she remembers now. Just a few crackers and cheddar. The clock shows it's past four a.m., which means she won't sleep again. She goes to the bathroom and gulps water from the tap, downs four Advils.

"Annnghhhhh!"

She washes her face. The fluorescent bulbs over the mirror are nasty to her already wrecked, flushed skin: even with her serv constitution, she's too old for that kind of drinking. It is not a new realization.

The arrival's tucked himself into the corner of the crate with his knees drawn up to his chest. He squints at the light pouring in from the bathroom, rubbing his eyes. The air reeks of urine and feces, the pull-up no match for the body's explosions. She gags at the lumpy liquid pooling on the mat. He starts crying, feeling at his nose with both hands, becoming aware of the stench. His legs move weakly; he tries to back farther away, but there's nowhere to go.

"*Hadj*," she says, tugging on the mat. *Move.* She loathes this. She loathes all of it. The thin, scrabbling arms and legs. The too-big head lolling on the stick-figure body. His legs swipe through his body's own waste. Pinpricks spatter her cheek. "Goddammit," she cries. She shoves the filthy mat to one side and drags him out, hissing her disgust. His legs are filthy and wet. He hugs himself, his big blue eyes fixed on her, exuding terror.

Guilt lances her. "It's not your fault," she mutters. "Don't worry about it."

He gazes at her in mute incomprehension, and she feels dumb for apologizing. He's an arrival, still compressing; he can't experience shame yet, or any complex thoughts or feelings at all, not until he's fully realized.

She guides him to the bathroom and into the tub, holding him by the armpits as he steps over the rim. He's so small. She cautiously lets him go. His arms come up to keep his balance. She removes his filthy tee shirt. His bumpy little spine runs down his narrow back to clenched buttocks, wobbling legs. She grips his arm to steady him, leans over and turns on the water, holding her hand in the stream till she feels it go lukewarm. There's no way he can do hot yet. She detaches the hand shower and pulls it free. The first spray of water jolts him; she knew it would and has a firm grip on his shoulder. It is like washing a mouse. She turns him in place, sprays the water down his front. His little penis and balls are retracted, his bony knees pressed together. The water drives the mess down his legs into the water rushing to the drain, and she turns him around, making sure he's completely rinsed. Back when these jobs first started, she'd use soap and shampoo. What's the point? Julian would say, and it got to where she couldn't stomach that truth, so she stopped.

She lifts the arrival out and wraps a bath towel around him. When she turns from rinsing the filth from the tub, he's shrugged it off. Too warm. He prods his belly, swaying. He's weak from hunger. He's in that dead zone, too exhausted and souped up on meds to feel the pain, and in this lull becoming conscious of the body and its needs. If he doesn't eat, he will weaken with alarming rapidity, upsetting the carefully calculated rate of compression Theo relies on. His body needs fuel to cope with the shock of its own existence, and soon.

She says, "*Badel een.*" *Wait here.*

She sucks in her breath, holds it, and leaves the bathroom. She stuffs the soiled mat into a garbage bag, ties it tight, then stuffs that one into another. She grabs the Lysol and paper towels, cleans the floor and the crate tray. All the while, the boy peers at her from his perch on the toilet. He watches without any sign he comprehends what he is seeing, eyes wide, hands on his knobby knees, big eyes following her every motion. His toes poke at the tile floor.

She digs through the bag of spare clothes, pulls out a tee shirt. She guides his head through the opening, then each arm. The tee shirt falls to his knees. With some effort, she manages to force his feet into the leg holes of a fresh diaper, drag it all the way up over his bottom. He prods the front with his forefinger. He looks pale and he's clenching up again, lips pressed white as the pain sweeps back in waves.

"Come on. You need to eat. Then I can dose you again."

SHE SETS ABOUT UNWRAPPING the sandwich Bernie left at the door. The arrival wobbles over to the window, stares at the buildings and winking lights and a few stars sprinkled across the dawn sky. She hunts around for a napkin. A cold breeze wafts over her. She looks up to find the window open and the boy clambering onto the sill.

"*Osh! Osh!* You can't do that!" she cries, tugging him inside. He stumbles, his numbed feet tripping over each other. She grabs the blanket from the stroller and wraps it around him. When he resists, she grips him and gives him a hard shake. "*Gedneh.*" *Sit.*

He obeys. She rubs his feet with a kitchen towel.

"Ah," the boy says softly.

She looks up. His lips are parted, damp hair falling over his eyes. His nose is running a little. He touches the snot with his fingers, then pushes his finger up his nose.

"*Osh,*" she says automatically.

He looks at her for a second before lowering his hand, index finger stuck out.

She brings him his sandwich. He devours the food savagely, unable to perform the simple motions required, his body moving in fits and jerks. Food gobs fall down his front. Lucy opens the baggie for his next dose. He goes still, eyes darting greedily, seeking the syringe. It's amazing how fast they become addicts.

His temperature is down to 126, so she sends a text, then settles him back in the crate. Once he's asleep, she takes a shower, spraying down the tub with Lysol first. She leans against the tile wall, her face turned up into the weak waterfall, trying to wash away the image of the boy in here a few hours earlier.

Afterwards, wrapped in a towel, she wipes down the mirror with the heel of her hand, combs her hair. In adulthood she's parlayed her strange looks into a kind of otherworldly attractiveness, but as a child she was a complete freak with that skin so pale and translucent. Ghost-girl, the other kids mocked. The Nafikh prefer extremes, stark contrasts, intensity of color and light, and those needs sometimes get reflected in the servs They create. Lucy has the palest blue eyes, pale lashes and almost invisible eyebrows, and her hair never lost the white-blonde hue of childhood. As for her smile, other kids in school got braces, but Eva couldn't afford them, so Lucy spent her youth with her lips clamped tight, till Julian ran his fingertip over her crooked teeth and called them charming. In bars men sidle up and ask where she's from. She enjoys turning the full force of her strangeness upon them, her face utterly still and eyes drained of emotion, so that they shrink away: Hey, man, no need to be a freak, I was just asking.

But I am a freak, sir. More than you'll ever imagine.

Her veins are a network of dark blue threads in her white forearms. They were easy to find. She turns her wrists this way and that, examining them. The scars never faded, thick brown slashes crisscrossing her skin. At work she wears wide bracelets to conceal them.

You be a good girl, Theo used to say, and maybe one day those will vanish.

The promise mystified her, as he himself did with his rich accent and smooth groove, the way he rolled cigarettes between his stocky fingers, how he pushed back his hair and chuckled at things she said like she was special. My Lucy-goosie, he called her, stroking her braids. How magical those first months were. Summer evenings on the porch at sunset, the meadows blazing orange. Getting stoned and playing tag, causing the brown horse to prance and snort along the fence. Theo told her that the Source was the remnant of their true selves, from when they had been Nafikh, that it was the key to their salvation. And just as it burnt out, so could it be fanned to life. And it must be. They had the right to live as they were meant to, as they once had. Why should they submit to mortal incarceration? It was their duty to resist, to survive, and then to help others break the chains of servitude.

They didn't tell her everything, of course, not right away. Not until she started Serving, got a real taste. After those first calls, she curled tight on the floor, banged up and bleeding, her body shaking so hard her bones rapped the wood. You will be rewarded one day, I promise, Julian soothed, cleaning her up with alcohol swabs, wrapping her in gauze. She couldn't imagine any reward that could make up for having to Serve Nafikh, though in hindsight, she didn't have it too bad in the beginning. After all, back then she still benefited from the high-end stuff to get through. Julian slipped the needle in, stroked her forehead, and off she went into heavenly numbness. When she visited Ayer, everyone coddled and encouraged her in the warm safety of the house, the snow whirling white past the windows. My brave little firecracker, Theo would say, stroking her cheek, promising it would be over soon.

And then, one Sunday, Julian held up a tiny vial in front of her eyes. The others smiled, and the room brimmed with a queer excitement. She stared at the silvery substance inside the vial. It seemed to be moving, like mist, and something glinted in its center. Julian said it was a grab, a portion of a Source, and if she carried on doing so well, eventually, she would receive this gift, and then again, and again.

How old do you think I am? Theo joked, leaning forward and stroking his own cheek.

He'd arrived over eighty years before, it turned out. Alita and Soren, around forty years. Ernesto and Julian were the most recent and hadn't been taking grabs for too long, but Julian explained his scars used to be way worse.

Lucy asked, But how does the serv live, if you take some of his Source?

If she were to go back and find the moment things started to go sour, that was probably it. The question was innocent enough, and she was too shocked to protest when it was explained that, in fact, the serv does not live; but nor did she conceal her distress. Julian put away the vial, and no more was said that day. But what she'd found out agitated her ceaselessly, and she kept bringing it up even though she sensed she shouldn't.

How many have you killed?

Does it hurt when you do it?

How do you choose? How *can* you choose?

You need to drop it, you're pissing Theo off, Ernesto warned one night, taking her outside where they could be alone. Why can't you understand? It's natural selection. We only take the ones who can't make it. They're weak, useless. They're a danger to everyone else in Service.

It's not natural selection if there's no breeding, Lucy argued, a dog with a bone. The Nafikh will just make more like them, right? It's not like anything changes. So it's not natural selection.

The ones who can't tolerate Service get mangled or killed, Ernesto insisted. What Theo does is a gift to everyone. It's a painless, gentle exit from an existence they can't hack, and it protects the servs they'd otherwise endanger. And at the same time, they provide for the resistance. They help us to be strong enough to help those who deserve it.

He made a good argument, solid, reasonable. Except for the playing God part.

She wonders how they justify Theo taking arrivals, which he does now as often as he can, probably hoping they'll turn him back into a Nafikh faster; arrival Sources are a thousand times more potent. As sick as it makes her, Lucy can't deny that for the kids, yes, it's a gift. But the older ones should at least get a chance, shouldn't they?

You think you're special, Julian would chastise her, the irony lost on him. You think you're better than us.

Theo put it another way. Your problem, Lucy-goosie, he said, is you lived too long with people.

THE NEXT FEW HOURS, while the arrival sleeps in his crate, she ties up the garbage bag and sends it down in the elevator for

Bernie to collect. She wipes the desk, washes the floor around the crate more thoroughly, adding bleach. Also the bathtub, the sink, the toilet. It's always like this. As the time approaches, she starts to clean. So she won't think about it. Like it never happened.

While she cleans, she dreams. She's going to save up, make a break for it. She gets email alerts from travel sites, and flights are super cheap in the off season. Dublin is way cheap right now. Southern Ireland is one of the havens, where the Nafikh don't go much. The closest Gate is in London, and it's not a Nafikh magnet by any means; They like snow and ice, not rain. The fantasies spin into a frenzy and she scrubs and wipes and scours. She's on the plane, then on a bus looking out at green rolling hills dotted with sheep. The country itself reminds her of flight, of freedom, the way the land pours away westward like streaming hair. She grew up staring at that map in Eva's kitchen, a red pin marking her ancestral village near Galway. Now she'll go, she really will. She'll send Eva a card.

Then, as they always do, the images break up into pieces. Even if she could scrape together the travel costs, the rest of it is beyond her—obtaining fake papers, getting a job with no references, finding affordable housing. Never mind her tag.

Anyway, there's Eva, alone in her house at the edge of the bay, phoning to ask when will you come see me again, as if Lucy wasn't just there. She can't just abandon Eva.

Sometimes she wonders, if in fact there was a Before, did she have a mother. Or if she was a mother herself. If there are mothers there at all. All servs are barren and sterile, so maybe the Nafikh are, too. She's heard it said the Nafikh always were and always will be, that They weren't created, They just are. Whether or not that's so, a bottom-feeder serv like Lucy will never know.

Lucy takes her place at the desk, smoking. It's so quiet she can hear the minute hand click forward on the bedside clock. She can see the arrival's feet from here, drooping to one side. Gradually, the slate-gray morning darkens and shifts, and within moments the sky is filled with swirling snow. It's a sight that always gets to her, it's so beautiful and wild. She peeks around the partition, but his eyes are closed.

She slides the shot glass over, spins the cap on the Jack.

THE BUZZER SOUNDS ON her phone, indicating Julian's almost here. She guides the boy out of the crate. He clings to her as she helps him onto the couch, propping a pillow behind his back. His head lolls on his skinny neck. His frame jerks with shudders, and he clutches his elbows, hunching over.

"Here," she says, handing him some saltines.

He munches, crumbs falling everywhere. Then he doubles over. He sobs, clawing at his chest.

His Source is spitting fiery pain at Julian's approach, just as hers is. You get used to it, she almost says. But he won't.

The key turns loudly in the two locks, then Julian steps in carrying a large duffel bag. He tosses it on the floor, takes off his gloves. "What's going on here? He's a mess."

"He's fine."

"Yeah? What's his temp now?"

"One-seventeen."

He looks towards the couch, nods. "O.K. Dose him, then go."

Julian unzips the duffel, hands Lucy a syringe, the contents formulated to halt compression. Lucy approaches the boy. He looks up openmouthed, a wet gob of cracker on his lip.

"*Alee*," she says, but her throat's packed tight and hard, and the word comes out a strangled croak. He's oblivious. He's noticed the syringe, and his eyes fix on it, hawk-like, shining with need. She pumps it in. He collapses sideways, and she catches him on her forearm, lowers him back onto the pillow.

As she pulls on her coat, she watches Julian unload the duffel: I.V. drip, oxygen mask, blankets. The drip keeps the compression process stalled. Something to do with tricking the body into maintaining a higher temp. Julian will stabilize him, then transport him to wherever Theo's set up this time.

Lucy's never seen the procedure. All she knows is a passageway is opened up to the heart, and the Source is released. With an arrival, the Source is still roiling with the potency of creation. It's a thousand times hotter, can throw off sparks that can burn a hole right through you. Lucy pictures a fireball roaring out from the boy's puny, narrow chest. Julian swears the procedure doesn't hurt. They go under sedation and never come back, is all.

Julian counts out $150 into her hand. She folds the bills, stuffs them into her pocket. She takes one last look at the couch.

"Quit it, Lucy." Julian snaps his fingers in front of her face, breaking her gaze. He leads her to the door, bending close to her ear, hot breath of spearmint and cigarettes. "Go home. Take a bath, have a drink, and think how you helped spare him a life of hell. It's that simple."

He goes back inside and closes the door. She stands there a moment, listening, but all she hears is the metallic slamming of the heating pipes in the walls and the faint rumble of traffic outside.

Lucy turns around and walks away, dragging the suitcase behind her.

Lucy Belle Hennessey
Arrival: 1983
*Dropped/tag: 2002
Stat: 29y 5'9" bl blu
Serv: 177/303
Loc: Eternity 02:23

"YOU WANT TO TAKE it again?" the sentry jokes, flipping the tablet so she can see.

"Ha, ha." The picture looks like a drunk and disorderly mug shot. What the fuck do they want at two a.m. Lucy digs in her bag for a compact.

"I'll never cease to be amazed," he comments, scanning the rest of her info to make sure it's all up to date, "that you weren't tagged for so long."

"Gabriel, I *exist* to amaze you."

"Always, baby," he flirts in his sexy British accent, uncapping the syringe. He's a scarred, hard mountain of muscle and impatience, but he's got a thing for her, and she can't say she minds. He arrived in London originally. He's dark with hooded eyes, lush lips. Indian, she's speculated, is what the Nafikh were aiming for. She's grateful every time he's on her call because he always slips in a little extra to make it all go easier. She holds out her arm for the jab, smooth lovely cocktail of goodbye-pain, and soon she's separating from herself like oil blobbing through water. She floats up and away, the searing chunk of hurt in her chest diminishing to a spec of nothing. The relief is a cosmic dose of joy. Truly, this is the only good thing about calls. Her eyes drift shut, insulating her from the dark, freezing alley, sleet whipping her bare arms. There are only two of them, waiting to go down into Club Eternity. It's not one of her favorite locations, but the call started way earlier, so their part will probably be brief. Last-minute replacing of servs who fucked up and got themselves killed, most likely. Who knows why, it makes no difference. Things don't develop one from another with the Nafikh. Shit just happens. It's all about getting through.

Just make it out: her mantra.

Her 176th was a cakewalk, a late-night stroll through the Gardner Museum, way after hours, no people to corral and protect. The two Nafikh had visited so many times already that They had more nuanced needs from this world: it was a choice call, the sort every serv longs for, all of two hours long and a total nonevent. The Nafikh skipped along in white dresses They might have seen in a painting and wanted to emulate. They had champagne in the garden. They ate fruits and sandwiches. They were merry as kids on shrooms, oohing over every swirl of marble. Then the sentries picked a few servs and whooshed off with Them in limos, leaving the remaining servs fucked with finding their own way back home because the location didn't qualify for a lift in a van.

She'd take walking the miles back to Somerville any day over limo duty, though. Even seasoned Nafikh can turn on a dime. Once, Lucy got called to an art auction. She had to sit with the Nafikh during the bidding. It didn't matter that Lucy didn't know what to do, she just had to play the part of the merry socialite excited about this object or that. The Nafikh sat very still, taking in the scene with Her weird, dark eyes. Later, Lucy rode in the limo with another serv, a young guy whose name she can't recall. He coughed. The Nafikh leaned over, took him by the neck, and squeezed. His eyes bulged, he turned all dark and puffy. He tried really hard not to struggle, so maybe She'd let go. Lucy should have done something. Clinked a glass, switched on the TV. But she was too terrified. She just froze. *I'm sorry,* she screamed inside her head. When the limo stopped in an alley off Harrison Ave, the Nafikh was led away on Her next adventure. A sentry pulled the dead serv out onto the sidewalk where he was bagged and loaded into a van, and Lucy walked in the freezing cold to the bus stop to get home.

Every second spent in Nafikh presence is a second too many, and Lucy is a pro at hanging back at the end of a call. Tonight she's in luck because the other serv they called in is Faithful, and he'll hop right to it, more power to him. He's all dressed up in a white suit with his hair slicked back like he's going to prom. Not that she's any better in her gold silk dress with a flower in her hair. The Nafikh need pretty things. Smooth things, light things, glittering things. And smiles.

"Get 'em on," Gabriel says, swinging the door open.

Her Faithful companion shapes his face in to the broad smile that the Nafikh prefer. He turns to Lucy. He looks insanely happy.

"I'm Jay, by the way," he says, holding out his hand.

"Who the fuck cares?" Lucy retorts, and shoulders by.

Gabriel chuckles, shaking his head. But why bother, the way Lucy sees it. Your new serv friend could be dead in an hour. There's a whole host of reasons that make it pointless to know each other at all, but that doesn't stop servs from clustering together like the aliens that they are, clutching at their pathetic doomed connections as if they have any meaning, freaking out every time one of them pops off like there aren't three more sweating out arrival around the corner.

It isn't to say Lucy doesn't ever socialize, but in the end, her work for Theo makes everything too complicated. A fellow serv might start asking questions, such as how she gets to stay in an apartment instead of bunking. And then there's her weird history, all those years living with people.

That alone makes her more freakish than the freaks they all are.

She plasters on her smile and heads down the narrow staircase leading into the club. Freezing air wafts up from below; the Nafikh have to be kept nice and cool in Their human bodies. Even elevated serv body temps get tested by the cold the Nafikh need, which is where the painkiller dose comes in handy as well.

She doesn't get why people come to this frigid club. Socialites in furs, hanging on lanky sallow guys with poufy haircuts and shiny clothes. They stand outside in all kinds of weather, begging for a chance to get in on the exclusive private party. The sentries, posing as bouncers, have to calibrate the numbers with a fine hand: the Nafikh yearn to be in the vicinity of humans, but They get all worked up, They want to touch, squeeze, sniff. A little too much, and They get hyperstimulated, end up crushing and mangling instead. It's the stench of mortality that They go off on, as every serv gets taught: They are tuned to the minuscule events occurring deep inside human bodies, a cell collapsing, a disease taking root. They can smell the rot clear as if the merry, oblivious host busting out moves on the dance floor is already bloating up on a gurney.

Servs have the rot, too, but less so, being powered on the Source rather than heartbeat, blood, cells. Servs are stupendously perfect simulacra, down to every hair, every deepening wrinkle, every sneeze. But they aren't real, so the Nafikh can tolerate their presence better. Which is in no way saying servs don't get targeted; it's just less certain.

For servs it's hellish having people around. So much can go wrong. Last year, one of the Nafikh went berserk at a gala affair.

A fire broke out and twenty people died. The official investigation was inconclusive, but the truth traveled fast through the serv world: the Nafikh had been in a male form and succumbed to the body's desires. His actions had been untoward and violent, someone assaulted Him in turn, and He got frightened. He blew out of this world from there instead of using the Gate. Hence the conflagration. As for witnesses, there weren't any and never are. The Nafikh travel on the bend of time, that is how Theo explained it once. Then time snaps back. All a person's left with is a massive headache and the feeling of having forgotten something. Provided he or she survives the departure, that is.

There are supposedly Nafikh called Stayers that can cozy up to real people without losing it. They've been visiting for hundreds of years and have built up Their tolerance. Lucy's never met one and never will, as They have no need of Service. She's heard Stayers can hang around the whole winter without burning out, that They're able to contain Their violence, that They just want to poke around and take Their pleasure. They live in swank apartments and have social lives with people, going to the opera, hosting dinner parties and the like, as if They're nothing more than wealthy foreigners on holiday.

All of which sounds like a load of crap: serv urban legend. Nafikh that don't require Service and wouldn't harm a fly? Right.

The stairs end in a short hallway with silver curtains. A sentry parts them to let the two latecomers into the bright room lit with chandeliers. A glass platform revolves slowly in the center, flickering with strobe lights. Lucy picks out the three servs among the dancers, subtly keeping themselves between the people and the Nafikh in the opposite booth.

Lucy hasn't seen either of Them before, a male and female, encased in the statuesque, muscle-bound bodies They prefer. She sizes Them up at once: not first-timers, but close to it. They're both sitting bolt upright, brimming with tension; the female's leg juts out from a high-slit lamé dress in an awkward pose, like She doesn't yet know how to arrange Her body; the male is in a white silk shirt and tight, glittering dark pants that He is currently prodding, His mouth an O of delight.

Their newness to visiting is both good and bad news. Good, because They'll tire more easily, unaccustomed to the strain. Bad, because newbies scare more easily. The Nafikh, for all Their power, basically spend visits in a state of fear. They're strapped in a rickety roller coaster hurtling on the wild ride of mortality. In these bodies, They could be hurt, They could die. They're here to taste that terror, but when it gets the best of Them, it means a world of shit for servs and sentries.

The Nafikh become aware at once of new servs in the room. They turn to look. Nafikh eyes are a punch in the gut: they shine bright and wet, but they're totally drained of emotion, like the empty stare of a wild animal. Deep within those awful eyes swirls a darkness, a sucking void that terrorizes every serv drawn into the field of vision. It's undetectable by humans, of course; to them, a Nafikh's abstracted glassy look indicates a drug-induced high, or just another league: the not-so-subtle presence of bodyguards and Their unusual height and physique suggest famous athlete or movie star.

"You're on drinks," Gabriel says from behind, "and you're on the female."

Faithful, grinning Jay oozes delight and moves towards the booth, which to Lucy is the pit of hell she wants to stay as far from as possible, thank you. She'll never get the Faithful. Never. Lucy's just glad she's on something easy. She ducks towards the bar, reveling in her good fortune.

"Well, if it ain't Miss PhD," the bartender says. She's a bitter old crab Lucy's worked with before, her name is Asa. She calls Lucy that for her fluency, a rarity among servs. "Why you so giddy?" Asa demands. "You not be all stuffed with yourself, you being here one hour ago."

"Well, I wasn't, and now is now."

"Mr. Fancypants brained pretty thing just like you," Asa informs her.

"Thanks."

"Just saying." Asa slops gin into the shaker and slams the lid on, planting her bleak gaze on Lucy all the while. They're out of sight so they don't need to wear their smiles, and Asa takes full advantage.

Lucy ignores her, aimlessly spinning the silver tray on the gleaming bar surface. Her reflection shifts and breaks. She glances up to see Jay and the female heading into the back room. Sentries always have to rustle up a Faithful for female Nafikh; a regular serv with a healthy, normal level of terror would never be able to get it up. The male, left on His own, now stares blankly at the floor, like He's winding down. This is promising. Lucy calculates two hours tops, including cleanup. Which means she'll get home in time to shower and have a coffee before heading out to work.

"Hey, who are they, anyway?" A fresh-faced college kid in a tailored plaid coat leans into their space, holding out a fifty for a refill. "Are they, like, important or something?"

"I heard they're Hungarian wrestlers," Lucy proposes, and Asa tucks a sly smile, shaking the mixer.

"Oh, yeah?" The boy looks at the Nafikh with admiration. "Wouldn't want to get pinned by one of them, huh," he jokes.

"That you would not," Lucy agrees.

He leaves a two-dollar tip in loose change, which Asa swipes off the counter into her apron. She sets a gin and tonic on the tray, gives it a nudge.

"Go ahead. Break a leg."

"Huh."

Lucy lifts the tray. She pauses to fix her smile, glancing over at Gabriel for confirmation that all's in order: a smudge of lipstick on a tooth can send a Nafikh into a tailspin. He gives her a small, tight nod, all business now. Lucy turns on her heel and marches forward, the tray held high, pushing as much merriment into her expression as she possibly can because the Nafikh like pretty things, happy things, grateful, merry, shiny things.

Just make it out.

She arrives at the table and pauses until the Nafikh lifts His head. The wet eyes bore into her, following her every motion as she carefully removes the drink from the tray, slowly hands it over. There is a pause, everything perfectly still. Then His hand lifts, the huge fingers unfolding. He grasps the glass, carries it to His mouth. Lucy gauges her options, and then, ever so slowly, backs away with the empty tray, her cheeks starting to ache from the broad rictus smile.

The Nafikh's eyes flit, fix on her. She stops. He stares at her with increasing focus. His skin glows in the flickering lights. His mouth drops open, and then the tongue emerges, licking the dried lips. The sentries teach the Nafikh how to use Their human forms properly—how to behave in public, in short. This one's losing His manners, which is the serv euphemism for a Nafikh about to blow a gasket.

Gabriel nudges her. "Keep going," he says.

He edges into the Nafikh's line of sight, blocking her slow retreat. It's a sentry's job to distract and diffuse, but a lot of them opt to just hang back; better a few servs get banged around or worse than risk their own precious skins. Gabriel is different that way. From the relative safety of the bar, Lucy watches him bend over the Nafikh, saying who knows what. Sentries have sway: they're servs whose strength has been boosted by the Nafikh for the sole purpose of protecting Them. The Nafikh heed their directions, most of the time. The rest, sentries get mangled and brutalized like any old serv, even killed.

Gabriel's a pro, however, and a few minutes later, the Nafikh slowly lifts Himself up, towering over the sentry: He must measure at least six and a half feet tall. The people on the dance floor stumble into one another, agape with clueless amazement at the muscles straining against the tight clothing, the comic book physique.

Three more sentries fan into the room, laying out the protective net around the moving Nafikh, so as to keep His fear in check. They exit the far side of the room in a phalanx. At the door, Gabriel glances back, gestures Lucy to stay put, snuffing her hope that she can duck out early.

She sinks onto a barstool, trying to quell her frustration. Service amounts to two extremes: terror or boredom. She'll have to sit here waiting for the female to come back out with Her Faithful dog, who'll sicken Lucy all the more with his postcoital satisfaction. She squashes the wicked hope that Jay gets offed: the Nafikh's rage could spin out of control and land right on her, no need to tempt fate.

"Drink?" Asa inquires, and places a Jameson neat on the counter.

Club calls do have a perk or two. Lucy takes the shot in one gulp, wondering if Gabriel will come back. She might be getting a thing for him, too. Though it could just be gratitude. Vague images of sex with him flit around in her head; any such contact between sentries and servs is forbidden, but that isn't to say it doesn't happen. It's been a while. With a person or a serv, that is; she hardly counts servicing Nafikh, which is like scrabbling along the brink of death, every second a silent scream.

She sits there, one leg swinging, watching the stupid frozen people gyrate and spin and laugh. Asa pours a few more rounds of drinks. They load up their purses with nuts and leftovers from the sandwich trays that went around earlier. It's a good yield. They wait, their eyes flitting every now and then to the clock, whose hands move with tormenting slowness. At last, the doors open, and out comes Jay. He's limping, tears streaming down his wrecked, swollen face. He looks around in total confusion. Lucy jumps off the barstool and hurries over, leads him away from curious onlookers.

"I thought for sure it would happen tonight," he cries, leaning against her. "I thought I'd get my boost!"

"You should be glad you're even alive," Lucy hisses, struggling to walk under his unsteady pressure. She heaves him forward, towards the door to the left of the bar, held open by an impatiently waving Asa. He blabbers on about his failed boost. He did everything She said, he did more, he was perfect. They're in the back office now, and Lucy can't shake him off. He's losing it. She squirms free, and he gropes at her, weeping, "I did everything right! I swear!"

"Stop!" she yells and slaps him.

There is a moment of total shock, his huge baby-blue eyes stunned and hurt. Then something changes in them. In the split second before she sees his fist coming at her face, Lucy thinks, *Oh, come on.*

SHE GETS HOME AT six thirty a.m., flips open her laptop to check in.

"Already getting pinged every two minutes, and they're saying it's gonna be the worst winter in years," Bernie complains, as if he's the one who was out most of the night on a call and now has to get ready for work. His face looks distorted on the screen as he leans in closer to peer at her. "That's a nice shiner."

"Boost-bum had a meltdown when he didn't get what he wanted. Now I have to explain this at the office. Fucking sucks."

"What're you wearing? Oh, that gold number. I like that one."

"You wish." She'd lay a string of curses on him, but overseers giveth and they taketh: she'll hardly forget that Bernie can slap a Service on her anytime, and he knows it, which is why he takes a moment to lift his fingers to his lips in the vulgar V-shape, then flicks his tongue.

"Go take a shower, Bernie."

"You're killing me." He sighs. "All right, you little tart. You're all checked in. Going strong at 177/303."

"Thanks," Lucy says. She hits the End Call button and he vanishes. He may irritate the hell out of her, but so far, he hasn't been unfair.

It's already seven, she has to be out the door at eight. She can't keep this up. The winter is predicted to be frigid, so things are going to go from bad to seriously hellish. She's got no choice, she's going to have consider forking out for a dupe, suck up the blow to her meager savings. But better to stay on the temp agency's good side. Her life is a cascading list of priorities, with keeping her job no matter what sitting at the top. There is no way she's losing this apartment and ending up in a bunk, even if it means not sleeping for a whole week.

She bums around the dupe sites looking up the neophytes, which is all she can afford. She's only hired twice. One time it paid off, the other, the dupe didn't make it and she got called in with three extra Services slapped on, hence her 303 quota. A neo is a risk she'll take again only if she's in the direst need.

The profile pics are either pale and defiant, *I can do this* conveyed in their grim stares, or else they exude the dreamy vacancy of the Faithful, who make up the majority of the dupe population. She settles on a sturdy-looking chick called Vivian as her first choice, if and when the time comes. Vivian lists her ultimate goal as owning her own home. Lucy likes that. It suggests gravity and purpose, unlike the rest of them. *I'm gonna sail around the world! I'll start my own product line!*

Lucy's considered hanging up a shingle herself. The problem is, a neo goes for shit at first; it takes ages to build a reputation. There are staggering up-front costs: advertising space on other dupe sites, a wardrobe, three or four cell lines. Typically, you go into serious debt to your sponsor dupe, because you can't hold down any other job to make ends meet; it's hard enough working a regular Service rotation, let alone back-to-back.

Still, if you make it as a dupe, you're in jet-set limo land, you can charge the moon for a Service. You're also more likely to get a boost. Regular servs mostly do the bare minimum in Service: their only goal is to make it out in one piece. Lucy falls squarely in that camp. But the long-time pro dupes who excel at giving the Nafikh everything They want without making a peep, they angle hard for a boost, every time.

Lucy's thought hard on whether she'd strive for a boost if she'd already socked away a fortune duping—as if it's a real possibility, but who doesn't need fantasies to keep going. Her conclusion: no fucking way. Sentries live way longer than regular servs, and they get to retire, so part of that long life is free of Service. But even that wouldn't be worth having to spend one more minute in Nafikh presence. She'll never dupe, and if she does ever bust quota, no way she's hanging around hoping for a boost. She'll finish her degree, get a decent-paying job. She'll get a place in the North End, her favorite part of the city and just a short ferry ride to Hull. She'll save up and take Eva on her longed-for trip to Ireland—

She regains focus on the screen. Bidding's currently hot on the high-end dupes. Because she's got a masochistic streak, Lucy can't help checking for Theo's aliases, so she can nurse that old wound of his broken promises. And there he is, bidding on Jade, of course. Bitterness wells up against whoever's getting Theo's gift. Jade is a legend. The counter on her website stands at 547, which is astronomical. To be a dupe like Jade, you have to love what you do, which in Lucy's view makes her fucking insane. Of course, she's Faithful. Her website shows a tall, muscular beauty with wavy black hair down to her waist. The photos aren't doctored, she looks just as startling in real life; Lucy's worked a few calls with her, and it was hard to concentrate, she's so jaw-dropping gorgeous. In all the photos she's with a Nafikh, any X-rated areas blacked out with exclamation points over the smudge. She's always smiling, the way They like it, and there's nothing fake about her joy. Jade's completely reliable.

The sentries cheer up when she makes an appearance. They know there won't be any shenanigans or accidents. She's so good at what she does, she keeps all the other servs in line and the sentries can sit back and gab among themselves. The prediction is she'll get boosted this season, and she's counting on it, too: a glittering banner flashes at the bottom of the web page: *My time has come!* with smiley faces on either side.

Crazy freak.

Lucy just can't fathom it. Come Nafikh season, she goes entire nights awake in bed, stiff as a board from all the tension, her eyeballs dried up and burning. Waiting, waiting, waiting. The little black burner cell Bernie bestows at the start of the season is the enemy. It terrorizes her, lying there on the bedside table, tucked into her bag at work, on the sink when she's in the shower.

It galls her that the Nafikh Themselves are so scared of dying, and yet totally indifferent to the plight of servs. She's got a recurring fantasy in which she finally gives one of Them a taste of Their own medicine. She swoops out of the darkness with a weapon—sometimes it's a sword, other times a gun. Those abysmal eyes go wide with shock, and the massive body crumples. The Nafikh screams. It can't blow out of this world to safety, It's too weak now, it's too late.

Your turn to die! Lucy screams.

Sometimes, after that, she's able to get some sleep.

ON CHRISTMAS EVE MORNING, Lucy gets herself together to go visit Eva. She has two gifts for her: a boxed set of scented soaps and an Amazon gift card so Eva can order a bunch of the trashy romances she likes to read. She wraps them in the glittery gold and silver Christmas paper Eva loves and ties them with multiple ribbons, dragging the scissors to make bunches of curls. The gifts look pretty good, almost like a store did the work. She tucks them into her knapsack with care, so they don't get crumpled on the trip.

Lucy makes her way to Hull about once a month in season, tries for more the rest of the year. It's a long day going back and forth from Somerville, so sometimes she spends the night, but never in winter in case she misses a call, and certainly not at Christmastime when the Nafikh show up in numbers. They love the lights and music and window displays. They can't get enough of the tuba concert at Faneuil Hall, the Holiday Pops, the Nutcracker ballet, never mind the parades. It's a nightmare with all the crowds. Servs run back-to-backs this time of year, and she's lucky her rotation worked out so she can make Christmas Eve, at least. Still, it's a risk being so far away; if she gets called in, she'll end up with a penalty for no-show.

Why the fuck go? Julian used to berate her, back when they still had some kind of a relationship. *It's not like she's actually your mother, so why do you have this obligation?*

You wouldn't get it, she'd say, just to piss him off.

Lucy loiters in front of the mirror, patting cover-up onto her bruised cheek without much success. That stupid Jay turned out to have one hell of a mean streak; the bruise is going dark and blotchy, and there's no hiding it. She'll have to say she slipped on the ice and put up with all the drama. And maybe next Service, she'll remember to keep her shit temper in check. You never know when someone's going to crack.

She gears up for the day: she swills coffee in abundance, picks out a few books and shoves them in her bag, makes sure she's got cigarettes, a granola bar, money, breath mints. The walk and ride to South Station take about forty minutes, but she has to build in extra time; then there's then the wait for the train, then the train ride itself which takes another forty.

She closes her door with care, so as not to aggravate Mrs. Kim down the hall. She heads down the stairs from the third floor, sensing the building's quiet, everyone away on holidays or visiting family except for the Syrians on the ground floor. They're Christian, but they've got nowhere to go, and she can hear the radio playing Arabic news; in summer when all the windows are open, Lucy has to wear earplugs to drown it out.

She reaches the lobby without having to greet anyone, and there finds a row of bright handmade Christmas cards taped to every mailbox. She unsticks hers, opens it. It's from the young couple that moved into 2E in fall. All Lucy knows about them is she's pregnant, they fight a lot, he's a machinist at some company in Waltham. Lucy reads the bubble-letter greeting, Merrrrrry Christmas and Happppppy New Year! She almost tosses it in the bin in the corner, then imagines it being discovered and shoves it in her purse, annoyed she now has to carry it around.

It was already snowing when she was getting ready, but now the snow's gusting down the street, blinding her. She stops to tie her scarf around her face. The wool goes damp and warm with her breaths as she trudges along. When she finally makes it into the subway, the scarf is soaked. Her skin itches in the heat, waiting on the platform for what feels like forever. A worry starts up that she'll miss the train, have to cancel. Eva's surely already in the kitchen, preparing a feast with carols blaring on the radio.

When she emerges into South Station and heads for the ticket counter, she feels the Source jolt. She finds him, it's one of the ticket sellers. He's wearing a Santa hat. His eyes dart her way, and he gives a grumpy nod. *Here we are, fucked together,* is what the nod conveys. He's currently enduring a tirade by some downtown suit with cheeks flushed a deep red. "Can't they hire people who speak English?" he demands of the people in line behind him. "Where are you from, anyway? Do you speaky Englishy? Do you understandy?"

The serv is unmoved. "Ticket not valid," he says.

"Then where's the goddam ATM?" the suit yells, as if the ticket seller's trying to conceal it.

"This way across room."

His accent is pretty awful, typical of most servs, who get just enough basic instruction to handle their crap jobs. The rule is, when they're in public, they have to speak the language of the country they've ended up in. Otherwise, they typically use the rudimentary Nafikh they arrive with to communicate with each other. Servs keep entirely to themselves. They have no call to explore the human world, nor to seek a place in it, and his bland disinterest finally gets to the suit, who marches off muttering. Lucy comes to the counter. He doesn't say a word when he passes her the ticket, for which she's grateful. Romeo, his nametag reads. What a joke, he probably can't even get with one of their own kind. Lucy holds her ticket tight, always gripped by an irrational fear she'll lose it and have to fork out for another.

The train's pretty much empty and Lucy gets a window seat. She opens one of her books, then tries the other, but she can't concentrate. She keeps going over what she'll tell Eva when the questions start coming. How's she been passing her free time, any men she's interested in, what jobs she's been getting from the agency—at least the jobs aren't lies. She wishes the same could be said for the rest. She wishes she really was the Lucy they think she is, depressive drop-out who pulled herself together and now pays visits from the big city. The lies leave her sick, no matter how necessary they are. It's because Eva loves her so, without guile or any regret for the years Lucy spent curled up in the dark weeping, or the times the cops rolled up to the house with all the neighbors watching. Loves her, and trusts her.

She knows she let Drunk Pete's curses stick too deep, but she can't help it. *Ain't no serv ever had a ma. You can't be loved.* If he could see her now, still clinging like a barnacle to her life in Hull, scraping her way through Services, he'd die laughing.

At Nantasket Junction, she finds Sean idling his truck in the fire lane. Usually Eva's neighbor Phyllis will do pickup, but not in any kind of weather; it's unnerving she still has her license at all. Lucy steels herself getting in, it's so hot and close with the fan blowing high to keep the window clear of fog. The car floor is littered with energy bar wrappers and crushed Coke cans, so she kicks her boots around to make space.

"Sorry," Sean leans over and kisses her on the cheek. "Merry Christmas, Luce."

"You too."

"Whoa: what the hell happened?"

"Fell on the ice."

He gives her a *Yeah, right* look, but she ignores it, saying, "You look all spiffy. You're gonna make all the little old ladies giddy."

"Yeah, sure," he chuckles. "That's date night for me."

"So—no more Janie?"

He shrugs. Lucy doesn't press; Janie is a selfish bitch who doesn't deserve him, so good riddance. He drives slowly with his wrist, the other hand tapping his knee. His plaid shirt is crisp and clean and he smells of cologne. He always has Christmas Eve dinner with his nana at the nursing home, then he comes back later to bring Eva to midnight mass.

"Aunt Eva says you can't stay over," he remarks at last.

"I've got work first thing tomorrow. It's a company fighting a takeover, they need extra hands. It pays double. I can't say no."

The lies pour from her like water. He gives her another sideways look but doesn't call her out. He thinks she moonlights as an escort, a theory he advanced when he was wasted one night, then laid into her about his right to worry, her being his younger cousin and all. You don't have to do it, he blathered. You're better than that! She had to dig pretty deep not to contradict him. It stung, that he pictured her stooping so low, despite the ironic parallels to the truth. But she saw the advantage of letting his theory stand. He'll never dare suggest it to Eva, who'd have an aneurism from sheer horror, so he ends up in a circuitous way serving as her ally, stopping Eva when she's pushing too hard lest Lucy blurt out the dreadful truth.

"Harry O'Neill finally kicked the bucket," he says.

"Eva told me."

"Remember when he caught us stealing all that gum?" He chuckles to himself. "What morons we were."

"Yeah. You puked, you were so scared."

"At least it hit his shoes."

Lucy laughs a little, surprised to remember, actually. Memories of her early years are fragmented, disconnected. The shrinks way back said it was due to trauma. Not remembering things, not sleeping, nightmares, all these symptoms would go, they promised, once she resolved her issues. Fat chance of that. Sean keeps talking, and she listens, tries to joke around, her hands clenched inside her pockets. They were two peas in a pod, once upon a time, that's what Eva used to call them. They used to make a tent in her room, hide inside, make plans for the future. Now he thinks she got clocked by a client while giving him sex for money. It just sucks, and as much as she berates herself that it's just how it has to be, the frustration builds up so much sometimes she could just explode.

He pulls up to the house. Single candles stand in each window, and the bush out front is draped with blinking lights. "What's up with you?" he frowns.

"Nothing," she forces a smile. Then leans over and gives him a quick kiss. "It's good to see you, cuz."

"You too, man. Merry Christmas."

"You're not coming in?"

"I'm running late."

She pauses halfway out, looking back. "Bullshit."

"What?" he asks innocently, though he knows damn well she's sussed out he's headed to Janie's.

"Come on, Sean. Christmas Eve? Don't be lame."

"You worry about your own shit," he says, waving her off.

She slams the door hard to seal her disapproval. He drives slowly away down the snowy street. He uses his blinker even though there's not another car in sight. He is a good man, that's what Eva always says, sighing.

"Why didn't Sean come in?" Eva cries from the doorway. She's in her Christmas housecoat with the embroidered trees and candy canes, clutching it tight against the cold. Her wobbly legs stick out from under the glitter-encrusted hem, ending in fuzzy red slippers.

"Because he's a moron," Lucy says, kissing her hello.

"But I told him to," she protests. "He should have had a sherry. My Lord, what happened to your face?"

"I fell on the ice. Get inside," Lucy says. "You'll catch your death."

Eva hobbles down the hallway towards the kitchen. Lucy smells the fish baking; the house is overheated and terribly close, with the ever-present odor of cat piss that no amount of delicious kitchen smells can conceal. Come winter Eva locks the house down and turns up the heat, and thus it stays until late spring, when she'll deign to crack a window or two. Lucy takes off layers of clothing, slips off her boots. One of the cats rubs up against a boot, its tail stiff in the air.

Lucy hurries into the half bath off the foyer. There's a new St. Jude card taped to the mirror. It gets to her, because Eva can't possibly suspect the quagmire that is her life: Lucy works hard to make it all look like things are just fine, so why the Judes everywhere, still? When Lucy was small, Eva prayed every day to an array of saints, begging them to lift the mental sickness possessing her child. Eventually, she cracked and went for Jude, the end-of-the-road saint. Lucy can't stand the green robes and the long-suffering gaze. She pees hard like it might snuff out her annoyance. The tiny framed flower paintings opposite the toilet are grimy with dust. So is all the edging on the door panels, and cat hair has collected under the vanity. Lucy will have to chew out the cleaners again. She washes her hands and dries them on the Christmas towels threaded with gold. They're stiff with newness. Lucy imagines Eva at the CVS, carefully picking them out.

"How are you today, Ma?" Lucy asks, pulling out a chair at the table.

"What?"

Lucy repeats her question louder.

"What do you think? I'm the same, just older."

Lucy ignores the crotchety tone; Eva's getting up towards eighty, so she's allowed her moments. The big-boned, stolid woman of Lucy's childhood has been worn down to a weaker, hunched version that can't stand her own diminishment. The sight of her fills Lucy with worry: that she might have to move back here, in the end, because who can afford live-in care or a nursing home, and then how will she make Service calls all the way from Hull? She imagines the penalties piling on no matter her efforts to get to calls on time. Eva complaining she's gone all hours of the night. The neighbors peeking out the curtains. In this doomed future, her quota climbs relentlessly until the

Gate labels her unfit, brings her in, and puts her down, the ultimate penalty for evading duty.

"It's not so bad," Eva says. "My hip's actually been all right for a few days. The doctor gave me some new pills but I threw them away. Who needs more pills! I even went up to the attic this week."

"That's not safe," Lucy protests. "You could fall."

"Look who's talking! Now, tell me about you."

"The agency's getting me into a really swank law firm."

"Oh, that's good news!" Eva beams.

"Yeah, the job won't start for a few weeks, though. They said it could become full time."

Eva is delighted, and Lucy falters under all that happy pride. The part about getting the job is true, but so long as she's in Service, she'll never be able to take a full-time position. She shouldn't have given Eva that hope. She turns away, unzips her knapsack to bring out the gifts. Eva cradles them in her hands as if they are rare and marvelous objects, then sets them on the kitchen table. It's always a ceremony, the opening of presents, there's no rushing. Eva makes her way over to the secretary desk in the corner. It's piled up with mailings and junk. A cup sits precariously close to the refurbished laptop Lucy got her so she can play online Scrabble. She picks up a present wrapped in wide cloth ribbon, expertly looped into a pretty flower, and gestures Lucy should open first. Eva watches with excitement, leaning forward.

Please, not another self-help book, Lucy thinks.

The paper falls away to reveal an album. Lucy opens it. At first she can't recognize anything. It's like there's a film over her vision, preventing her from identifying the curly-haired woman in the wool skirt suit and little tilted hat. The man in the loose undershirt grinning next to a bright blue boat, holding a paintbrush dripping white. The name half-finished, Lucy Belle, their darling baby just adopted, dream come true. The same boat that's now dry-docked under a tarp, so wrecked it might as well be firewood, except that Eva can't bring herself to have it hauled away.

"You're always saying how you can't remember," Eva says. "So I pulled together pictures for you, you know, so you can have your own album. You're a grown woman now, after all. You should have an album."

She says it the way another mother might say, You should have a family.

Lucy's eyes smart. She blinks hard, her hands flipping the pages. The pictures are all from the first years. Nothing from later, she realizes, when everything went to shit. None of the blood, the razors, the screaming and weeping, the ambulances and stitches and pills and shrinks. It's never spoken of, not by any of them. Eva likes to dwell on the time when the life she'd fantasized about still lay ahead. The boat freshly painted, the sun shining, the baby draped in white at the christening, screaming, as well she should to let out that devil.

Lucy can hardly remember, and Eva doesn't want to. What a pair.

"Do you like it?" Eva begs.

"Yes. Thank you. I do."

Eva sits back, deflated, but there's no way for Lucy to make herself sound more enthusiastic. She turns back through the pages, pretending to examine each one though her vision's blurring with the strain. There she is at about four or five, petting a kitten she can't remember; she thinks it might be one of the decrepit beasts wandering the house now till she realizes that's impossible, it's been what, at least twenty-five years since that picture was taken.

On the next page there's a small cropped black and white of her and Sean in swimsuits, side by side at the beach. She glares out from under her bangs, clutching a plastic shovel like it's a weapon. He's grinning, gap-toothed, his scrawny body all joints and shadows. No more than eight or nine, gripping her hand like a big brother. She turns the page. Comes to a photo of her infant self in a onesie. The lack of chronology in how Eva arranged the album is bizarre. The picture is terrible to look upon, the tiny face etched with grief, the little O-shaped mouth. Eva reaches over and taps the page, smiling.

"I remember that day. You were less fussy than usual, so we took pictures. You were such a demanding little thing," she says. "Do you know we thought you might have some sort of disorder?"

Lucy knows. She's heard it a thousand times. Eva carries on with her favorite tale of the doctor who threw his hands up in despair and said they must go to another specialist, he couldn't take it anymore. Lucy goes back through the photos, considering Eva in her middle-age, grinning with delight next to the cradle. As for her da, Frank, he looks unsettlingly happy: she never knew him like this. Not that she can recall, anyway.

"Don't be sad," Eva admonishes. "I didn't mean to make you sad."

Lucy is suddenly affected by a horrible tenderness for the sagging, soft pale skin, the sparse hair swept back so carefully with a salon brush. She bends her head, struggling against the urge to leap up and out of here.

"We all wish we could be young again," Eva sighs. "That's time for you."

Eva opens her presents, gasping and oohing with childish delight. She inhales the soap aromas, unwraps one and places it on the kitchen sink. She props the Amazon card on the secretary desk like it's an award. They eat. Lucy clears the table, shooing Eva away, You cooked, I clean, stop it. She sets a pot on for tea. Eva retreats to her easy chair in the parlor where she likes to look out the picture window at the bay and read her romances. While the water heats up, Lucy trudges up the stairs to perform a cursory check on the house. It smells stale and musty, more so than downstairs. Her bedroom's to the right, the door ajar. She glances in to verify there aren't any leaks. Eva keeps the room just the way it was when Lucy was carted off to foster care: purple bedspread, stuffed animals waiting in a row, books with their spines lined up flush. It resembles the enshrined room of a dead person, as if Lucy never actually came back. When she does spend the night, sometimes she feels like a ghost.

At the opposite end of the hall is Eva's room, a stifling place of draperies and patterned covers, ancient, dusty lamps, a vanity table with the never-used family heirloom brush, comb, and mirror laid in perfect symmetry. All seems in order, but when she checks the hall bath, it's particularly close and damp. Upon inspection, Lucy finds scattered mold dots above the shower that indicate poor ventilation. She flips the switch for the ceiling fan. It isn't working, and who knows how long it's been. She'll tell Sean to see to that. She gives the sink a quick rinse, knowing Eva can't see the soap scum on the porcelain, then opens the medicine cabinet, sighing at the jungle of bottles large and small, expired creams, medications, old toothbrushes, used Q-tips, ancient makeup. She notices a steady drip from the bathtub faucet, another repair to deal with. She counts one second, two seconds, *plink*. One second, two seconds, *plink*.

The pot starts to whistle, and it's built to a screech by the time she comes back downstairs. She pours two cups and carries them in on a tray, the way Eva prefers. She compliments the miniature plastic tree with its blinking lights and crowded ornaments, some of which Lucy made in grade school: a pair of mittens with her handprints, a camel colored with crayons. They sit in silence for a time, and then Eva gradually begins to talk, as is her wont, and Lucy listens as best she can. Eva tells about how she used to swim right out to the sandbar. How she and Phyllis used to steal old McManny's boat and take it out to the islands. She tells about clamming and cook fires and the summer her father painted this house and it all started peeling a week later. She stays back in her own childhood, and it's not senility, Lucy knows. It's because she's happier with it than what came later.

When it's time to go, Eva calls Jonas Wheeler to give him a heads up he's got a fare on the way. Lucy promises she'll come again soon. She leaves twenty-five dollars in the secretary drawer for Eva's next trip to Hingham, reminds Eva several times it's there. An eldercare van picks up Eva once a week to take her on errands. Eva loves it. She dresses in her Sunday best and acts like she's going to visit the queen. She starts talking about how this week she'll be getting cut flowers, even though it's such a luxury, and so Lucy digs around for an extra ten bucks and sets it aside. Then, mindful of Eva's failing memory, she withdraws the money from the drawer and places it under the jade cat figurine on the table in the front hall.

"You're fine with your bills, I did them all online," she reminds her, "so don't send any checks, O.K.?"

"You're too good to me, honey," Eva says tremulously.

Lucy embraces her. She smells lavender oil, and beneath that, the unmistakable odor of a body collapsing.

"Are you sure you won't stay?" Eva asks.

"I'm sorry, I can't, Ma."

"There's always a next time," Eva says brightly. Her smile exudes sorrow and affection and the longing for Lucy to come back sooner than they both know she will. Lucy turns away. At the bottom of the steps, she gives a last little wave.

"Get inside," she calls. "It's too cold."

She trudges fiercely down the street, her head bent in the wind. The walk is a good twenty minutes through residential streets, the houses strung with icicle lights, driveways clogged with the cars and trucks of those visiting for Christmas dinner. The town's festooned for the holidays, dripping with greens and ribbons and giant blow-up Santas bobbing in the wind. She passes the convenience store with its broken payphone and broken people loitering outside, smoking; she passes the restaurants and shops and the hardware store where she was once caught stealing a box of nails. She walks fast and with purpose, dreaming of the train and the South Station bar where she'll buy an outrageously priced whiskey and have a smoke before she heads on to her ten p.m. call. As she sets off across the parking lot behind the Wheeler's, she sees a truck sweeping past; Sean hits the horn once, a cracked little beep that's barely audible, and then he's gone.

BACK WHEN SHE FIRST got tagged, she kept calling and visiting Eva like usual. She didn't think it mattered. But eventually, it came to Theo's attention.

You must forget your past life, he told her. It was a falsehood.

She'd felt that way herself, but still, the way he said it sounded harsh. Can't I visit just sometimes? she pleaded. I mean, Eva, she gets all worked up if I fall out of touch.

We do not spend time with people unless we have to.

I know. I just thought—

You thought what? That you would be exempt?

She blushed with embarrassment. Of course she'd thought that. She was Lucy-goosie, his special find, his treasure. I won't visit again, she promised.

She did try to stick to her word, but Eva kept calling, and besides, she was homesick. Theo didn't have to know, she reasoned. If she just went occasionally, it would be all right. She was possessed of that dumb sense of invincibility particular to youth; the Nafikh made them perfect, after all. So a mere few weeks after he'd given her that lecture, she went to Hull, ate pie and shot darts at Maggie's Shack with Sean. She spun tales about how she was making money, she hadn't needed college, she and her boyfriend would get married soon—that one was for Eva's sake.

She came back to find Julian smoking on the stoop, butts scattered around his feet. He was livid. You can't ever go there again, you hear?

What does it matter? He'll never know!

Julian seized her by the arm and hauled her inside, up the stairs to her room, shaming her in front of her smirking bunkmates who loitered in their doorways, ever hungry for a scene.

He *will* know, Julian said, slamming her door shut. He will know because I will tell him, do you understand? I will *have* to tell him! he exploded.

She cowered in shock, and he turned contrite immediately. Luce, please, you have to listen, he begged her. He's not going to buy you out, not if you keep talking the way you do, and not if you disobey him! Why can't you understand?

Lucy shrank away, sat on the edge of the bed. It couldn't be true. It just couldn't be. She drew her knees together, recalling the last Service, the blood whirling down the drain after. She'd been called up six times so far, and every time she wanted to die, but what kept her going was that promise of moving into Theo's home forever: the crackling fire, the polished curved stairs, the fields swaying under the starry sky. And now she might never have that? The servs he didn't buy out were drubs, losers. They ran errands, worked shit jobs, Served without any break. They were excited when they got an extra ten bucks to spend on dope.

Now you're hearing me, he said, coming to her side and sinking down. I'm sorry, Luce, but you can't go against him. I don't even know why you'd want to. I mean, do you really want to stay here?

Of course she didn't want to stay in this dump, a ramshackle house in Dorchester with six bedrooms, each one occupied by bitching, strung-out servs. There was no restriction on how many to a room, male or female. She had her own room because Julian set it up that way, but her bed was a plank with a thin foam mattress, and Joe Brynn, who creeped her out and seemed to hate her, said she wasn't some princess to have it replaced. Freezing air seeped through the ancient windows, so she had to keep a blanket bunched along the sill. At night, the radiators hissed and banged, and there was always the noise of weeping from somewhere in the house.

She recalled the painted floors of her rental in Charlestown, the snug double-paned windows framed in shining white plastic. Right now, she'd give anything to be with her merry people housemates listening to their people gossip and people problems.

How could you? she turned on him. How could you even let me get tagged?

Whoa—

I hate you! she screamed, shoving him away so hard he actually stumbled off the edge of the bed, his knee cracking on the wood floor. I want to go back! I want to go back to where I was before!

He didn't strike her or shout. He turned eerily calm. He stared at her with a weird detachment. She wanted to scoop up her words and shove them back into the dark pit where they'd come from, but it was too late.

I really thought you belonged, he said.

Those words were the biggest punch in the gut. *I do belong,* she tried to say, but he was already gone.

SHE SPENT THE FOLLOWING months trying so hard to make things right again. But it was like the argument had torn right through them, left a wound that couldn't heal. The time they spent together dwindled, and days would go by before he'd return a message. Joe Brynn dumped a second bed in her room, and another serv moved in. She didn't make a peep about it, but her compliance made no difference. Theo grew increasingly aloof, and the rest of the family sensed her fall from grace and distanced themselves, so there were no more hugs and pity fests for the Services she had to endure.

Maybe it was the pain of her increasing isolation, or maybe it was just inevitable, but when she sat cross-legged on the living room floor obediently listening to Theo's lectures, she found herself thinking there was no way they'd ever been Nafikh. Servs were just what they seemed, beings made by indifferent creators, with no meaning to their existence other than to try and stay alive as long as possible. He'd been too long out of Service, she thought bitterly. He'd forgotten what it was like to grovel under a Nafikh's hungry stare, powerless as an insect.

She kept her her mouth shut, of course. But it was too late. They all knew she was the jagged bit from another puzzle, no place for her here.

And then, one evening when she was supposed to be picked up for dinner, Julian called. He informed her she wouldn't be going out to Ayer anymore. She'd be moved from the bunk, though, to one of the apartments. She had him to thank for this, he emphasized, because he was the one who'd convinced Theo to keep that promise. She'd work for Theo, and she was responsible for the rent. If she failed to meet her obligations, well, then.

And that was that.

They no longer cared what she did so long as she did her job. When she finally understood that, it was early spring, and yes, she appreciated the change of season in a whole new way. She got on the ferry to Hull. Snow was melting everywhere, birds sang. She walked the mile to Eva's house and the sea wind whipped her hair about her face. She hadn't been back in forever, and she hadn't called first. Eva wasn't home and the door was locked. Lucy went around back, noting the broken fence and wondering how come Sean hadn't fixed it. She dug the key out from under the stone cat and let herself in the kitchen door. She went straight upstairs to her room and curled up on her purple bed and passed out.

When she woke, she was under a blanket and there was the smell of meatloaf and the tinny noise of Eva's afternoon radio show. Her door was ajar, the way she'd always liked it. She lay there a long time. Eventually, she heard footsteps on the stairs. Eva pushed the door open and stood there with a wounded, wary expression.

Where have you been all these months? she asked. Sean even went to your old place. No one had heard from you. We thought you were dead.

Lucy said, I'm sorry.

Eva sighed. She came over and sat on the bed, patting Lucy's hip.

I knew that bozo was no good the first time I laid eyes on him, she said. What did he do to you? Did he do that?

Lucy's hand crept to the healed cut on her jaw, sure to scar. A sentry up in Montreal had smacked her around during the last Service of the season, when she tried to duck out early.

I fell, she said.

Eva didn't buy it. Striking a woman was the worst possible crime, in her book. She always said about Lucy's da, Frank: At least he never raised a hand.

I'll send Sean after that lowlife, she threatened, show him what's what!

Don't do anything, Lucy begged. Please, just leave it alone.

Why did you stay with him so long?

I couldn't help it. It was—it was kind of like a cult, I guess.

A cult! Eva cried.

Nothing to do with the devil, Lucy scrambled. It wasn't really a cult. It was just like a close group, you know. They said I couldn't see my family. I just wanted to belong.

You belong here, Lucy Belle Hennessey, Eva stated. A cult. Of all things! I sure hope you're finished with him now.

I am, Lucy lied, and it came easy, because it was all she'd done for years, tell lies. She added, because Eva looked dubious and worried, Really. I swear I am.

Well, get washed up for dinner, Eva said. I told Phyllis to come, and Sean, too.

You did not!

A cult, Eva marveled on her way out.

It wasn't a cult! Lucy called after her, uselessly.

To this day, they still refer to it. That time you were in the cult, they say. It's lucky you got out of the cult, they reminisce. You realize not many are able to get out of that kind of thing.

Yes, she might say. Do I ever realize that. And how.

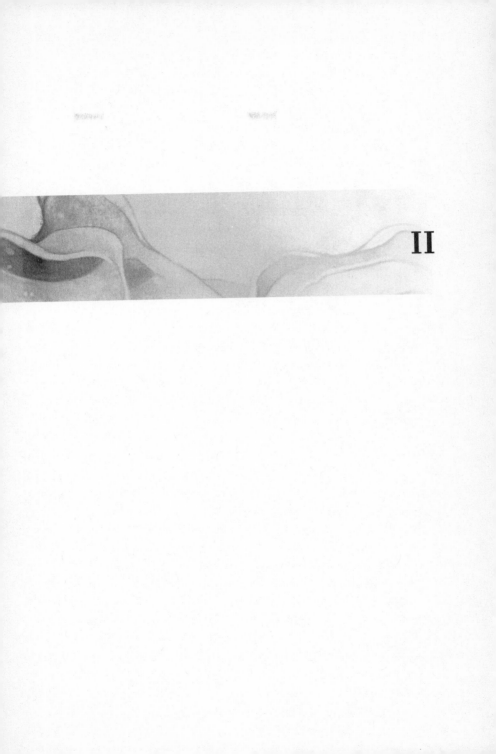

II

SNOW. MORE SNOW. THE coldest winter in ages. Then the freezing rain comes. Ice crackles all night against the windows, driven by a wailing wind. In the morning, a crystalline silence falls. The trees shimmer and glint, studded with icicle points. The world comes to a stop. Businesses shut down, hampered by collapsed electric and telephone wires, stalled busses, employees too nervous to venture forth. Schools close. Children hurtle down the empty streets, their sleds spinning out from beneath them. Flecks of ice continue to swirl out of the dark abyss of the universe above, and the ice settles in deeper, crackling.

It's so wickedly cold that more Nafikh than ever pour into the world. They need twenty-four-hour entertainment; They don't sleep, They just keep going and going. Typically, the Gate schedules driving tours to fill up daytime hours, usually to some secluded part of the Maine coast where They like to dip Their hands in the frigid ocean, or else a snowy expanse in the countryside. Last season, pictures went around of figures They built out of snow and ice, bizarre, twisted shapes, like stalagmites on acid. Everyone went nuts speculating on what they represented: Was it the home world? Was it what They actually look like? Who the fuck knew.

Montreal runs low on servs, and Lucy gets packed into a van along with about fifteen others, all Boston can spare. It's always a hellish trip to Canada, seeing as they have to cross over illegally on foot, passports being hard to procure for servs. The grueling journey's followed by back-to-backs with a cliquey bunch who fancy themselves on a higher rung in the serv world, given how many more Nafikh visit Quebec, suicidal snobbiness that Lucy finds hilarious. Their Boston group is reduced by two during the Services, so Lucy claims the back seat for herself on the way home. She calls Eva. She's been on assignment in Montreal, she explains. "Lucy went to Montreal!" Eva brags to Phyllis, who visits every evening for a glass of sherry. Phyllis hollers in the background, "You go, girl!"

Lucy can't help feeling glad to make Eva proud, even if it's all a crock.

The bus rolls into Boston at about six a.m., stops at three different bunks. Lucy gets off at the last, which is a few blocks from the Lechmere stop on the Green Line. She'll have to transfer, so she's looking at a good forty minutes before she's home, but it's the best she'll get. The other servs are too thrashed to notice she's walking off down the street; they can't be bothered to ask where she's going, where does she live. As for the sentry driving the bus, she could fall down a drain for all he cares. She rides the line with early-morning commuters, zombies in scrubs, a few drunks, suits bent over their smartphones. When she finally emerges from the T at Porter Square, the sunlight slivers into her eyes, makes her sneeze. People look as she goes by, but she's used to it and her whole demeanor communicates, Don't fuck with me. She's got a fat lip, ripped stockings, and a slight limp from a Nafikh kick to the thigh. Her cheeks are still dusted with glitter, her eyes smeared with kohl. One lady even goes so far as to stop her and ask with grave concern whether there's anything she can do to help.

Lucy ducks into a convenience store, in need of coffee and a pastry. She didn't land any assignments for today, so thank

God she doesn't have to turn around and go to work. She's going to have a hot bath, eat a lot, and hopefully sleep. Inside the store, it's hot and steamy and already full of regulars, their puffy parkas cramping up the space. She feels it then, a jolt in her chest. Looks sideways. His name is Ivan. He bunks a few blocks over on Summer Street. He's a tremulous, worn-out specimen who's spent too many years on the cheap dope that's all bunkers can afford. Lucy's always surprised to see he's lived another day.

"Hey, Lucy," he says. "You O.K.?"

"Same old, same old."

"Get me a coffee?"

"Sure," she nods. "Grab a Danish, too."

She gathers up a newspaper from the pile, pulls out her wallet. Someone says it's mighty cold, and she ought to be dressed better for a day like this. She ignores him, unfolding bills on the counter. There are murmurs all around, disapproval, mostly. She picks the paper up, scans the front page.

And sees his face.

Black hair, staring blue eyes, pinched little lips.

It is like being socked in the head: everything goes dark at the edges of her vision, a cold metallic band presses like a vise around her skull.

A beat. Another beat.

Then awareness of her breath caught in her chest, tight as a fist. She lets it go. She makes herself move, pushes out the door, and almost trips down the steps. She walks up the sidewalk clutching the paper with his face turned in, so no one sees. All the way up to her building she keeps the paper clutched this way: it's someone else's face, it's got to be.

But it's him.

As she goes down the landing, she hears the click of a lock undone.

"Why do you do this?" Mrs. Kim demands. "You are a rude young thing."

Lucy stares at the slight, hunched, malevolent Mrs. Kim without comprehension. She cannot process this. She cannot.

"Haven't you anything to say for yourself? It's seven o'clock in the morning. I need to sleep till eight. My bedroom's right there"—she jabs her finger at the wall as if this is fresh news—"and yet every time, there you go, waking me. Is it too much to ask? Is it?"

The rage whips up and out, too late to prevent. "Can you fucking leave me alone?" Her voice rising, as if from another place. "If you harass me again, I'll fucking kill you, you understand?"

Mrs. Kim's wizened face collapses in fear and astonishment. Lucy falls into a half run. She fumbles with the locks, all the while aware of Mrs. Kim's shocked stare. She ducks inside and slams the door. The newspaper falls from her grip and lands at her feet, and yes, it's him, and, *Oh my God I shouldn't have yelled. Don't draw any attention to yourself, ever. Ever.* But what does that matter. What can it possibly matter?

She bends down, gathers the paper, and brings it to the table.

Boy Found Dead in Junkyard, the headline reads. The inset photo of the arrival looks a little strange, and Lucy realizes it's actually a computer-generated image. Of course: it would be too offensive to show a picture of the actual corpse. But it is unmistakably him. The small, bony shoulders, the neck too thin, the head too big, blue eyes wide over a sprinkling of freckles. She sees the water wash over him: the bumps of his spine, the shuddering legs. She lights a cigarette, snapping the lighter three times before the flame takes. The distinctive deep blue eyes stare up at her, vacant, lifeless.

The junkyard has to be one of Theo's way stations. Some serv on Theo's payroll, clueless about the chain of events, would have been slated to collect the body for delivery to the closest sentry van. The sentries wouldn't care how or why he died, they'd just log him and load him up for disposal at the Gate.

Except, instead, the body was found by people. Theo will go out of his mind, when he hears.

The main photo splashed across the page shows a bleak asphalt foreground and a chain-link fence strung with police tape. Farther in, surrounded by towering piles of crushed cars, a group of police officers and detectives mill around a blue sedan with a missing rear door and a crumpled hood. Next to the heaps of wrecked cars and twisted metal there's an office trailer with a CLOSED sign in the window. The manager is considered the main suspect, but he's gone missing. Theo never has people in his pay, so this manager has got to be a serv. Given his lowly position he'd never be duped up, so most likely, he bit it on a call, leaving the junkyard untended.

She scans the article. It was truants from a nearby school who found him. They'd climbed the fence to look for interesting stuff in the junkyard. There was a funny smell coming from a car. When an arrival dies before realization, the body gives off an oaky, licorice smell; Lucy had no idea how long it lasts. The truants pried open the trunk and saw something in a blanket. They knew right away it was something really bad, but they couldn't help themselves, they had to look. The boy was in diapers, no other clothes. His eyes were half open and so was his mouth. His chest was wrapped in bandages. *It was all dried up black, but I knew it was blood. You could see a hole through the bandages, like an inch wide. It looked burnt all around the hole.*

His narrow, ribby chest, the skin so pale.

A wave of nauseating darkness pushes Lucy into a huddle over her lap. She remains that way for several minutes, till it passes. Then she lights another cigarette, crushes her hands together, but they won't stop shaking. She chokes on exhaling smoke, her torso ratcheting each cough till the episode subsides. She stamps out the cigarette, forces herself to get up, makes her way to the bathroom. She leans her elbows on the sink, bent over, periodically sloshing cold running water over her cheeks and eyes.

When she's able at last, she reads the article the whole way through. The police have it all wrong, of course. They're saying they can't be precise because the severe cold messed with decomposition. Their best guess is the boy has been dead anywhere from three days to two weeks, when Lucy knows it's actually been over a month.

The body was wrapped in a blanket, which according to the police indicates possible remorse. The victim's age is estimated at nine years old, and he is most likely of Irish descent. His perfect teeth and signs of good health suggest he was raised in this country in a fairly affluent family. The police are working closely with the Department of Children and Families and the State Police. No matches have been made yet with known missing children. The police would like to encourage anyone with information to call the anonymous tip line.

"The killer or killers are somewhere out there," a detective is quoted. "Someone knows them. Someone saw something. We need the people's help on this one."

She reads again, more slowly. But there is nothing more to glean.

The image of Julian carrying the dead boy into the junkyard keeps playing through her head like a film, looping over and over. He trudges through the chain-link gate, the corpse wrapped in the blanket over his shoulder. Or no, in the duffel bag he brought to the hotel. The boy was so small, just a twig. Julian jimmies open the trunk, drops the body into the well. He walks away.

The detective said the blanket indicates possible remorse. What a joke.

Alee, she told him, over and over.

"Stop it, you stupid cunt," Lucy blurts out. Her voice sounds harsh in the empty air. She flips the paper over to hide the little white face. She grabs her cell phone, punches in Julian's number. He answers almost at once.

"I was just about to call," he says. "Don't get your panties in a twist. This'll blow over."

"Fuck you." Her voice is a rock thrown hard. If he was in front of her, she'd smash him to pieces. "Is that all you care about?"

"Zip it, Lucy."

"How am I supposed to believe he didn't suffer? Did you even read what those boys said?"

Julian heaves a sigh. "He didn't suffer, Lucy. With arrivals, the Source is just one big motherfucker of an explosion, O.K.?"

"No, it's not O.K.! It's never been O.K.!"

There is a shuffling sound, like he's switching ears. "Luce, you better take a deep breath, now."

She struggles to pull herself together. Spewing her views is unwise, even to Julian. "What about the Gate? They'll know. Every serv in town will know."

"That a serv bit it? Happens every day."

"Not with cops all over, that doesn't happen."

"Another throwaway kid that no one claims. It'll blow over in a week, then everything goes back to normal."

"Yeah, well, I don't want those jobs anymore, Julian."

There is a pause. Then he says, "That's not your call."

"I'm asking."

"And the answer is, that's not your call. Do you have a problem with that?"

Lucy grips the phone hard.

"Lucy. Do you have a problem with that."

She says, "No."

"Good. You've got a drop tonight for Bernie. Package will be with Joe."

Click.

"Asshole," she snaps at the phone, tosses it aside. She gathers up the paper and shoves it under the couch. Her body's a stiff, sore mess from last night. She's starving but feels too nauseated to eat. The image in the newspaper is stuck in her vision: freckled, wide-eyed, head too big on a thin neck. *Big motherfucker of an explosion.*

She closes her eyes, presses on the bridge of her nose. She's getting a motherfucker of a headache. She herself might explode.

THERE'S A LIGHT SLEET falling when she gets to Joe Brynn's bunk at a little before seven. His old Camaro is out front, the same one they used to ride around in when he was training her to be Theo's lackey. She'd sit in the passenger seat, quaking with nerves because he was one of Theo's oldest hands, he was important, and she could tell he didn't like her.

He thinks you're a mistake, Julian explained. Don't worry, you'll prove him wrong.

That's not how things went, and now, when she has to swing by Joe Brynn, she aims to get in and out as fast as possible. She climbs the stone steps, pushes open the front door. There's a serv in the entryway, touching up her lipstick for a call. She brushes by Lucy without a word, shrugging her coat on as she goes, trailing a flowery perfume. Lucy walks through the shabby living room which hasn't changed an iota since she lived here. The glass coffee table, the ashtray piled with butts, the rows of empty beer cans and whiskey bottles in the bookcase instead of books.

Joe Brynn's office door is ajar, so she slips in. He keeps a tidy place of gray cabinets, oversized desk with papers squared off, executive black leather chair. There are stacks of car magazines going back to the dark ages, and a darts area complete with rubber mat, lighting, chalk scoreboard. He's lined up for a throw. She waits quietly, aware of his stiff-shouldered annoyance at the interruption. He throws. Another triple. She wouldn't want to play him.

He turns to her. He's got the mangled face of a boxer, but his skin's as taut and smooth as a teenager's due to the regular infusions courtesy of his boss. "Bit early in the season for you to look so raggedy," he comments.

"Thanks," she says.

He doesn't smile. Even after all these years, he still creeps her out, and she's eager to be gone. He bends to unlock a drawer, giving her a view of his bald head, which has a puckered blotch of a scar on the right side, something recent that no doubt the grabs will take care of soon enough. He hands over a small brown parcel, then pulls it out of reach at the last second, leaving her hanging.

"Stay on your toes, princess," he smirks, and drops the package into her hand.

Outside, sleet prickles her cheeks. She hopes it doesn't get any worse, as it's a good half-hour trudge to the hotel. She bends over her phone to check the main Twitter feeds, discovers the closest Service is only a few miles off. She sets a fast pace, keeping an eye on the updates and adjusting her route to stay as far away as possible.

BERNIE'S ASLEEP ON HIS couch, snoring. Unfortunately, he's not alone: his on-again-off-again girlfriend Alicia is perched on the couch arm chatting on her cell. Lucy raps the metal bars in warning, then comes around through the door. Alicia acknowledges her with a glance, then rattles on in the broken shorthand English typical of servs. "I say you wanna go? He say sure baby less go an stupid mofo believe me an we go an then but did I get him trade me drinks for . . . " Lucy tunes her out, drawn to Bernie's desk computer, which displays a grid tracking every serv in his district. Name, date of arrival, etcetera, underneath all of which GPS coordinates update in real time. She bends close to peer at the names, scrolls down to find herself. The picture's from Service checkout last night, they update automatically. God, she does look raggedy.

"Just a few clicks," Bernie says. "And your quota's, imagine, poof," he shakes his fingers like confetti's coming down from the ceiling.

"Go ahead, then," Lucy says.

"Oh, baby, I wish I could, for you." The couch springs squeak and groan as he sits up. Alicia slides down to where his feet just were, still chatting. "Gimme," he crooks his finger.

Lucy hands over the package. There's an open pizza box on the coffee table. She leans over to investigate. It doesn't look that old, and she hasn't eaten since morning, so she grabs a slice and tucks in. Bernie rips open the package to reveal a small box. He removes the lid. "Oh, yeah," he mutters.

She looks up, wiping sauce from her chin. He's holding a tiny vial to the light, twisting it between thumb and forefinger. She glimpses the tell-tale silvery mist within, and almost chokes.

He gives a sly grin. "Finally got a pay raise."

Alicia's watching now, too. "Hey," she says, "I get some?"

"You skedaddle," Bernie snaps. "I'm sick of all that noise. Didn't anyone ever tell you how bad it sucks to hear one side of a conversation?"

"Yeah, whatever." Alicia unfolds her legs and gets up, taking one last envious glance at Bernie's prize before heading out. Lucy doubts she even knows what it is. Making grabs isn't that common, as it takes resources most servs don't have, and whatever cuts might come on the market are priced way out of reach.

"You really gonna take that?" Lucy asks, tossing the rest of her slice back into the box, her appetite gone.

"What do you mean?"

"I dunno. It's always seemed kind of sick to me."

"Huh." Bernie drags a lockbox out from behind the couch, opens it up. His butt crack shows when he bends over.

"It's like being a cannibal," Lucy insists. "It's gross."

Bernie's done squirreling away his treasure, and now he turns to face her. She's clearly pissed him off, which is never a good idea with an overseer. She makes to leave, but he stops her with one fat hand on her belly, tutting. Now that he's close she can smell his sweat and mixed in that, Alicia's perfume. He says, "I got a soft spot for you, Lucy. Just the story of you, it's so fucking strange, and look at you. But this," he waves a circle in the air, "it's not anything. It just is how it is. So don't fuck around with it, you hear? Because that's fucking around with me. And you don't wanna do that," he wags his finger in warning.

"No," Lucy agrees, "I don't."

"And might I advise you not to fuck around with Julian and whoever the hell he works for, either."

"For sure. I wouldn't."

His hand slides away, releasing her. He says, "You watch your back."

Whether that's another warning or him showing concern, she can't tell. She exits the room, aware of his gaze tracking her past the barred window. Her whole body feels so wound up, she could just bust out screaming. When she gets out the front door, she breaks into a run, makes it all the way up the street and around the corner before she collapses against a wall. She puts her hands on her knees, bends over. Her breath makes white clouds around her face. The sleet's changed over to softly falling snow.

She sinks onto her haunches. It was dumb to have expected anything different from Bernie. Fundamentally, he is incapable of giving a shit, like pretty much their whole goddamned race. Or, more accurately, he's just not motivated to show it, because there's never any point. It is how it is: if there was ever a mantra common to all servs, that would be the one. She's tried to reach that numbness, she has, because what else can she do. You can't care about stuff in the serv world. You just can't. She can't think about how that arrival ended up, or any of them. It's done. It just is how it is.

Her Source churns fire and hurt. *That is me,* she used to think so delightedly. Theo said they had been potent as burning stars, and one day they would be again. He'd smile and chuck her under the chin, You too, Lucy-goosie. It shames her that she can still miss those long-ago days, even after all that's happened. She closes her eyes and tilts her head back, exposing her bare skin to the snow, letting it float into her mouth and melt down her throat. If only it could put out the burn once and for all.

LUCY CARRIES HER GROCERY bags up the three steps and shifts them to one hand. She fumbles through her keys searching for the right one, but her fingers are frozen numb so the keys drop into the filthy slush on the stoop. "Dammit," she curses. She plunges her hand into the freezing mess and gropes around the soaked welcome mat. The door swings open, releasing a blast of hot air from the lobby.

"Need some help?"

Lucy's got the keys and raises herself upright. The woman who addressed her smiles in an open, friendly way and steps aside, propping the door open with her foot. Lucy's never seen her before. She's holding a thick black binder under her arm. Pantsuit and cream shirt, and on her chest a badge hanging on a cord.

Lucy thinks, *Just keep going.* But there's another cop inside the lobby, a big guy leaning against the wall, turning a pen between his fingers.

"Terrifically cold out there, isn't it," the woman carries on behind her. "Never seen such cold, it feels like."

"It's pretty bad," Lucy agrees.

The other cop steps into her path, blocking her. He's foreign-looking, with thick dark curls, bushy eyebrows, sad-dog brown eyes. "Would you be Lucy Hennessey? Apartment 3W?"

He sounds impatient. She nods.

"Ah, good. We've been waiting a while."

"I went shopping," Lucy stutters. "What's going on?"

The woman comes around from behind. She offers her friendly smile. Her tidy, short gray hair and crisp attire make Lucy feel frazzled. "Lucy, I'm Detective Miller, and this is Detective Bedrosian. We're with the homicide department." She lifts her shield so Lucy can see.

"We need to talk with you," Bedrosian says. "Shall we go upstairs?"

"Why?"

"We're investigating the death of that little boy they found last week," Miller tells her, smiling her smile. "Have you heard about it? They're calling him the Christmas Boy? It's all over the news."

"The Christmas Boy?" Lucy echoes dumbly. Her arms go weak holding the grocery bags. She clutches them tighter. She tries to look confused, polite. "Yes, of course I have. But what do I have to do with it?"

"We're just following up on some tips," Bedrosian says. "We're talking to a lot of people. Just routine, Ms. Hennessey."

"It shouldn't take long," Miller smiles.

"Can't we just talk here?"

They exchange a glance. "We'd like to sit down," Miller offers, as if she's admitting something a little embarrassing. "Is there a reason you don't want us to come in?"

Beneath the question, the faintest edge. Lucy says, "No, of course not. It's just a mess, I guess."

Bedrosian steps forward. "Here, please, let me help with those."

Before Lucy can answer, he reaches out and seizes the grocery bags. His hands brush hers, causing her to flinch, but he doesn't apologize. He heads towards the stairs. He has a noticeable limp, dipping with every step. There's nothing left to do but follow him down the narrow, hot corridor that's filled with the smell of fried onions and cumin from the Syrians in 1A. They can't just come in to her place, Lucy thinks frantically. She has the right to tell them they can't, she's pretty sure she does. But if she protests, then they'll read into it. They already have.

Her heart's beating too fast. She has no lie prepared, nothing. She tries to compose her face, her shoulders. What tips would lead to her? Who could have possibly seen anything? Her mind skates through choppy images of the hotel rooms, the grimy windows, herself stepping out at the end with the suitcase. The arrival was always hidden. It makes no sense—

Margot.

It can't be. She would never.

They cram into the narrow stairwell, Lucy behind Bedrosian, Miller following.

But she must have. Margot would probably like nothing more than to bring down a serv like Julian.

Like me, she realizes in a cold wave.

She focuses on Bedrosian's back. He's broad, with a thick neck, gray in the curls. He gives off a tangy aftershave smell. *Say nothing*, she thinks. *Just play dumb.*

Miller speaks from behind her. "This is a funny old building, isn't it? Kind of like a warren."

Lucy nods.

"You'd never know how many apartments they've tucked away in here."

Bedrosian snorts over his shoulder. "Well, we do now. We went all around looking for you."

"What a mix of people, too," Miller observes in her soft melodious voice. "Are you friends with any of them?"

Lucy shakes her head.

"That young couple in 2E, the Davies, they seem very sweet. She's about to have a baby. How long have you lived here?"

She tries to remember. Her mind is a wasteland of rising anxiety. "Since—I don't know, about ten years."

"And no friends in the building?" Miller protests, astonished.

"I mean I know them," Lucy adjusts. "They're just not really friends."

"Well, that's the city for you."

But Lucy hears in her reply the faintest judgment, some hidden understanding. They step into the third-floor corridor. There's a click, and Mrs. Kim's door opens an inch, stopped by the chain.

"Ah," she says. "You found her. Good."

The door shuts on Miller's thanks.

Lucy's apartment is several yards farther down the hall. She pictures the two detectives ringing the bell and waiting, ringing again, while she traveled the aisles at Market Basket, shuffling through coupons. She grapples with her key. "The lock always jams," she apologizes. She feels their eyes on her back, finally gets the door open and steps in. Bedrosian says, "Where do you want these, here?" and sets the bags on the counter dividing the kitchenette and living room. They stand around, turning this way and that, their eyes taking everything in with fast, steady concentration, like there are little computers in their brains registering the details of her life—the cheap couch in the bay window with its old quilt throw, the stained coffee table, the full ashtray and whiskey bottle on the kitchen table. She feels ashamed, and angry she feels that way.

"It's pretty cold in here," Bedrosian observes, squinting at the thermostat. "Fifty-five? Wow."

"When the radiators come on it overheats," Lucy says.

"I hear you," Miller says sympathetically. "My place is the same. How long did you say you've lived here?"

Lucy knows what she's getting at. "I don't really need stuff," she explains. "Just the basics."

"What do you do for work?" Bedrosian asks.

"I'm a temp."

"Administrative?"

"Yes."

"Tough job, huh. Couple days on, couple days off," he wags his hand.

"I like the flexibility." It's her rote response, delivered as she watches Miller lower herself into a crouch to examine the jumble of newspapers on the floor. There is a week's worth, multiple publications. Mostly folded open to stories about the boy. Bedrosian wanders across the room to the shelf that holds some books, the album Eva gave her, and framed photos. He picks up the one of Eva and Sean, years ago on Nantasket Beach. "Who are they?"

"My mother and cousin."

He frowns at the image. "You look nothing like her."

"I was adopted."

"I see." He sets it back down, adjusting it with his forefinger till it's back in place.

"You seem quite interested in this story," Miller observes.

She's holding up a newspaper, the front page from that first day, the one with the face.

Bedrosian joins his partner. He roots through the newspapers to pull another one out. "What an abomination," he says, shaking his head. "Never seen something quite like this. I can see why you'd be so—taken with it."

The oddness of the word *taken* hangs in the air.

"I still don't understand why you're here," Lucy says after a moment.

"Well, Ms. Hennessey, we get many tips with a crime like this, and some of them, we take more seriously." Bedrosian hikes his pants, sits down. He squares the newspaper on the coffee table in front of him. Miller takes the other chair and opens her folder, leafing through pages of tightly written notes. She looks up with her friendly smile, gestures Lucy to sit on the couch. Lucy crosses the floor, makes her way to the couch and sits. She places her hands on her knees, then withdraws them to her lap.

"So, Ms. Hennessey," Bedrosian begins, "may we call you Lucy?"

She nods.

"Good. So, Lucy, we got a call in saying the boy was seen with you the night of the nineteenth, the week before Christmas."

Margot, for sure. Her heart bangs. "I don't know why someone would say that," she says.

They remain quiet, watching her.

A sliver of clarity in Lucy's brain: she's fucking this up. Completely. There was a time when she had some wherewithal around cops. That time is gone. It's a muscle that hasn't been used in a while.

Miller frowns at her notebook as if considering a list. "Lucy, did you go out that night?"

"What night?"

"December 19."

"How am I supposed to remember?"

Miller jots a note. Sound of the pen scratching paper.

"It was a Wednesday," Bedrosian says, eyes fixed on her, unmoving. "Middle of the week, before Christmas. Maybe you went shopping after work?"

"I don't think so. No."

"You're sure?"

"Yes."

"So you do remember?"

There is a long silence during which she can no longer withstand their steady gaze. Her neck trembles and she lowers her head.

Bedrosian says, "Lucy, it doesn't seem like you remember one way or another."

"I said I was in."

"But you might have been out."

"Yes. I mean, no."

They sit back. Bedrosian maintains his steady stare. Miller consults her notes, still wearing her placid, kind expression. She taps her pen on the paper. She looks up. "Why don't we move on from this question of were you here, were you not here. All right?"

Lucy says nothing.

"Maybe you're just uncomfortable talking to us? We understand. Believe me, it happens all the time. But if you have nothing to hide, then you don't have to worry."

"Look, you seem like a decent young woman," Bedrosian offers. "We can see why you'd be so affected by this." He holds up the newspaper, tapping the photograph. "But then again, there's so much here. All piled up like this."

He looks to Miller. She shakes her head at Lucy as if to say, Sorry, it's true.

"So your interest becomes a little striking. Understandable, of course. But striking." He pauses. "Look at that face. Little angel of a kid. Nobody knows who he is. But he belongs to somebody out there, Lucy. Somebody loved him. Somebody held him as a baby."

No, Lucy thinks. *Nobody ever did that.*

"Is there something you want to say?" Bedrosian asks.

"I don't know what you're talking about."

"Is that so?"

"I didn't see him."

"Didn't see him where?"

"I didn't see him anywhere."

"You didn't see this boy, on that night?"

"No. I didn't."

"And what about a man, Lucy? Did you see a man, maybe?"

"A man?" Lucy stutters.

"The caller said you and a man know what happened to the boy. Who's the man, then?"

Lucy feels faint. "I don't know what you're talking about."

"Do you know Enrique Maron? He's the manager at the junkyard. The one who's gone missing. You've never met him?"

It's a relief to answer something with total honesty. "No, never."

There is a pause. Miller's pen scratches, scratches. She looks up. She asks, "Your neighbor, Mrs. Kim, you know her?"

"Yes."

"She says you were pretty upset last week. When the news broke."

"What?"

"She says you yelled at her. You were holding the paper—" She gestures, and Bedrosian holds up the boy's face again. Lucy stares at it blindly. "And you were visibly shaken and upset. Maybe you knew this boy?"

"I didn't. I already told you."

Bedrosian leans forward, elbows on his knees. "Do you get upset often? You seem upset."

"I'm not upset."

"Mrs. Kim says you threatened to kill her."

"That's ridiculous. I mean, she just annoys me."

"So you just said that because you were upset."

Words jumble inside Lucy's mouth. They watch her struggle. She feels sweat sliding down her sides. "She's always harassing me."

Miller smiles. "All right, then. Well, maybe we should continue this interview at the station. What do you say, Vic?"

"Seems like a good idea."

"But why? Do I have to go with you?"

Again, the shared look. Miller says, "Lucy, if you choose not to come with us, then we might have to interpret that a certain way. You see?"

"And we'll get a warrant and then you'll have to come with us anyway. So you might as well do it now."

Don't get in a twist, Julian's words come back. It'll blow over.

The words scream hysterically inside her, utterly senseless.

Lucy looks from one to the other. Her gaze travels past them to the window, the blinding winter sunlight. If Theo finds out she was hauled in—

Miller leans forward. "Is something wrong?"

Lucy gazes at the woman's clean, open face, full of smile wrinkles. She thinks, *You have no fucking idea.*

FOR AGES SHE'S BEEN in the room with the green peeling walls and the metal table and chairs, their questions coming at her relentlessly. She tells them over and over that she knows nothing. That's what she decided and she sticks with it because there's no alternative. Her mind is so bleak, so bare, it's like the surface of the gray metal table, a dull gleaming uncreative expanse from which she can draw nothing at all, nothing to help her out of this mess. Julian said not to get in a twist. Julian said it would blow over. But the boy was seen on the night of the nineteenth during the snowstorm, with a man and Lucy Hennessey. Of this, the witness was certain, and repeated the information in two separate anonymous calls. The witness said: Lucy Hennessey knows what happened to that boy.

It could be a different Lucy Hennessey, she offered up in a flash of genius, but the caller described her: blue eyes, hair so blonde it looks white.

You know, people pay to get that color, Detective Miller complimented.

They haven't mentioned Bernie or the hotel, which is not surprising. It's bad enough what Margot's done, let alone bringing cops down on an overseer. Lucy has tried to suggest it must be someone getting back at her for something. But she couldn't offer up any enemies who might do such a thing to her.

No friends, no enemies, Detective Bedrosian mused.

The detectives keep insisting they know that Lucy wants to cooperate. That she'll break in the end, admit her part, and tell them who that man is. Because they don't think she did it, the killing. No, they don't. They can see it's not in her. All she needs to do is spill everything out. She'll feel better, they promise. They know how tormented she is. She seems extremely tormented.

"That's because you're tormenting me," she says.

Her small joke gets no smiles.

Before her lie three large black and white photographs of the arrival's corpse. These aren't computer generated, they're real. Lucy keeps her eyes averted from his hollow little face. She doesn't need to see it. It's glued to the insides of her eyes.

She's acutely conscious of herself. Physically. Arms wrapped tight and hair hanging limply over her eyes: it's how she used to look in front of the shrinks. This is her forte: shutting down, waiting things out. Just watch. Loopy Lucy is what they called her at school, when it first came out she'd hurt herself. The pain from that time is a sliver inside that's opening her up with hurt. It hurts. It hurts. It hurts.

There's no getting away: that is the terror that keeps swamping her. She is so completely fucked, and she's going to be locked up in jail. Because they have a witness, as they keep reminding her. The witness saw the boy and a man and Lucy Hennessey.

But that's all they really have. Margot didn't identify herself, and it looks like she hasn't called back. Lucy clings to this: all they have other than the anonymous tips is a pile of newspapers.

Which means they'll let her go home, eventually, and then when Theo finds out—

"I don't know anything," she says exhaustedly, again.

"Who are you scared of?" Bedrosian repeats.

She feels herself shrinking under the weight of his gaze. No more sad-dog demeanor now. He's zeroed in on his prey, he means business, his jaw's set hard. She's come to know every inch of him, they've been sitting here so long. He's got hair on the backs of his hands and sticking out of his shirt collar. Thick, square-tipped fingers, no wedding ring. She wonders if he's ever killed anyone.

"Lucy, I know you're scared. I've been in this business a long time."

She shakes her head.

"We can protect you, if you help us."

"I can't help you."

"I think you can."

His examination of her is relentless. She feels bored into, peeled apart.

"What?" she demands. "What do you want from me? I don't know anything."

He gives a minute shake of the head. He gets up and leaves, shutting the door softly.

THEY COME AND GO. Each time with a new angle. Cajoling, insisting, asking the same questions.

Now they've dug up her past. Suspensions. Juvenile delinquency. Her stints at McLean.

"You're a real piece of work, you know that," Bedrosian comments. He runs the words together: piece-a-work.

She says, "I think I want to go home, now."

"Well, we aren't quite finished here," Miller says.

"Do I need a lawyer? I don't understand."

"Do you think you need one, Lucy?"

Lucy shakes her head. She retreats back into her silence.

"That's some history you have, Lucy Hennessey," Bedrosian muses. "A real troubled girl. Violent, too."

"I wasn't violent."

"Says here when you were sixteen, you laid into an aide, cracked three ribs and messed up his face pretty good."

"I had a good reason."

"Because he was inappropriate with one of the younger girls. He denied that."

"Of course he did!"

"Relax. I believe you." He peruses the file. "You were with your adoptive family till you were fourteen?"

"Yes."

"Then the state took you out of the home. You lived all these places, pulled it together and got your GED. You in touch with Eva Hennessey?"

"Yes."

"Is your relationship with her O.K., then?"

"Sure."

"So you have some education, you work, you have contact with your family. Honestly, you've got it pretty good compared to most kids coming out of the system. So what happened?"

"What do you mean?"

"I mean, what happened, to bring you to where you're part of this? This little boy, he went through hell. The coroner said he bit himself. Nobody knows that detail, Lucy. I just shared it with you now, and you don't seem surprised. You already knew, because you were there," he concludes, his tone flat with certainty.

She shakes her head no.

"Coroner said he'd never seen anything like it. Why'd he do that to himself? We know you were with him, so tell us why."

"I wasn't with him."

"Yes, you were. Did you get paid? Is that it, money?"

Detective Miller leans forward, her motion cutting off Bedrosian. "What I think is you've had a tough time in life, you have lots of bills to pay, no steady income. And maybe you were offered some help, is that right? And you're upset about what happened. I think maybe you got involved in something and maybe you didn't know how far it'd go. Is that right, Lucy?"

It's close enough to the truth that Lucy could weep. The arrival huddles, his face turned to the light. His scrabbling stick legs on the mat. *Alee.* Lucy squeezes shut her eyes, pressing her fingers to her eyelids.

"Are you feeling sad, Lucy?" Miller asks in her gentle voice. "It's normal to feel sad about something like this. It's a terrible thing, what that poor boy went through. But he seemed well-cared for before he died. Maybe that was you, caring for him."

Lucy blurs her vision, stares down at the table.

"It's hard to be precise, with the cold we've had," Miller says, thumbing through some pages, "but the coroner's estimate means the boy was alive for several weeks after the date you were seen with him. What happened to him during that time? Where was he? Did you take care of him?"

Lucy shakes her head. They're way off, they have no clue. They'll never be able to tell the arrival in fact died right away, because their calculations are based on human biology. She's so exhausted, she can't sort out if that means more problems for her or not.

They can't hold her here forever, they don't have anything. Even Bedrosian, who told her he's got all the patience in the world, even he's looking a little wiped out. Sweat stains at the armpits, constantly scrubbing his jaw with his hand. His frustration gives her a small measure of pride.

She says, "I've told you a thousand times. I don't know anything."

They respond with silence. She listens to them breathing. She stares at a minuscule crack in the beveled table edge. She presses her fingertip into the sharp space. She imagines a muscled convict smashing his handcuffs against the edge, trying to get free.

IT'S BEDROSIAN WHO WALKS her out. He leads the way, his left shoulder dipping with each step. There's the whir of machines, fluorescent lighting, telephones ringing. She follows with her head down, barely keeping up. Her body feels wrecked. She was in that room for six hours, except for bathroom breaks. They turn down another hallway, get in an elevator. He punches the button with the heel of his hand. She can tell it's how he always does it. He stares up at the lights counting down the floors. The doors slide open, and he stands aside, his arm thrown out in invitation. The look on his face does not match the politesse. She slips past him. She thinks that's it, so she says, "I'm sorry I couldn't be of any use."

Instead, he takes her elbow and guides her across the lobby. It's snowing, the world outside dim with nightfall, streetlamps lighting up the gently floating flakes. He follows her out the door, right behind so she feels his weight against her, causing a twist of panic.

"Don't you apologize to me, Lucy Hennessey," he warns. "Look at me when I talk to you."

She obeys.

"Don't play me for a fool." He measures out each word, his breath puffs of white. "You're a part of this thing. I know it, and you know it."

"I told you—"

"Be quiet." He leans closer, forcing her attention. "You don't fit. Nothing about you makes sense. But I will figure it out, do you hear me?"

She takes a step back. "Can I go now?"

"We'll be in touch."

At the corner she glances over her shoulder. He's still standing there, watching her.

SHE WALKS. SHE'S CONSCIOUS of her own weight moving forward, or rather the lack of it. How thin and frail she is out here in the cold dark city, the buildings soaring up all around and rush-hour workers hurrying by with no mind for anyone but themselves, she's a rabbit. A cold, exhausted rabbit. She walks with her mittened hand cupped over her freezing nose. She passes a pizza joint, and the aromas make her woozy, but that's money she can't waste right now. Ideas are forming, vague swirls in the back of her mind. About the coming days, how to get through this. She won't be able to keep what's happened from Theo, no matter how much she wants to. She doesn't dare.

Preempt, she thinks.

She stops at a payphone, digs around her pockets for change. Dials Julian's cell. It rings and rings. He doesn't pick up unknowns. She waits through the interminable voice mail options, finally gets the beep.

"It's me. The cops came by. I thought it was better to go with them, so it's not like I'm hiding anything. I didn't say a thing. They've got nothing, I swear." Her voice cracks at the end. "I'll get a burner on the way home. I'll explain more later, O.K.?"

Julian will put two and two together just as she did, but she can't help that. Margot made her bed: what the hell was she thinking, calling cops? How could she be so stupid? So goddam full of herself and her bunk-boss superiority. Why should Lucy have a single thought for that prissy bitch, when she turned Lucy in without a second thought?

Depleted, Lucy sags into the payphone, her hand still gripping the receiver. She's been so wound up, now it's like the mechanism just snapped and she can't even move. The photo skims her vision, over and over: his white, dead face, lips slightly parted, the narrow little shoulders. But there was nothing she could have done. She can't let what the cops said get to her. She'd like to show them a kid serv getting torn to pieces by a Nafikh: *I'll show you murder.*

She blinks hard. Focuses on the crushed dirty snow around her boots. Cigarette butts, a candy wrapper. Graffiti all over the phone base and the phone itself. Call Josie for good head. You suck. Piano and guitar lessons by established musician. When she was a kid, Eva got her one of those electric keyboards, but Lucy quit after the first few lessons. She couldn't stand doing scales, the ladder of notes like nails scratching a board, the Source twisting in agony. Poor Eva. Everything she put up with. All that money on lessons for this, tutors for that, never mind the equity loan for college. *And for what. Look at me, I'm nothing.*

And now this.

The current jolts and races under her skin. She whips around, but it's just a serv a little way off down the sidewalk, her eyes already fixed on Lucy. They can never just pass each other. Always checking, who are you, what's your status, are you a danger, are you of any use. The serv's in sweats and sneakers, darting through the rush-hour crowd. She makes a beeline for Lucy.

"Scoops!" she hisses, and then she's gone, her long hair swinging on her back.

Lucy turns in place, peering up and down the street. There's nothing worse than getting scooped—a random call that a sentry can slap on anytime, mainly to provide insurance via numbers, cast a wider net around the Nafikh. Scooped servs usually have to stand outside a venue or trail a limo, nothing like the dangers of a regular call. But scoops don't count towards quota: they're just pointless drains of energy and time, one more noose around a serv's neck.

The sentries are still a good block away, coming down both sidewalks. She can pick them out even before her Source stirs. They're always in dark, baggy, nondescript clothes, wool hats pulled down low. They're nameless, faceless, forgettable, shadows moving through the unsuspecting world of real people going about their daily lives. But their black unmarked messenger bags are stocked with firearms, Tasers, full syringes, a tablet for logging stats. The best bet is to get out of sight, and Lucy feels a pang of pity for the clueless serv stepping out of a diner, right into their path. He immediately kicks up a fuss.

Pointless. He's screwed, even though there are two Faithful up ahead on the corner, ready and willing.

Lucy ducks away from the payphone and breaks into a jog. It must be so weird to be a sentry on scoop detail: all they see are servs scattering like ants. There's no subway nearby, which is unfortunate since in a pinch, the T is the safest place to hide: scoops don't waste their time going all the way down to a platform that could be empty by the time they arrive. At least it's approaching rush hour, so there's no way the Nafikh are going to be taken on a bus ride, one of Their favorite activities. She runs a few streets up, finds the 11 just about to leave, manages to leap on before the door closes. The Source pulses warning, causing an instant of anxiety, but it's just an ordinary serv sweating in the corner, flushed and miserable, his knapsack held to his chest. He registers her presence with a vague nod, then resumes staring out the window.

BY THE TIME SHE gets to the Essex Street stop, though, she can't help it, she gets off and heads for the T. She meant to keep going, make her connection, go home. But she's got an idea stuck in her head of confronting Margot and she can't shake it. She hurries down the steps and into the tunnel, into the blast of heat and fumes and screeching that signals a train pulling in. Sweat instantly prickles her scalp and she drags off her wool cap and mittens, unbuttons the parka all the way. It sucks for a serv to ride at this hour, to endure the sweltering press of bodies cramming in on all sides. She surreptitiously examines everyone around her, but no one seems interested: Bedrosian hasn't had a chance to pull his shit together and keep tabs, if he decides to do that at all. Now's her only chance: it won't take long for Theo to exact his revenge on Margot, and they sure as hell aren't going to let her stop in first to say her piece.

She gets out at Ruggles, scrolls through chat rooms for the kid bunk address. It's a few blocks away, not such a great neighborhood. She walks fast, keeping her eye on the street signs. She cuts through a small park. The benches are scrawled with graffiti. The primly trimmed bushes lining the path shelter butts, used condoms, crushed cans and cups. Guys in oversized coats and wool hats wander the perimeter, snickering come-ons when she walks by. One of them steps into her line of sight, postures and preens, flashing his teeth.

"Come on, loosen up, baby. You think you too good for me?"

They chortle together. She manages to shoulder by, lengthening her stride almost to a run. They don't press on, which is a relief, because one or two she could take, but they were too many.

The bunk turns out to be in a ratty tenement next to a vacant lot strewn with garbage. She climbs the stairs to the top floor and rings the buzzer. It takes way longer to get a response than she has in patience. She rings the buzzer over and over. At last, Margot opens the door.

"How could you?" Lucy snaps, and shoves her hard.

Margot stumbles backwards, almost falls. She teeters over to a chair and hangs onto the back. Lucy realizes she's stoned out of her mind, probably on the good stuff, too, seeing as she's a boss.

Though she's not so far gone she can't screw her face into that imperious, know-it-all look. "What's the matter, Lucy? Are you in some kind of trouble?"

"You know I am! What the hell is wrong with you? How could you do this?"

"What else could I do? I tried to tell a sentry. Fat lot of good."

"You told a *sentry*?"

"You know what she said? 'The Gate doesn't care about some dead serv,' she said. As if she was never one of us."

Lucy drops her bag on the couch and sinks down beside it, at a loss for words. Margot stumbles her way around the chair, seats herself. It's dead quiet except for an oversized white clock ticking above the kitchen table. Across from where Lucy's sitting, a doorway gives onto a room where three bunk beds stand in a row. All the beds have matching red plaid blankets. The whole place is weirdly tidy, like all Margot does is clean up.

"Where are they?" Lucy nods towards the bedroom.

"I only have two right now. They're on a call."

Lucy stifles further questions: How long have they been out, who were the sentries, how many Nafikh. She sets her jaw, says, "Can you just tell me why?"

Margot sighs, as if the answer should be obvious. "Because, Lucy. Someone has to pay."

"But they won't pay."

Margot shrugs. "Better than nothing, you taking a ride."

As in, a ride in the crazy car: when a serv gets picked up by cops, he can either spew the truth and be called crazy, or say nothing and feel crazy. Until now, Lucy never appreciated the full meaning of that. "Well, thanks a lot. It really sucks, if you want to know."

This elicits no reaction, so Lucy leans forward, raising her voice. "Do you even understand the trouble you're in? They won't let you get away with this."

Margot drops her head back, her motions muted by the drugs awash in her veins. "I don't care anymore."

"If you want to check out, you're picking one fucked up way to go. You realize how bad they could hurt you?"

"Maybe I deserve it."

"Oh, come on. Get a grip."

Margot looks around the empty room. "You know, Lucy, I had the highest rate last year."

"Yeah?"

"I work so hard, to train them, so they make it out. But there's no point. They come home, but then there's the next call, and the next. So tell me, what's the point?"

The rawness of her plea makes Lucy uncomfortable. Servs don't share this kind of stuff out loud. Because, ironically, there's no fucking point to doing so. "It is how it is," she says, repulsed to be falling back on that tired phrase.

Margot barely reacts, as if it's all she expected. "And now my last two, they might not come back."

"Well, it doesn't help you're in no shape to pick them up."

Lucy's effort to break through falls flat. Margot's bleary eyes fix on her, full of sadness. She asks, "Why do you work for them?"

Lucy rubs her forehead. She's wiped out. Totally thrashed. "I've got no choice."

"You do so have a choice. The only one we get."

"I can't just check out, O.K.? I've got someone I have to take care of. I owe her."

Margot squints her eyes, trying to grasp this bit of news. She shakes her head, as if it's too much and she can't be bothered. "You could try to stop them. That's what you should do."

"Right—me? Like you said, even the Gate doesn't care. No one cares, Margot."

"Can't you just get a gun and shoot them?"

Lucy almost laughs. "The one who does this shit, I haven't laid eyes on him in years."

"But you know who he is. Where he is."

"Not even. I'm telling you, Margot. There's nothing I can do."

Margot shrugs again. "That's how it is, for us."

She keels over slowly, curls up on her side. "I always thought you'd get out," she mumbles into the chair arm.

"Why'd you think that?"

"Cause there was something different about you. You were smart, educated. I mean, it took me years to learn how to read, right? No one helped. They keep us low, but you, you were already up there. You had your fancy office jobs and all. I just figured you'd get out."

"Yeah," Lucy says after a moment. "I guess I thought that, too."

"Yeah. Well."

There is a silence. Margot's breaths soften, lengthen. She's passed out. Lucy gets up, goes to the bedroom doorway. Curtains with sashes, fringed carpet. A kiddie table and chair set, a few books. It's too much to absorb, all the kid servs that have passed through here, season after season, the beds filling and emptying. She always thought of bunk bosses as having it easy, but this kind of bunk, the way Margot keeps it, no way. All those kids, clothing them, feeding them, then saying good-bye. No wonder she's checking out. A handful of servs go that way every season, even without all that extra sorrow. The only reason so many hang on at all is just animal instinct, that recoil from death shared by all living creatures, even skinners.

It's a nasty question that's lingered around the edges of Lucy's days for years: would she be able to gut it out, if she didn't have Eva to think of. If all she had were the testy, changeable alliances forged in bunks and Services. It's hard to imagine the answer being yes.

Outside, she stands on the sidewalk for a time listening to the traffic, flecks of snow dancing down from the black sky above. She wonders where Margot's kids are, if they're waiting for their ride that isn't going to come. Who'll end up with them. Last she checked there were three ongoing Services. They could be anywhere, or already gone. More will arrive soon enough, get dumped at the overseers all around town. One day soon, Margot's phone won't pick up, and someone else will get her job. The beds will fill up, and then they'll empty, then fill again.

She dials Bernie. He answers with his mouth full, TV blaring in the background. She tells him wherever Margot's kids are, they'll need a ride home. She hears him chewing as he checks their location. He tells her there's only one left, and he'll text the sentry to give her a ride, they're almost done now.

She hangs up and walks on, head bent into the snow.

LUCY UNLOCKS HER DOOR, steps into the dark hallway. The bulb's burnt out, but the ceiling's so high in this old building that replacing it requires the super and his ladder, and she can't be bothered to ask. She dumps her keys on the kitchen counter, drags her new bottle of Jameson out of the paper bag. Her card is carrying debt again, but what the fuck after a day like today. The answering machine is blinking; the phone set dates back to when she first got her own place, and she's never bothered to upgrade. She presses play, and Eva's gravelly voice fills the empty air, asking where she's been and why hasn't she called, and then describing the minutiae of her day. She ate a bologna sandwich for lunch. She's having a sherry and looking out the picture window. Her latest library book is a bore.

Lucy's hands fumble as she lights a cigarette. The groceries Detective Bedrosian deposited on the counter are still there. A numbness creeps over her: she stares at the rumpled fleece blanket on the floor, the pile of newspapers the detectives sorted through, the chairs where they sat. The ghost of herself perched opposite them with her hands tucked in her lap. And now here she is, in the same space, what feels like a month later, and nothing's changed and everything's changed.

She makes herself move. She empties the grocery bags, opens the milk and sniffs, shoves it in the fridge. The rest she unloads into the cabinet: cans of tuna, refried beans, tomato soup. Then she folds up all the newspapers, stacks them near the front door to take to recycling later. She dusts the coffee table, washes the entryway floor where the detectives didn't wipe their shoes.

When she's finished, she finds herself on the couch right where she sat this morning. Maybe she thought all this activity would bring some kind of revelation, yield a plan. But she's got nothing. All she's got is herself, sitting in the dead quiet. Fighting the dread pooled inside her belly.

The words, unearthed from their dark place, won't quit repeating in her head: *He became a liability.* The dank, mildewy smell of the basement, the noisy dehumidifier in the corner. The wooden crate loaded with machine guns for transport to Eden, to be added to the stockpile in case the Gate ever came down on them. Joe Brynn sat on the edge of the crate, his slick egg head shining. He opened his hands, asking, You get it? Julian nudged the serv on the floor with his foot. He'd been beat up pretty bad, and he wasn't moving. Lucy didn't have to get any closer to know he was dead.

She got it.

She'd been after Julian ever since he moved her into the apartment and made clear her new role as a nobody. I don't deserve this, she kept insisting. I can hack it. I'm fine with the grabs, she even wept in hysterical sobs after a Service. That message, she regretted even as she left it, because it was over the top, not at all the way back into their good graces. To make up for that debacle, a few days later she left a message on Theo's line, real friendly and logical, reminding him of everything she sacrificed to be with them, reminding him of his promise that he'd dupe her, stuff like that. Inarguable truths.

That she could go so far kind of amazes her now; but she wasn't in her right mind. All she dreamed of was getting back to Ayer, where she'd giggle with Ernesto and munch on Turkish Delight. All she yearned for was to stand outside under a sky full of stars and put her cheek to the brown horse's muzzle, secure she'd be there forever.

But now, she got it. She got that she had to stop dreaming, that it was really, truly over.

She followed Julian out of the basement, into the kitchen of Joe Brynn's bunk. A serv was there frying sausages, and the air was heavy with greasy smoke. They stepped out onto the back stoop. Julian gave her a cigarette. She screwed up her courage and asked, Can't I just go my own way? I won't tell anyone about Theo or anything.

He narrowed his eyes at her through the smoke. What about your ma? You haven't said anything to her, have you?

Her Source flared, a blast of agony that left her gasping.

Because, Luce, that would be a big mistake.

I'd never! Lucy cried. Julian, you know that! She's got nothing to do with anything!

Julian felt bad: she saw it in the twist of his mouth, the way he buttoned up whatever threat he was supposed to deliver next. Instead, he said, Look, all you gotta do is as you're told, Luce, and quit your whining. You do that, everyone will be O.K.

I promise, she said, nodding her head like it was on a spring, desperate to be believed.

He tossed his cigarette and went back inside. The unlatched screen door creaked on its hinge in the breeze. The serv who was cooking stepped out with a pan of grease, poured it over the railing into the dirt, and only then did Lucy find her legs, take off down the steps.

For years, she hasn't thought about that day other than in passing. The chaos of that time faded long ago, molded into the robotic rhythm that now defines her existence. The phone rings, she answers, she does what she's told, comes home. The phone rings again, she does what she's told, on and on. Even the tiffs with Julian, the bouts of despair she endures in privacy, it's all part of the clockwork routine, neither here nor there. It's just how it is.

And that's the point, she tells herself.

She's never once stepped out of line. She's always done what she's told, even if she complains now and then. *I am not a fucking liability.*

She lights another cigarette, holds her hands out to examine her trembling fingers, curls them slowly into fists and squeezes. She spins the cap on the near-empty bottle of Jameson, finishes what's left in one gulp. She opens the new one.

By the third shot she's found a modicum of relief from the ache in her chest. She activates the burner she bought along with the whiskey, dials Julian's cell. It rings and rings.

"Hey, it's me," she says. "Call when you get a chance."

WAITING FOR THE PHONE to ring, Lucy opens the windows to let in the winter cold. She lies on the cool tile floor in the kitchen, folds her hands on her chest and presses down hard. *Stop it, you fucking former self,* she begs. The fantastic, grand sensation of *me* she felt at Theo's is a long-gone dream. She tried to hang onto it. She really did.

You came to us, Theo lectured, the first time she dared to beg for a dupe. You were free as you were. But you came to us, because in your heart, you understood the truth that you were *not* free.

She lay on his couch wrapped in a blanket, bruised and sore, and now humiliated. She'd come on her own after an all-night Service, sure her pitiful state would move him. Instead, she was getting this lecture in front of Alita, who was visiting from Maine. Alita listened in amusement, her legs crossed over the chair arm, dressed all in black, svelte as a movie star. Being around her made Lucy feel clumsy and dumb.

Do you understand, Lucy, that you were not really free?

Yes, Lucy whispered.

You lived a coddled life, Theo explained. Real people cannot begin to grasp the *notion* of what it is to suffer. In what way did you suffer, Lucy? In what ways do you *think* you suffered?

He wasn't looking for an answer, though she had one or two. Sean's da Uncle Seamus, huddled over a glass of gin and ice, leeching bitterness and rage. Eva hollering for him to stop beating on Sean, her bare feet skidding out on the slick floor till she landed on her knees with a crack and Lucy screamed. Her own wrists over the white sink while Eva rinsed away the blood.

She said, We didn't suffer.

Real people, Theo went on, are oblivious to what they have. Just as you were. But now, you will earn your freedom. You will deserve it. Do you understand?

She nodded. There was a bit of cork floating in the wine, and she worried at it with her fingertip, gave up. Tears rolled down her cheeks.

You'll see, Lucy-goosie, he said, and he came to her side, held her close. I will take you on a journey you can't even imagine.

She becomes aware of the painful stiffness in her joints from lying prone on the cold tile floor, drawing her back into the present: the narrow kitchenette with its crappy brown cupboards, the pipes dripping a permanent rust-colored stain down the wall, mouse turds under the stove.

A journey she couldn't imagine, he had that right.

HER CELL PHONE RINGS, buzzing hard and thunking on the wood table top. She scrambles to her feet, rushes over to answer.

"How in hell did you end up downtown?" Julian demands. "What do they know? What'd they ask?"

Her heart pounds furiously. It's all she can do to speak, let alone cultivate the indifferent tone she's planned on. "Did I see a man and a boy," she manages. "Did I know the boy. Was I there that night. Blah, blah. They don't have anything. I told you."

"They have the boy," Julian retorts. "And somehow the fuck or other, they have you."

Lucy's throat is a wad of hurt, blocking speech.

"How?" he demands. "Was it that kid boss who showed up?"

Margot made her own bed, but it still feels like shit to give her up. "It must've been."

"Tell me what you said."

"To who?"

"The cops, Lucy. The cops!"

He makes her go over the whole interview. What they asked, how they seemed, did she give anything up. She becomes aware of the tautness in her frame, feet pressed hard on the floor like she might spring up at any moment. Her throat is raw from cigarettes. Julian won't quit asking the same things over and over.

"Jesus, enough," she interrupts. "I already went through this today."

"Don't even," he warns.

Lucy bites her tongue, sets her jaw. Waits for her orders.

"Is there anything at your place that ties you to us? Anything at all? No scraps of paper, no pictures?"

"Nothing."

"Make sure you clean, you hear me? I don't want my prints popping up."

"You haven't been here in ages."

"What's that?"

Lucy hesitates. Then says through her teeth, "I'll clean."

"Now you listen. It's dead in the water, you understand? He's a runaway kid with no name, they can only expend so much effort on him. It's just a matter of time."

"O.K. I understand."

"You just act normal. Go about your normal business."

"What if they come here again? I mean, do I talk to them? Don't I have to?"

There is a pause. The hiss on the phone goes muffled, as if he's placed his hand over the receiver to consult with someone else. Theo, probably, which pricks her with unexpected hurt. Because this is such a special circumstance, you'd think he might speak with her directly, but no.

Julian comes back on the line. "Do you think they're onto you, Lucy?"

"No! I swear."

She holds the phone hard against her ear. Inside her head a frenetic spool of images: the detectives holding up the newspaper; herself, guilt pouring off her like an odor.

"We'll just take this day by day," he says. "And Lucy—"

"What?"

"Don't screw this up, or else."

He hangs up without bothering to say goodbye.

Lucy sets the phone down on the table. She'd forgotten, really. She's gotten so complacent over the years, talking back, getting snippy as he calls it. She'd forgotten the actual mind-numbing, draining terror of that day in the basement, and what he said after, about Eva.

Or else.

Just this morning, she was standing in the grocery store fretting over whether to indulge in Barilla pasta or stick with the cardboard-flavored store brand. The stupid, pointless scene brings on the sting of tears, and she shoves her palms against her squeezed-shut eyes, she's so pissed, so helpless, she's gone round and round in circles her whole life, always back to this same shit place. Service, running errands, riding up the elevator with whatever arrival they've dumped on her, it's the same crushed, mangled feeling of being trapped with no way out.

She's tried and tried. She even enrolled in online courses last year to become a paralegal. To have a real career ready for when she hits quota. What a joke. She couldn't even keep up for one semester, and is still paying off the debt.

And now—she'll be out all the extra bits of cash she relies on. Till this blows over, there's no way Theo's giving her any work, even crap errands, not so long as she's taking a ride.

There's no stopping her spiraling panic: what if she loses this apartment? If this drags on, she'll have no value. He'll boot her, and there's no way she can get a place on her own, not without first month, last month, security. She'll end up in a bunk with a bunch of bottom-feeding, drug-addled, thieving servs. Her professional life will go down the tubes: there's nowhere in a bunk to keep a wardrobe, shoes, bits of jewelry, and no boss would approve her doing that kind of work, anyway. Which means she won't be able to pay off Eva's loan. Eva will lose the house.

Jesus, pull it together!

Think.

She has a couple hundred stashed in the bank. Julian might be guilted into helping: he knows damn well this mess isn't her fault. All she needs is a room somewhere. She doesn't need a whole apartment: she's been spoiled. A room, a closet, she's good to go. Theo can go shove his precious apartment.

It would be a relief to get out of here, actually. Just pack a box and go. She doesn't have much, and most of it she'd just leave here. The shitty oval coffee table and armchair from the Salvation Army. The couch that was already here when she moved in. She tossed a patterned quilt over it, something Eva's friend made to celebrate the adoption: a relic concealing a wreck. In the kitchenette, there's a plastic folding table with one chair. The cupboards are mostly empty. Even her bedroom consists of just a mattress on the floor, no matter if she draws up the sheets and blanket and sets the pillow square and fluffed.

It's salt in the wound to imagine how, exactly, the detectives saw this place when they walked in: it's just so pitiful, this ramshackle, poverty-stricken scene with the near-empty Jameson bottle, more like the clustered belongings of a squatter than a young woman who takes temp assignments in fancy offices. She wonders what they made of the few artifacts from her real-person life. Bedrosian mentioned the books and the picture, but did they notice the album Eva gave her for Christmas, next to a glass bowl filled with pebbles from Nantasket Beach? Or the old postcard of Paragon Park taped to the wall right above it? She's had it since she was a kid. The picture was taken sometime in the 1950s, at sunset, the clouds sweeping the giant sky above the graceful curve of the rails. It's all gone now, of course. The picture's an echo, a little winking light in the dark.

You came to us just a year before they broke up Paragon Park, Eva used to sigh nostalgically, and Lucy always felt bad, as if she'd been the harbinger of all that ruin.

The blinking on the machine reminds her of Eva's message. She pictures Eva leaving it, then treading heavily across the floorboards away from the telephone stand (cordless phones kill you with radiation, she insists) back to her post by the window. Eva loves that picture window. On a clear day, you can see out to the islands.

She picks up the phone and dials while arranging the couch pillows and sinking down, dragging the blanket over her legs.

"Hey," she says when Eva picks up. "Sorry, I was out most of the day."

"I just wanted to say good luck on Wednesday," Eva says. "Are you excited?"

The new assignment—the one she told Eva about, that might lead to something permanent. With all that's happened, Lucy actually forgot. "Yeah, I am," she says. "I can't wait, actually."

"Will you come on the weekend? We can celebrate."

"I hope so. Yes, probably," she corrects, swiftly calculating that the way the Service roster stands right now, there's a good chance she'll have Friday or Saturday off. "Can you do the meatloaf?"

"Of course," Eva gushes, always delighted when Lucy puts in a request. "I'll shop tomorrow."

They chat about the cats and how Sean repaired the exhaust fan in the bathroom. Eva has tickets to a play in Hingham on Thursday. She and Phyllis are going.

After she hangs up, Lucy lights another cigarette, her leg jiggling nervously. Nothing will happen, she reassures herself. It will all work out. She's taking a ride, is all: there's always a first time for everything. She just has to hang tight and not fuck up, or else.

It's the story of her life. She's a pro.

LUCY SHOWERS AND DRESSES in her office clothes: cream button-down, navy skirt, neutral hose. She switches to tan slacks, back to the skirt. Arranges her hair into a chignon and finally opts for a tidy ponytail. She's been temping for years, but with every new assignment, she still gets nervous, preyed upon by the need to impress. She carefully rolls a pair of socks over the hose; she'll wear boots and change into her pumps once she's in the building. She stands in front of the mirror, staring at her expressionless, weird face, the skin so white. Ghost-girl, the kids at school used to call her. Vampire. She smoothes her hair back, redoes the ponytail. Blots her lipstick again.

She never looks quite right, as if it shows, the sickness of her hidden, alien life.

But that's pure fancy. Like anyone would ever think.

She's cautiously hopeful that things will all work out. She's heard nothing from the cops for days, and she got a message from Julian via Bernie to just hang tight. The papers are full of new headlines already. It's going to blow over, like Julian said.

She lingers in front of the mirror, staring at the self she creates for the outside world. She takes pleasure in wearing these clothes. She looks forward to the methodical filing and copying, writing tidily on Post-its, fetching coffee from the communal kitchen. It's a big law firm, this one. The kind that, if they like her, they'll support her finishing up her paralegal degree, maybe help her go beyond that.

This feeding on the leftover crumbs of all her old dreams is a bad habit. But she can't help it, especially at times like this, on the brink of what should be all kinds of possibilities. When she accepts a job, when she travels to it and performs it, when she gets her paycheck, no matter how measly it is: these are the only times she feels like she might still have a normal life.

At least yesterday's Service was a breeze. She sent Bernie a few pizzas in exchange for switching her to an early shift, so she'd be able to get some rest before her first day. The call was way up in Rockport. The Nafikh were styled as tourists on a visit from Austria who wanted to see this famous attraction even if it was the dead of winter. They walked around in the freezing cold, stared at the harbor for a while, then entered a pub. The bet was it'd be empty on a weekday afternoon, and it was. Lucy and her two fellow servs scored beers and burgers, so as to make their party seem normal. The only hitch was one of the Nafikh started losing His manners over the bartender pestering them so much about Austria, wanting to know where to stay if he traveled there, which he might in summer, he didn't know yet, but it would be cool. Lucy had to flirt him off, giggle him back to the bar, where she gave him all sorts of advice, things she'd gleaned from TripAdvisor.

If she can just hold this balance, if Bernie stays good with her bribes, it could all work out. With less than two months left in the season, and enough servs this year to keep the rotation reasonable, Lucy's letting herself dream a bit about saying yes, if a full-time offer comes out of this new job.

She's in good cheer when she steps out of the building, till the Source tugs, sending darts of hurt into her ribs. It's the teen serv who showed up in the neighborhood about a week ago. She's halfway down the block, fleece hat tugged low over furious green eyes.

"You need anything?" she hisses, stepping into Lucy's path.

"Do I look like I do?" Lucy retorts, dodging the girl's outstretched hand.

"Fuck you." The girl steps back, disappointment etched all over her gaunt little face. Lucy speeds up, impatient with the pity she feels. It's hardly Lucy's fault the girl got stuck dealing. She'll earn her bunk bed and daily rations. She could very well be in some cockroach-infested motel opening her legs for the same, or worse, forced into duping, so all things considered, she's not so bad off.

Lucy stays close to the wall, out of range of tires spitting salty slush. People hurry down the sidewalks, eyes glazed over, giving wide berth to the guys huddled disconsolately around the steps of the convenience store. The bell jingles, and the owner barges onto the sidewalk, yelling curses at a car parked in front of the hydrant. The driver's side door swings open, and to Lucy's dismay, Detective Bedrosian gets out. He looms over the guy, holding up his badge.

Lucy stumbles, she should turn around, get the hell out of here, but he's seen her. Of course he has; she's the reason he's here at all. He watches her approach without expression, making her feel clumsy and anxious. He's wearing a furry Russian hat with the flaps tied up and a thick wool coat, a hulking figure amid the fast-walking commuters. She's got no choice but to stop in front of him.

"I can't talk now," she says. "I'll be late."

He shrugs. "First day, you need to be on time, I get it. I stopped by the office," he adds. "Spoke to your supervisor."

It takes a moment to absorb the chilling news that he's been at the agency. "What do you mean? What did you say?"

"You like your work, Lucy?"

"Sure," she says, confused. "Yes."

"I hear you turn down a lot of assignments."

"Not really," she stammers. "No, I don't."

"Well, according to your supervisor, you do. The last one was, let's see," he licks his thumb and flips pages in his notebook, "first week of January. You hadn't worked for a while already, and it was choice. Care to explain?"

Lucy's mind scrambles, alights on the endless nighttime bus ride to Montreal, the on-board toilet stench, the miniature bags of pretzels and weak coffee. She says, "I had a flu. I couldn't kick it."

"The flu, huh. Too bad."

She glances down the street, starting to feel desperate. "I'm going to be late."

"Won't take long. Why'd you drop out of Bunker Hill?"

The turn's too sudden to catch up. "What?"

"You had decent grades. You were, I quote, 'attentive and enthusiastic.' That was your Intro to Law prof. She remembered you."

Lucy is aghast. "You spoke to my teachers?"

"Just the one. So why did you drop out?"

"I don't see what that has to do with anything."

"Why does it bother you, me asking about college?"

She doesn't answer. The thick, giddy fullness of that time, buried so long, wells up in a choking lump. Books piled on the floor, her notebooks, the feel of the padded chair in the lecture hall.

"Maybe it was a mistake you regret," he proposes. "Young people make dumb mistakes all the time. I know I did. Why'd you leave, then? What happened?"

"I'm going to lose this job!" she blurts. "Please, just let me go."

He looks at his watch, his bushy eyebrows furrowing. "I guess you might. You better get going, then. Oh, and Lucy?"

She's already leaving, has to turn around. "What?"

"Your old roommates, what were their names?"

"How should I know? It was ages ago."

"Try and remember."

"Angie. Angie Leavett had the lease. I think one of the others was Sabine. She was from Ethiopia. I can't remember the other one. Why do you need their names?"

"Just routine."

She stares at him a moment, her mind scattered with confusion as to why he'd need that information. He taps his watch, indicating she'd better get a move on. She whips around and breaks into a jog, her heart racing hard and the Source tweaked and loosing darts of pain, signaling fear. Her neck goes stiff from the effort not to look back. But she succeeds. She gets around the corner, goes limp, slows down.

"Have a good day," he calls, jerking her to attention.

He's done a ueuy. He waves out the window, then the car tears off down the street.

The subway ride is a torturous, tense event, her anticipation of the day obliterated. She sits hunched with her hands wrapped tight around the burner phone till the surface is slick with sweat. *Call. Don't call. Call. Don't call.* Julian might never find out. They can't possibly be watching her every second. Best not to trouble trouble: if it does come out, she'll just say it didn't seem important. Downplay all the way.

The guy opposite her unfolds his newspaper, flips it, and a full-page ad for Aer Lingus appears, clover leaf against a blue sky, glorious green landscape beneath. It's ludicrous, seeing that right at this moment, like the universe is mocking her. She twists in her seat, closes her eyes.

The image of Bedrosian visiting her supervisor torments her. She pictures him asking questions, grunting uh-huh, and what about this, and what about that. What could he have possibly said to explain why he was asking about Lucy Hennessey? She feels sick. And her old teacher, what the hell did he say to her?

He's not going to give up. He'll keep digging around, bothering her. And what about when Julian finds out? She can only downplay so much.

She almost misses her stop she's so distraught. She jumps to her feet, squeezes and pushes her way to the doors, earning angry looks. She's sweaty and tense climbing the steps out of the subway, dimly aware of the Source flashing pain but paying it no attention. Until she practically walks right into a sentry.

No, no, no, please.

The sentry's her own height, Asian with bright, perfect skin, jet-black hair in braids on either side of her face, wool cap pulled low to the sharp curves of her eyebrows. Lucy feels like an insect being pinched in tweezers, the way the sentry examines her with cold, mathematical precision. "Name," the sentry commands. She taps the answer on her tablet. "Lucy Belle Hennessey, dropped as an *infant*? Picked up at nineteen?" the sentry marvels. "Wow, that was shit luck. 182 out of 303, five calls so far this season. *And* Montreal—that's a drag."

"Please don't scoop me," Lucy begs. She points at her destination. "I have a job, I really need it. I just Served the other day."

"So you did."

"If I don't show up, I'll lose this job. I can't lose it."

The sentry squints at her, bemused. "One of those, are you."

By which she means, a serv trying to shape a life so she can have one beyond quota. As in, a total idiot. Lucy nods, mentally scrambling for excuses she can give her supervisor.

"Go."

For a second, Lucy doesn't understand. The sentry widens her eyes, parodying Lucy's amazement, and thrusts her chin in the direction Lucy was headed.

"Thank you!" Lucy blurts.

The sentry's already moving on down the sidewalk, scanning for others.

Lucy makes her legs move, though they feel wobbly and weak. She trips and almost falls flat on her face. Someone seizes her arm, keeping her upright. He's already gone before she can say thanks, swallowed into the crowds rushing in both directions.

The world whooshes back into focus. Her job, the time, the way the day was supposed to go. She hurries through the crowd, just another worker bee on a frenetic weekday morning.

THE FIRM'S LOCATED IN a glass tower near the harbor. The building has shining marble floors, and farther ahead Lucy sees a serene atrium with aluminum tables and chairs scattered among the potted ferns. The voluminous space rises all around, silent, dignified. Lucy stops inside the entrance to change out of her boots into pumps under the concierge's understanding gaze. She tells him her destination, and he says, "Thirty-second floor to the left, miss," and politely indicates the elevators. Inside the quiet elevator with its gilded mirrors and panel of gold buttons, Lucy straightens her shoulders, willing herself into the state of bright, pleasant alertness required of her position.

The office manager's Polish last name is unpronounceable. "Everyone calls me Mrs. M.," she says with a cheery wink. "Now where are *you* from originally? Sweden? Denmark?"

"I don't really know," Lucy says demurely. "I was adopted."

"Oh—" Mrs. M. shapes her mouth into a pitying smile. "Well, wherever you're from, you come quite highly recommended, don't you!"

Mrs. M. goes over Lucy's tasks with fastidious care, every step from start to finish. "We just want to be sure you're comfortable here," she says. Lucy examines her in secret as Mrs. M. works her way down the detailed list: the lightly powdered skin, faint rose blush, square no-nonsense fingernails a pale pink. She smells clean and well-rested. Her gray hair is gently waved and caught in a barrette. Lucy wonders how long it took to be elevated to her managerial position. She pictures herself years from now in a similar charcoal skirt suit, a string of pearls resting on her neck, greeting the temp as she arrives.

If she plays her cards right, the supervisor said. Lucy was so full of anticipation for this job starting, but as she trails Mrs. M. through the office, nodding polite greetings as she's introduced, all she can think about is Bedrosian's ambush, the menace in his questions and how he looked at her. She fights to hang onto her earlier satisfaction, but it fritters away under the anxious memory as surely as the hundreds of documents she has to feed through the shredder, her first task of the morning. We just have to get this done, Mrs. M. apologized, then we'll get you to proofing, don't worry. But given Lucy's current state of mind, the tedious, solitary work is welcome. She's in a narrow, white-walled room stacked floor to ceiling with office supplies. A gigantic copier studded with various feeders and handles stands against the wall, blinking and beeping now and then as if it has its own agenda. The shredder is located under the window. She sits on a stool whose wheels slide on the linoleum floor every time she makes any motion. She clutches at the floor through her shoes, and soon her leg muscles start to hurt. She feeds the documents into the machine. Other secretaries pop in, merrily checking on the temp, and she obliges them with mindless chitchat. She empties the shredder bin into a big plastic bag; shreds cling to her skirt and hose, they float up with uncanny lightness and settle on her arm hairs, resisting her vigorous brushing, glued down with static. She starts shredding the next batch.

Lucy's Source prickles deep within, and she looks up, startled. After a few minutes, when the pain doesn't abate or increase, she gets up, peers out the sealed window, searching the street far below.

A sleek white limousine is stuck at an intersection and the light's gone red, sending everyone into a fury. A policeman approaches on horseback. The limousine door opens. From within, first a pair of long legs in white leather boots emerge, followed by a tall, splendid Nafikh in a swirling silver dress and an elaborate feathered hat. Lucy lets out her breath, relieved she's so far up, or else she'd be bent over puking, and that wouldn't go over too well in the office. The Nafikh turns in place, Her face lifted upwards. It is radiant with pleasure; They always love a good dose of the Financial District with its mirrored buildings, ornate facades, and the glistening bay with its fleet of bobbing white vessels. Passersby slow down, craning to see what's holding up all the traffic. A group of tourists snaps pictures, assuming the lady with the limo must be famous. Servs mill on the sidewalks, subtly blocking people from getting too close.

The policeman arrives just as the Nafikh's sentries usher Her back inside the limousine. The horse is tense, high-stepping and tossing its head. A path clears, and the limo glides away, carrying the Nafikh towards whatever new adventures lie in store.

Lucy steps back, sinks onto the stool, which promptly swoops off to the left, carrying her smack into the metal shelving.

She clutches her dinged elbow, gritting her teeth against the lancing pain. *Fuck, fuck, fuck.*

The room returns to itself: a close, hot space full of white and gray things.

She starts feeding documents again. The air fills with the whirring noise, the machine giving off heat that prickles her cheeks and neck. She stuffs the documents in ten at a time, even though the label on the front cautions against it. The feeder slows, groaning and grinding, and comes to a stop. Lucy stares down at the tightly crumpled stack of papers poking out of the dead machine.

After a time, she unplugs the cord and lifts the top part of the shredder out of the bucket. A volley of shreds flies up, plasters her pantyhose anew. Lucy works with anxious concentration, dragging each sheet out. She's probably wrecking the machine, so she works fast, before someone catches her in the act.

A SECRETARY CALLED MARCIE invites her to lunch. "It's tradition!" she waves off Lucy's protests. Lucy stops in the bathroom first. The lighting is dim, the counters and walls a gray granite, the stall doors black. She carefully applies a new layer of powder in the tomb-like silence. She rinses her hands, closes her eyes a moment, listening to the water trickle from the faucet.

Marcie suggests they eat in the atrium downstairs. Sunlight filters through the glass ceiling, but the temperature's thankfully calibrated towards cooler. Marcie buys her a turkey wrap and a cappuccino. "Oh, you shouldn't pay!" Lucy cries, as is expected. They carry their trays to one of the polished tables and sit. Marcie is in her early twenties. She graduated Wellesley College last spring. She's working a year then she'll apply to law school. She's infectiously happy and lively, her bobbed brown hair constantly falling from behind her ears so that she has to keep tucking it back as she talks.

"You look like a model," she praises. "Did you ever model?"

"Oh, no," Lucy demurs. "I'd never have imagined."

"So what's your story?"

Marcie leans forward, her eyes bright with curiosity. Lucy knows how she appears. Older, unfulfilled. No BA on her resume, no permanent positions.

"I like to work, save up, then travel," she says.

Marcie's eyes widen.

"I've been up to Montreal and Quebec City a ton of times. Nova Scotia, Halifax in particular. I like the winter festivals. This year I'm planning another Scandinavian tour," she elaborates, now drifting into lies, but they aren't, really, in the sense that she's read so much about these European destinations she might as well have been there. She can answer any question. "One of my all-time favorites is Dublin," she carries on. "You can take a bus all around the country. You should see the western coast in winter. It's so grand, practically mythological."

"Wow," Marcie breathes as Lucy winds down. "You are *so* lucky."

"It's good not to be stuck on one track," Lucy advises sagely.

"Yeah. I have to remember that. It's so great to meet you. We should do this every day."

"Sure," Lucy nods, "though sometimes I have to work through lunch, so I can leave early."

She explains about her aunt in Jamaica Plain who relies on her preparing dinner and getting groceries and so on. It's always a challenge. Marcie explains how awesome Mrs. M. is, not to worry. She never questions a sick day, she's so kind. Lucy files this information away, wondering if taking this job full time might be feasible after all. The hour passes, and Lucy relishes being part of this world with her little red tray with its crumpled napkins and wrappers, professionals milling about, the noise of her heels smartly tapping the marble floors as they head back for the afternoon shift.

In the elevator, her Service phone bleeps a text inside her bag. She ignores it, waving off Marcie's curious expression. "Just a med reminder," she says. "Antibiotics from a cold last week."

"That sucks."

She checks the message on the way back to the supply room. It's just a routine scheduling, not a last-minute replacement, which would have entailed a call from a sentry. She's on for nine p.m. Plenty of time to get home, eat, and power-doze for a few hours.

"How is your day going?" Mrs. M. inquires.

"Great," she replies, stuffing the phone in her bag, and in that moment, she actually means it.

SHE COMES IN AT three a.m., rings Bernie on Skype to check in. He looks misshapen on the screen, his fat face looming over the camera. Maybe Julian dicked him over on his first cut, because he doesn't look any better at all. He licks his lips once, then again, slow and suggestive.

"In your dreams, baby," she says tiredly. "Come on, Bernie. By my tally I'm at 183."

"And you would be . . ." he leans forward, dragging it out, eyes narrowed. "Correct," he sighs. "How's it feel to be over halfway?"

"I'm not counting my chickens."

"Address the same? Phone number? Yadda yadda?"

She nods. "No updates to speak of. Sleep tight."

Lucy reaches to switch off the session, but he holds up his hand.

"I heard you're taking a ride. Is it true?"

"Yeah," Lucy shrugs, as if it's no big deal.

"You tell me if you turn toxic, you hear?"

"No way that's happening, Bernie," she says. Bedrosian looms up in her memory from this morning, pen poised over his notebook like a threat. Actually—yesterday morning. She's been working nonstop since she saw him, and in three hours has to start all over again. "It's not going anywhere. They've got nothing."

"You keep it that way."

"Trust me, it's the last thing I want."

If Bernie thinks she's toxic, she'll get taken off the roster so as not to draw attention to her Serving. But for every call she misses, she gets penalties.

"What a cock-up," Bernie sighs. "You know Margot's gone back to the Gate," he adds, drawing his finger across his throat. "Had her picked up yesterday."

Lucy knew this was coming, but the news is still a shock. "That was fast."

"Yeah. They don't fuck around. You watch your ass."

"I'll be fine," Lucy says, and taps the key, stares at the blank screen. The tidy bunks in a row, the shining floors. She wonders what happened to that last kid, who's boss now.

It's Joe Brynn who usually does those jobs. The thought of him stepping into that space, Margot dozing on her chair, it makes her sick.

She gets up and draws the blinds, checking the street below. She can't tell if Bedrosian's there or not, or if any one of Theo's guys is watching, either. Her heart races hard, pumped up on anxiety. She can't even think of sleeping. She sits on the kitchen chair, smoking, staring hard at the floor.

Just because they got Margot doesn't mean the same will happen to her. It doesn't. Margot lifted the curtain, she gave real people an inroad to their existence. Never divulge: it's the biggest treachery a serv can commit. Whereas Lucy herself has done nothing. Nothing at all. She's holding up her end of the bargain.

Except for concealing she saw Bedrosian again.

She wipes the sweat off her hands, shakes them out. Flips open the burner and dials. Julian, a career insomniac like herself, answers on the third ring. "What?"

"Just checking in."

"Yeah?"

In for a penny.

"Well, I just want to get an idea of where things stand. I thought you said it'd blow over. So why's that cop still on my case?"

"Is he, now? What'd he ask this time?"

"Same old shit. Look, he bought the tip, O.K.? That's what it boils down to."

"Well, your friend's out of the picture, so she can't do any more harm."

"I know. So what do I do?"

"Well, Lucy, whatever you *are* doing, it doesn't seem to be helping."

This was not the direction she'd meant things to go in. She grips the phone tighter, says, "Julian, that is so fucking unfair, O.K.? This is your mess. I'm doing everything I can. Help me out here."

"Help *you*? You help *me*. You tell me those cops aren't coming back. You tell me you haven't said a word, not to them, not to anyone!"

"Of course I haven't! Jesus!"

"So what's to discuss? Just keep your mouth shut and trash this line."

"I'd never—"

He's already hung up. Furious, she digs in the kitchen drawer for the hammer. She drops the phone in the wooden box she keeps for this purpose, lifts her arm over her eyes, and brings the hammer down with a ferocious stroke. It crunches into plastic and metal bits. She tilts the box and empties the detritus into a plastic bag, ties it shut. She'll dump it in the morning. Then she'll have to shell out for another one, all because of Theo's fucking paranoia.

She goes to the bathroom and washes up. Under the blue-tinted economy bulb lighting, her reflection is reminiscent of a cadaver. It's past four a.m., and there's no hope of looking even halfway decent in a few hours. At least she didn't take any blows in Service: it was an outdoors call in Billerica, a long wait in a snowy clearing under a low-hanging full moon. The Nafikh just stood there, turning in place, staring up at the stars. One of the servs literally fell asleep on her feet.

She drags herself to bed, her body a dead weight. Her mind fills up with memories of Joe Brynn's bunk, the top floor deck at night, chain smoking and gazing at the city lights. She spent a lot of time up there. Margot moved in during Lucy's last few weeks, when Julian hardly came around anymore. That's why she didn't name him when she called the cops; she probably never even met him. She found Lucy on that deck one evening, complained about how she never cleaned up the kitchen. Fuck you, Lucy told her. Margot sat with Lucy nevertheless, arms wrapped tight around her knees, gazing at the lights. She bummed some smokes. They didn't talk much that night, or after, except to say hello. Lucy borrowed band aids from her once, but never gave any back.

Lucy pushes her face into the pillow, curled up tight, staring into the dark.

ON LESS THAN TWO hours' sleep, the workday passes minute by grinding minute. She's finished with the shredding and has moved onto the filing backlog in a glass-walled room where the attorneys store all the firm's cases, going back five years. She moves back and forth from the manila folders shelved on the metal rolling cart to the tall, stately mahogany filing cabinets. The work is steady and thankfully mindless. She has lunch with Marcie and a few others, casually mentions that she'll need to start bringing in lunch, she can't afford to eat out every day. They leap on this idea as practical and smart; from now on, they'll all bring sandwiches and find fun places to go eat them.

"Already done so much?" Mrs. M. praises in the late afternoon. "You are such a gem."

"Thanks," Lucy replies, unable to help feeling proud, though a monkey could do this work. She's looking forward to proofing briefs, which should start next week.

She sits on the subway seat, arms around her purse, staring at the lights blinking each station, the announcements drowned out by the roar of the train and screeching brakes. She imagines herself, shrunken and huddled with her white face turned upward. Blank, sticky, exhausted. The being segmented by the time frames in which it operates: wake up, prepare for work, work, return from work. The dryness on her fingers, microscopic paper dust, the thumb sore from separating thickly packed files.

She texts Bernie: *Tell me I'm clear.*

A few moments later, the reply: *All good baby.*

She sends back a few smileys and a thumbs up.

She's not on the roster tonight, but it's good to have confirmation, and this little exchange will tip things in her favor should Bernie need to tack more servs onto a call. The train careens around a bend, and she tucks her legs to avoid the swelling crush of off-balance strap-hangers. At her stop, she elbows her way to the door, pushes out the moment it opens. She becomes part of a stream of people moving with harried urgency along the platform, bottle-necking at the stairs, climbing. The blast of cold sweeping down from the street is dizzyingly welcome; at the top, Lucy steps to one side, leans against a pole to recover, breathing deeply.

When she rounds the corner onto her street, she finds the idea of climbing up to the dingy apartment unbearable, her only prospect being to sit in stoic solitude under the oppressive weight of all her problems. So she walks right on by the house, loops back towards Porter Square where her favorite local bar serves affordable shots.

Now we're talking, she thinks, and downs the first shot of Jameson in one gulp. She signals for another. The bartender Ewan's already on his way: Lucy is not exactly a regular, but her distinctive looks and surprising capacity to hold her liquor make her hard to forget.

Lucy turns in her seat, finally relaxing a little. There's a folk band setting up for seven p.m. Banjo, fiddle, drums, a sweet-looking young woman warming up her voice. Judging by the tone, she'll be offering up ballads. It's Eva's favorite kind of music, that sad, Irish-sounding stuff. Lucy typically can't stand listening to music, she prefers silence. But tonight, she could be in the mood. She could stay till bedtime, skip the whole sitting around staring at the walls part of her day.

She feels someone maneuvering onto the stool next to hers, turns a little to make room.

"Hey, there," Bedrosian says, crushing the little bit of pleasure she was just starting to feel. "Mind if I join you?" While Lucy watches in consternation, he removes his hat, the Russian thing with fur and flaps, and sets it on the counter. He eases himself onto the stool, and Lucy shifts away, his leg uncomfortably close. Ewan steps over. "Just water," Bedrosian says. "I'll have a burger, though. Medium. No onions. You hungry?"

Lucy shakes her head and throws back her second shot, slides the glass forward for more.

"Wouldn't want to try and drink you under the table," Bedrosian comments. "Long day at work?"

"Yes."

His water arrives. Her shot glass is refilled.

He uses the stirrer to poke at the clumped ice, then takes a long drink. "I just have a few more questions," he says, "but they can wait. You take some time to unwind."

Lucy's mouth is all dried up, and she doesn't trust her hand to pick up her glass without spillage, but her Source is sparking, and she's got no choice. She grips the glass and drinks up, relishing the blast of alcohol. He just watches. She knows it's deliberate, what he's doing, to get her on edge, and it's working, the not-talking making her jumpy. She leans back a little, trying for casual. "What kind of name is Bedrosian, anyway?"

"Armenian. Bedros means Peter. Petros. Rock. The name means 'son of Bedros.'"

There's a pause in which Lucy wonders why the hell she asked and what to say next.

"My great-grandparents came over," he offers. "Diyarbakir." The word is a jumble that means nothing to her.

"They had five children, and only one survived. That was my grandfather. When I was a boy, he used to tell me how much I looked like his little brother Viken. I'm named after him, Viken Bedrosian. I have his curls," he gestures at his hair. "All his siblings, they died in the genocide by the Turks. Have you heard of that?"

"Yes," Lucy says, "I think so."

"It's a tough life, immigrants. Sticking together, never really belonging, and all because. It never ceases to confound me, what people are capable of," he says, slowing, with emphasis. "They were just little kids. Maimed and killed."

Lucy stiffens. "That's very sad."

"You're a good liar," Bedrosian shakes his head in admiration. "You probably lie all the time, get a lot of practice."

This is sliding hard at the truth. Lucy maintains her bland, emotionless stare.

He lifts her empty glass, gestures to the bartender. "Let me get the next one."

"I need to get home, actually."

"No, you don't. I have some questions."

"Shouldn't this be at the station, or something? Is this even allowed?"

This amuses him. "You prefer to go to the station? We can go there, if you want. You want to go?"

The bar is filling up with energetic young people in print tee shirts, porkpie hats, sideburns. The fiddler starts tuning up, each note slicing through the jabber. Lucy wills herself to just leave, but she can't, in case Bedrosian stops her. Pulls out his badge, yells she's under arrest: that's the scene that swoops into her head, paralyzing her.

"So," Bedrosian says, leaning over his elbows and watching her sideways. "Detective Miller and me, we paid a visit yesterday to your old roommate Angie."

Lucy watches Ewan fill her glass again. "Oh, yeah? Does she still have that bouffant hair?"

He indulges this with a faint smile. "She's married in Winchester. Two kids," he holds up two fingers. "Husband in finance."

"Huh."

"She said you went out to Ayer a lot with some boyfriend called Julian. She couldn't remember his last name."

It's a blow that leaves her quaking. She manages to tip the glass to her mouth, sip real slowly, buy some time. "That was a hundred years ago," she shrugs, wiping her mouth. "I can't remember either."

"He couldn't have been too special, then."

"He was just some guy."

"Yeah? Angie said he's the reason you dropped out."

"I don't get what my failed college career has to do with anything."

"Looks to me like a lot," he replies. "You still in touch with him?"

"No."

"What did he do for a living?"

"I don't know."

"How do you pay for all those shots of Jameson?"

"You're paying for this one."

"How do you pay off Eva Hennessey's loan every month?"

"Jesus!" Lucy snaps. "You have no right."

He merely looks at her, waiting.

"I work my ass off, O.K.? That's how."

The noise level has really ramped up now, with drums getting adjusted and the banjo in the mix. They are surrounded by laughter and the noise of clinking glass. It's getting hot: Lucy wants to take off a layer, but that would signal she's up for staying. Bedrosian leans in close. "You must have cash income, Lucy. No way you cover rent, the loan, groceries, utilities—uh-uh. Want to tell me what other jobs you got?"

"I don't have other jobs."

"It's simple math," Bedrosian shakes his head. He twirls the stirrer between his fingers, pops it between his teeth and chews, considering her. "You get paid to do something with that kid, Lucy?"

"This is ridiculous."

"Yeah? I know your kind, Lucy."

"What's that supposed to mean?"

"Selfish," he says. "Thinking only about your own survival. Beat down, desperate, just making it day to day."

"Wow. I didn't think I come off that bad."

He meets her weak joke with a flat stare. "You've got bills to pay, Lucy. A lot of them. I don't know how you pull it off, in winter. You being so sick all the time, I mean."

Their eyes lock.

He knows: the thought flies at her out of nowhere.

She goes clammy and weak, and a few seconds pass, an eternity. Then she says, "I really have to get home." She slides off the stool.

"Not so fast," Bedrosian says, blocking her with his arm.

"Yo," Ewan sets the burger down, sliding a paper mat into place first. "What's up? He bugging you?"

Yes, Lucy conveys with all her being. Bedrosian reaches under his jacket, flips the badge into the bartender's line of sight. The look of surprise on Ewan's face shames Lucy to the core. He retreats down the bar. Bedrosian looks at her, then slowly lowers his arm. "It's not you I'm interested in, understand? You help me, you'll make out fine. Think about it."

He spins the stool, directs his attention to his meal. Lucy winds her way through a bunch of guys who grin, flirting, holding up beers in invitation. Outside, she breaks into a clumsy half run, hampered by the treacherous wet sidewalk. She checks over her shoulder, but he isn't following. She's a high hum of wordless panic that pushes her along down one road, across the next.

He can't know, the rational side of her keeps insisting. It's absurd to think this guy, this cop, could know the truth about her. The stuff he said, it could be taken any which way. It's nonsensical to assume the worst.

She gets inside her apartment at last, rams the two bolts home. Stands there, out of breath. She becomes aware of how hot she is in her down parka, huddled in the corridor in such a state. Sweat's leaking down her sides into the waistband of her skirt. She kicks off her boots, pulling off her coat at the same time and dumping it on the floor as she strides across the room. She flips open her laptop, keys in her password.

The Google search on Bedrosian does little to help her out. He's been a detective for a number of years. He's quoted in a few older articles on homicides. There's a piece on his role in a soup kitchen in Watertown, which is full of Armenians, apparently. He's got a review on Amazon of some book on Armenian cooking, unless that's a different V. Bedrosian. He only gave it three stars; why, who cares.

She slams shut the laptop. She's supposed to alert Bernie if she thinks a real person knows something about them. It's the rule, make a report to whoever, an overseer, a sentry. But no way she's doing that: he'll stamp her toxic before she's done talking.

She can't even think about what if Julian hears. Never mind if he knew Bedrosian has his fucking *name*—

Although, she could alert him, make it like a warning, like she's helping him out. She stares blindly at the floor, imagining the way such a conversation might go. *Why would I tell you if I'm the one that spilled? Jesus, Julian, get a grip!* She could push hard for them to get rid of Bedrosian. He knows about servs, he poses a major threat. Things are worse than any of them ever thought, and so on.

It could work.

Except, going after a cop, that's a whole other league. They wouldn't take the risk, not when they can just get rid of Lucy herself.

A loud rapping makes her jump. Lucy stares down the corridor, frozen. The rapping starts again. Filled with dread, Lucy tiptoes to the door, looks through the peephole. It's the super, staring back at her with bored resolution as if he knows he's being examined.

"Ms. Hennessey," he calls, rapping the door again. "I know joo can hear! I just saw joo come in!"

"What is it?" Lucy says.

"Package! I sign for joo!" He holds up a large envelope, blocking the view of his face. "Looks *muy importante!*"

Her hands hover uncertainly over the bolts. It could be from Julian. Maybe they're using the mail because it's safer.

"Who's it from?" she asks.

"*Puta*, I'm your secretary?"

She hurriedly undoes the bolts. "Fine, sorry, give it to me."

Bedrosian steps into view. "I'll take it from here."

"*Siento*, is police, what can I do," the super shrugs at Lucy. He trundles off down the hall, the envelope that tricked her under his arm.

Lucy tries to push the door closed again, but it's too late. "You can't come in," she protests. "You have to go."

"Well, no," he corrects, and shuts the door. "I have to talk with you, is what I have to do."

He fills up the close little corridor with his thick woolen coat giving off the odors of the bar and the frigid winter outside. There are dark circles under his eyes, and he seems weary and burdened by whatever he sees, looking at her.

She backs away slowly, his possible intentions filling her with new alarm. She could put up one hell of a fight if need be, but he's a cop, he has a gun.

"Lucy," he shows her his empty hands, "I'm just here to talk. Settle down."

"What do you expect, you come barging in here?"

"I didn't barge."

"I want you to leave."

"When I'm done."

When he's done, he says, as if this is supposed to make her feel any better? She stumbles, going backwards, into the kitchenette table. Rounds it, putting it between the two of them. Now there's nowhere left to go, she's backed up against the counter, but at least the butcher block's in reach.

He stops on the other side of the table with a contrite look, as if to oblige her. Then, he pulls out the chair, hitches his pants and sits down. He doesn't take off his coat, which is a good sign; though it could just be due to how cold her apartment is. He opens his hands again, a silent inquiry if his sitting down is all right, as if she has any say. She doesn't move a muscle. He rubs his jaw, thinking. He says, "Just so you understand, so you see things from my perspective, O.K.? We have a victim with no ID. We have no evidence, no witnesses, no nothing, just you, and you aren't talking. This is the kind of case that ends up in a box for years, maybe forever. And it gets to me. He was just a little kid."

"I told you, I can't help."

"Bullshit. Let's cut to the chase."

He looks at her from under his brows. She shrugs, as in, Sure, whatever.

"That boy was a serv," he says slowly, "and you are, too. No one will ever sort that out. That's why the case is dead in the water. But not for me, see."

A strangeness comes over her. It's a dream, this man in her apartment, saying the word *serv*. It leaves her floaty and abstracted. She pictures a needle under a microscope, pushing against the bubble of a cell, piercing it: *That boy was a serv.*

"Are you listening?"

He comes into focus: big face tilted to one side, eyes boring into her. She says, "I don't know what you mean. You need to leave."

"You want to play it that way for now, I understand. Just, you know, don't push it too long. I'm only so patient, O.K.?"

Meaning what, she wonders. Her heart drums faster, and her Source surges, causing her to buckle a little. There's a bottle of Jameson on the table, and he leans forward, slides it in her direction. "I know you're just a pawn, Lucy. I know it because look at this crap," he indicates the bottle. "Step up from rail, sure, but it seems to me you're doing some really hard jobs, and you don't even get decent dope?"

It's almost a joke, how on the mark he is. She says, "I don't know what you're talking about. It sounds crazy."

"You are one cool cat, Lucy Hennessey. Look at you, just standing there, sucking it up. But I've been thinking about you a lot," he taps his temple. "You didn't grow up with servs. You had to live with it for years, all on your own. So maybe you have a higher tolerance. Is that it?"

"Tolerance for what?"

"Yeah, yeah, O.K." He shakes his head, chuckling a little, but she can tell he's starting to lose that patience he was talking about. "You servs," he says, "all you care about is let's get from point A to point B in one piece. One of you gets bumped, and instead of grieving, the rest of you fight over a cell phone and a pair of shoes. One day you're best friends, the next you find the ten bucks you worked so hard to save is gone. Am I right or am I right?"

He can't possibly expect her to just come out with it. When he loses his patience, he'll try and force her. Every muscle in her body is tightening up. She measures in her mind the distance to the knives, how fast she can grab one, spin around and lunge.

And then what, after attacking a cop?

"But I get it, see?" Bedrosian places his hand on his chest, as if to indicate the depth of his sincerity. "You can't help being that way. It's a case study in nurture. Not nature. Maybe at first, you start out with the capacity for compassion, for forging real bonds and real friendships. You're kind of like, *tabula rasa.* Anything could happen. But we know what happens. And all that potential, it's squeezed out of you, day after day, year after year, till there's nothing left. You're incapable of empathy. Most of you, anyway."

She wills herself to exude total blankness, because it's as good an option as any. She can see herself, pale blue eyes voided, face empty as a wall.

"That's what I saw first, when I walked into this shithole of an apartment. Just another serv who's maneuvered herself into some kind of a life, even if it means killing little serv kids on the side. But from the start, you didn't fit the mold. I couldn't get my head around it. You grew up with people, you went to school, you even tried college. How the hell did you end up here? Was it a mistake you made, maybe with that boyfriend? I can tell I'm onto you, Lucy," Bedrosian wags his finger at her, "you just lost your cool there for a second. There's something off about you. You work like crazy, all to repay a loan Eva Hennessey took out for you, when you could just walk away."

"Why's it strange I should pay back my mom?" she snaps, unable to help herself.

"Because she's not your mom," he states flatly. "Because if she knew what you were, she'd run screaming. Because if she knew the things you've done, she'd fall apart. Are those enough reasons?"

His retort flattens her plan to talk her way out of this. She clamps her mouth, furious that he's cut right through to the fears that plague her about Eva: If she knew. If she ever found out.

"What I'm getting at is, I think you care, Lucy. You do have empathy. Look at all you do for your mom. Look how hard you work, all for her. I don't think you killed that kid yourself. You feel bad about it, you kept all the newspapers. Maybe you kept playing back over it all, could you have done something, could you have saved him."

She stares at Bedrosian, wondering what on earth he wants from her, really. To spill everything, a final act of contrition, is that what he wants?

"Lucy, I'm already on the paper trail for this apartment. I don't care how slick he is, whoever you work for. I'll find him. Do you understand what this means?"

Her palms are in a sweat now, her legs going soft. She understands what it means, yes. There's no way Theo hasn't been keeping tabs on Bedrosian; he probably knows he's here right now. And that he went to Ayer, and he's looking into the apartment—

"You want to skip that outcome, you can help me out. If not for your own sake, how about for Eva Hennessey. If you're gone, who'll pay off that loan, huh?"

He rubs his jaw, waiting for a response that does not come.

"Man, you are a sphinx," he sighs. "Why are you so loyal? Are you scared, is that it? Believe me, we'll take care of them. I have friends."

His words conjure men in a pickup, slung with guns. It is ludicrous.

She says, "I don't know what you're talking about."

"Oh, cut it out!" Bedrosian swats the table, making her jump. "How long do you want to play this game?" He reaches into his jacket, pulls out a piece of paper, unfolds it. "Look at him, Lucy. He was just a little kid, for Christ's sake! Tell me you're not sick enough to think it's O.K., what happened to him! Tell me I'm right about you!"

She sees the boy's freckled skin white as snow, lock of dark hair plastered to his forehead, eyes closed. Bedrosian thrusts the paper closer to her, insisting she not look away. "How many more have they killed? Because you don't just do this once, take a Source. That's a professional job, there. They're doing it again, and again, and you're helping. Do you appreciate how he died? Do you realize how much blood there was?"

Her vision blurs to tiny limbs splayed on a wood floor, head tilted all wrong, blood pooling into the crevices between the planks. Earlier in the season, up in Montreal. Does she realize how much blood, he's asking. For all the time Bedrosian's put into psychoanalyzing servs, Lucy doubts he's ever witnessed an actual Service.

After a minute or two, he lowers the picture slowly, and she sees his shoulders sink a little, like a weight's come down on him. It strikes her that he's carrying this picture all the time—the paper is crumpled, the folds show a lot of wear. He actually cares, she realizes. He thinks he can be this dead serv's champion, when the only ones who could make a difference—sentries, overseers, the Gate—couldn't give a shit, just like that sentry told Margot. Bedrosian thinks he knows so much about the serv world, that he's got friends who'll help put away the bad guys, fulfill some hero fantasy he's got going, when the reality is, if he pokes around any deeper into their business, he'll end up dead in an alley right alongside her.

She almost wants to warn him.

The phone rings, startling them both. It rings, and rings, and rings.

"You gonna get that?" Bedrosian asks.

Lucy shakes her head. She knows it's Eva, wills her to hang up instead of leaving a message.

"Hi, baby," Eva's tired voice speaks into the machine. The voice slips through the air, inserts itself between Lucy and Bedrosian. Their eyes lock. "It turns out the play is on Friday, not Thursday. So come on Saturday if you can. Just make sure you let me know, hon, so I can get the ingredients for the meatloaf. All right, then," she trails off. "I guess I better get going. I have my sherry waiting. Call me when you have a moment."

There is the hiss of the phone line, as if she might say something more. Then the click.

After a moment, Bedrosian says, "So that's Eva Hennessey."

Lucy nods.

"So, you grow up with the nice mom making you meatloaf, and him, what does he get?"

It's a jab that should have no impact, seeing as the arrival was hardly looking at a childhood like the one she got. But it stings nevertheless, and badly. How many times she's imagined a kid arrival compressing too fast, telling Theo it's too late. Taking the kid home, buying him or her out of Services. Dumb fantasies that always founder on reality. She can barely pay the rent, let alone keep another serv out of rotation.

Bedrosian is nodding, as if he's reached some internal decision. He eases himself up out of the chair, adjusts his coat, tucks the chair beneath the table. Then he waits. And waits.

She grudgingly meets his eyes.

"I want to give you a chance, Lucy. I don't know why, but so help me, I do." He drags his wallet out of his back pocket, opens it, and flicks a business card onto the table. "I'll give you a day or two. And Lucy," he pauses halfway down the corridor, looking back over his shoulder, "you think long and hard about your mother. Think what she'd want you to do."

After he's gone, she waits a breath. Another. It takes all her courage to get in motion, make her way across the floor, at every instant expecting him to walk back in. But there is no sound except that of her own breaths and the soft padding of her bare feet. The door stays closed, the handle does not turn. She rams the bolts home, backs away to the wall. She slides down to the floor, tucks up tight and buries her face in her arms.

She sees her earlier self entering the pub, filled up with pleasant anticipation, the day's drudgery draining away. The thought of waking up tomorrow, dressing, returning to the office is farcical. How was your night? Oh, lovely. How was yours?

Bedrosian's got no right to judge her. What the fuck does he know? How dare he bring up Eva. Him and his friends, whoever they are, as if they can keep Lucy alive if she betrays Theo? It's a joke. Then who will take care of Eva? He hasn't thought of that, of course.

And even if, for argument's sake, even if he managed to keep her out of the mix, succeeded in taking down Theo, then what? It's not as if her own life changes. In fact, it gets worse. Word will get around she ratted to a human cop, so then she goes toxic, probably beyond hope, and before Bedrosian can stop by for an I-told-you-so, she'll be bundled in a van and headed for the Gate.

Then who'll be thinking of my mother, asshole?

She can't dispute his intentions. His outrage over the arrival's death is genuine, that's for sure. But he's out of his depth, fancying himself some hero thrusting his sword into serv amorality, making it known justice will be had. He's living in a movie.

And in doing so, he's nailed a bull's-eye to her forehead.

He knows that well enough, she thinks bitterly. He thinks he can pressure her, as if she hasn't lived every day since she got tagged under threat, as if she'll crumple like a flower.

She pulls the knives from the butcher's block, checking them one by one. The search triggers a long-ago era when she kept tucked away any number of sharp objects with which she scoured her skin, gouged her flesh. There was a time when she would not have fumbled over blades, unsure of their efficacy. *I'm out of practice,* she thinks with sick humor.

She selects a paring knife. Compact, but with a long enough blade. She sharpens it, soothed by the rhythmic metallic sounds. Closes her palm around the handle, finding the balance.

All it takes is one hard thrust, Julian instructed, guiding her hand towards the dummy.

She needed to learn to defend herself, he said. She'd stepped into a different world now, and more often than not, she'd be on her own. You hit with all you've got, he told her. Then you run and call me.

Now, there's a sad joke.

The steadily blinking light on the answering machine intrudes on the surreal memory. She goes over to the couch, lies down, dials.

"Hey, baby!" Eva exclaims. "Well, I didn't expect a call back so soon! What a nice surprise! What have you been up to?"

"Nothing much, just the usual."

"What's wrong? You sound terrible."

"I'm just wiped out," Lucy forces more strength into her voice. "It's been a long day."

"Oh, honey, you work so hard."

"It's not that bad. Today it was just filing, actually."

"Filing. Oh dear. Can't they give you something more interesting?"

"It's O.K., I'll get to proof soon."

There is a pause.

"So, baby, what day do you think you'll come, then?"

"I don't know yet. I might be able to do Saturday, stay over."

"That would be a treat," Eva says. "Let me know when you can, then."

"O.K., Ma." Her voice cracks. "I have to go. Long day tomorrow."

She holds herself, stares around the room, caught in a slow-motion dream. The telephone primly in its cradle. The chair where Bedrosian sat. Her parka still on the floor in the hall. She shouldn't be so distraught. She's lived most of her life expecting to be offed from one day to the next. Just because it might be Theo, not Service, what difference does it make.

She shouldn't have promised to visit, she realizes. Who's to say she'll even make it to Saturday? It would have been better not to make the promise.

She imagines Eva calling. The phone ringing here, in the empty room.

A WHILE LATER, SHE activates the new burner she picked up in the morning and dials Julian. The singsong beeps indicating a disconnected number are so loud that she jerks the phone away from her ear.

Theo's number yields the same. As she suspected.

Let it not be said that she didn't do her best. She flips open her laptop, Skypes Bernie. It takes a number of rings before he appears, wall-eyed and droopy from whatever hit he's just absorbed.

"I need to talk to Julian. Do you have his new number?"

He lifts an eyebrow. "He don't want to be reached by you, and I'm supposed to go against that?"

"Bernie, come on. It's important."

He narrows his eyes, leaning in close. "What's going on? Are you toxic?"

"Not at all," she forces lightness into her tone. "I need cash, is all. I need some jobs."

"I'll pass the message along, then."

It's all she can hope for. Downplay, act normal. The cop being here, it was nothing, she held him off for one more round. It's a breeze, getting through this. She can do it.

TIME PASSES, THE CLOCK ticks. The night deepens, settling all around her now quiet, wide-awake, rigid body laid out on her bed like a corpse. She doesn't check the clock; it's a rule she has. If she sees the time, realizes how little is left, then for sure she won't sleep. And she needs her rest, because she's got no choice but to get up, go to work, come back. Go through the motions. Whoever's keeping an eye on her for Theo, they'll report all is normal.

She grips the knife close to her chest, staring into the dark with burning eyes. She lets her mind slip away to worn, pleasant fantasies of making quota and moving on, taking night classes, maybe paralegal, maybe something more ambitious. She makes money, moves somewhere hip like the North End. She fixes up the house for Eva's twilight years. She repairs *Lucy Belle*, chugs around the bay on weekends. At dusk, she stands in the cold wet sand under the dock and digs in with her toes, seeking the sharp edges of clams.

MORNING. SHE'S DOZED MAYBE one hour, if that. Her skin feels papery, loose, everything underneath a soggy blob held upright by sheer will. She stands in the lobby for several minutes, the metal blade tucked in her skirt waistband, heating up her skin.

"What's wrong wi' joo?" the super criticizes. He's got the vacuum out, preparing to do the narrow strip of worn carpet running the length of the hall. "I don't want no more trouble with *la policia*, joo hear?"

"There won't be," Lucy says flatly. She fixes her disarming gaze on him. She knows what she looks like: a total lunatic, huge pale eyes ringed with dark, her body rigid with tension. He backs off, grumbling.

She peers up and down the street through the grimy windows, but Bedrosian's nowhere to be seen. Her plan of just keeping up her routine is completely absurd, but she's too exhausted to contemplate a change. She tried to think of alternatives, but there are none, short of just getting back in bed and staying there. And that won't pay the rent.

Once outside, she still can't see Bedrosian's boat of a car. The absence of him sets her more on edge. Maybe he went ahead last night after all. Maybe he went back to Ayer, or to some serv contact, asked more questions. He could be lying dead in an alley somewhere, and here she is going down the sidewalk, the easiest target on the face of the planet. She finds herself hurrying, almost running. By the time she gets to work, she's envisioned so many scenarios in which she's fighting for her life with her pathetic little weapon that she's in a sweat, dumbfounded to be alive.

She pauses just outside the office to change out of her Kamiks into her pumps.

"My Lord," Mrs. M. exclaims. "Are you all right?"

There is the soft rustle of heads turning. Lucy thought she'd done a passable job with makeup and hair: evidently not.

"Dear, you look unwell," Mrs. M. says in a hushed voice. "Do you have a fever?"

"Food poisoning," Lucy confesses. "I'm O.K. now. I promise."

Mrs. M. doesn't buy this. She follows her down the hallway. "You can take the morning off, you know. We aren't ogres here."

Lucy fixes her face in a smile. "I'm O.K., really."

There's nothing Mrs. M. can do but retreat. Lucy's back in the storeroom for the day, and she feels like a dog guarding her close little territory, the humming copy machine, the shredder waiting with its malevolent row of curved teeth. She sets about her work, ignoring everyone's anxious stares. They're overreacting. How she looks today is nothing compared to how she's showed up at other jobs. There are no bruises or lacerations. She just looks like she didn't sleep, and that's no big surprise, because she barely did.

When she goes to the bathroom, she rips her panty hose with a broken fingernail. She's extra careful, but pulling them back up causes a run to flee down her leg. She doesn't have an extra pair. The dilemma leaves her teary-eyed. She knows it's just because she's so shattered, but she can't help feeling self-conscious, walking fast to get back to her haven unseen. Another hour passes. And another.

"Hey, you." Marcie leans in the doorway, cradling a steaming cup in her hands. "How's it going?"

"O.K." Lucy manages a smile.

"Where are we going for lunch?"

In the agonizing haze of her morning routine, Lucy forgot to pack a sandwich. But nor can she deal with chitchat today. She can barely function in her solitude, let alone in a bright café surrounded by people, with this happy person prying for information, sharing bits and pieces of her own unbearably easy life.

"I need to work through. Which reminds me—I forgot to ask Mrs. M. if I could."

"O.K." Marcie hesitates, disappointed. "See you later," she says awkwardly, and heads off down the hallway.

Her departure causes a tug of pain, as if something inside Lucy is unraveling, getting dragged away along the carpet behind her new friend. She should have just said yes. Stuck to the pattern, gone along. *You have to act normal,* she berates herself, trying to tamp down the desperate spiral of her thoughts. Bedrosian keeps appearing in her mind's eye. Here, in the small room tucked high up and far away in an office building, their conversation feels smothered now, muffled and unreal. Her mind deflects, goes running in the opposite direction.

He's been going around asking questions, and Theo's already gotten wind. There's no way he hasn't. She's deluding herself, thinking if she just goes to work, acts normal, she'll be off the hook. The papers slip from her trembling hands. She bends to collect them, her fingertips brushing the carpet, gathering static. She sits very still, squaring off the paper, trying to get a hold of herself. Beyond the humming sound of the copy machine, there's the faint tinkle of laughter from one of the cubicles. Ringing phones. Prim hurried footsteps going this way and that, muffled by carpeting. What's happening with Theo, with Bedrosian, it's all just so far away from this.

Her life is like this explosion and she's a faint little dot now on this side, now on the other. There's no thread, no connection.

Her phone rings, and she digs frantically through her bag to answer. She shouldn't have it on at work. Eva's number shows on the screen. *Shit*, she thinks, switching off the ringer. She turns her mind to her tasks, wishing she could be put back in the file room where the temperature is lower. The sooner she gets this stuff done, the sooner she can get out of here. Her fingers fumble and shake, and she can feel the pink heat in her cheeks, the way she gets when she's at the end of her rope. Maybe take the lunch break after all, but sleep somewhere. She pictures herself curled up in a stairwell somewhere in the building.

Her phone hums inside her bag, alerting her to another call. Eva again. Frowning, Lucy backs up to the far side of the storeroom, tucks herself between the shelf and the window. She keeps her eyes away from the dizzying drop to the street, stares out at across the harbor, frothing whitecaps on the slate-gray water that melds with the colorless winter sky. She answers the call, hisses, "Ma, what is it? I'm at work!"

It's Sean who replies. "Luce, where the hell have you been?"

"I'm at work like I said! What are you doing calling?"

"Are you in some kind of trouble, Luce?"

"What do you mean?"

She hears Eva yammering on in the background. "No, we have to tell her!" he snaps in response. "Luce, a cop came by here this morning, asking all sorts of questions. He said you're a possible witness to something, and he thinks you're protecting some bad guys. That's what he said, 'bad guys,' like Aunt Eva's a two-year-old!"

Lucy's gasping for air. She leans against the window, trembling. "Put her on."

"No. You tell me, and you tell me now!"

"I need to know what he asked!"

"Why?" he bellows. "What the fuck, Lucy! What did you do? Is this something to do with you-know-what?"

For a second, she has no clue what he's talking about. Then it comes to her: his escort service theory. She hears Eva demand what he means by you-know-what. *Ohmygod, ohmygod, ohmygod.* She pushes her fist against her teeth, biting hard. Deep breath.

"This guy's a freak, O.K.?" she blurts out. "I didn't do anything! He's been following me around. I think he's some kind of maniac."

"Oh yeah? And how did you meet him?"

"At a bar," she improvises.

"Great. That's just great, Luce. A maniac you picked up in a bar. It's a good one, I'll hand you that, because it's so damn believable!"

There is a rustling sound, the muffled sounds of them arguing. Eva comes on the line. "Baby, don't pay attention to him. You know he's just worried. Are you all right?"

Lucy closes her eyes. *Breathe.* "I'm fine. I'm sorry he bugged you. Are you O.K.?"

"Oh, he was nothing but polite. He was very professional"— Lucy pictures her turning to Sean as she says the word with extra force—"and he did not say *you* did something wrong. Sean, I told you this already! Honey, if you're covering up for someone because you're scared, then you need to just do the right thing, all right? The police can protect you!"

Lucy's faint at the image of Bedrosian seated at the kitchen table, Eva fussing over the antique porcelain cups she pulls out for visitors. She no doubt gave him her special almond cookies, too. She's got an almost worshipful regard for the police, maybe because they'd periodically scoop Seamus Hennessey off the floor of a bar and lock him up, which meant for at least one night, Eva, Lucy, and Sean could all relax and watch a movie, spill popcorn on the furniture, and laugh as loudly as they cared.

"Ma, what did he ask?"

"Oh, he wanted to know about you, and people you knew in the past. I mean, there isn't much from the present, is there," she forces a laugh.

The memory pops right up, inducing panic: Julian's visit, when she was still in college. There is a picture of them among her stuff in the attic, standing on the dock with their arms around each other, two grinning brutes, poor Eva compliantly snapping photos. Maybe Eva's forgotten.

"I said you've always been a bit of a loner. No friends to speak of, except for that boyfriend."

Lucy's insides lurch.

"Julian whatever-his-name-was. He was a rotten piece of work, I told him."

Lucy swallows, her mouth dry as dust. "What else did you say?"

"I said if he's involved, it'll be about the cult, and you're not in it anymore. Is he involved?"

"I don't know."

"I said you're a good girl, you're a hard worker, I told him. Now you do the right thing and assist the police. They're here to help us, and we have to help them."

"O.K., Ma."

"Don't 'O.K.' me!"

"No, I will, I promise. This is all a big misunderstanding. Don't worry about it. He won't be coming back again."

There is a rustling sound as the phone exchanges hands, then Sean says, "Luce, are you sure you're not in trouble?"

"Yes," she says. "It's fine. I promise. I have to get back to work."

She hangs up, presses her hands to the window, her legs shaking. *Breathe.* Looks back over her shoulder, turning in place. The solid pile of paper sits on a low table, her stool next to it, the shredder waiting with its bright green light. She stares uncomprehendingly at these objects, clueless as to how she'll pull through the next—she lifts her phone, checks the time—five and a half hours.

A ferry chugs towards the harbor. She wonders if Bedrosian's on it, or if he drove. She stares at the boat, aghast. He might come here.

"You really should go," Mrs. M. chastens her from the doorway. Lucy turns around, blinking.

"I've already called the agency," Mrs. M. warns. "You shouldn't come in when you're so sick. There's a flu going around."

"I don't have the flu, I promise."

"They're sending someone right now."

"But I need this job!" Lucy blurts, then feels herself blushing hotly.

Mrs. M. stiffens, looks up and down the hallway. "How about you leave a message early tomorrow, Lucy," she concedes. "If I haven't heard from you, I'll send for someone else."

"O.K.," Lucy agrees, surprised and grateful for this concession. "I appreciate that so much. I'll call, I promise."

"All right, then. Get along. Get some rest."

She can feel everyone staring as she leaves. She doesn't blame them. When she hasn't slept, her pale skin goes white and her blue eyes get huge, shadowed by dark rings. Crackhouse Casper, that's what Sean used to tease, and she'd punch him till he took it back. "Are you all right?" Marcie asks, popping out from her cubicle and falling into step. She gives Lucy's back a quick, circular rub, as if to boost her into a better mood. It takes monumental effort not to shrink away from the contact. Even through her shirt, her abnormal body temp might be sensed. Lucy manages to edge away. "I'm fine, I thought I was doing better this morning. My mother keeps calling," she adds with a roll of the eyes, a moment of genius to explain away the ringing phone.

"Yours is like that, too?" Marcie laughs merrily. "I wonder if we'll be the same."

"Yeah," Lucy smiles. "Probably."

"Do you want kids?" she asks with her disarming enthusiasm.

"Sure."

"Do you have a boyfriend?"

Jesus fucking Christ. "I did. He died."

"Oh—" Marcie claps her hand over her mouth, eyes wide with dismay.

The elevator dings its arrival. "It's O.K. But I don't really want to talk about it."

Marcie complies, her expression flooded with empathy. Lucy steps into the elevator. The doors thump shut, closing her off from Marcie's concern. The ride down in the roomy, quiet space tightens the knot in her stomach, balled-up sick fear of the outside and what if Bedrosian's there, waiting. Or tracking Julian down, right now. When the doors whoosh open on the ground floor, two elegant men in the midst of a soft, chuckling conversation step inside, carrying their suit jackets draped over their forearms. "Hey," one of them says, throwing out his hand to block the door's automatic return. Lucy starts, mumbles apology, and hurries out onto the marble floor. She finds herself yearning for the close, hot little storeroom with its laden shelves and soothing machine noises. She could go back up, she fantasizes, sneak in and hide there.

In the lobby, the concierge watches her discreetly as she changes into her Kamiks. All is silent at this time of morning, the atrium tables unoccupied but for a few lone coffee drinkers deeply engrossed with their laptops. "Short day?" the concierge inquires. Lucy nods. She turns away and trudges towards the main doors, her boots squeaking faintly on the shining floors.

SHE WALKS IN AN aimless daze, unable to conceive of going back to the apartment so early in the day, just sitting there for hours, doing nothing. She comes to a crosswalk, waits for the green signal. People shoulder past since there's no traffic, and she joins them, skidding through the narrow, slushy passages formed in the heaped snow on either side of the street. She edges close to a wall, pauses over her phone to check if Nafikh are anywhere in the neighborhood. Her nose is running from the cold, and she sniffles, wiping the snot on her mitten. The first Tweets she reads provoke anxiety: there are two Nafikh heading east from Beacon. She turns in place, scanning the streets. No scoops yet, but that doesn't mean they aren't coming. Trying to make Park or Downtown Crossing at this point is a big risk, which means heading all the way back to the Aquarium stop.

For a moment, she stays put, huddled against the icy wind blasts. She could just give in, wait here till it happens. Scooped, carried along on the wave, mindless robot getting told what to do with no decisions to make. It would be so easy, too, to just trip at the right moment, bumble into one of Them. End it all.

She comes back to reality as she scans another feed, this one spitting out a new message every few seconds. There's a first-timer in town, nicknamed Rambo because He looks like Stallone. First-timers rarely stay out long, but Serving Them is the worst, They can't control Themselves for shit. Lucy's only been on a few of those Services, and they were hell. This one's already racked up three dead servs and scores others injured: any scoop would be sending her that way for sure, no chance of getting assigned to the more seasoned Nafikh having a stroll through town.

Lucy desperately casts about for a safe haven. No malls or department stores—the Nafikh love escalators. No small shops, either, nowhere to hide. No jumping on a bus, as They might want to go for a ride, and it would be just her luck.

There's only one place to go, painful as it may be, and Lucy makes for it at a jog. It's on a winding narrow side street paved with brick, of which there are so many downtown that she finds herself on the wrong one, has to stop to get her bearings. At last, she catches sight of the small bronze plaque nailed into the brick wall, the Nafikh symbols engraved above the house number, fanciful scrollwork to the unknowing observer.

She climbs the three stairs and rings the buzzer, staring boldly up at the camera bolted to the overhang. After a moment, the door clicks open, and she ducks inside, at once enveloped in the soft, acrid odor of Faithful incense. It's dark and cold, the hallway narrow, more like a tunnel. Someone steps into the doorway at the end, his tall form outlined in the light beyond. Though he's in shadow, Lucy immediately recognizes the sloped shoulders, the thick, wavy hair.

"You shouldn't be here, Lucy," Ernesto says. "What gives?"

"I am lost," she says with exaggerated meekness.

"Shut up."

"Truly," she begs. "I need guidance. I can't take it anymore. I just need meaning."

A fractional smile. "Come on. But keep it down."

She hasn't been here in forever. Once she fell out of grace, it felt too shameful to hang around Ernesto. He is Theo's prized mole, who climbed the ranks in the Faithful Church till he actually was made a priest: Theo cracked open champagne that day, and they all howled laughing, partied all night. Not that Lucy was invited. Julian told her about it, to rub in everything she was missing.

She follows Ernesto into the main room, and is at once engulfed by the vaulted, hollow quiet of the place. The walls are plain white plaster, the floors natural wide pine boards. A few Faithful are scattered about the labyrinth of pews, staring with fervent attention at the central dais, from which the priest every morning unloads his torrential Sharings about Nafikh glory and serv salvation. At the moment there is only a fountain trickling water, meant to enhance prayerful meditation. Lucy switches off her phone, sets the Service one to vibrate. She edges into the outside row, being unworthy of penetrating the labyrinth more deeply, not that she'd want to.

Ernesto settles at a distance, as befits his status. He crosses his legs, and she notes the polished tasseled loafers, the expensive-looking jeans. His shirtsleeves are rolled halfway up his forearms in perfect symmetry. He whispers, "You look like shit, Lucy. What's going on?"

"Nothing."

He doesn't buy this, examining her with a long sideways glance, his brows furrowed. He, of course, looks fantastic. Glowing olive skin, thick dark hair with a touch of stately gray brushed back from the temples, lush lips she kissed once a long, long time ago, when they were young and drunk. He says, "You aren't up on the roster, are you? There's a first-timer."

"No," she says, then adds nonchalantly, as if she does it all the time, "I'll use my dupe, anyway."

"Good. I'm glad to hear it."

"Things seem to be going well for you," she remarks.

"They are."

The conversation dies out. What is there to talk about, after all? He's Theo's darling, she's a grunt. They aren't on equal footing anymore, haven't been in years. And yet there's the connection still there between them, like an invisible, shimmering filament. She could reach out and touch his hand, and in an instant, they'd be laughing and gossiping on Theo's veranda, the frosted fields sweeping away into the mist, a deer frozen among the birches, its delicate face turned towards their noise.

An incalculable exhaustion creeps over her; she yearns to lie down the length of the pew and close her eyes. The fountain trickles softly. The air is refreshingly cool, the temperature perfectly calibrated for servs. She drags off her mittens and hat. Her vision swims.

"You could join," Ernesto whispers. "Acolytes get a long time off."

He thinks it's Service that's brought her to this low. She'd laugh if she weren't so wiped out. *I've got a cop on my back who knows we're all servs,* she imagines telling him. It would be one way to check out, finally. Just confess—she's in the perfect spot, after all—then sit back and let things take their course. Maybe Ernesto would do the deed himself, for old times' sake.

"It's not so bad," Ernesto carries on. "I've actually come to like it here."

"You don't have to Serve," Lucy points out, partly in genuine annoyance, and partly to keep him thinking this is the root of her problem. "Of course you like sitting around here all day."

"I do more than that," he retorts.

"Oh, come on."

He sets his jaw. "They are all servs, just like us, Lucy. All just trying to make do."

That's classic, coming from the guy who used to go on about natural selection, but she doesn't have the energy to argue. She blinks, trying to focus through her drowsiness. The stone fountain is carved with Nafikh symbols she cannot comprehend. She sees among them a relief of two figures holding a flaming sword aloft: the biblical cherubim at the entrance to Eden, reinterpreted as Nafikh protecting the Before, to which the Faithful hope to be returned. Stirred to irritation, she sits up, shaking off her tiredness.

"The problem is," she whispers, "they *aren't* just trying to make do. They're making shit up, all over the place. We have nothing to do with real-people mythology."

"How do you know it's mythology?"

She lifts an eyebrow. "Are you kidding me?"

"Lucy, of all living creatures on this earth, we see evidence every day."

"The Nafikh aren't gods."

"No, but maybe They're angels, subject to a god's will. Isn't it possible the Nafikh dwell beneath a higher power?"

The worn, flawed notion pricks her ire. That even he is now spewing this poppycock, it's beyond her. "Does Theo know you're cracking?"

He shrugs. "He likes to philosophize as much as the next person."

A quick envy flares: he's so secure, has no idea what it's like. "Well, philosophize this," she retorts. "There's no mystery about what we are and why we're here. You can't just glom onto real-people stories and pretend we have some deeper meaning or purpose. The stories don't even fit! The Nafikh don't go around with fiery swords, and it's not like we were kicked out of a garden."

"Lucy, myths aren't literal."

"No, but there has to be some thread, some connection to the reality we're in! There's no way They're angels, Ernesto, just like we aren't people. Suck it up."

A silence falls, during which she reads in his expression the worst possible thing: pity. She sets about gathering her stuff, furious.

"Don't," he says, reaching out his hand and grasping hers. "Don't, Lucy. It's not worth the risk. Stay here."

"Fuck you," she says.

"Come on," he smiles, seeking reconciliation. He was always like that. Always letting go of his anger so easily, like it's nothing. She tugs her hand out of his, sits back resolutely, ignoring him. After a few moments, he gets up and walks away.

Lucy's eyes fall shut against her will, her whole body succumbing to the sweet tinkling noises of the water. She sinks into a deep doze, distantly aware of footsteps now and then, the murmur of voices. She wonders if this is why Ernesto's come to like being Faithful, for the heavy quiet draping everything, the certainty of belonging. God is kind and good in ways you can't possibly imagine, Eva used to tell her. He will forgive you anything, anything. *Forgive me!* Lucy begged hysterically in her mind, every night. Forgive her weirdness, her rage, her selfishness, her inclination towards knives. Forgive her wicked hatreds, her cruelty towards her ma, her detailed plans for killing Uncle Seamus because he beat Sean. Forgive her for being crazy and believing she was a serv like Drunk Pete told her. Forgive her for deep-down not believing in Him at all, for hating church, for taking the wafers and grape juice nevertheless. The day of her Communion, the other kids tittered and elbowed one another, they called her Bride of Casper.

Fuck you all, Lucy tells them across the expanse of time and space, and tries to push back her thoughts, sink away again.

But the memories have done their work, slipped in like crochet hooks and tugged her brief time of peace apart. She reluctantly sits up and looks around, refreshed, blinking. The pews are filling up for evening Share. Ernesto is at the lectern, studiously squaring off papers. She slides down the pew as quietly as possible and gets up.

"May she come back when she is ready," he announces, his voice booming across the room.

He has to call her out, of course, she gets that. But still. Lucy flushes as the entire congregation rustles, turns, stares.

That's something to be said for St. Mary's, no one would ever yell like that. She ducks out fast.

WHEN SHE SWITCHES HER phone on again, she discovers two messages from an unknown. *Julian,* she thinks, with a speck of hope: not written off after all, still worthy. But it's not him. It's Bedrosian, the first message about visiting Eva and what a good woman she is, how he has to hand it to Lucy for the cult story, and asking if she's made a decision. The second more impatient, telling her curtly to call, to quit being so obstinate.

While she's listening, the phone rings again, same number.

She stares at the screen, lets the call go to voice mail. When it bleeps, she plays back the message. "I know you left work, Lucy, so you're just choosing not to pick up. You listen to me. I've made inquiries. You'll be off the hook if you cooperate. It's that simple. The sentry I work with, his name is Aaron, he isn't happy with what's going on. He's ready to take action. He'll leave you out of it, if you cooperate. So you call me, you meet me, and let's do the right thing. I'd hate to see Eva Hennessey have to go through losing you. You do this for her, you hear?"

Click.

Lucy presses play again, listens in a daze. A sentry? It has to be a trick. She racks her memory for an Aaron, can't come up with anyone, but that doesn't mean much, she's been in so many Services over the years. She listens again, trying to decipher whether Bedrosian actually gave out her name. Because if this Aaron really isn't happy, he'll just trace her tag and make her talk, and Bedrosian can go piss in a pond. She listens a fourth time, chewing her lip, bent away from the wind so as to hear every word, every intonation. It doesn't sound like he gave her name. He's not that stupid, she considers. He's been around the block.

She wipes the moisture from the screen, considering the number displayed there, unsure. Then she opens chat rooms, Twitter, keeping tabs on scoops just out of habit. She's kind of amazed by the extreme mix of emotions blocking her from giving up Julian, Theo, the rest of them, despite how far she's been thrust from the fold. The idea of revealing his name, *Theo Elander,* it goes against everything. It just hurts.

But it's not only that. Even if this sentry lets her off the hook, as Bedrosian said, her worst scenario will still unfold. No more extra income means no more apartment, and into a bunk she goes because she won't have Julian to guilt into helping her get a room.

Julian.

If it's hard to imagine betraying Theo, with Julian it's way worse. She wonders if he felt bad at all, disconnecting his number like that, cutting her off. It's sinking in, that they've done that. They'd have been in touch otherwise. They'd have wanted to know what's going on.

Since they aren't calling, they probably already do.

Her vision readjusts to the text flickering on the screen. *Fuck:* scoops a few blocks away. She breaks into a jog, heading for the Aquarium stop. She gets the latest on Rambo on the subway. A dozen dead servs, and he's being taken out of town to minimize the risk to real people. *God help me,* Lucy prays involuntarily, perhaps still under the effects of the church, but if there was ever a time to hope a deity exists and that it outranks the Nafikh, it would be now. All the way home she wills the Service phone to remain silent, and to her immense gratitude, it does. She runs up the stairs and bursts into her apartment, bolts the door. The memory of the night before slams into her—Bedrosian, sitting right there at her table—but she can't think about that right now, her priority is to avoid this Service, no matter what.

She flips open her laptop, hunts around, trying to gauge how long Rambo will last, whether she should sink money into a dupe or ride out the visit with her fingers crossed. A first-timer will burn Itself out much sooner on the brand new sensations of inhabiting a body. Rambo's been out at least twelve hours already: it's got to be almost over. She agonizes over her decision, biting her lip hard, staring at the reports. There are three bids on Vivian already, the highest at $175. It's a lot of money. A lot. But He's a first-timer. The per-call survival rate is less than 50%. The luxury dupes never do first-timers. The neos do them because high-risk calls are a fast track to the capital and prestige they're desperate for.

The minutes tick by with nail-biting slowness as she watches the screen. The bidding creeps up to $190, then holds. Lucy waits. In the last seconds before close, she keys in $200, sits back with fingers crossed tightly.

Moments later she lets go her breath. She pulled it off. She has a dupe on deck. Vivian will transmit her stats to Bernie, who will plug the update into Lucy's file, redirecting any sentry who calls her up for Service. If Lucy doesn't get called at all, she'll owe Vivian her base rate of $75, which is painful, but it's actually the lowest rate for peace of mind; Jade's base starts at $300.

Lucy makes a tuna sandwich and sits on the couch, taking pulls off the almost-empty Jameson bottle. The apartment falls to silence. She keeps glancing at the bolted door, half expecting Bedrosian to come knocking again. Or worse. If only she'd pulled the curtains. She can't now, imagining herself in someone else's eyes, a shadow creeping to the window, tugging, the stupid loops getting hitched and stuck as they always do. She sinks lower into the couch, unable to eat. After a time, she pulls the cushions around, lays herself down, and closes her eyes.

It's still dark. She blinks at the green clock numbers, trying to get them in focus. A little past two a.m. Too early for the alarm. Why is she awake?

The Service phone beeps and buzzes angrily on the floor next to the couch.

No.

It won't be Rambo. Surely that's all over with now. It's another Nafikh, it has to be. *Do it. Just get the fuck up and do it.*

"On call," she says flatly.

"Your dupe's gone. Pickup in half an hour. Formal attire."

LUCY'S SOURCE FLARES, FLOODS pain through her chest, into her arms. She tries to dredge up the guts to say no, but the lost dupe's already incurred three extra. Outright refusal will cost as much as the sentry feels like slapping on. Or worse, a trip to the Gate.

The sentry's hung up anyway.

She steps into the bathtub, sprays hot water into herself, scrubbing her labia and vulva and soaping her pubes. They're supposed to douche, but she'll have to take her chances, it's this or be late for pickup.

She dries off and rubs herself with scented jojoba oil. The sight of her pinched, white face in the mirror jolts her: how many years she's raced around this same bathroom, scrambling to pull on the lacey underwear she despises, her heart smashing with anxiety that she'll be late, late, late, that she'll be hit, that she'll be pushed to the front line under the Nafikh's gaze. No matter how much she tells herself it will be fine, she can't control the waves of sickness and fear. She takes several pulls off the Jameson, reaching for that dull I-don't-care state, but she's too wild with nerves, running this way and that, where's the shoe polish, the eyelashes, that pink lipstick.

There are a few minutes left, so she taps her laptop screen to life while doing her blush, puts in a call to Bernie. After numerous rings, he leans into the camera, an unshaven walrus drooping with sleep. Before he can complain about being woken, she says, "My dupe tanked. Just tell me, how bad is it?"

He closes his eyes, shakes his head.

"Fuck," she says. "Bernie, please, get me out of this one."

"Baby, you can't afford that. Just keep your head down."

He sounds genuinely sympathetic, for which she's grateful, though she'd rather he make good on all his avowals of affection and get her the hell out.

"Call me when you get in," he says.

"Thanks for the optimism."

She slams the laptop shut and heads out in stocking feet, carrying her heels so as not to wake Mrs. Kim. The building lobby is cold and dark and smells of fried onions and dust. She huddles in the shadows, peering out at the empty street. Even her higher body temperature can't withstand the freezing air seeping under the doors, and she holds herself tightly, practically naked in the skimpy, backless lamé dress. Time passes. God forbid a serv be late, but sentries can do as they please. They're ten minutes past due now. She should have douched. She frets that she might not be able to see the van, what if it parks in front of the wrong building, waits and leaves, then she gets penalized anyway.

She unlocks the door, steps outside. The sight of Bedrosian's car up the street is a punch in the stomach: her legs wobble and she backs a few steps to the wall. He's seen her, but he doesn't move, just stares from under the furry brow of his Russian hat, a big dark heap in the dim glow of the street-lamp.

There's the noise of an engine, and the van swings around the corner, coming fast. Lucy hurries to the curb with her arm stuck in the air like she's hailing a cab. The door slides open with a thunk. She climbs in. The van careens away at once, the door sliding shut as it moves. She falls heavily onto the seat, blinking hard, her vision taking a moment to get accustomed to the dim interior. Then becomes aware of the unusual number of sentries—three, one crouched between the two up front. It's the Asian she ran into a few days ago, Lucy realizes. There's the sound of breathing, and stifled sobs. The van is full up, the heat of all their serv bodies and breaths warming and then rapidly dampening her bare skin to the point of discomfort.

She looks around slowly. There are a dozen of them crammed in. Mostly female, all dressed to the nines. The one in the back who is sobbing is no more than twelve years old, dressed in a garish sequined top that ties at the back.

Oh my fucking God, Lucy thinks. They're cattle going to slaughter. She hisses at the kneeling sentry to get her attention. "Is it Rambo?"

The sentry nods, her mouth a tight, hard line forbidding more questions, but Lucy ignores that.

"I didn't get a chance to check updates," she insists. "How bad is it?"

"What do you think?"

"But how much longer can He go?"

"Shut up and shore up."

"What's your name?" Lucy demands. It's important to get their names, always.

"Sina. Now shut the fuck up."

Lucy sits back, hands in fists under her thighs.

You will get out, she starts her mantra: *You will get out.*

She wonders if Bedrosian knows what's going on, where they're headed. The information's bare for the taking all over the net, provided you know what you're looking for and can make sense of what you find. She twists around in her seat, suddenly and irrationally hoping to see his car out the back window. Instead, the street yawns away into the dark, empty but for the cones of light on the shining asphalt.

THE DRIVE TAKES AGES. No one talks. The little girl's sobbing subsides after a while. Lucy tries to doze, willing herself to rest, to gather strength, but her eyes keep flying open. She eavesdrops on the sentries. The driver's name is Roy, the other guy is Malik. It's good to know their names, it personalizes things, gives you an advantage when you try and guilt them into helping you out. She gleans very little from their stilted, whispered conversations. There's another Nafikh with Rambo called Gretel. Lucy's Served that one before, She's hit or miss. They are both getting tired, and the sentries are concerned about timing, should they be getting Them out together, or just focus on making sure the first-timer doesn't burn out. An issue comes up around a dupe no-show, and Malik spends a solid five minutes on the phone, cursing in loud whispers at whoever fucked up. She can see Roy's glare in the rear view, his hands gripping the wheel like he might tear the whole thing off. It's no good when the sentries are strung out. Sina's sitting on her butt now, arms around her knees, her face set in that grim stare, like she's gathering herself up inside.

Lucy almost feels kind of bad for them. It's not like they have the easiest job. But it's rare that a sentry goes down, whereas this busload of flesh and nervous blinking eyes and tinkling sequins, they may as well be carcasses.

The bus speeds northwards, alone on the empty highway.

You will get out.

THE MANSION STANDS AGAINST the starred sky, the pale stone lit by moonlight. They're somewhere in Maine, Lucy overheard. Lights flicker behind the drapes. A limo is parked in the circular gravel driveway, waiting to deliver the Nafikh back to the Gate.

A murmur rises inside the bus as they pull up. Hisses, intakes of breath, groans as their Sources respond to the nearby Nafikh. They creep out of the van one by one, proffering their arms for the doses being administered by Malik.

"Add some extra," Lucy pleads.

His eyes flick away. "Just go through the motions. You'll be fine."

She leans back against the van, feeling the powerful drugs take effect, like syrup sliding through her limbs. The relief is monumental. She wishes Gabriel were here. She detects the salty smell of ocean in the air, wonders how far they are from a beach.

"I don't want to," the little girl complains fearfully. "I want to go back to my bunk."

"You're going to be fine, Annabelle," Malik reassures her. "Just stay out of sight after presenting, O.K.?"

"What's with the little princess," someone whines. "How about putting her up front and getting it over with?"

One of the more seasoned servs whips around, furious. "How stupid are you, Cora?"

"Who the fuck are you to call me stupid, you hag!"

Lucy edges away, not wishing to get involved. The whiner is a pretty young thing in her twenties, her hair in a sharp bob, lips bright red. She can't have done too many Services; you never put a kid up front. They can't control their reactions, and before you know it, they've upset the Nafikh and all hell breaks loose. The best bet when kids are called for, unless they're seasoned and know the ropes, is to pass them by the Nafikh and then divert Their attention away quickly. Lucy watches from some distance away as young Cora gets schooled on these facts, looking petulant and pissed off.

When it comes to Annabelle's turn for dosing, Malik goes down on one knee to administer it. He strokes the girl's arm before slipping the needle in. The dose is far more than what a girl her size can tolerate. She'll get presented, pass out, and the sentries will smuggle her out of sight. It's all in the timing.

THE OPIATES RELAX AND muffle and diffuse. It is like gliding through a wonderland of painlessness. A serv's life is pain:

Our currency is grief, that's how the saying goes. But in Service, once that needle's bled out its treasure, the pain lifts away, a kite wafting and fluttering up and away, and the body's left light and airy. Lucy's feet lift and fall. She's drifting on a wave, smiling. She doesn't want to smile, but the Nafikh require that. They want their servants to be happy. She doesn't feel happy. She feels nothing, which makes her happy, not in her body but far away in the kitestream of her mind.

You will get out.

They file in. The mansion is aglow with candles giving off the thick scent of roses. Lucy blinks, taking it all in: marble floors, swirled marble columns, a majestic stairway curving up and away to other levels. If her life slid just a little bit sideways, she'd be a princess entering a castle, not what she is. She floats forward, her fear a bed of coals deep inside her belly. There's a fountain up ahead. A sculpture of three cherubs dancing with jugs, water pouring over multicolored jewels. The Nafikh like color and light. There is one naked in the sparkling water, Her yellow braids dripping, ivory skin shining wet. That's Gretel, Lucy has Served Her before, She's all right. She is enchanted by water. Her long hands swirl in the water, round and round. Her muscles ripple, Her every motion fluid like a predator cat.

Some of the servs are sent into the fountain to help Her play. Gretel tugs at their clothes. They undress immediately so as not to distress the Nafikh, whose desires must be met without hesitation. Their dresses lie strewn on the wet floor, which sucks because they'll have to put them on again later, and it's so cold out. But they've got the better deal, Lucy knows. Gretel is in a dreamy, mystified mood, and She's tiring out. She just wants to touch and stroke, She craves softness. Water, cushions, lips, snow. Attending a Nafikh in this state is a cakewalk. Lucy edges forward, hoping to get chosen, her smile wide and inviting. Gretel's gaze shifts towards her, big bright green eyes, and Lucy senses at once the roiling void within, sucking at her, hungry. Sickness swirls in her stomach and she fights to keep her balance, to keep smiling. A sentry grips her arm, guiding her away.

"No," Lucy says, pointing at Gretel.

The sentry—it's Roy, the driver—gives her arm a warning squeeze, as in, *Shut up.*

Up ahead are doors decorated with painted vines and angels. Lucy blinks, trying to take stock. She should have grabbed something to eat on the way out, she thinks regretfully, the emotion inordinately overwhelming. If only she'd eaten. If only. Roy comes into focus. He is consulting his tablet. He points at them one by one. "Lucy, Patrice, Cora. You're coming with me. Keep your wits. Go with the flow."

"We have to bring in the girl," Sina reminds him.

Lucy turns her head, every movement slow, dreamlike. Sees Annabelle pressed close to the sentry, her huge eyes glassy and distant.

"We'll do it fast," Roy says. "Who's diverting?"

Lucy hangs back with the rest of them. Her cowardice is hideous. She can't help it. Far away in some other part of her mind, she pictures herself heroically stepping forward, but her actual body is leaden, motionless.

Sina says, "You do it."

For a second Lucy's stomach clenches up with dismay. But Sina is addressing Cora. Her face is a mask of shock and outrage. You reap what you sow.

"Ready?" Roy nods. He shoves the doors wide open.

"Fuck," Sina mutters. The Nafikh is on His hands and knees, retching. This isn't good. His huge, muscled body heaves and shudders, mouth wide open. He has no clue what's happening. The sentry manning the room is getting a jug ready for washing up.

"Khajja reyyk!" The Nafikh bellows, scrabbling in His vomit. *"Khajja afeel!"*

Lucy has no clue what He's saying. It sounds like cursing. She sidles to the left, making sure to steer wide of Cora in case the sentries decide she needs a hand.

The Nafikh stops all motion, going from bestial lunacy to dazed stillness in a heartbeat. The sentry moves forward, gently inserts a needle into the Nafikh's back. He actually does look like Rambo, with hooded eyes and damp black ringlets plastered to His forehead. He is meek before the sentry, allowing the ministrations with barely any movement.

The sentry backs away. Sina steps forward with Annabelle. "*Dalla,*" Sina says. Lucy knows that word. All servs know it. Child.

The Nafikh twitches, turns. He rises to His full height. He is monstrous, towering over the diminutive girl. Nafikh are always big, but first-timers are so scared They'll be harmed, They tend to be slabbed with crazy muscle, like body-builders on steroids. Annabelle tilts her head back, looking up at Him as instructed, and Lucy assumes she's smiling as hard as possible; she can't see as the girl's back is to her.

Rambo bends, reaching out with His forefinger. Annabelle sways at His touch, almost falls over. She's on her own now. The sentries always back off, it's what They want.

Annabelle's long hair is tied in a blue bow, her sequined top glittery in the candlelight. The Nafikh prods her, turning her this way and that. Somehow, she manages to stay on her feet despite being handled. Her face is a dull mask, mouth dragged open in a sagging smile, like she's really trying to make her face keep doing what it's supposed to but the drugs are winning out.

The Nafikh's thick brows come together in an exaggerated frown, His whole face working the expression. His unhappiness with the stumbling, unresponsive child is obvious.

"Go," Sina hisses at Cora.

Cora utters a squeak. Her red-nailed hand claws at the sentry's arm in mute resistance. Sina gives her a shove. Cora pitches forward, her heels clattering the marble. The Nafikh swings His head, fixates on her. The sentry who just dosed Him glides forward and gathers Annabelle in one smooth motion, strides away. Rambo doesn't even blink, riveted by Cora's glittering silver dress. He reaches out, grabs her by the neck, and yanks. She opens her mouth to scream, then remembers it's the noise the Nafikh hate most, fixes her face in a rigid smile. The Nafikh rips her dress off. He lurches backwards, holding the dress aloft in both hands, turning it so it catches the light. Cora just stands there, rictus grin in place, her knees locked together because she's peed herself. While the Nafikh's back is turned, another serv rushes over with wipes. Cora's so stricken she can't do it herself. *She's gonna pay for that,* Lucy thinks, noting the savagery with which the other serv wipes her down. *Stupid cow.*

LUCY CAN'T MOVE. SHE can't believe she has to go in again. The first-timer's lasting longer than anyone expected. Who knows why, He just is, but she won't go back in. She can't. She shakes her head, No, please, no. Realizes her mouth is opening, closing, no sound coming out. The bass beat booming through the golden doors threatens to topple her. Her legs are breaking toothpicks, her insides mangled and hurting. She only just got dressed again. Malik shakes his head, gestures her forward. She can tell he feels rotten about it. *I can't,* she mouths. She gives in to the tears that have threatened all evening. She's ready to grovel, weep, do anything but walk through that door.

Someone grabs her elbow and shoves her forward. It's Sina.

"No!" she cries. "He already had me twice! Send someone else!" She's sobbing like a baby now. "They won't want me this way, They'll get mad," she blubbers. "What if They blow?"

"If They blow, it'll be on you," Sina snaps. "Come on, pull yourself together. It's gonna end any minute."

"Please don't make me," Lucy begs.

She hangs on Sina's arm, dead weight.

"You want ten more penalty?" Sina whips around, slaps her. "Get. It. Together!"

That does the trick. Lucy ceases all protest. There's no point. There's never any point. She takes the offered tissue and wipes her eyes. Her whole body is shaking. Sina waits, breathing heavily, not meeting her eyes. She feels bad, Lucy acknowledges. Of course she does. They all do.

"Ready?"

Lucy clenches her teeth. She nods. Malik leans a little, shoves open the door.

THE NAFIKH TURN SIMULTANEOUSLY, sinuous and animal in Their motions. Rambo lost His manners way back, if He ever absorbed any to begin with, and Gretel is losing Hers. Lucy's heard it said that the Nafikh in Their true form are fire, and maybe it's true, the way They flicker this way and that, the way They dance when They walk.

Somewhere along the way Gretel became more enchanted with Her companion's antics than the fountain. She's wearing a top hat with a long red ribbon, and is otherwise naked. Blood smears Her stomach and legs. Cora is curled up at Her feet. She's still alive, despite the screams they all heard a short while ago. Rambo has changed. He's in a tuxedo, the white shirt stained and rumpled, hanging out of His unzipped pants.

"Help me," a tiny voice cries.

Lucy whips around. It is Annabelle, peeking out from behind a column etched with a green vine pattern. The stone is so shiny, Lucy notes. The room is gorgeous, lofty, marbled, hung with portraits of long-ago, stern figures in capes and soft caps. She doesn't know why Annabelle is back in here. The Nafikh must have asked for her, then gotten distracted again. She signals

Annabelle to stay hidden behind the column. It is too late. Rambo steps forth, alight with curiosity. His eyes bore into the child.

Annabelle's mouth collapses open. She's trembling violently. Lucy lifts her finger to her lips. *Shhh,* she mouths. *Shhhh.* But Annabelle can't make a sound anyway, she's so petrified. This is good. *Smile,* Lucy mimes. *Smile.*

She can't, she's a crumpling mess, her face stretched in all the wrong ways, terrified. Rambo takes another rigid step, and another.

Malik edges into view. He murmurs at Rambo, making a sweeping, inviting wave to the other side of the room, where Lucy is standing. Lucy plasters on her smile, anticipating the Nafikh's response.

Instead, He raises His arm, backhands Malik across the face. The sentry flies several feet through the air, lands in a heap on the floor.

Annabelle screams.

Rambo's head swivels instantly, teeth bared in a grimace.

"Hello," Lucy croaks, to offer diversion.

The Nafikh turns towards her.

Lucy stands openmouthed, staring. She hasn't said a word. She's just imagined it. She can't do it, she doesn't have the guts. The Nafikh is still fixated on the screaming girl. Her shrill cries fill the domed room. Gretel spins around, Her face drawn with dread. Both Nafikh dart towards Annabelle with speedy, hungry grace. Lucy is dimly aware of the door opening, more sentries rushing in.

Though what can they do? What can they possibly do?

Gretel reaches Annabelle first. She seizes Annabelle by the neck, lifts her into the air, choking off the noise.

There is the shuffling, grunting noise of the girl fighting for breath, her thin legs kicking in the air. Gretel goes into a state, turning this way and that with Her catch, legs bent in a crouch, defensive panic mode. Sina approaches, speaking swiftly, soothingly. It does no good. Annabelle squirms and shudders, driving the Nafikh into more of a frenzy. She hurls the girl aside. Annabelle hits the marble wall hard, falls to the floor.

Stillness.

The stick-thin legs, the jumble of elbows and knees, the thick hair tumbled all over the floor, glint of red sequins. One pointed red shoe on its side, some feet away.

Roy holds up his hand. Lucy sees his mouth moving but can't hear. There's a roaring in her ears. Gretel wends towards the sentry, willing to take him up on whatever he's saying. She spins a braid around Her forefinger, staring back at Her companion, Her round face slack and bored under the top hat. Rambo crouches down next to Annabelle. He prods her with His forefinger. He lifts the arm, then starts to twist it.

"*Pajjeh*," Gretel commands suddenly, blue eyes boring into Lucy.

For a moment, Lucy does not know what the word means. Then she starts singing, the first song that pops into her head: Silent Night.

The Nafikh listens, head tilted. The top hat slides a little, falls off.

As Lucy sings, Rambo drags Annabelle's corpse away from the wall. He starts pulling it apart. Lucy glimpses bone in the clumped red flesh, and an upturned, open hand. She shifts a little, blocking the sight, and sings. Eventually, Rambo approaches the dining table, peruses the selections, picks out some cake. He stuffs His mouth, avid, curious, examining His sticky fingers. He comes towards Lucy, crumbs falling from His smacking lips. Gretel walks away. She lifts Her hand in farewell. "Thank you very much," She tells Lucy in stilted, slow English, per Her lessons at the Gate. Rambo lifts Lucy's hair. He runs His fingertips over her forehead, her cheeks. He smells of wildness and blood and sweat and urine. His breathing is shallow and hard, His head bobbles on the thick neck, crusty with serv blood and tears.

"*Lakhidj,*" He gags. *Finish.*

The visit is over.

Malik is back on his feet, approaching with the syringe aloft; a first-timer at the end of His rope has to be dosed, to prevent involuntary departure. Rambo stares down at Lucy. His hand comes up slowly, and He points at her. "*En Nafakhsht,*" He says. *I made you.*

Then He collapses in a heap, revealing Malik standing behind.

"You know what that means, right?" Malik asks, zipping the syringe back into its bag. "Don't read anything into it. He's been saying it all night."

"Sure," Lucy agrees, "whatever."

There was a time when a Nafikh saying those words stirred her up, like a kid coming upon a long lost parent. Thankfully, that time is long gone. It's a rite of passage for every serv, to get from one side of all that longing for compassion to the other.

Now, all she wants is to make it across the room without falling flat on her face.

LUCY FADES INTO A semi-doze on the back seat of the van, her body lulled by the engine. Cora's strapped in the front, probably won't make it, but the rule is save the serv if they can, so she'll be carted to a doctor. The ride takes forever and Lucy doesn't want it to end, she wants to fly along the highway in this dulled state, on and on, and never have to step back into her life. She's afloat in dreamworlds of rolling green hills and rain-smacked black roads and the ocean smashing her wooden boat and licking brine off her lips and the Matterhorn rising against a cobalt sky, herself gazing upward in a handmade hat trailing braided ties and pompoms. Every so often she's yanked from her doze by the van slowing down or the sudden loud ticking of the turn signal. Then the truth of where she is heaves up and displaces the pretty scenes, and she smells engine oil and metal and stale leather and feels her hip bone digging into the wood plank beneath the thin upholstery. The sentry's tuned the radio to some news station, as if real-people news matters. Lucy can't make out any words, just the sound of voices. The space in the van feels huge and hollow, filled up with engine noise and those static murmurs. Only two of them left, and just hours ago full up and hot, the windows misted over from so many breathing bodies. Lucy stares at the leather seatback a few inches from her eyes, the lights from passing cars playing over the cracked surface. She pokes her fingertip into a tear and pulls, releasing a wad of yellowish foam stuffing.

When the van pulls up to her building, Lucy struggles to open the door. Something's wrong with her arm, she realizes. The sentry gets out without saying a word and rams the door open. Sunlight stings her eyes, and she closes them for a moment to adjust. It's late morning, she can feel it in the angle of light and the brightness, the steady frozen air and the empty streets, everyone already where they're supposed to be. She steps out gingerly, gripping the sentry's shoulder. "Epsom salts bath," he advises as he helps her onto the curb. When he climbs back in and slams the door, she feels unaccountably abandoned. She watches the van drive away.

She turns around. Distantly hears the thunk of a car door, then becomes aware of Bedrosian limping towards her. She tries to head up the steps more quickly, but she trips and then his hand is under her elbow, helping her up to the landing. "Don't touch me," she tries to shout, but her voice comes out a cracked whisper.

He lets go. They stand there in silence, some feet from each other, the locked door a torment, her hand digging in her bag for the keys.

He says, "I didn't think you'd make it back."

She has no capacity for deception. "Leave me alone," she whispers. "Please."

"You know what your mom said? She said you've got a good heart."

Lucy's shoulders crumple inward.

"That woman loves you, Lucy. Losing you is gonna kill her. You know that, don't you?"

She stares woodenly at the door, the keys dug into her fist.

"You could walk away," he says. "The sentry I told you about, he'll make it happen."

"What do you mean, walk away?" she whispers.

He leans in, galvanized by her response. "You won't be held responsible. It'll be like you weren't part of it at all."

Her smidgen of hope is extinguished. She thought he meant not having to Serve anymore.

She hears him breathing, he shifts his weight, coming a little closer. "Do you need a doctor? I can take you. I know the ones that see servs."

She shakes her head at this bizarre offer. She withdraws the keys and fumbles to find the right one. He edges even closer and she freezes, but he doesn't touch her, just bends close, talking urgently. "Look at yourself. You're a mess. You're standing here protecting these assholes, whoever they are, and they won't even get you dupes? They don't give a shit about you. Or else how can they let you go through this? Huh? Look at me. Look at me," he insists, turning her by the chin. She refuses to meet his eyes. Focuses on his stubbled jaw. "Lucy," he jiggles her chin, "You're not being reasonable. They probably haven't Served in years. Tell me I'm wrong. What do you get out of this? Nothing. Wake up. Think about it."

She shakes her head, a minute motion hampered by his grip on her. He goes still, then, and his hand relaxes, releasing her chin, and she sags into the door, barely able to stay upright.

The cold surface feels good against her cheek. She wants to close her eyes and just sink away from him, from all of it.

"They're living high off grabs," he says, "and you're barely making it. They're living off him," he says, patting his coat, where the picture is folded in the pocket. "He was a living, breathing kid, Lucy. Tell me where they are."

The blue, blue eyes. The shoulders sharp like pebbles in her hands. Annabelle, screaming. She lets out a sob, catching it in her throat, ball of pain. "There was nothing I could do," she says.

"I know, Lucy. Tell me where they are."

"Go away," she whispers, and turns the key. She can't push the door open, so he does it for her, and in this way, he ends up inside the building, too. He holds her by the elbow and they inch their way across the lobby, start up the stairs. On the third step, she crumples. He slips his arm around her to keep her upright, her head rolling against his shoulder as they climb. A gaping pity wells up for him. He is so earnest with his folded picture of the boy, carrying it around in his pocket. He doesn't understand anything. He thinks he does, but he doesn't. Kid servs shouldn't exist. The arrivals with their stumbling, gangly bodies march through her mind. They tread her doorway, dripping waste and tears. They fall, cracking their slender bones on the floor. They scream, scrambling to hide from the monsters with their abysmal gazes, mouths hanging open like animals.

He leads her into the corridor, closes the front door. The apartment is flooded with cold sunlight, illuminating the dust, the shabby upholstery, the worn wooden floor scattered with yesterday's paper. There's a cut on her thigh that hurts tremendously; the pressure of walking causes blood bubbles to erupt through the congealed parts. She goes into her room, drags off her stained skirt and soaked underwear, stuffs them in the corner. She tugs on a pair of sweatpants and a sweatshirt. She lights a cigarette. Her hands keep shaking, her body convulsing with shudders. Hunger claws deep inside her belly: she didn't eat, not since the day before.

Bedrosian is here, she realizes, as if it's a long-ago memory. She limps back to the living room. He just stands there, watching her. His coat's draped over the back of the kitchen chair. She is overcome by the acute strangeness of being here at this time of day, with him.

"I need to check in," she whispers.

"Do what you need to do," he replies.

She goes to her laptop, tilts the screen away. She plugs in her earbuds so Bedrosian won't hear.

"You made it," Bernie says, amazed.

"Am I set?" she asks, her voice dry and cracked. "I'm at 184-306. I got a dupe penalty."

His expression changes. He looks about as sad as he's able. He can't meet her eyes. He says, "I'm sorry, Lucy. You've gone toxic. Julian called—" He lifts his shoulders, like he had no say.

"No," she begs. "He's wrong."

"You try and get things sorted, you hear? Maybe they'll let you be."

He's gone before she can say another word, coward that he is, sitting back not lifting a finger. He can't face her, knowing they've marked her good as dead.

"What was that about?" Bedrosian juts his chin in question.

She closes the laptop, ignoring him. The machine is blinking. She pushes play. Her agency supervisor's toneless voice fills the cold room, lecturing her about commitment and professionalism, and how could she promise to call and then fail to, and how they need to meet to resolve issues that have come up, especially regarding the matter of recent police inquiries. Lucy listens to the very end, utterly numb. She presses delete.

She looks at Bedrosian, who has filled two glasses of water. He hands one to her. She drinks, every swallow a cool slice of relief. When she's finished, she wipes her mouth with the back of her hand. She asks, "Do you have seven grand?"

He is taken aback.

"You don't have a wife, you probably don't have kids. Do you have seven grand?"

"I have savings, sure. Why?"

She steels herself. "Buy me out. If you buy me out, I'll talk."

"It's seven grand to buy you out?" he frowns. "That's it? Man, that is sad."

"Yeah? You can pay off my ma's loan, too."

She can see his jaw working, and it's gratifying, to have nailed him like that.

"Fine," he says. "Talk."

She points at the phone. "Buy."

He sets down his glass, comes to the couch. He digs in his jacket for his cell phone. "I just tell Aaron, or what?"

Lucy nods. She's draining away, overcome by what's happening.

"And it's O.K. if it's me who pays?"

"The Gate doesn't care where they get their money."

She tilts her head back, closing her eyes. She's done it. It's going to happen. She listens as he talks to the sentry, sorting through the details of how he'll pay, when, and so forth. She wonders how it all works, when they'll cut off the tag. How it will feel.

"O.K," Bedrosian says. "It's done."

She looks at him as if from a dream. The words form in her mind, *Theo Elander*. And then, at last, she speaks them out loud.

IT TAKES AGES FOR Bedrosian to get through questioning her. He dissects every piece of information, compelling her to dig for the most innocuous bits of memory associated with it. Recounting the story of how she met Julian, then Theo, the visits to the house in Ayer that had so enchanted her, she finds herself getting sick with shame. It's a whole different thing to tell it all in order, out loud. She's used to pushing aside memories that crop up, burying them where they can't torment her. He can tell when she holds back, too: he reads her every hesitation, pushes harder till she yields. She didn't want to tell him about the summer parties, the way the porch felt warm on her bare feet, or the horse dancing along the fence, but she ends up doing so, because he asks, and asks, and asks. Most especially, she planned to keep Ernesto out of it. But he keeps asking who else was there, as if he's looking into her mind and can see another shadow farther down the porch, sprawled on the chaise lounge, reading. He warns her about lying, that if it turns out she did, he can't honor the buyout deal. So she cracks, and then curls up, face to the cushion. He instructs her to look at him, but she can't. He tells her she's not the first to go down the wrong road, that she has to hang onto the fact that she's doing the right thing now.

"It doesn't feel right," she says.

"It's a betrayal," he replies. "Of course it doesn't feel right."

She glares at him over her shoulder. "Like you would know."

"I do," he says, and folds his notebook shut, sticks his pen into the spiral at the top. "You still have my number?"

She shrugs, just barely.

"Go home to Hull, then. Keep your head low."

The question's been nagging at her something fierce, and his motions to leave spur her to turn around, face him. "Why does that sentry Aaron even care? Just another dead serv, that's how they think."

"I convinced him."

"How?"

"It takes money to have a house, never mind the equipment for that kind of surgery, or paying employees such as yourself, or leasing apartments such as this one. So I said, where's the money coming from? How much is there?"

"And is the Gate getting their cut," Lucy finishes for him. "God, that's all they care about."

"Yeah. If there's one thing I've learned over the years, the Gate can't abide servs with too much money."

"So you're on their side."

"I'm just doing my job. Someone was murdered. I find who did it, and I make them pay."

A whirl of anger fills her limbs. "What about the rest of us getting murdered?"

"That's not on me, Lucy."

"It's on nobody, right? It's just how it is?"

"It's not something I myself can stop, is all I meant," he says. "Although, let's not forget, I'm getting you out, O.K.? That was my Alaskan cruise right there."

"Fuck your cruise."

"Agreed," he says, rising. "My luck, I'd go on my shore visit and walk into a bunch of you lot and a Nafikh. Go home, Lucy. I'll call when it's over."

She watches him pull on his coat. How does he know so much about servs? It's mystifying, but she has no energy to ask. She doesn't really care, she realizes. She's so terribly exhausted, the need to pass out overwhelms her. She sinks back against the cushion, drawing her knees up to her chest. She hears herself ask, "How long will it take?"

"They'll mobilize by tonight, I've got no doubt. Hey, wake up."

Her eyes won't stay open. She can barely see the blurred shape of him looming over her.

"Lucy, a storm's coming in this afternoon. They'll stop the ferry."

"Three o'clock," she mumbles.

There's a period of quiet when she hovers a little above the vast abyss tugging at her limbs. Then she starts awake, eyes flying open, aware of a presence. It's Bedrosian, still. He's draping his coat over the kitchen chair again.

"Aren't you leaving?" she asks, confused.

"I'll wake you up in a few, take you over to the docks. I'll make the call from here."

She can't argue. It seems like a good plan. She hears him moving about, the wood floors creaking under his heavy footfall. Then there's the familiar metallic thunk of the front door bolts driving to, one after the other. More footsteps. He must have gone into her bedroom to make his phone call.

Silence. Cold. The thrum of his deep voice, from way over there.

A dislodged, floating tiny part of herself thinks in astonishment, *It's over*. And then she allows herself to fall away into the darkness.

III

BEDROSIAN WAKES HER AT four thirty. The ferry's running later after all, so he thought he'd let her sleep some more. There's drool on the pillow, and her eyelashes are crusty. She feels awkward padding back and forth getting clothes, having a shower, toweling off, all the while acutely aware of the silence beyond the bathroom door. She pictures him sitting at the table drinking the coffee he made to help wake her up. Her whole body hurts, head to toe. The cut on her thigh opens, and she has to spend several minutes compressing it with gauze, and then snipping butterfly band aids because she's run out. She needs stitches, no doubt, but that's not happening. She disinfects with iodine, clenching her teeth in a silent scream, then sets the band aids in place, wraps her leg, and gets dressed. In the kitchen, she shakes four Advil into her palm, downs them with water.

"You O.K.?" Bedrosian asks.

"It'll pass."

It's beyond weird that she's getting used to him being here all the time—at night, in daylight, and now at dusk. He pours her a coffee, stirs in some sugar. He tells her there are several sentries involved now, so it looks like things will go down fast and smooth. Lucy figures he can be as optimistic as he wants, but she's not counting on anything. She preps herself while she sips her coffee, rehearsing in her head, and then calls Bernie. She lays into him the second he answers.

"I've been thinking, you tell Julian if he believes I said one fucking word, he's a true bastard! I'm the one who's been putting up with this since day one, and I get shafted? What the hell am I supposed to do to prove myself? This cop won't leave me alone, and it's *my* fault? How about leaving the body in a car, huh? How about not duping the guy watching over the yard, huh? I mean, could they be any cheaper?"

"Baby, I hear you, just stop yelling," Bernie begs.

"I just need to know someone's on my side, someone cares," Lucy says pitifully. "I mean, you understand where I'm coming from, right? Can you just tell him? He'll listen to you."

That's not true at all, but there's no harm in stroking his overseer ego.

"I'll do what I can, O.K.? You take care of your end."

"I swear I am, Bernie. You know that."

"I know, I know."

"If I could just—"

He hangs up. It's irritating, but he could've done so a lot sooner, so she can't complain. Overall, it didn't go badly. With any luck, he'll advocate for her, tip the scales in her favor just long enough to see her through to tomorrow.

"Nice to have an overseer in your camp," Bedrosian comments.

Lucy empties her cup and sets it down. "How do you know so much, anyway?"

"I've been around a while."

"You know what I mean."

"A long way back, I stumbled into things, and here I am," he says. "Important thing is, here you are, and you have a ferry to catch."

She ends up on the 6:05. Storm swells rock the harbor, filling the air with eerie clanking sounds. Bedrosian holds up his hand in farewell, walks away into the snowfall, back to his car. There wasn't anyone tailing them, he reassured her on the way; she's just glad she made that call to Bernie, her last piece of insurance. Anyway, there's no other serv on the boat, so that's that.

The ride is choppy and takes longer than usual, and by the time she gets off at the terminal, the storm's picked up something considerable. She opts not to call Sean, however. She slings her backpack over her shoulder and trudges the long walk home, the lone pedestrian on the streets in the blowing wind and snow.

When Eva opens the door, her face goes blank with surprise, then she cries, "Lucy, what are you doing here?" She ushers Lucy inside, pressing her to remove her boots, her coat, is she cold, how could she not call for a ride, why didn't she call to say she was coming?

"It just kind of happened," Lucy explains. "I didn't want you to go to any trouble."

"I don't have dinner," Eva frets. "I'm meant to go to the play with Phyllis. But now there's this snow. I called Sean so he can take us in the truck, but he didn't answer."

"Call him again."

"It's Friday night," Eva demurs.

"Don't tell me he's with Janie again?" Lucy groans. "All the more reason to call. Get him away from that stupid cow."

"I keep telling him he's too good of a man," Eva agrees. She rummages through the fridge, saying, "You were supposed to come tomorrow, so I don't have anything."

"You always say I don't visit enough, and now you're complaining," Lucy points out. "I can have a sandwich. It's fine."

"Don't be silly. I could make a stew, but I only have a few potatoes," Eva worries. "There's no time, though."

"Ma, really. Stop." Suddenly weak, Lucy sits down hard on one of the wood chairs. She wonders where Bedrosian is, if he's with the sentries, or waiting like her. If any of it is actually real.

Eva approaches but doesn't touch her, she knows better, and for this Lucy is grateful. "What's wrong, baby?"

Lucy shakes her head.

"You'd tell me if something was wrong?"

"Nothing's wrong." Lucy rubs her eyes, tries to straighten herself up. "Actually, things are good." She makes herself say it, because it's true, and she needs to believe it herself. "I mean, things are going to change. It's going to be a lot better, going forward."

Eva brightens a little. "The job—they want to keep you?"

"No. But it's O.K.," Lucy says quickly, "there's always another job to be had. And I think I'll finally be able to get back to school. Maybe go traveling, too."

Eva's looking a little suspicious of all this good news, and Lucy thinks, *Too much, too fast.* Her own head's swimming, like she's tipping over an edge, barely hanging on. She's only just started thinking of how her life could change, really change. "Never mind, I'm so tired right now, Ma, I think I'm kind of crazy."

This, Eva can handle. "You lie down while I make a sandwich," she commands.

It's an appealing notion, but Lucy heads for the secretary desk. "If I fall asleep now, I'll wake up at two in the morning. Lemme go over your papers. I haven't gone over things in a while." She notices the Amazon gift card still standing at attention on the secretary desk, the centerpiece. She swipes it up between two fingers, shakes it at Eva. "Didn't you order yet?"

"I haven't decided what to get. I like browsing."

Eva busies herself at the counter, the fridge, pulling out turkey, cheese, mayo, lettuce. Lucy shoves aside all the junk mail on the desk, hefts a sheaf of papers out of the file cabinet and starts separating things into piles: bills, bank statements, correspondence, donations.

"Eva, you can't give this much to the SPCA," she groans.

"Those poor animals have no one."

"I give you my hard-earned money so you can save a cat?"

Implacable, sturdy in her cause, Eva does not relent. She sets to chopping a red onion with vigor, her arms flopping with the motion. It comes to Lucy that maybe, after all, the animal's a better investment than the girl ever was. Though that's going to change.

She wishes Bedrosian would call with an update. Instead, when the phone rings, it's Sean. Eva puts him on speaker, announces Lucy is here. They exchange greetings, Lucy hollering from her position bent over the lower drawer of the file cabinet. Eva asks him to pick Phyllis up first so she can get the window, which Lucy finds pretty funny. It's too much, Sean with two old ladies in his truck on a Friday night: it's a wonder what he puts up with.

Time passes with Lucy going over statements and bills, munching on her sandwich while she works. Eva changes into a navy blue wool suit she got on sale two winters ago, adds a string of fake pearls to the ensemble, and fusses endlessly over her hair in the front hall. When Sean pulls up, Lucy helps her down the steps, then scatters deicer on the way back up. She waves and Sean honks. They pull away.

She'll be able to come home whenever she wants, she realizes. Every weekend. She can stay over Christmas.

She enters the house, closes the door and locks it. One of the cats meows, rubbing figure eights around her legs. She gazes at the polished table with its rectangular lace doily and jade cat, Eva's snow boots primly stationed on a boot tray next to the door, the little wooden plaque hanging on the wall with its merry painting of a sandcastle and pail above the scrolled words: *Gone To The Beach!* Lucy made it in grade school. She wanted to open a shop and sell such knickknacks to tourists. Eva got her paints, wood scraps, ribbon and string to hang up her creations. She made about ten, sold them for two bucks each to Eva's friends, then lost interest. She's seen this plaque a thousand times and not once before has it ever made her feel like crying.

Get a grip, she chastises herself.

The fact that she's getting bought out keeps swooping into her mind out of nowhere, leaving her stunned all over again. It's going to take days, weeks, to come to terms. To really, truly grasp that it's real. She pops open Eva's sherry and pours herself a stiff portion. She picks up her knapsack, carries it and the drink upstairs to her room. She dumps the knapsack on the bed, sits down. The room is dusty and dim; the nightstand light's burned out, and the ceiling fixture gives off a blue glow, which was what she liked when she was a kid, to be encased in a womb-like darkness, hunched up on her bed with her knuckles digging at her ribs. The walls are bare except for a Dürer print of the grim reaper. The book shelves still hold the sci-fi and fantasy series she was reading back then, a snow globe, a wooden recorder, a Tarot deck.

Alone in this quiet, exhaustion setting in once again, her elation at her freedom dissolves into an acid pool of guilt for the betrayal that bought it. Especially Ernesto: it pains her even more than Julian.

They wrote you off first, she reminds herself.

It's weird she's not that distraught about Julian, but maybe being in this room is keeping her in check. That one time she brought him to Hull was just so wretched. Why the hell had she, anyway? He'd wanted to come, that was the main reason. But also because, truth be told, she couldn't stand to go a day without him—that's first love, sick and cloying and blind to everything till it's too late.

Julian, who'd never had a real family, wanted to see. It was like a circus attraction for him, to peek into the musty tent of Lucy's childhood, to look upon the strange creature called mother. That was how it felt, after all the giggling and making out on the ferry, once they stepped into the house and Lucy saw the avid curiosity on his face, the sneering way he looked around like he was in a place beneath him. In that moment, Lucy wanted to take it all back, swoop backwards in time, the ferry flying backwards across the waves, them trotting back to her apartment, back to the moment when she said, Sure, come along, when she should have said, No.

Eva sensed it. She was guarded, welcoming but suspicious, and a little scared, and happy, too. All her conflicting emotions were so pathetically obvious, laid bare for Julian to see, and Lucy couldn't help it, the skewed resentments she'd felt as a child resurfaced: Eva had no spine, no ability to discern, to conceal, to put up a fight. She was weak, flaccid. It was why she'd given Lucy up, in the end.

At the same time, Lucy knew she should protect Eva, shield her from Julian's nasty curiosity, from the whispered comments, I can't believe you lived here, and, What a dump. Because in his and Theo's view, the Before was infinitely superior to this world: servs were like princes driven from their thrones, they did not belong here, they deserved better. Anything in this world was shit, and Lucy's little brown house in this working-class neighborhood was a cesspool.

But Lucy was too cowardly to protest. She hung on Julian's arm, mimicking him. They filled Eva's house with meanness and snobbery, they ate her meal, went out drinking, they came home and fucked on this bed.

Lucy stands up, repulsed. The memory is a pit of awfulness, of everything she just wants to forget. Most of all Eva's collapsed look, a few hours in. Her resignation, a sheep headed for slaughter. Plodding back and forth with dirty plates and silverware, making bright conversation, putting on a show that all three of them knew was a farce.

I'm sorry for everything: that's what Lucy always says, and maybe it's really just for that one time. It's the most awful thing she ever did, because it was conscious. Not the ravings of a bewildered serv child with no guidance. It was calculated: she made her choice, and she chose Julian.

In the morning, Eva took her aside. She said, I don't like that man, Lucy. She sounded resolute, despite her total humiliation. You stay away from him.

Eva doled out some good advice over the years, all of which Lucy let pass through one ear and out the other. It might be time to start paying heed.

Time: the word itself fills her with new wonder.

She's got time. Time lies ahead, pouring away, and all she must do is step forward into the stream. It's just not believable. She's never made a plan more than a week ahead. Even in the off-season, she's never dropped her guard, not ever. A host of threats lurks right around the corner, always. No serv makes a plan without *we'll see* or *let's check in again*. They live day to day, week to week maximum. Even without Nafikh in town, there are cranky overseers slapping on penalties, other servs trying to edge into a choice bunk, squabbles over jobs and tasks. Even privileged with her own apartment, there is dealing, maneuvering, wrangling, all in the effort to position oneself for the coming season. There is the desperate quest to put away extra cash for bribes, drugs, emergency dupes, and in her case, Eva's loan, her rent, utilities, food—

She lets out a sudden laugh, more like a choking sound. The urge to call Bedrosian practically topples her: *Is it real? Did you pay yet? Is it a trick?*

The first gong of the doorbell jolts her out of her reverie, followed by the ladder of merry notes echoing through the house. She peeks out the window, sees Sean's truck idling in front of the house. She rubs her eyes. She needs to change the sheets, replace that dumb blue bulb, eat some more. And hit that bottle of sherry again for sure; she can get Eva another one before she leaves. There's no way she can go out. She needs to rest, think, get herself in order.

She opens the door and leans against the jamb, arms folded. "What, no Janie to keep you busy?"

"It's over for good this time. Let's go for a drink." He flicks his wrist, miming a dart toss. "Come on. If you don't, I'll lose."

Lucy hesitates. It's not every day a serv gets bought out. Maybe she should celebrate. "O.K.," she says. "Lemme get my darts."

IT'S THE WITCHING HOUR and Maggie's Shack is crammed. The two boards are already occupied, so Lucy signs up for the next round. She heads for the only stool left, at the far corner of the bar next to the cash register. In the mirror behind all the bottles she glimpses her drawn, hollow-looking face, her nose and cheeks pinched red from the walk across the parking lot. Sean lags behind, nodding hellos, cracking a joke or two. Mayor Sean, that's his nickname, because he knows everyone, and everyone loves him. A woman with streaked blonde hair latches onto his arm, all twinkle-eyed and adoring. It's obvious they had a thing at some point. Sean can't shake her off because, as usual, he's too nice for that. At least Janie is out of the picture.

Lucy goes ahead and orders a Jameson, fixes her gaze on the scratched and dirty bar, letting all the noise wash into her, the band setting up in the corner, people crowding in already on second and third drinks and getting loud. The guy next to her is digging into a burger, smacking his lips, fingering the balled-up napkin. Lucy thinks of Eva's fridge and decides she'll go shopping with her tomorrow, so she can really stock up with Lucy there to carry the bags. She turns on her stool, finds Sean approaching. Something about him takes her back what feels like a hundred years to the wet stadium grass seeping through her shirtback, Jamie O'Conell's groping hand making a try for her tit. How old was she—eleven? Twelve? O'Conell was fifteen at least. Then Sean barreled out of the dark, waled on the older boy with whirligig fists. The last she heard, O'Connell works for some consulting firm in Boston, drives a BMW, and can't be bothered to get to Hull for his own mother's birthday. Asshole.

"How long we got?" Sean asks, peering over the crowd to try and see the boards.

"Maybe half an hour." She downs the Jameson and pushes the glass forward, signaling her need for another.

"Already on number two?"

"You were busy chatting up boobs over there."

"You could get padded cups, you know."

"Ha-ha-ha."

She feels his weight pressing in on her space as he fits himself between the barstools. The bartender slides a pint down the counter without comment. Sean takes a long drink. "So are you gonna tell me what's been going on, Luce?"

Her mood sinks a little. "There's nothing going on."

"Yeah? You look like the cat dragged you in."

"Wow. Thanks."

He chews on his lip, leaning over the bar with his arms folded. "Seriously, Luce. I mean, that cop?"

She shakes her head, downs the rest of the Jameson in one gulp. She meets his eyes in the mirror, between all the bottles. "It's nothing, Sean. Just drop it."

"Drop it?" He draws in his chin, amazed. "Boston Homicide comes to the house, and you say drop it?"

Lucy's starting to wish she stayed home after all. "I know how it looks. I'm sorry. But I swear, it's all taken care of."

He regards her with obvious distrust. "That just sounds like a lie."

"Well, it isn't."

It's pretty ironic that the one time she's telling the truth, he still calls her out. The girl who cried wolf, she supposes. She turns to survey the room. There are so many familiar faces in here: Pat McGill, Georgie whatsit, Ellie from middle school, her red hair cut short now, still with the tattoos and now a snake circling her bicep. And Damian Leary, who used to pepper her with spitballs. He's a freaking cop now. He turns, catches sight of her. His round freckled face breaks into an awkward smile, and he lifts his hand in greeting. Lucy waves back.

"Luce, Jesus," Sean hisses. "Now will you quit telling me everything's O.K.?"

Her sleeve rode up when she waved, exposing the dark mottle of bruises. She tugs it down. Her surroundings are momentarily obliterated by the memory of the Nafikh clenching her forearms over and over, fascinated by the way the skin changed color when He let go. The muscles in her face tense up, automatically ready to shape the rictus smile. She bends her head. "I said, just drop it."

"Is that what it's all about, some asshole beat you up? Was it one of the 'bad guys' that detective was talking about?"

"No, Sean."

"Because I can take care of that shit, you understand?"

She is momentarily baffled. "What?"

He leans in, subtly points to Damian, then another guy in a black leather vest, his name is Call. He's beefy and short, he plays drums in a local band. "All I have to do is say the word."

Understanding dawns. "Uh, Sean, hello. They hate me."

"They don't hate you. They just think you're weird. Which you are. Anyway, they like me," he points out, "so they'll do what it takes."

She pictures them in the doorway to the mansion, the Nafikh turning His gaze upon the intruders. "No, I don't think so."

"It's all some kind of joke to you, is it?"

"It's not a joke."

"Do you realize how worried Aunt Eva is? 'Find out what's going on, Sean.' 'You have to make her talk, Sean.' That's all I got, all the way to Hingham!"

"So that's why you wanted to go out?"

"God, you take the cake, you do!"

"What the hell am I supposed to think?"

She turns away, furious at this interrogation, but he won't let up. He leans in, forcing her to look at him. "I wanted to go out because I care, too! Aunt Eva said you're talking big about things changing and going back to school? That sounds nuts, Lucy, especially with cops after you!"

"There aren't any cops—Jesus! Things are looking up at last, and I get criticized? What do you want from me?"

"What do we want—?" He's gripping his glass, white knuckled, and his mouth clenches into a hard line. She's rarely seen him so worked up, and it leaves her off balance. "What we want," he says through his teeth, voice low and hard, "is the fucking truth, for once. That is what we want. It's the least we deserve."

Her eyes blur and she turns abruptly, blinking hard. The van turning on the circular drive. The mansion against the moonlit sky, Cora whining why don't you just put her up front.

"You know what, forget it," he snaps, shoving his half-empty glass so that it totters, almost falls. Then, to her shock, he throws some bills on the counter and walks away, headed for the door.

It takes a moment before she's confident she can pick up her Jameson without slopping it everywhere. She drinks slow and deep, sliding the liquid in a tiny stream along her tongue and down the back of her throat. To feel the fire of it. To obliterate the sting of tears in her eyes. He's drunk, is what it is, already worked up about Janie, and then Bedrosian's stupid visit.

Although, he's got a right to be so mad. She has lied to his face for years, after all, every single fucking time, a lie. Same with Eva. And he knows it. He just doesn't realize how deep things go.

She slides off the stool. She makes her way across the crowded room, erases her name from the lineup. Damian notices her, waves in farewell. She forces herself to acknowledge it, gives a little smile, because after all, it's true he'd beat someone up for her. At the door, she pulls on her parka and ties the belt, pulls her wool hat down low. When she steps out she discovers it's snowing heavily now. They're predicting up to two feet. The sea wind picks up the snow and tosses it in mist-like swirls and eddies across the parking lot. At the end of which Sean's truck idles with the headlamps pouring cones of light through the snowfall.

She stands there, not sure. Then she's walking forward without having really decided to, but she can't turn back so she keeps going. Her boots make tracks all the way, and he doesn't get out or drive forward, just sits there waiting. She can hardly blame him. The walk towards him feels redemptive in some way, like she's doing her penance.

She waits at the passenger side till the lock thunks, giving her permission. She gets in. It's hot and noisy with the fans blowing high to keep the windshield from fogging. He's sipping coffee from a thermos. The whiskey in it perfumes the air. She feels the Jameson now in the heat and in his proximity. She drags her wool cap off.

"You going to be sick?" he asks.

She tilts her head back against the headrest. "I'm not sure."

A few minutes pass. He turns down the defogger, and the silence between them gets so loud, she makes herself go first.

"You're right about the cop, Sean. It sucks he came here, and I need to reassure Eva again. But I swear, it's all over."

He rubs his forehead, pushing back his hair and gripping it. "Can we be straight, just for once? You're not an escort anymore, is what you're saying?"

She grits her teeth. "Yes. It's over."

"Why'd he come here asking all those questions?"

"There was an investigation. I can't go into it."

"God," he mutters. He makes a fist against the window, closing his eyes briefly. Then he says, "You know, Luce, I always thought the hospital made you all weird and cagey. But I've been thinking, it's just how you always were, right? I mean, even as a little kid." He turns half around in his seat to consider her, like he's taking stock. "I can't figure you, Luce. I just can't. I mean, how can you not tell me what's going on, after everything we went through?"

Jet-black lashes around his blue eyes, the freckles over his nose, so deeply familiar. She might throw up after all, she thinks, it's so close in here, the boozy air. "Please don't, Sean. Not now."

"Oh, yeah? When would be a good time, Luce? All those emergency room visits, all the blood everywhere, the suspensions from school, Aunt Eva ripping her hair out from worry. How about me getting beat black and blue for sticking by you all the time. At my house, when you did it with my da's razors. You want to know how bad he beat me for that? Yeah, that's right. I never told you. I didn't want to upset you more. Doesn't that count for something?"

An image of Uncle Seamus flashes into Lucy's mind: a crooked, angry man with eyebrow hairs sticking up like wires. How terrified she was of him. When he died, there was a crappy funeral at St. Mary's. Lucy was in McLean so she couldn't go, but Eva told her Sean cried, which Lucy doesn't get. "Look, I'm sorry all that happened. You know I don't remember much."

"Yeah, well, Aunt Eva said they were doing shock therapy on you, and all kinds of drugs. She said she'd visit and you wouldn't even know who she was. So I guess I shouldn't be surprised. But still, it sucks, you know. It's like everything we did means nothing."

Lucy thinks, *Ma visited me?*

She feels memory slithering past like an eel in total darkness, and then it is gone.

"Here's the thing, Lucy. The whole fucking world revolved around you. It was this little, tight world," he shapes it with his cupped hands, fingertips pressed together so hard they're white, "comprised of me, Aunt Eva, and you. That was it, that was your world. And all we did was focus on keeping you alive. We were like your own little ambulance crew. One day it's pills, the next day it's razors, the next it's pulling you off the bridge just in time. You were like this vortex. This black fucking hole."

I didn't realize, she wants to say. But of course she did. She just wasn't able to stop.

"And now here I am," Sean goes on, "all these years later and I find myself thinking, why did I bother? All those years waiting to hear from you, worrying about you, thinking about you, all that effort. For what? For you to end up like this? It's over, you say. But you know what? I don't believe you. Do you know if Aunt Eva knew, she'd fucking *die*? Is this how you repay her? Jesus, all she went through for you!"

The shell has cracked, opened, the wisps of angst seep out like poison, that indefinable longing carving out a hole inside. The heat from the Source grows hideous, coming in waves so staggeringly painful she might pass out. Lucy edges down the automatic window in fits and starts to suck in the cold air. She jams a fist against her sternum, hunching.

"Oh, man, you still get that?" Sean grips her arm, shakes it. "Are you O.K.?"

"I'm fine," Lucy stutters. "I'm O.K."

"I thought they gave you something for it."

"Not really."

"But it's stress! They have pills for that!" Sean fumes.

"Getting mad won't help."

He withdraws his hand. "Sorry. Luce, I'm sorry, I shouldn't have said that stuff."

"It's not your fault," she shakes her head. "You're right about everything."

"When things went bad, you could've just moved back home," he says in a bewildered tone. "I just don't know why you'd do this to yourself. What are you trying to prove?"

"I should've come back," she agrees, though that would never have been possible. "I didn't want to be a burden."

He nods, looking out his window. She watches the patches made by his breath expand and contract on the pane. "You know, when I was a kid," he says, "I saw you as my way out. You probably don't remember, but you told me this story about being an alien. You remember that? You were nine."

Her eyes flutter away. She stares down at her lap.

"I thought one day, a spaceship'd show up and cart us both away, whoosh." He moves his hand in slow motion towards the sky. He chuckles. "I'd watch *Star Trek* and *Dr. Who* and shit, you know, thinking about all that. Like what if there's another world, please God let there be, and let me find it. I was jealous, if you want the truth." He slides a humorous glance at her. "I wanted to be the alien."

There is a pause.

She says, "I don't think it was a good thing."

"Eva said it was how you coped."

"What do you mean?"

"She read some diary you had. You had the whole story in there."

In a flash, Lucy recalls that morning: the pages turning in Eva's hands. *It hurts so much. I want to die. I come from another world.* The diary's still in Lucy's room, in a drawer.

"She'd say, 'Sean, don't be too hard on Lucy. She's finding her place in the world.'" He mimics Eva in a fake high-pitched voice that sounds nothing like her, then speaks his part in exaggerated bass. "And I'd say, 'Aunt Eva, she's crazy,' and she'd say, 'Sometimes crazy is what you need to get by.'" He chuckles to himself drunkenly. "Anyway, I guess what I'm getting at is, Nothing matters, that's what you always said. Everything we did to try and help, and you'd say who cares. And here's the irony, right? Here we are, all these years later, and I drive around this fucking town and pick up my paycheck and head to the bar and hang with my friends, and no, I don't have a woman in my life that I actually love, I got no kids, no aspirations, no way out of the debt that crept up on me like fucking lava, and you know what, Luce?"

Her body's so stiff it might crack if she moves. He's way drunk, spewing stuff she doesn't want to hear, like the bottle burst and out it all comes.

"Nothing matters. I finally got there, Luce. I get it. And the only person who might understand is you, and you don't give a fuck! Pretty dumb, I mean, I see it now. Why should you care? Look at your own life. I mean, God, I think *I'm* in a mess? Of course you don't care."

There's a silence. The heating ticks and stutters.

She says, "I do care."

He laughs out loud. "That's all you're gonna say? I swear, Lucy, you've got an extra Y chromosome."

He spins the thermos cap, drinks. He passes it to her. There is a sense of the space between them untwisting in the silence, settling. Going back to normal.

She shapes fists and squeezes hard. "Things really are changing now, Sean. I swear. You'll see."

He looks at her. The hardness in his face yields a little. "O.K., Luce." He bends his head, slowly turning the thermos cap back and forth. "But when you say change, you mean, getting hurt—"

"Trust me, it's not happening anymore," Lucy interrupts. "I swear."

"You sure?"

"Yes."

Their eyes meet. She pours sincerity into her gaze, willing him to accept it. He nods. He puts the car in gear, drags his seat belt around and clicks it in. He pulls out slowly, and the snow whirls towards the windows in silence. They drive along the crashing bay, then turn onto her street. When he pulls up, she leans sideways to give him a hug. "Have fun picking up the ladies. You're a good man, Sean," she jokes.

"God help me."

They share a laugh. Once she's unlocked the front door, she turns and waves to signal she's in and safe. The truck rolls away into the darkness, headed for Hingham. She waits till the brake lights vanish around the corner, and then waits a little longer. The street is empty and quiet, snowdrifts building up along the fences.

IN HER ROOM, LUCY empties her knapsack, goes through the stuff she brought, checks all the compartments twice, but she has indeed forgotten the yoga pants and tank she likes to sleep in. She opens up all the dresser drawers, finds a pair of pink pajamas that were a Christmas gift one year. For when you forget your overnight things, was what Eva said, with maternal prescience.

Lucy pulls off her clothes and gets into the pajamas. They're thin cotton, because Eva knows Lucy runs hot, and musty from lying in the drawer so long. She looks at herself in the mirror, expecting, she doesn't know, expecting something else. But what she sees is the girl she ever was, glowering in the dull blue light, her blonde hair the same, her stance the same, herself the same.

Plus ça change, she thinks. *Fuck.*

She sits on the bed and checks her phone, finds three missed calls from Bedrosian's number. Her stomach lurches. She swiftly dials, shaking. He answers right away.

"You made it O.K. Good. I was wondering."

"That's it?"

"Yeah. Nothing happening on this end. I just checked in. They're still getting their ducks in a row."

Lucy's still trying to wrap her mind around him calling three times just to check on her. "Well, they can't trace tags, maybe that's why."

"He said something about that. Listen, I gotta go. You keep your phone next to you. I'll call the minute I hear."

She hangs up, feeling weirdly conspiratorial, tied up with him. She can see his big face and sad eyes, his jaw working with all the tension. She wonders where he is.

She lies down, not with any hope of actually sleeping, but just to let her body rest a little. The argument with Sean wound her tight, even though they made up. He'll see, soon enough. She actually could move back for a while, she decides. Why not? It's not like she'll be keeping that apartment. She wants nothing to do with it. She should've just taken her stuff today. It would fit in a small box: the afghan, the album, the knickknacks, the photos. She could have exited once and for all, and now she'll have to go back.

She lifts her phone, checks, in case she had it on mute by mistake. No calls.

It's only been five minutes, if that.

She lies there, staring at the ceiling, then abruptly flings herself up and out of the room, heads downstairs. She builds a fire, which Eva always likes in a snowstorm, and sets the grate once it's going strong. Just as she's pouring a sherry, she hears the front door, Eva's merry good nights, then the door slams shut.

"What are you doing up?" Eva cries happily. "Sean said you were so tired. I told him I hope she's tucked in by now."

"Here you go," Lucy hands her the sherry. "How was it?"

"Such fun," Eva says with delight. "We never go enough. It's hit or miss, but this one was a good one."

Lucy clinks her glass in salute. "Wanna play Scrabble?"

The suggestion lights Eva right up. "Let me change," she says excitedly. "Get the board set up. Oh, and Luce," she adds, mischief in her eyes, "there's a new sherry in the kitchen."

"Music to my ears," Lucy sighs in relief, pulling the game out from under the chair. "Hurry up or I'll cheat."

PAST MIDNIGHT AND STILL no updates to speak of, but that's because all the sentries got pulled out on four simultaneous Services, as it turns out. It's so strange to hear Bedrosian say that, lying in the semi-dark of her bedroom in her pink pajamas, tucked under a blanket, never to Serve again. Never. Again. She doesn't have to keeping checking Twitter. She doesn't have to text Bernie begging not to get bumped up the roster, nor does she have to haggle over what it'll take to ensure that. Never again.

Is it real? she couldn't help asking.

Better be, he replied, seeing as there's a hole the size of Alaska in my account.

She can't sleep for the excitement of it: she stares into the dark, wide awake, feeling the thump of her heart and the faintly hurting Source. That she might be here tomorrow, the day after, is unfathomable. She wants it, but in the wanting, too, the hard memories press up all around, rustled up by the bow in the mattress, the smell, the house creaking in the wind perpetually blowing in off the bay. She thinks of her da Frank for the first time in years, and wonders where he went and what became of him. She thinks of the street in summer with its scrubby lawns and sprinklers and squealing kids in bathing suits, the feel of the stairs under her bum, her stiff little body in the shade, glowering. She didn't want to be slathered with the pasty sun lotion: the other kids made fun of her even more. But if she exposed herself to the sun, her fair skin practically caught fire, like a vampire, which was another of her nicknames, along with Ghostie. Sean always sat with her for a while, because she was his cousin and he was older, protective like a brother. Sadness pricks her, for the long-ago silent, intense communion and closeness they'd shared. Maybe it was inevitable that it got damaged, just a part of growing up. Especially if you grow up in a loony bin.

After everything we did for you, he accused her. But that went the other way, too. How many times she stuck with him, hiding from Uncle Seamus when he was on a rampage. In closets, behind bushes, under the porch while he slammed around inside the house. There was that one time when she thought for sure he'd kill them. She was so terrified. Uncle Seamus's boots thunked the wood floors, reverberating through to where they crouched, and now and then he shouted obscenities and threats that came in pieces: Fucking little . . . I'm going to . . . git your ass . . . . They groveled in the dirt under the porch floorboards, hugging their knees. It smelled like cat shit and beer and dried up leaves. Lucy was ten and Sean was twelve. Sean's eyes were big and wide and wet staring up just waiting for his da to bust out the front door and start searching outside. Lucy held his hand so tight her fingertips went white. The Source hurt awfully right under her ribs, like being stabbed over and over; it always got like that when she was scared. She pushed her fist hard against the spot which helped a little. Uncle Seamus stomped onto the porch. His boots were dark shadows between the boards.

Sean you little fuck I'm gonna git you!

Their hands went sweaty gripping each other. They did not breathe. Uncle Seamus mumbled and paced. Then he went back inside and they heard the screen door squeaking loosely on its broken hinge.

Everything went quiet. They waited, their breaths like whispers. They heard motorboats slowly cruising by, the slap of water on the sand. How long did they sit there? Lucy thinks maybe up to an hour. Like little animals, sweating and breathing, clinging to life. Eventually, Uncle Seamus must have passed out. They agreed on this theory without speaking, just breathing, looking at each other. They crept forward on their scraped bare knees. It started to rain, big hot fast drops splattering them as they raced across his scrappy yard, then the asphalt drive poking their bare feet, down the sidewalk to her house and her own grass which was plush and bright the way Eva labored to keep it.

Where've you rascals been? Eva looked up from the stove as they went racing by. And Lucy knew they'd be safe for the time being because Eva never let Uncle Seamus after them, not in the territory of her own house.

In Lucy's room they closed themselves into a tent made from her bedspread and an old sheet. Sean was tall and skinny and barely fit inside. He had to tuck himself up, a jumble of bruised and bony limbs.

He said, When the spaceship comes, can it take me with you?

Lucy feels tears well under her eyelids, remembering.

The small long-ago Lucy replied, Yes.

Sean looked relieved. Lucy already knew there were no spaceships. Drunk Pete had told her. What he said was: There are no spaceships, you stupid little creep.

She said, It's a long, long ride.

How long?

Really long. And when we get there, we'll be other beings. We'll change along the way. We'll be made of fire.

(Drunk Pete said the Source was a kind of fire, that it was what they used to be.)

If we're made of fire, how can we talk?

Lucy didn't know. She didn't like lying to Sean, even though it made him happy. She said, You can't ever tell anyone about me, O.K.?

I know.

I mean it.

I won't tell. I promise.

They hooked their pinky fingers together and intoned, Never divulge. And he didn't, and the years went by, and gradually she realized he'd stopped believing, the way you stop believing in Santa Claus. She was eleven years old. He looked at her with his sad blue eyes and he said, Cuz, you need help.

It hurt. But she didn't correct him.

Don't ever tell them, Drunk Pete warned time and again (he said kids blabbed the most, and he was right). Is that what you want? You want the only people who give a shit about you to be killed?

Who'll kill them?

The Qadir.

She pictured black-caped figures emerging from swirling mist, mythical avengers with swords dripping blood. The image terrorized her.

So when the time came, instead of insisting, she said, I'm sorry I lied.

Yeah, whatever, Sean shrugged.

And there it was: the truth of her folded up and tucked away, the subject closed forever. Her real-person body mechanically put the dishes in the washer—it was after Easter Sunday lunch, the table centerpiece a festive bowl of decorated eggs and cheap plastic greenery and flowers—and Sean washed the pots and Eva chatted with Uncle Seamus in the living room as if he were always a gentleman in a suit with a folded hankie poking up from his pocket.

Lucy stares into the dark, her palm sweaty and hot against her chest, imagining the impossible, what it'd be like to tell Sean it was all true, she's from outer space after all. How he'd roll his eyes and laugh.

How she'd have no way to prove it, other than to make the cut.

LUCY'S DREAMING. SHE'S AT the edge of a vast, undulating ocean. Her feet are in the sand. The water's coming closer. There's a terrible dread about being here, but she can't remember what it is. She's worried it's the Before. It's strange that she's frightened of the Before, but she is. She tries to run away but slips and falls backwards into the sand. Now she's looking up at the sky, and she can't see the ocean, but she knows it's coming closer, the mass of water heaving towards her paralyzed body. Her terror grows. She squirms in the sand. Now there is a boulder on her chest. The boulder's weight is crushing. She has never felt such agony. It starts in her center and then sprays out like fireworks through every part of her flesh. Aah, she cries. Aah, aah.

Her eyes fly open.

In the same instant that the room emerges from the dark, she becomes aware of the figure in the hallway and the Source's subsiding response.

It takes ages. What feels like ages. Then her body jolts into motion, she sits up, fumbling for the lamp. Her hand crashes into it, causing it to topple, and she scrambles to keep it upright. "Who's there?" she whispers, groping the lamp, unable to find the switch.

He pauses, turns. He moves towards her room. The door stands open to the hallway, a blue glow emanating from the nightlight Lucy installed so Eva wouldn't trip on her way to the bathroom. The light gives shape to him, and she recognizes the dome of his head, the thick neck and shoulders.

"No," she whimpers, scrambling backwards on her bed.

"Shut up so you don't wake up your darling ma," Joe Brynn hisses. "She was supposed to go first. Up to you if you want her to watch."

She goes dead still, her breath caught tight and high in her throat.

"I always told J," he shakes his head disapprovingly, "she's gonna be a fucking problem, I said. You need to unload her now. But no, he was all starry eyed and optimistic. You can't turn black to white, I told him. You can't turn a cat into a dog."

Lucy's mind is hurtling around her bedroom: books, lamp, clothes, stuffed animals. Nothing she can use. There's nothing. Despair floods her, turns her weak. *Keep him talking.* "But why, Joe? What did I do?" she whispers, all earnestness. "Can you at least tell me why?"

"She asks why," he addresses an invisible audience, arms lifted. He approaches as he talks, step by step. She's got nowhere to go, pressed up against the headboard. "Because you're a loose end. Loose Lucy," he adds jauntily, impressed with his pun. "I always told J, she's not like us. She's weak. She'll cause problems. Who'd you talk to, Loose Lips Lucy? Did you tell your ma? I bet you told her."

"Joe, I swear," Lucy stammers, "I swear on my life, I did not tell her. She does not know."

"Yeah, O.K. Sure, Loose Lips Lucy. What about anyone else? I bet you told this whole armpit of a town. Yappety-yap."

"I swear," she blubbers. "I really swear."

"But you told the cop. You told him everything."

"No," she whimpers.

"Don't you lie to me, you rotten little skinner."

Her hands grip the blanket. She could fling it around his head, duck by, run like hell. It's her only chance. An utterly pathetic one that will never work. And how will she save Eva.

Eva! a voice weeps inside her head, a child's voice.

"Does Julian know?" she asks, in the same tiny voice.

"Does he know," he chuckles, as if her question is a punch line. "Yes, he knows. Or I should say, he *knew.* Theo doesn't like naysayers. No, he does not."

"What do you mean?"

"You know what I mean. I told Theo, you better watch him, he's got a weak link and it starts with an L. And now *I* end up in bum-fuck nowhere doing his work." He reaches into his jacket and withdraws a knife, which he balances on his palm for her to see. "Murder-suicide. Crazy girl finally does it. It'll be a real tragedy. Now, hush. I was told your ma is deaf as a doornail, but you're getting a little too noisy."

She realizes she's wheezing. She can't breathe. *I'm hyperventilating.* The noise fills the room, a high keen. She fights to bring it under control, but it only seems to get louder, and now her whole chest heaves with every breath, a pinprick of air each time, not enough.

Julian said no, she understands, as if from an impossible distance. *Julian.*

"Like I need this shit," Joe says, and leans in and slaps her once, hard, so that she almost falls off the bed. The breath getting knocked out of her interrupts the panic, and she gulps air. "This kind of weather, I have to drive the Explorer, and then I have to park a mile away and hike, and you know what, it's not my thing. I hate snow. Us true servs, true in our hearts," he pats his chest, patriotic, upright, "we hate snow, Lucy. How about you? Do you hate it? Or do you not hate it enough? Because, you know, I told Theo, I told him a thousand times, she's gonna be trouble. She's not one of us. And sure enough, as usual, I was right."

"No," Lucy pleads. "No." Her body thrashes to life, tumbling off the other side of the bed. She scrambles on all fours, desperate to get to her feet and run. She hears the heavy tread of his boots, then they are in her face and there's a wrenching pain as he hauls her upright by the hair. He slaps her hard. And again. The slaps explode through her head, paralyzing her. She dangles there, stunned.

His face is inches from her own, the expression flat and purposeful, eyes just off-center from hers. "Don't fight."

"No," she utters. "*No!*"

She pushes at his face, his neck. Her legs resume their flailing dance. In a distant part of her head she's aware of how pitiful her efforts are, but she can't stop.

Motion, muffled noises. Bare legs, the scalloped lace hem—

It's Eva, tottering in her bedroom doorway, her face a mask of shock.

Lucy spasms violently, then twists, sinks her teeth into Joe's arm.

"Jesus!" he yells, and throws her off. Her head snaps back against the bed rail, crumpling her, the blow an explosion of sparks in her skull. "Stop fighting, you little bitch, or I swear I'll make her suffer, you hear me?"

"Run!" Lucy screams at Eva, and launches herself at Joe's legs. She's wild with rage, infused with a strength she thought had drained entirely away. She comes into him with such force that he almost falls. The knife clatters to the floor. She clambers up his body, onto his back, wraps her legs in a vise around his waist. He spins around, slams her into the wall. Lucy glimpses Eva's horrified stare, she's backed away, clutching the landing railing with both hands. She's only gone about three feet. She can't reach the staircase, Lucy calculates in some distant part of her brain, not before Lucy loses this fight, which is sure to happen.

She screams, and claps the heels of her hands against Joe Brynn's ears, as hard as she can, as if she's going to crush his skull. She saw a Nafikh do that once and the serv went down like a stone, but Joe just teeters, then his hands reach up, groping for her. She slams again, and again. His hands drop, and he sways a little.

"Go!" she screams at Eva.

Eva totters along the rail, barely able to stand. *She's not going to make it,* Lucy realizes. Joe Brynn is recovering, she can feel the bunching in his body, the muscles heaving to while her own strength dissolves. She clamps her legs tighter, but their grip is too weak.

"Run," she begs Eva, who totters one more step, then stops again, clinging to the railing just to keep herself upright.

"Stay there," a voice warns. "Let her go now."

Lucy feels Joe go still and hard as rock. Then he swings her off his back, locks her to his body, forearm across her throat.

"Let her go, asshole!"

Recognition is slow, fumbling.

It is Bedrosian, coming up the stairs, both hands on a gun pointed right at Joe.

"Let her go!" he yells again, and in the instant before Joe's arm tightens, Lucy feels a kind of pity for his assumption that he'll be obeyed.

She claws at the concrete block of his arm: *I'm going to die!* A darkness presses into her eyes, compressing her brain, her chest. Scenes pop into her fading vision in fits and jerks as her body lurches: Bedrosian advancing one step at a time, gun eye-level, the demonic rage on his face; Eva sinking down the railing to the floor, her hands to her mouth. *I'm sorry, Ma,* Lucy begs. *I'm sorry.*

She feels herself drop, then there's a sudden upward rush, and her body gets tugged forward, held tight.

Bedrosian's holding her up. His other arm is still outstretched, the gun fixed on Joe.

There was a shot, she realizes. Joe. He's down, slumped against the wall. For a confused moment, she can't figure why. Then she registers the tracks down his face, the shattered cheek. His eye is gone. Blood, a lot of it.

"You O.K.?" Bedrosian demands. "Lucy, hey. Stay on your feet. Look at me."

"Source," she whispers.

He releases her, and she fumbles her way along his outstretched arm that brings her a few feet from Eva. She takes a few steps on her own, drops to her knees. "Ma," she whispers. "It's O.K. It's O.K."

Eva nods, white with shock.

"Come here," Lucy says, and pulls Eva to her chest, maneuvering to block as much as possible what is happening with Joe Brynn's corpse. The Source is just now being released. It snakes out from deep within, through bone and muscle and skin, seeping through his shirt. Lucy looks over her shoulder, shifts her position, frantic Eva might see. Bedrosian moves into Eva's line of sight, his sizeable bulk providing more of a buffer. To Lucy's relief, Eva remains huddled into Lucy's chest, mumbling about how she felt the vibrations, she thought Lucy was up and about, she was worried Lucy was sick, and then she came out. "I know, Ma," Lucy whispers, "it's over now. It's O.K."

The Source thickens to silvery white, floats lazily up behind Bedrosian's shoulders. Eva starts to lift her head, but Lucy says, "No, don't look, Ma," and Eva slackens, willing to obey. Even across the hallway, the heat of the Source seeps into Lucy's back. She glances up as it wends its way ceilingward, loosening, scattering, until the last glinting wisps vanish.

"Get a blanket," she tells Bedrosian, indicating her bedroom with her chin. Source aside, Joe Brynn is a gruesome sight that Eva shouldn't have to endure. Bedrosian hurries into Lucy's bedroom and returns with the bedspread, tosses it over the body.

There is the sound of all of them breathing, and a clock ticking somewhere in the house.

"O.K.," Lucy says. "Ma, let's get up."

Bedrosian helps Eva to her feet. She stares at each of them, her face drained of color. "We have to call the police," she says.

"Mrs. Hennessey," Bedrosian says gently, still cradling her forearm in his palm, "I *am* the police, all right? I'm going to handle this. You don't need to call anyone."

"But—"

"Ma, you need to trust him. He knows what he's doing."

"If you say," Eva says uncertainly.

Lucy meets Bedrosian's eyes over Eva's head, urgently mouthing, *What do we do?* He makes a mollifying gesture.

"Let's go downstairs," he suggests.

Eva makes no protest, clinging to his arm, taking the stairs at the cautious pace he sets. He speaks comfortingly in her ear as they go, exuding a calm authority that starts to ease Lucy's concern, because there's no way Eva won't defer to him. Downstairs at last, Lucy sinks onto the window seat while Bedrosian settles Eva in her wingback chair and arranges the afghan over her knees, as if he's always caring for shaken old women.

He says, "The important thing to remember, Mrs. Hennessey, is it's over. It's all over. Everyone's safe."

Eva trembles as she adjusts the afghan. Lucy touches her knee, squeezes. Eva lifts her watery eyes to meet Lucy's. "But— why did he come here? Why did he want to kill you?"

"Now, you listen," Bedrosian says, sinking into a crouch next to the chair. He covers both her hands with one of his own, jostles them a little, as if to shore her up. "That man was after Lucy because she was ratting on him. You understand? She was doing the right thing, and helping me out."

"Ratting about what?"

Bedrosian shoots Lucy a glance. "The investigation is ongoing, Mrs. Hennessey. All I can say is it's about drugs. This guy is part of a much bigger organization, all right? Lucy's helping to bring them down."

"You were involved with drugs?" Eva asks Lucy in despair.

"I—I needed money. I just—it was a stupid mistake."

"She's made up for it in spades, Mrs. Hennessey. Trust me," Bedrosian insists. "But it's imperative that we keep what happened here quiet for now. We need to buy ourselves some time. It's for Lucy," he adds gravely. "It's to keep her safe."

"Please, Ma," Lucy begs.

After a moment, Eva reaches for Lucy's hand. "All right, then," she says, exhaustion in her voice. "If it's for Lucy."

EVA'S IN HER WINGBACK chair, Lucy's on the window seat, cold seeping through the glass against her back. The cats mewl, huddled together under Eva's legs, staring out wide-eyed. Lucy can see through to the kitchen, the tablecloth with its checkered pattern, the twin cherries set in merry squares. The pot whistles, then is set aside. Bedrosian moves back and forth, pouring tea. He brings it to them. He says he needs a tarp. Lucy directs him to the basement. They listen to him move about downstairs.

Joe Brynn, sent after her, now lying there upstairs. And Julian. *Theo let it happen.* It's unreal. Herself, she can buy, but Julian—maybe it was a lie. Joe Brynn just said it, to break her down.

Her scattered thoughts are swamped by grief anew. It was no lie. Julian is dead.

She'd never have guessed she'd feel so bad. It's the gift he made, at the end, of refusing to come after her. Her mouth turns down, tight effort not to cry. He couldn't have imagined what would happen. He just assumed he could say no to Theo. *You idiot.*

Lucy stares hard at the floor: golden oak, the finish worn to bare wood in places. A memory swoops in: her da so many years ago, sweating and grumbling, his undershirt stained with dirt and sweat from the labor of sanding this same floor.

Eva says, "I knew something was wrong. A mother knows. But there was nothing I could do. You never tell anyone what's going on."

"I didn't want you to be upset, Ma."

"Well," Eva tries for a shaky laugh.

Lucy draws her knees closer to her chest, hugging them. She's so angry she could pick up that fireplace poker and ram it right through Bedrosian's head. This is his fault. He did this.

"Why couldn't you tell me you were in so much trouble?" Eva asks, despairing.

She looks so frail and old, Lucy feels a lurch of fear. "You don't have to worry, Ma," she says. "I swear, it's all over."

Bedrosian emerges from the basement, carrying a badly folded blue tarp that obscures his upper body and head. He rounds the door, kicks it shut, heads up the stairs.

"Are you O.K. alone for a minute?" Lucy asks.

Eva nods, picking up one of the cats and placing it on her lap. It arches, hisses at Lucy. She touches Eva's shoulder, then goes up the stairs after Bedrosian.

He's on the floor, rolling Joe Brynn up. The plastic crackles harshly in the quiet. Thuds and thumps.

"How the fuck did this happen?" Lucy hisses. "This is your fault, you know that?"

He pauses, speaks around his shoulder. "This is not my fault."

"In what universe?"

He gets back to his work. "No tags for the higher-ups, as you know, so the rest of the list you gave me, those were the only leads. But every one of them was up in thin air, or turning up dead, and Aaron said they were throwing in the towel. In their view, the network was broken up, Elander would take his business elsewhere, the story was over."

Bedrosian sits back on his knees, wiping his forehead. Lucy averts her eyes from the big blue package. He can't carry Joe Brynn alone. Which means she'll have to help. An image comes of the two of them maneuvering down the stairs, visible from the parlor. "So what happened?"

"I didn't like how Elander was closing up shop, and what he might have in mind for you," Bedrosian says, "so I went to Bernie Poor. Sentries had already worked him over, but I figured no harm trying. I was too late. I found a hysterical girl, blabbering on about how she was behind the couch when it happened."

Alicia, Lucy guesses.

"He was finished," Bedrosian mimes a slit throat. "It was chaos. He didn't go down without a fight. Girl was behind the couch, she said, the whole time. She said it was Joe Brynn, and he made Bernie log on and say where you were, before he ended it. So I came as fast as I could. Wasn't easy with the snow. I was almost too late."

He seems to be fishing for a thank-you, but Lucy's not ready to give it. If he had just left her alone from the start. She's gagging on the dark splatter all over the wallpaper, the sweet, thick smell of all that blood. She's seen such things a thousand times, but it's different here, at home. Eva downstairs in her chair, still shaking. Lucy can't ever make up for this.

Something in what he said comes back to her.

"When you say the whole list," she says, "do you mean—Ernesto, too?"

He makes his way up to standing, the floorboards creaking under his weight. He nods.

"How?"

"I don't know. Aaron said he was in the church."

Lucy swallows, sick, her stomach twisting up with grief. Julian, and now Ernesto. His flashy smile and olive skin, the thick black hair he liked to shape with product, as he called it. *I got some new product,* he'd say. He was vain, and funny, and the only real friend she ever had in that house. It was just a few days ago she saw him. He was so nice to her, even after all this time.

He'd thought he could philosophize, as he'd called it. He'd assumed he was safe, tucked up inside Theo's inner circle. But he never was. None of them were.

You fucking bastard, Theo.

Bedrosian hoists Joe Brynn's middle off the floor a few inches, testing the weight, then sets him down. "When you're ready," he says.

The splatter on the wall is thick. It has brain in it. Wallpaper can't be cleaned. It'll have to be replaced, and it's such a job, removing the old, patching the plaster. It'll cost, unless she does it. But she can't live here. Eva won't want her here anymore.

"Lucy, pull yourself together."

The disturbance in her belly curdles upwards, and she claps a hand to her mouth, careens into the bathroom splurting droplets on the carpet, the lino floor. Then heaves a gush of liquid into the toilet. The tea she just had.

"Jesus," Bedrosian mutters behind her.

She gulps and spits, dragging toilet paper over her streaming nose and mouth, aware of Bedrosian's hulking shape filling the doorway, watching.

"All done? Clean up," he says.

Her face in the mirror is hideous, her neck purpling, one side of her face puffed up and red from when Joe slapped her. Her mouth fills up with a rush of spit. She buckles, spews another stream of acid into the sink.

Bedrosian leans over, twists the faucet on hard. She washes her face and rinses her mouth, elbows propped on the sink to hold herself up, she's so shaky. Their eyes meet in the mirror. "I wish I'd just said no," she says, her voice a dried-up crackle. "I wish I'd let them kill me. Then none of this would ever have happened."

"No use looking back. You're doing the right thing now."

"The right thing," she repeats. "You keep saying that."

"Lucy, we have to move," he says, taking her arm. "It's getting light soon."

She disengages stiffly from his grip. "Like what I did was so wrong. Like it was this terrible crime, and I have to make up for it."

"What are you getting at?"

"It's not black and white the way you think! You just don't understand. You have no idea."

"I think I have an idea."

Lucy suddenly pushes him hard, with both hands. He falls back a step, surprised. "No, you don't!" she snaps. "They can't hack it! They—they scream, they make noises. It happened the other night! The Nafikh can't stand it, and no one could do a fucking thing!"

"Lucy, settle down—"

"Just quit telling me how he was just a kid and didn't deserve it, like he'd have had some great life instead! That's not what they get. That's not what they ever get!"

She steps abruptly backwards, rigid, hands in fists. A few feet of empty space between them. They stand there in the close, damp space, eyeing each other.

Bedrosian says, "O.K. I hear you."

"I don't care if you hear me. You'll never understand."

"That is correct."

His capitulation disarms her. She slackens, leans against the sink.

"Shall we?" He indicates the hallway.

She takes a few breaths. Then she nods.

HE SEIZES JOE BRYNN under the arms, and Lucy gets the legs over her shoulder. They inch their way down the stairs. The front door slams. They freeze. Boots tromp the hallway. Sean appears, dragging his baseball cap off his head. Eva must have called him while they were upstairs. He's in his uniform; he tows cars for extra cash. Lucy imagines him barreling down Route 3, freaking out.

He looks up, finds them on the stairs. He gapes, shaking his head, as in, *What the fuck?*

"Wait with Ma," Lucy says.

"Are you kidding me?" he retorts, but his voice is high and thin, no real fight in it.

"Go on," Bedrosian says. "We got this."

BEDROSIAN UNLOCKS THE TRUNK of his car. He shoves aside stuff: a toolbox, a pair of boots, a pile of *National Geographics* tied with twine. They lower Joe Brynn into the space, and Bedrosian slams the lid. The plows heaped snow at the end of the driveway when they went by. He'll have to dig out to leave. The houses on the street are still dark. It will be dawn in less than an hour.

"You have a real problem on your hands," he tells her.

"Which one?" she says.

He smiles a little. She looks back at the house. Kicks at the snow, arms folded. "I'll think of something. What will happen now?"

He rubs his jaw in that gesture that is all too familiar. He's badly in need of a shave, and his eyes are ringed with dark, making them look bigger and sadder than ever. He's leaving in a minute, and she doesn't want him to go. She doesn't want to walk back inside, face them on her own.

"The question is," he says, "why's Elander doing all this. He's got ample means to just take off, disappear."

Lucy's been wondering that herself. "He's a neat-freak. It could just be that."

"A lot of risk," Bedrosian shakes his head. "Doesn't sit right. And he'll know soon enough this here was a fail, and then what?"

"But they'll find him," Lucy says, his questions touching her with dread. "They're sentries. It's the Gate. They have to be able to find him."

"You'd think," Bedrosian agrees.

There is a pause. Lucy doesn't want to go back in. She wants to climb into the car, go with him.

"You should get inside. Even you must be getting cold," he says, nodding at her pajamas.

She folds her arms tighter, suddenly aware of her nipples. He clears his throat, looks away, having embarrassed himself. It's a ludicrous moment, but she can't bring herself to laugh. She turns around and hurries back up the path, her boots sinking into the piled-up snow. At the door, she looks back. He hasn't gotten in the car yet. He's just standing there, phone to his ear, and he lifts a hand in farewell.

SHE PAUSES IN THE doorway to the parlor. They both look up. The silence goes on too long, and her Source starts spitting anxious hurt, tingling fire through her limbs. She says, "I'll clean upstairs."

Eva's shoulders sink. Distress seeps from her, tears in her eyes, hands clutching the cup of tea that must have gone cold by now. "Is that all you're going to say?"

Lucy takes a step into the room. "I can't tell you anything."

"Sean told me," Eva says.

Told—? Lucy looks from one to the other.

Then she understands. Eva's stern, whitened face, the sorrow in her eyes as bad as it's ever been. Sean's tight-lipped, angry stance, like he's daring her to deny it.

Jesus. He's told her I'm a prostitute. My mother thinks I'm a prostitute.

"I should go," Lucy says helplessly. "I'll clean up, Ma, O.K.? I'll do the best I can. Then I'll go. You don't have to worry. I swear."

Eva clenches the cup. She stares without seeing, her whole body stiffened at Lucy's words, lips tucked in so her mouth is a line. Then she hurls the cup, shattering it on the floor. Both

Lucy and Sean start in shock, and one of the cats snarls and darts away, belly to the floor.

"You do not get to just go!" Eva shouts. She pounds the chair arm, beating out her words. "You stay here, young lady, and you explain just how the hell you could do this to me!"

Hell, Lucy registers. She can only recall one time Eva's ever used that word, and it was when she was excoriating Uncle Seamus.

The effect is almost immediate: Lucy topples forward, makes her way to the chair on the other side of the round table with the doily. She leans into the lamp light. "Ma," she says. "Ma, I just can't—I swear, I didn't mean for any of this."

"Well, I hardly think you did!" Eva snaps. Then her anger suddenly deflates, turns to disappointment and sorrow. "Why, baby? Why? How could you?"

Lucy bends her head. There is a silence. The story of what she is, all she's done for so many years, is a wild jumble about to burst from her, because she can't bear what they're thinking, she can't. But she can't give them the truth. Eva's known Phyllis for forty years. Sean's leaning up against a bar every night. They will talk. They won't be able to help it.

But this? They'll never breathe a word. The shame of it.

"I needed the money," she whispers, head bent in humiliation. "I am so sorry, Ma. But I was trying to make things right."

"Lucy," Bedrosian says from the doorway. They all turn to him. He holds up his phone. "You need to get dressed."

"WHAT'S HAPPENING?" SHE WHISPERS in the hallway.

He pulls her a little farther along, out of sight of the parlor. He keeps hold of her arm as he speaks. "Don't go into a panic. Aaron said you're wanted at the Gate. They were sending a pair to pick you up, in fact. I said there are civilians here, I'll bring you in myself."

Lucy's knees are melting to nothing. He keeps her standing, looking in her eyes, nodding with grim encouragement. "I bought you out, Lucy. Don't you forget that."

"You don't come back from the Gate," she says. She muffles a sob with her hand. *This isn't real.* "Is it Theo? Why do they want me? I told you everything," her words tumble over one another. "You have to call him back, explain I'm useless. I've got nothing."

He just grips her arm tighter, conveying in his stare that no, she has to obey, there's nothing to be done about it, and she must pull herself together.

She nods, wiping her nose. Then, she calls out, "Sean."

He appears in the doorway, steps forward, full of worry.

"Come up with me," she says. "We need to talk."

"Not a good idea," Bedrosian warns.

"Not your business," Lucy retorts.

SEAN SITS ON THE edge of her bed as she changes into jeans and a tee shirt. She doesn't ask him to leave, or to look away. In her mind, she sees herself in his eyes, thin, white, bony. "Listen," she says, "you need to stay with Ma. I'm going to have to go."

"What the *fuck*," he says, hard and low. "Why?"

"I can't tell you. It's part of the investigation."

"That guy tonight, was he the one that hurt you?" Sean demands.

"No," Lucy says.

He looks defeated, his theory blown. He bends over his knees, fingers gripping the back of his head, cursing to himself. Then his long arm sweeps out, his fingers gather something up off the floor. He holds out his hand. It is Joe Brynn's knife.

"What's this?" he demands.

"That was his weapon."

"Jesus," he mutters, and looks about, then sets it on the bed. "So who the hell was he? Oh, wait," he says bitterly, "let me guess, you can't tell me."

The Source spits hurt, and her hand moves reflexively to her chest. She can't bear how he sees her, especially after the talk they had earlier in the night. Sean: her cousin in the dim dawn light filtering through the curtains, all tall and gangly and grown up. In a blink of an eye, they might be kneeling together under the bedspread tent.

"Remember the spaceship we wanted to build?" she says.

He goes still, then he nods.

"It's just that—I—"

There's a gentle rap on the door. Bedrosian leans in, giving Lucy a warning look. "We should get a move on."

"You get out of here," Sean warns.

He's ready to leap across the room, pummel Bedrosian to a pulp, if she just says the word. Family sticks together, he always growls, like it's some fundamental cosmic law.

She says gently, "Sean, he's right. I have to go."

"Jesus, Lucy." He's up and across the room in two strides. He wraps her tight to him. "No way," he says. "No way you have to go."

She presses into him, breathing in the smells of engine oil and cigarettes. She pushes her face into his chest. "You'll need to change the wallpaper," she says.

"The hell with the wallpaper."

"And make sure you stay on top of the cleaners. I have an account. I'll get the money out on the way. Detective Bedrosian can bring it. And he's supposed to take care of Ma's loan, too. He said he would."

"You're talking like you're not coming back!"

"She *is* coming back," Bedrosian interrupts from the doorway. "But right now, we have to go. Now, Lucy."

She shifts against Sean's tight embrace, and his arms loosen, fall to his sides. She gives him a tight little smile, trying to convey a promise she doesn't herself believe. He follows them down, his treads heavy on the wooden stairs. In the parlor, Lucy bends to hug Eva in her chair, holding her as close as possible without hurting her.

"I love you, Ma," she whispers.

It's not something Lucy's said in years. It causes a depth of sorrow in Eva's eyes that Lucy wishes she could draw out and destroy.

"You come back home when you're done, you hear?" Eva says.

"Sure, Ma. As soon as I can."

Lucy stands back up. Sean kisses her forehead, hard, gripping her shoulder. Bedrosian turns to follow her when she passes. Maybe she will come back, like she told Eva. *I got bought out,* she insists to herself, but the concept is already drifting out of her reach, unreal, a dream. Through her daze she sees the kitchen, the tidy sink and folded towel draped over the side. The piled-up secretary desk, the Amazon card, the laptop. She meant to get Eva a new one, as a surprise. She ought to feel sad, but weirdly, she doesn't feel anything. It's as if she's been transformed into a void, floating along in silence through the familiar spaces, her home.

But it's not her home, not anymore. That's why she's so numb. Her life here was never meant to be, after all.

Ain't no serv ever had a home, she thinks, and closes the door behind her.

IT'S A LITTLE AFTER six a.m. when Bedrosian suggests they pull off 93 for a pause before continuing on to the Gate, and Lucy doesn't argue. The turn signal ticks loudly in the silence as he eases the car down the ramp towards the gas station. He drives with his wrist on the wheel, without hurry. He pulls into a parking spot. It's still dark, and they're the only ones there. She pulls down the passenger visor to inspect her face: a blotched mess, her cheek dark and puffy.

"I can't go inside like this."

He indicates the shrubbery and trees with his chin.

She creeps past the picnic bench, finds a spot behind a bush. The pee generates hot steam all around. She almost falls-face first into the dirt patched with snow and cigarette butts. The engine shuts off, and Bedrosian makes his way to the small, brightly lit shop with its buzzing neon signs. He disappears inside. She pulls her jeans back on. At the picnic table, she sits down, digs through her parka for her cigarettes. Just put them in the same pocket every time, Julian would say, impatient with her frantic searches. She stares at the sky, seeing Joe Brynn's whitened face and the slump of his dead body. There is a weird opacity to it all, a dream that was fierce in the night, now fading away. But it happened: the feel of it whips back up, again and again, a shock every time.

That she's on her way to the Gate is not something she is able to dwell on: it races at her, glances off the dull closed surface of her brain.

She waits for him, smoking, taking in the shabby picnic table carved up by lovers, the sickly trees, the detritus of countless others who paused here, their moment of rest so infinitesimally unimportant they will never recall it again. Not for the first time in her life, Lucy wishes she were one of them. She wishes she were resting on some mundane trip, about to carry on towards the next thing, and the next, on and on. Another car pulls in, the headlights blinding her for a moment. The car is yellow, smart and compact. A lady in a fur coat tumbles out. She laughs, waving off whatever her boyfriend's saying. They sway into the shop, their staccato merriment pricking the still night air. Bedrosian exits on the same door swing, tromps towards her carrying two cups.

"Here," he says gruffly. "Well, do you want it or not?"

She puts her hands around the cup, warming them. He's put milk in when she always takes it black. She drinks. Her throat hurts when she swallows.

"Better?"

She nods. She takes a deep drag off her cigarette, exhales a plume of smoke. Her breath, after, clouds before her, visible in the light cast from the shop.

He says, "You want to know how I ended up banging around in your world?"

She shrugs assent, watching him through the steam rising from her cup.

"I'd just become a cop," he says, "and we had this family friend, he was like an uncle to me. A Russian Jew, Amo Iakov, married to an Armenian. That's one hell of a combo."

He pauses to chuckle. It beats her, why. She says, "O.K. Go on."

"So one day we're drinking and Amo Iakov, that means uncle, he says I think I'm a big know-it-all, now that I'm police.

It's true I was a little puffed up in those days. Why shouldn't I be? It was a big deal. But he was a hard old man, he didn't brook any sort of pride, so he says let me show you the truth of the world. That's what he called it, the truth of the world. He wasn't someone you argued with, so I went. We end up in the basement of a house somewhere in Dorchester. There's a guy there, tied up with duct tape. I start freaking out. Amo, you can't do this, what the hell are you doing, who is this guy? And he leans into my face with all that crazy gray hair on end and those googly eyes, and he says, He is not human!"

"Great," Lucy says drily.

"Yeah. So I argue, and protest, and even try to untie the victim, but Amo kicks me out of the way. He says, watch this, and before I could say a word, he's pulled out a knife and hauled off and stabbed the poor guy in the heart. It was instantaneous. I'd never had such a shock. I thought I was in some nightmare, for sure, and now I'd wake up.

"And then," Bedrosian dances his fingers above his chest, fluttering them skyward. "That was when I found out about servs."

"Lemme guess. He thought we were demons."

"No. He thought you were an alien invasion. He was picking servs up whenever he could, with the help of three of his cronies, interrogating them, and then executing them."

"Interrogating," Lucy repeats slowly.

"I know. It wasn't pretty. It's how they'd learned about Nafikh, the Gate, all of it. But it was distorted through this lens of an alien threat. In his mind, the servs were all lying, see. They weren't slaves, they were foot soldiers. The Nafikh weren't just visiting, but here for reconnaissance. They were setting up funds, making alliances with human traitors, that kind of thing. The Qadir were Their generals."

"You believed all this crap?"

"It's about as crazy as the actual truth," he snorts. "But yeah. I believed it, for a while."

She eyes him. "Does that mean you helped?"

He drinks, then bares his teeth in pain, the coffee still too hot. "I thought I was doing the right thing."

"By torturing helpless servs?"

"We've all got our share of regrets," he replies.

It takes a moment for her to gather his meaning. "You can't compare. Don't even try."

"I suppose so," he concedes. There is a pause. "Anyway, eventually, you come to a tipping point. The voice in my heart finally got louder than the arguments in my head. I knew it was wrong, what Amo Iakov was doing. All I saw were scared, broken wrecks, one after the other. So I set out to change his mind. This is my Amo Iakov, for Chrissake, we play tric-trac on Friday nights with a bottle of vodka. But then, he took down a kid. Couldn't have been more than twelve or thirteen. I didn't know about it till after it was over. That one, I think it shook him up. Because after all, you are made perfect."

He tests his coffee, then takes a few bigger swallows, wipes his mouth.

"And that was it, for me. It was like a door opened, I stepped through, and it closed behind me. I kept walking and I found a sentry. I explained to her what had been going on and that it needed to be stopped."

"You're kidding."

"Next thing I know, I'm in a basement myself, and a couple of them worked me over like you would not believe. I gave them every piece of information I had stored in my brain. Anything they asked, I replied, just so they'd stop. But I deserved it," he nods, "I know I did."

"Is that why you limp?"

"It is."

"And then what happened?"

"Amo Iakov disappeared, along with his friends. Their bodies were found a few months later up in Revere. They'd been tortured, then shot in the head, execution-style."

So he did understand how she felt, turning on everyone. Though by the clenched-up way he spoke those words, he's a good deal more burdened. As well he should be. She's having a hard time wrapping her mind around him taking part in those sick acts. *How many,* she wants to ask. *How.*

But she doesn't want to know.

She says, "How come the Gate forgave you?"

He huffs at this. "They didn't. They use me to investigate serv business on the low. The day my usefulness expires, I will get my due."

"You really think that?"

"Lucy," he chides, amused, "are you really asking?"

She holds herself a little tighter, bending over her arms. Her breaths puff white. "So you're like us, basically."

"If by that you mean I, too, live under the Gate's boot, then yes."

"You hate them."

"There's no point. Like hating a machine."

She hasn't thought of it that way before. It rings true. The Gate just performs its function, day in, day out. It doesn't let anything stand in the way of that function, which is to keep the Nafikh happy and in line on every visit.

No wonder they don't give a shit about a dead serv here, another one there.

Bedrosian pours out the remainder of his coffee, splattering brown across the slush. He crushes the cup, tosses it at the bin, misses. "We'd better get a move on," he says, and tromps over to the car. Once he's started the engine, he drops his head back against the headrest, eyes closed. Slowly, Lucy climbs down off the table, stiff and cold. She collects his cup and drops it in the bin with her own, turns around. Without warning her chest is a searing nugget of pain, whirling faster, hotter, before exploding.

A van roars to a stop next to his car.

"Watch out!" she screams.

She sees his face turn towards her, open with surprise. The van door slides open and two sentries jump out. One of them is Gabriel. The relief she always feels when she sees him transforms instantly to fear when she reads the disgust on his face.

"I couldn't believe it," he says, striding over to her. The other sentry, it's Sina from the Rambo Service, is crooking her finger at Bedrosian, indicating he should get in the van. Lucy hears him asking why. "But no, it's really you. You have broken my heart, you little treacherous bitch."

Before Lucy can utter a sound he's on her, lifting her up by the neck. She gags, all the pain from earlier flooding up.

Then finds herself slammed onto her feet, pinned in place by his grip. Her teeth feel like they might crack to pieces, he's crushing her jaw with such force. When he speaks, spit flies onto her face.

"You will be executed for this!"

"For what?" she ekes out through her clenched jaw. "What did I do?"

"Where is he?"

"Who?" she begs. Her eyes drag this way and that, seeking Bedrosian. She can't see him. He was in the car, and now he's gone.

"Where is Theo Elander?" Gabriel thunders.

"I don't know!" she sobs. "I don't understand—can't you find him?"

His dark eyes bore into her, peeling her apart. "He has taken a Nafikh, do you hear me? He has a Nafikh!"

Everything goes dead still. She can feel her heartbeats, each one a lucid thud. The pain of the Source is obliterated by the high hum in her head.

"Where. Did. He. Take. Her." With each word, Gabriel jolts her, hard.

She crumples, black washing over her, a cold sweeping wave. She almost faints, but he keeps her upright. She stumbles along, propelled by his grip, and then he picks her up and flings her inside the van onto the hard metal floor, leaps in after her. The door slams shut and the van careens backwards.

She clutches at the wall, trying to pull herself up, unable to make out his dark features in the dim light. "Gabriel, I don't know anything! I swear! Are you sure it's even Theo?"

He looms over her, legs planted in a wide stance against the van's motion. "Ernesto Vaja was in on it, so yeah, it's your Theo. Did he ever say anything to you?"

She shakes her head. "But Theo took Ernesto out," she says, miserable under his increasingly visible glower. "Gabriel, I swear, I don't know what you're talking about."

"Well, then, you'd better start thinking, Lucy Hennessey. You'll have to do better than that for the Qadir."

He backs off, lowers into a crouch, phone to his ear. Her body slackens against the wall, and she curls up against it, her bones rattling with every bump and turn. It's not Sina driving. She must have gone with Bedrosian in his car. But no. He is here. Maybe she didn't want to see, at first. He's in the far corner, unconscious, his face a bloody mess. His huge body lolls this way and that with the movement of the van. Lucy stares, trying to make out if he's breathing. She concludes that he is, but her worry's going strangely abstract, meaningless. They're going to the Gate, and this fact slices all else away.

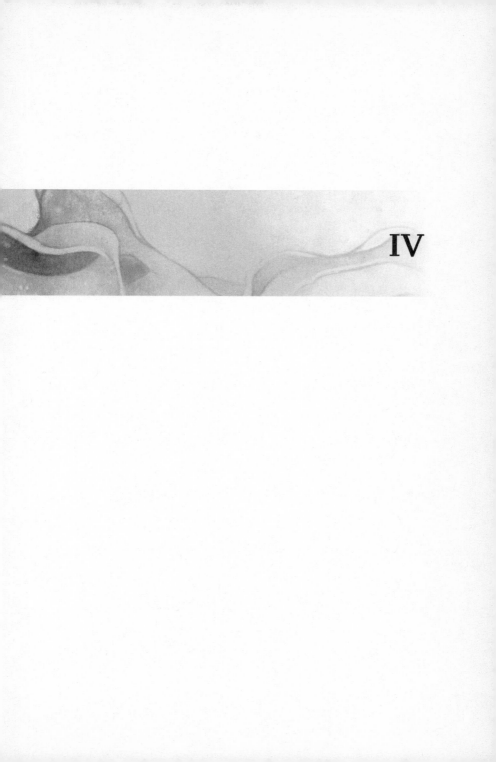

IV

"GET OUT," GABRIEL SAYS.

Lucy levers herself up off the van floor. She's weak, sore all over. She hears Bedrosian groaning as Gabriel rouses him. She steps out onto gravel and snow, squinting in the harsh sunlight, trying to get her bearings. They're parked at a loading ramp, behind a massive brick warehouse. The river's nearby. There are weedy asphalt lots to either side, empty and windswept with snowdrifts. The main road's a distance away. There's no one about.

She takes a few steps, rounds the back of the van. A biting wind whips her hair around her face. Beyond the corner of the warehouse, a walkway leads to a long, low white building, windows in rows. She numbly takes in the covered portico, dead plants in clay pots at either column, the smattering of cars parked across the way. The name *JetSet Limo Rentals* is stenciled on a window.

She turns around to see Bedrosian clambering out of the van. By the looks of it, Sina cracked a few of his ribs; he's sweating, pale, and wheezing. He wasn't kidding about not being forgiven. Gabriel leads them up the stairs to the loading dock. Bedrosian huffs behind her, helping himself along with the railing. "Lucy," he whispers. "I bought you out. Don't you forget that."

"I know," she says over her shoulder. He seems to need to hang onto that fact, and who is she to pop his bubble. She wonders if he'll get his money back, or if he's not getting out of here either. The overhead door rolls up with an awful metallic racket, and two sentries who look pissed as hell come outside. Gabriel asks, "Where are they?"

"First's in observation, Second's with the Nafikh that just came a while back."

Gabriel pushes Lucy towards the interior. "Not you," she hears one of the sentries say. She looks back, finds Bedrosian standing awkwardly between them, his form a dark outline against the blue sky. The door's clattering back down, and Lucy stops, anxious at Bedrosian being left with those two. Gabriel takes her by the elbow. "He's not your concern. That way, hurry."

The ceilings rise up in a daze of gloom and dust. The dirty windows allow in some light, the rest provided by buzzing fluorescents. They go up a worn wooden ramp leading to a freight elevator. Gabriel hammers the elevator button with impatience. Another ramp leads down to the main floor, where rows of shelves are laden with shipping crates. There are guys in overalls standing around, making notes on clipboards.

"What is all this?" Lucy asks.

"Imports from South America."

His flat tone forbids further questions. It's bewildering that the Gate would need to pull income from real-people business. Nafikh visits are funded by serv enterprises—drug trafficking, grabs, running whores, and all the rest of it. But imports? Limo rentals? It leaves her unsettled; the whole place does, with its dilapidated fixtures and paint peeling off the walls. A few hundred years ago it was probably bustling with workers. Now, the few guys in sight are servs with no paycheck or family and no interest in the goods under their care.

Gabriel has to nudge her into the elevator because she's going wobbly with fear again. Inside, she comes face-to-face with herself in the brushed metal wall: skinny body, stringy hair, scared face. She pulls her fingers through her hair, then realizes the Qadir probably won't be influenced by how she looks. She lowers her hand.

"How much will it hurt?" she asks.

"It's about as bad as coming up on a Nafikh," he says. "They might let you get dosed."

"Can't you tell them I don't know anything?"

The quaver in her voice shames her, but she can't help it. Gabriel looks away. She wonders where Bedrosian was taken, tries to put him out of her mind. He's been through it before. He'll make it out. She should be more worried for herself.

The elevator lurches to a stop and the door slides open.

They step out into a narrow corridor running the length of the building, doorways set at intervals. The walls are unfinished particle board, the doors plain wood. It has the air of a construction site, but some doors are open and Lucy glimpses plain metal beds and tables, some stuff hanging on the walls, images torn from magazines, a few books. Window cutouts reveal only empty space, some interior part of the warehouse. The rooms must be sentry quarters, is all Lucy can figure. There are what look like offices, too: old desks, wooden chairs, lamps without shades.

"I thought you all had it better than this," she says.

He gives her a dry look over his shoulder. "Yeah, champagne with dinner and a few cigars after."

"You know what I mean."

"Every spare penny goes for the visits," he shrugs.

She's unable to ask more questions because her chest suddenly spasms. She steels herself against the steadily increasing pain. They've traveled halfway around the building, she calculates, and by the time they've gone ten more steps, she's hunched over, her hands in fists. Gabriel ignores her struggle, for which she's grateful, because it's bad enough without having to endure his pity. She'd like to just sink down to her knees and buckle over, pass out from the fireworks lighting up her chest, her limbs on fire, every muscle tautened against the burn.

"Ready?" Gabriel asks, his hand on a door they've reached without her noticing. "You should know this Qadir's on the fritz, O.K.? He's already pissed. Don't fuck around with him."

Like I'd ever. She nods, unable to speak. It's news to her that Qadir can fritz.

He goes in first, so all she sees for a moment is the broad block of his back. She hears the distant crackle of his walkie. She's sucking air hard now, and it's noisy, but she can't help it. He steps aside.

The room is a little more finished than the rest, with white walls and a fringed carpet. At a table over to the left, a serv sits with a laptop. He glances up, leaving a brief impression of dark eyes magnified behind lenses. A window, this one finished with glass and a frame, gives onto the same dim, empty space as the others. Lucy glimpses scaffolding across the way, staircases, rows of windows.

"*Esh hun talar Elander?*"

"*Aji,*" Gabriel says, and he turns Lucy by the shoulder, pointing her in the right direction.

A figure moves towards them from the other side of the room, where she glimpses a couch and a coffee table, another smaller carpet. He's got a cane; it raps the floor loudly with every step. She blinks, her vision blurring from tears, because she's petrified now, she can't help it, she can't hold it together. The Qadir is gigantic, like the Nafikh are when They first visit Earth, Their bodies unnaturally oversized. But the Qadir doesn't have the animal, precise grace of the Nafikh. He's awkward and slow, shuffling with all his weight on the cane. It must be because he's fritzing. She doesn't want to look up from those massive black shuffling shoes and the ebony shine of the cane, but she can't help herself. The sight of him causes her to cringe, backing into Gabriel, who stands there like a wall, preventing escape. The Qadir is monstrous, his face scarred with taut red patches, as if he was dunked in boiling water. His mouth drags down to one side in a leering smile. Wisps of white hair are combed across his skull. He's dressed in fancy clothes, the sort the Nafikh prefer, a burgundy satin shirt and dark, glittery pants, and they hang on his bony, trembling frame.

But for all the signs that he's on the way out, his eyes are the same bright, horrible pools sucking at her, a whirling abyss from which she has to retreat, she has to run. But her movements are like the frivolous battings of an insect against Gabriel's solid bulk.

"Hold still," Gabriel says, annoyed.

She obeys instantly, clutching his arm.

The Qadir comes closer. His clothes release the odors of sweat and rotten food and dampness. She can't imagine why he smells this way. Someone should tell him. But he's a Qadir, maybe that's how they smell. Or maybe it's because he's fritzing. She's never witnessed a fritz. All the dying she's seen, it's been in Service.

She crumples, the world going black from the pain. Gabriel hauls her up, shakes her.

"Does it hurt, to be near me?" the Qadir inquires. His deep voice has a gurgle, like he's got something stuck in his throat.

"Yes," she whispers, her chest a roiling pot, the boil spilling into her arms, to her fingertips.

He tilts his head back to look down his cheekbone at her. "Do you want relief?"

"Yes," Lucy begs.

"You do not deserve it."

Lucy sways and teeters, unable to think of a response.

"Where is Theo Elander?"

Gabriel hoists her up again, as she is almost on her knees. She shakes her head. "I swear," she whispers. "I don't know."

There is an instant of shear mind-melting agony, and then Lucy discovers herself on her back, the Qadir looming over her.

She squeezes shut her eyes, curls up, anticipating another blow. "I swear," she tries to say, but her voice is no more than a whisper.

"There's a place in Maine," a voice intrudes. Lucy's shuddering so hard she can hardly hear. "It's in the information she provided, but there's no address. Ask her the address."

Lucy's mouth opens and closes. She hears Gabriel speaking in Nafikh, then the Qadir responds. She senses the heat of someone closing in, and she curls up tighter, locking herself up like a clam. But it's Gabriel, not the Qadir. He lifts her arm, and she feels the cool slide of the needle into her skin. She could weep. She gasps, staring hard at the floor, waiting for the relief. It comes so slowly, a tanker edging over the horizon, the bright expanse an endless crossing, it will never happen, she'll die right here, it wasn't enough.

But then, at last, the pain begins to recede, the waves slipping forward, then back, retreating farther with every breath. Exhaustion sets in. Her body is a limp, ruined blob. Gabriel reaches under her, pulls her to her feet. "Get it together," he commands. The Qadir watches, leaning hard on his cane, leaking his odors of disuse and age and sickness. He brims with anger not just directed at her, Lucy now intuits, but at his own weakness. "What is the address?" he demands.

Oh God, she thinks. *Here we go again.* She's so exhausted, the relief from the pain is so immense, she could just pass out. But she needs to answer, even if she doesn't know, so the Qadir won't strike her again.

It doesn't matter. The truth returns with fresh surprise, like something she'd forgotten. She's not getting out, either way.

Ain't no serv ever comes back from the Gate.

"I have no idea," she says, every word an effort, her longing to collapse so overpowering she can hardly see. "They never took me. I don't know if Theo ever even finished building it."

There's a sound, and Lucy turns to see the serv getting up and rounding the table. Lucy finds herself ashamed of her pathetic state, confronted by this short, brisk guy who moves so easily in the presence of the Qadir. He comes right to her, peers up at her face like he might find something. "So they never mentioned a road, a mountain, any landmark?"

She shakes her head.

"Did they say how long it took to get there?"

She struggles to find an answer. How long did it take. How long. Did. It. Take.

She drifts far back in time to the white house in Ayer with its rolling meadow and open door, Theo beckoning her closer. The tile floor in the kitchen, violets dropping purple, the scent of candles. Ernesto, his huge brown eyes wet with emotion. Alita and Soren, down for a visit, always so elegant. "It was far," she says, remembering. "Alita said once it took them all afternoon to come down to Ayer. She had a truck. It was black. She always wore black, and I thought it was funny the truck was black, too. And then I couldn't picture her there, because they called it Eden, and that word always makes me think of white."

Shit, she's rambling. She sways, liable to keel over. Gabriel steadies her at the elbow. Whatever he gave her was way more potent than the usual. She wouldn't say no to more.

The serv gestures impatiently. "Don't stop. Tell us anything you know."

"It was in a valley. Julian said that once. It was in a valley, and there was a river, and fields. It sounded boring to me, but I never said that. I never got to see it. They cut me out."

"Did he ever describe it?"

"He called it a compound. I always thought, wow, it must be really big, lots of houses, because there were supposed to be a lot of freed servs up there, eventually. Everyone was supposed to be there together."

He frowns. "Freed servs?"

"The ones he buys out. Well, whoever he thinks is worthy, anyway," Lucy adds bitterly.

The Qadir raps his cane for her attention. "You wanted to live there?"

The way he asks, she feels ashamed of the wanting. "Sort of. Not really."

"What about your duty? What about your Service?"

He can't possibly mean she's supposed to feel an obligation. But apparently he does, as he grows incensed by her obvious surprise. He lifts his gnarled hand, points to his livid face. The hideous scars blur in Lucy's vision. "The Qadir should Serve, but you go free?"

"But—what about—" Lucy struggles to piece together an argument, finally grasping her point. "But the Gate takes buyouts."

"Only because we have to. Freed servs!" he spits in disgust.

"I don't understand," Lucy says weakly. His gaze feels like it's drawing on her insides, churning them into a whirlpool.

"You are all the same, ungrateful and stupid," he accuses. "We have given you quota. You can come and go as you please when the season ends. What more do you want?"

What more—? She twists in place, staring up at Gabriel in confusion. He indicates sternly that she should return her attention to the Qadir, who is edging closer. She cringes, his rotting odor making her gag. "I was told Elander believes servs used to be Nafikh. Is this true?"

She nods.

"He kills other servs so he can live longer. And now he thinks he can live forever, with all the power of the Nafikh, by killing Dara-Lin. Am I right?"

Dara-Lin: She's the one that strangled the serv in the limo that time coming back from Swampscott. The name is Her own mangling of what the Gate called Her, perhaps its own form of sick humor: Darling.

Then what the Qadir said penetrates the woolen muffle of Lucy's thoughts. It's like bits of a puzzle falling into place at last. She always assumed Theo would combine grabs, create a megadose to restore what he called his true form. It never crossed her mind that he'd grab from a Nafikh. It's totally insane. "I guess," she whispers. "No one ever told me."

"Do *you* think you were once Nafikh?"

He leans in close, glaring at her. She glimpses yellowed teeth, receded gums. His lip trembles. She averts her eyes. "I don't know," she says. "No. I think."

The Qadir grunts, stands back. "We were never Nafikh. They do not have Sources that can be grabbed. He will kill Her for nothing. And we will pay. And pay! And pay!"

He drums out the last words with his cane, causing her to want to cover her ears.

For nothing.

They were never Nafikh. But Theo was always so certain. She wanted it to be true, she realizes now. There was always a tiny spark of longing, never completely extinguished, from that time with Theo. Maybe she was once a Nafikh. Just maybe. Instead of being just nothing. Nothing to Them, or the universe—

"Lucy," Gabriel shakes her, and she opens her eyes, startled. "You have to try and think. We're just a few hours behind them right now. Dara-Lin is probably still alive."

She wishes she could help, because she doesn't want him to think badly of her. But she's at a loss. "Maybe there's something in Ayer?"

The serv who was interrogating her says, "We're still searching. I'll keep narrowing things down on the map, but it's a needle in a haystack."

"Try," the Qadir nods. He looks like he's really ailing now, leaning so heavily on his cane. She swallows, swaying against Gabriel. She might throw up, she realizes. That wouldn't be good. She swallows again, her whole head rocking with the effort. The Qadir struck her in the stomach, that's what happened. That's why it hurts in this thudding, distant kind of way, muffled by the cocktail Gabriel gave.

The thudding: it's not from her stomach.

"What's that?" she whispers.

"More Nafikh," Gabriel mutters. "Eric, how many now?"

The serv is back at the table, shutting his laptop. He tucks it under his arm. "Of the three already out, one's in a burn and won't last. The other two are freaking, but it's contained so far. There are two in holding, still under. And whoever's coming now."

Lucy follows Gabriel to the window. They are high up, under the roof. The center of the building, she understands, has been gutted to create an empty space two stories high. The floor down below is empty but for what looks like a giant iron safe in the center. Scaffolding covers all the surrounding walls, with metal stairways and landings giving access to the quarters, Lucy surmises. Sentries are coming in now. They take up position in a wide circle around the iron structure.

"That's the Gate," Gabriel says curtly, when she lifts her eyes in question.

She's too exhausted to feel embarrassed, but really, it was dumb, to imagine the Gate would be anything more elaborate. The Nafikh can come and go as They please; every season there are one or two that blow. What They need is privacy, security, a structure that can contain the explosive violence of Their travel. Something just like this.

The other Qadir is down there, too. Lucy presses her forehead to the glass, hands to either side of her face. She is as massive as the First, but without sign of any weakness as she steps into the circle, towering over the sentries. She has long gray hair in a braid and is dressed in dark, shining clothes, leather boots. She looks up, as if aware of Lucy's gaze. Her face is chiseled, gray, a landscape of deep-etched lines, like an ancient tree. Her stare is hard as a punch, filled with anger and hatred.

"She's not happy," Gabriel states.

No shit. Lucy drags her eyes away, feeling sick again.

There is a thunderous roar, and the sentries edge closer to the Gate. Through the narrow windows at the top, Lucy glimpses blue licking flames within. The thunder is so loud that she presses her hands to her ears, her whole body humming with the reverberations. The ring of sentries tightens, rifles drawn. Sina is among them, sweat pouring down her face, hair plastered to her skull. They're all aiming in one direction, a door Lucy couldn't make out before, now outlined by the shimmering smoke seeping out the sides.

The flames explode.

One second there's a flickering dance of fire, the next there's an inferno whirling inside the iron walls. She almost misses it, it happens so fast: the door swings open with a crash, and from the depths, two figures hurtle forth.

Just as suddenly the fire is gone, leaving only the bland dark interior, the door already being shut by a sentry.

The Nafikh leap to Their feet, turning in place. They are naked, muscled like stone statues come to life, Their skin sleek with sweat. One female and one male, both with long, white hair. Lucy can't tell if she's Served Them before, Their faces are so distorted from screaming, the cries shattering the air. The cords in Their necks stand out, Their faces purpling, every muscle in Their bodies ripped.

"What's the matter with Them?" Lucy asks.

"They're always like this when They get here," Gabriel says. "We dose Them till They're stable, then They go out. Except today, They'll want to go out fast. They'll want to find Dara-Lin."

The Nafikh lope around dumbly, arms and legs loose as rags. The female succumbs first, holding Herself on hands and knees for as long as possible before collapsing. The male takes longer. The sentries fire at Him, one shot after another, with calm precision.

Within minutes, They lie crumpled in a heap, twitching.

The sentries shoulder their rifles, move towards the prone Nafikh. They bend in pairs, two at each end, to lift first the female, then the male, onto gurneys. The Second Qadir turns her stern face to the window where her counterpart stands. She mouths something, then holds up two fingers, then three, wags her hand.

"*Aante ey gosh. Khadji,*" the First steps back, leaning heavily on his cane. "*Osh bey. Osh.*"

"*Neyyel en adar,*" Gabriel says.

"What's going on?" Lucy grabs at his arm, but he shakes her off, goes over to the Qadir. He talks low and fast in Nafikh.

She turns to the serv. "You, Eric, what's happening?"

He swallows, his knuckles white, clutching the laptop to his chest like a shield. "The ones that just came, They're Hansel and Gretel. You've probably Served Them."

"Gretel, I have," Lucy nods.

"They're old-timers. They'll be out fast, and They'll push the others out with Them."

"So dose Them, keep Them here."

"Too much can kill Them. The risk is too high. Gabe, the Qadir's right. We're out of time!"

Gabriel whips around. "Shut up and get to work. Get what you can out of her."

The Qadir makes a gasping, stifled noise and sags, clutching his chest. Gabriel seizes him under the arm, helps him over to a couch at the far end of the room. The Qadir lowers himself onto the cushions, wheezing. His furious eyes rove the room. Gabriel levers up a blind above the couch, revealing one of the tall exterior windows framed in stone. Lucy blinks at the sunlight pouring in. She glimpses the silvery motion of the river, a tugboat moving slowly against the current. The Qadir sits back, staring out, hands pressed to his chest. His breaths sound ragged, hoarse.

His earlier accusation returns, about giving them quota. He's Served since arriving. Now he'll fritz, and all he's ever had of this world is what he sees out windows. Come and go after the season, he said. How could he go anywhere? Look at him. He's like a creature out of a fairy tale. He suddenly goes rigid, knees drawn up. A shudder racks his frame, and he hisses against the pain.

"Why can't he be dosed?" she whispers to Eric.

He gives his head a small warning shake, as if she's made a faux pas. "It just isn't done."

"Get a move on," Gabriel drives them out, closing the door behind him. "Work fast," he warns Eric, and lopes off down the corridor.

Eric sets off in the opposite direction. Lucy half runs behind him along some corridors, down a set of stairs, into yet another corridor. She can't get the Qadir out of her head. That he could seem so pitiful is too much to fathom. Her whole body feels soggy and weak from the dose, and it's difficult to think clearly. The Source barely tweaks at all, now. It feels like a bruise, if that. It must be what Eric's on, and all the rest of them, to be able to endure being with the Qadir.

Eric holds a door open for her and she steps through. They're on the Gate level: the iron safe looms in the middle of the room, the silence huge after all that just happened. She looks up, turning in place, until she finds the window where they were just standing, opposite from where they are now. They aren't alone, she notices; sentries are posted here and there beneath the scaffolding, the crackle of their walkies alerting her to their presence.

"This way," Eric says.

He guides her through a nearby doorway into a long room humming with computers, metal desks stationed at intervals. There's a rustling sound, murmurs from the servs peeking around their screens to see who's arrived. Lucy feels like a zoo specimen. "What is this place?"

"We keep in touch with the overseers from here, and the bosses, and so on. We also maintain contact with all the other Gates around the world. It's 24/7 in season." Eric talks over his shoulder, leading her to the far end of the room, where a more imposing desk with three screens is located perpendicular to the rest. He's got his own window cutout, no glass, giving onto the Gate. Lucy thinks, *Window office,* and almost laughs. A sentry across the way meets her eyes, causing her to flinch. She can just hear what he's thinking, that she's the serv who worked with Elander. The one who fucked them all up.

Eric's already hunched over his keyboard, eyes darting from one screen to the next. She says, "Can I ask something? Is that where servs arrive, too?"

"It is."

Lucy blinks at the image of herself, minuscule infant, wailing and thrashing in the midst of the whirling fire. "How do They make us?"

"We don't know. They do it in Their world, then send us over."

"So—we're there for a little bit, before we come here?"

"I guess. We're not really finished till we get here. There's a whole phase of cooling down, compression. But you know about that," he says, with a sideways glance.

"I guess I do," she says flatly.

She sits down on the empty chair next to him. He's perusing columns of numbers, and there's another screen with some kind of satellite feed. It's all gibberish to her. *Ice. Endless. Darkness.* How many times she recorded these memories for Theo. They could mean anything. They could describe the Nafikh world itself. Or, the place where servs are created, a frozen womb from which they are pushed out into this world. There are servs being made right now, most likely. Clueless, staring dumbly into the dark.

She becomes aware of the others in the room, watching. She feels awkward about her bedraggled, bruised appearance compared to these tidy servs in their clean clothes. They seem soft and weak. Like they've never done anything but sit at these desks, clicking away and gossiping.

"Does anyone here ever Serve?" she asks.

Eric shoots her a glance. "It's not like what we do is a cake-walk."

I'd beg to differ. "How did they educate you?" she asks, trying to keep her tone more neutral. She juts her chin at all the fancy screens on the desk. "Did you go to M.I.T. or something?"

"We don't get to go to school," he says. He gives his glasses a push up her nose, and his magnified, dark eyes fix on Lucy. "The Gate keeps a percentage of arrivals. If they're lucky, they get training for jobs like this. Otherwise, they stay on the sets."

"The sets?"

"The Nafikh have to be taught Their manners," Eric says. "Even old-timers need refreshers. The whole west side is just stage sets where They practice real situations. We've all put in our time."

The remark's meant to shame her, which gets under Lucy's skin that much more. She's in a roomful of servs who, by the luck of the draw, work on computers all day. She's hard-pressed to care that they put in their time. "Where do you all live? Those rooms up there?"

"Some do."

"And the rest?"

"There are apartments in Chelsea."

He says it boldly, in her face. Daring her to object.

Fuck him and his cushy job and apartment. She turns her attention to the jumble of information on the screens. If Eric thinks she's supposed to understand all this, he's dumber than he looks. She folds her arms and sits back. "I don't get how you think I can help."

"Look at the map, is all I want you to do," he says, pointing with a pen. "It's a topographical map of Maine. We know wherever he's built his Eden, it has to be out of the way, and probably protected with security apparatus which, if anyone looked closely, would seem irrational. I've already set up possible areas, marked with those red circles, and I'll keep adding to them. There's got to be a pretty deep underground component, so that other Nafikh and servs can't detect

Her presence. That limits where it might be built, so, uh, not where the land is rock, for example, or with a high water table."

"But what am I looking for?"

"Anything. The name of a town. A mountain he might have mentioned. A cavern, a river. Just keep looking. Maybe something will jog your memory."

"This is nuts. That's your plan?"

"That's all *you* can do," he says irritably. "Everyone in here is working on this. You can't engage in that kind of construction without leaving a trace. We're assuming the house was already being built when you met Elander. We're scouring fifteen years' worth of town records, permits, newspapers, electrical usage, sewerage notices, security firms, looking for anything that might hint at construction that includes rock blasting, for example."

"He complained about the contractors," Lucy suddenly recalls. "Maybe there are old receipts or something."

"We're done searching the Ayer house. There was nothing. They sent in footage. You can see if anything jogs your memory there, too."

He toggles through screens, and stops on a video, clicks play. Lucy starts with recognition: the wide hallway, sunlight pouring across the pine floors and kilim runner. The camera moves through the living room with its scattered couches and imposing mantelpiece, panning over the draperies, paintings, bookshelves. The scene calls up sitting cross-legged on the floor, smoking joints and laughing. The flicker of candles, the silver tray of amaretto being passed around, the haze of smoke.

"I can't believe a serv has enough money for a house," Eric says, and Lucy's surprised at the envy in his voice. Although, judging by the shabbiness of the quarters here, his apartment's probably a hole in the wall. She wonders what he'd make of the fact that she's got a house of her own, too.

Or did, before she walked into the Gate.

"Can you answer something straight up?" she asks.

"What?"

"Are they going to kill me?"

He has the grace to go a little red. "It's a big crime, what's happening."

"But I wasn't involved."

"It won't matter to the Qadir. You helped with all those grabs. A few here and there, they don't care, but something so systemic, with the purpose of defying the Gate," he shakes his head. "They'll probably put you on the sets."

He can't meet her eyes, and she's going cold and blank with the knowing sinking in that it's really true. A few bleeps draws his attention, and he swings his chair, giving her his shoulder as he taps rapidly at his keyboard. She hears him muttering.

"So why should I try and help, then?" she demands, irritated by his disregard. "What's the point?"

He stiffens. Then he turns, rolling back a little to give her a view of his laptop. "I guess because of this," he says.

There are multiple windows open. Reuters, AP, various online newspapers, all showing live feeds of an office building engulfed in flame. It's one of those tall mirrored ones near the harbor; it could be the one she was working in the other day. Jagged footage loops over and over of a bloodied figure stumbling down a sidewalk against a backdrop of billowing smoke.

She leans forward, shocked. "Is that going on now? What happened?"

"They're calling it a terrorist attack, but it was two Nafikh that blew. We've got a dead sentry and others that were badly injured. And countless people injured or dead."

She can hear the accusation in his tone. "That's hardly on me."

"They can do a whole lot worse than that before it's over."

"You think I haven't seen what They can do?" she retorts, pissed that she's being judged once again by this serv with his nice combed hair and button-down shirt and no clue.

He motions at the third screen, changing the subject. "This is satellite courtesy of Montreal," he says. "The Nafikh emit a particular heat signature. Every visiting Nafikh in every part of the world at any given moment can be located by satellite, unless we've got weather or cloud cover. Elander knows this, because he took Dara-Lin when the storm was still going strong." Eric taps his keyboard, causing an inset box to pop up. He points at the grainy black and white image: it's a highway, a clot of trees. "We discovered the Nafikh was gone from Nahant Beach at 4:27 a.m. At 5:38, the weather cleared enough to start scanning. We located the limo at 5:56. By this time, the Nafikh had been gone two hours. We calculated a radius of 150 miles possible travel distance by car from the limo, which is generous given road conditions. But there were no Nafikh within that radius, excluding the ones that have arrived since, of course. And now, we've expanded the search farther north, west, and up the coast, and still nothing. We're also keeping an eye on all watercraft. Nothing. Which leads me to conclude," he directs her back to the map, "that he's got Her somewhere beneath solid rock, or in a man-made structure with walls of iron, the only substances that can block Nafikh communication. Like I said, based on the travel time, and taking out the most unlikely areas"—he points back to the map of Maine, indicating darkened zones around major cities and towns—"he could be anywhere in all those circles."

Lucy's mouth has gone dry as sawdust. Eric, oblivious to her state, turns back to his other screens, starts tapping rapidly on one of the keyboards. She swallows hard, staring obediently at the map, her eyes blindly taking in the names of towns and rivers. There are so many.

I've got nothing.

Eric's laptop flickers with the destruction at the harbor. Black smoke billows over the Boston skyline. A string of cop cars races down an empty road towards the inferno. The Nafikh-fire generated by a blow doesn't last that long, but it can't be put out, and before it dissipates it sets anything it touches ablaze.

Lucy wonders if Eva's watching. She digs in her pocket, but she doesn't have her phone. It's probably in Bedrosian's car. She imagines it ringing. Eva's probably called twenty times by now.

A series of bleeps, and Eric swivels at once, peers at a message in a chat window that's popped up in the corner of the satellite imagery.

"Oh no," he mutters. "All right, keep your heads down," he announces, half rising from his chair. Worried murmurs fill the room. Lucy cranes to see the message: *Nafikh loose.* "He's not likely to come in here. If He does, just go about your business, am I clear?"

Murmurs, whispers.

Eric's exuding a sick anxiety that's got her on edge; it's the Gate, you'd think they'd be used to Nafikh here. There are more bleeps, a conversation unfolding. *Where is First. Is he on same level? Can't see.*

Eric points out the window. Lucy follows the line of his finger.

A bare-chested Nafikh is standing in the window, up where they were before, His hands splayed on the glass. It is Hansel. His breath spreads circles of mist that grow, shrink, grow, shrink. Even from here, she can feel the sickening chasm behind His eyes. His mouth hangs slightly open, and Lucy's stomach clenches. Right. They're coming out too fast. He looks the way They do towards the end of a visit, not the start.

How they are on the sets, Lucy realizes. Where she's headed when this is done.

She swallows, closing her eyes, faint with a swell of nausea.

"He's leaving," Eric says in relief. "The First's probably talked Him down."

She looks up. The window is now empty, smudged with oversized handprints.

Eric chews hard on his pencil tip, hunched close to the satellite screen. "They're more than three hours out now. We'd need a chopper to make up that kind of time." He shakes his head, speaking in quick, abrupt sentences, like an echo of the tapping keyboard. "They're all going to want out now. This is the worst-case scenario. They could do some real damage. I mean, some real serious damage. At least the Stayer is out of town," he adds with a nervous laugh. "That's something."

"Stayer?" Lucy echoes dumbly. *I didn't think They were real,* she almost says, then buttons her lip, feeling stupid. "So where is He?"

"Took a cruise up to Halifax."

"But Nafikh can't be in a closed environment like that for so long. It's too dangerous."

"Stayers are different. They can go wherever. He took just one sentry."

"One sentry?" Lucy shakes her head in amazement. "What are they doing, having martinis and playing the slots?"

Eric opens his mouth to answer, but instead goes silent, jaw dropped, horror filling his eyes.

She twists in her chair, following his gaze. The Nafikh Hansel is back in the window, holding something in His arms. The First Qadir, Lucy realizes. He's twisting, resisting, but even though he's large, he's much more frail than the massive, glowing Nafikh.

There is a moment swollen with quiet, a bubble of time in which no one breathes, nothing moves, the air is completely still.

Then the Nafikh hurls the Qadir through the glass, shattering it. The Qadir's arms and legs flail for an instant before his body drops two stories like a stone, landing on the wooden floor with a loud thump.

The Nafikh's harsh, wet breaths fill the air as He surveys the wreckage, leaning on the windowsill jagged with glass. His eyes rove the warehouse as He becomes aware of the gasps and calls erupting from all sides.

The Qadir is unmoving, a huddled lump on the floor. He must be dead. There are no sentries anywhere. None up there, with the Nafikh, whose mouth hangs open, His distress obvious at the steadily increasing cacophony of noises coming from everywhere within the scaffolded edifice—frantic voices, footsteps. The sentries who were stationed at Gate level are gone.

Suddenly He starts, turns His head slightly. Lucy eases out her breath, watching. She knows that behavior, it's when a sentry's talking the Nafikh down. She glances back at Eric, who is ashen. She says, "I think it might be O.K., now."

"O.K.?" he hisses. "Yeah, sure, everything's just fine!"

"I mean that," Lucy retorts, nodding up.

Hansel backs away from the windows. With the Nafikh out of sight, servs pour in from all sides, dash over to the Qadir's prone form.

"He looks dead," Lucy says, craning her neck.

"You can't kill a Qadir that easy, even if he's on the fritz." Eric is ashen, cracking his knuckles. "If he died now—I can't even think about it."

"What would happen?"

"A new one comes right away. There are always two, no matter what. But it won't know us, it won't know anything about what it has to do here. It'll walk into this chaos and make everything worse. I have to let Montreal know. And Q.C."

His fingers fly, spreading the word of their situation. He crouches at the keyboard, neck craned forward like a chicken, both legs jiggling. Someone's turned over the Qadir's body. He sure looks dead from here, Lucy thinks. Gabriel's arrived, along with one other sentry. There are a couple of servs there, too, not doing much, just milling around looking panicked. The rest of the sentries must be on Hansel, and Gretel's probably running around somewhere, too. And there were two others, she recalls Eric saying. Chaos. She can't say she isn't glad to be tucked away in here, with the cushy office servs. She rolls her chair out of the window's view. She tries to get control of her breathing, but it's tough with Eric in such a freak-out, tapping his foot, twirling his pen with dizzying speed between his fingers.

None of it matters, she reminds herself. Her fate is the same, regardless of what happens today. She wonders what the sets are like, how long she'll last. Maybe the Nafikh will blow the whole Gate up, and the question will be moot. She realizes she's feeling for her phone again. Eva must be out of her mind with worry.

She can't think about that. She peeks out the window. The Qadir hasn't moved. He's dead. He's got to be.

The Ayer footage is still playing. The kitchen comes into view: the imported Italian tiles Theo was so proud of, the farmhouse table with the long wood benches. The camera pans to the French doors with their pretty latticework, pauses on the idyllic view of field and dark smudge of tree line, calling up mornings stepping out with a steaming cup of coffee, the deer hesitating, noses aquiver, mist rising all around. Slowly, the camera moves on, swinging to a framed antique map of the USSR Theo picked up at an auction. Lucy used to gaze at those roads, a million worlds away, yearning to know more about Theo's mysterious, violent past. He had a lot of maps, all the places he'd been. He kept them stacked on a shelf.

It's so different now, no one uses paper. The memory slips up out of nowhere, herself tucked into the Camaro with Joe Brynn, the noise of unfolding paper, her hand hitting his ear as she spread the map open. He got so pissed. She was always the map reader when they had to run errands. Where are we? Are you sure we're on the right highway? Check the map! Joe pestered her endlessly. He couldn't bear being lost, just the idea of it set him on edge. Always pulling over, demanding she check again, Show me, where are we, are you sure. It drove her nuts. When GPS units were first invented, he bought three.

Lucy narrows her eyes, tugged by a notion she can't quite get a hold of.

Maps. Joe Brynn's obsession with having the latest TomTom.

"Oh my God," she breathes. She grabs Eric's arm so hard he winces, eyes wide in surprise. "Joe Brynn's GPS, from his car. The address might be on there."

"Who?"

"He's Theo's right-hand man. He'd be going to Eden. I'm sure of it. I need your phone."

"Why?"

"Just give it to me!" Lucy leans forward and snatches it off the desk, rolls her chair out of reach as she punches in Sean's number. "I can get the Maine address, O.K.? Just wait."

"Who are you calling?"

"My cousin."

Eric looks at her with suspicion. "Those people, you mean? The ones you lived with? You can't call them!"

She twists away from his grasping hand. "Shut up, O.K.?"

He's surprised enough to quit snatching for the phone, but he remains fixed on her every move. *Come on. Come on. Come on, answer!* she cries frantically in her head. The phone rings and rings. Goes to voice mail. Sean always screens unknowns, worried it'll turn out to be some needy ex. "Sean, call me at this number, *now!* It's *urgent!*"

"Give me the phone," Eric snaps.

She moves farther out of reach, one finger held up in warning. *One, two, three—*

The phone rings, and she hits Reply.

"Where are you, Luce? Jesus, have you seen the news?"

"Yes, I know," she interrupts. "Listen, this is major, major important, are you listening?"

"Are you O.K., then?"

"I'm fine. There's something you have to—"

"Aren't you going to ask how Aunt Eva is?"

He sounds angry and frayed, ready to pop. She grits her teeth. "Sean, I am sorry, O.K.? I know how awful it all is. But you have to listen. Please just listen. The guy who attacked us last night, he had a car. I need you to get in that car and pull addresses off the GPS."

There is a pause. "Luce, what the hell?" he says helplessly.

"It's an Explorer, that's all I know. He'd have parked it off the main road, out of sight. No more than a ten-minute walk, I'd guess. Break in if you have to. Just get the GPS."

"Is that detective with you? Let me speak to him."

"He's not here. He's in major trouble, Sean," Lucy says, with a flash of inspiration. "This is for him. We have to help him. Everything's gone to shit, Sean. You have to get that GPS!"

There is a pause. Lucy imagines his desperate, sweet face as he tries to make sense of things. She hears him breathing. Then he asks, "Is it safe to leave Aunt Eva?"

"Yes, yes, for sure. I swear. You have to go, now."

A movement in the corner of her eye: Eric jabs his finger, pointing, his face stricken. She turns slowly in her chair.

Hansel is coming down the stairs.

"Sean, get everything off the GPS," she whispers into the phone. "Text to this number, O.K.? It'll be in Maine. Look for something in Maine."

"O.K., Luce."

"Hurry," she whispers.

She switches the phone off. Edges to the window, staying to the side. The servs around the fallen Qadir are still as stone, watching the Nafikh's slow approach down the stairs. Whoever tried to talk Him down failed. He's worse off now, Lucy can tell by His faltering manners, the widening eyes and flared nostrils, the chin jutted forward. He's dressed only in a pair of jeans. Sweat dribbles down His forehead into His eyes, causing Him to blink. His glowing skin is damp, dripping. The muscles beneath bunch and ripple as He moves.

He reaches the bottom of the steps and pauses there. Rivulets of sweat shine down His broad chest. His mouth hangs open, huge hands cupped as He turns, staring hungrily. His chest rises and falls faster. He sounds like a winded horse. The air is filled with murmurs, sniffles, sobs coming from all sides of the vast warehouse. A chair in the room she's in suddenly scrapes the floor, noise like nails on a blackboard. The Nafikh twitches, mouth drawing back to bare His teeth.

Not good.

"Tell them to shut up," Lucy hisses. "Do it! *Now!*"

Eric starts, as if she smacked him. Gets to it, loping around the room, making silencing gestures. The room goes dead quiet.

Hansel paces the floor, loose-kneed and panting. Sweat pours into His eyes. He's still an inferno in a skin sheath, and for a few moments He becomes preoccupied with wiping His eyes, then staring at His splayed fingers in dismay like they're infected. The sentries flick their hands subtly, sending the cowering servs away. They slink off one by one, duck into doorways. They don't have enough experience, is the only reason why Lucy can think they received that gift.

Hansel prods the Qadir's humped form with His toe. The action provokes a low, deep moan that swells into the empty air. The Qadir can't be aware, or he'd never be stupid enough to make that noise. He's broken, unconscious, just a reaction.

Hansel bends at the waist, His face twisted into a mask of revulsion.

Lucy becomes aware of a new presence in the room: the Second Qadir, moving forward with her towering, strict grace. Hansel turns His head. Gabriel joins the Qadir, and the low timbre of his Nafikh speech carries across the room. Hansel stretches upward, listening, rippling muscle and sweat.

He lifts His arm and backhands Gabriel across the ribs, sending him smack into the iron wall of the Gate. Gabriel struggles to stay upright, clutching his side.

The Qadir looks over at him, then back at the Nafikh. To Lucy's shock, she bends her head, retreats one pace, then another.

"What the fuck?" Lucy hisses.

"The Nafikh blame the Qadir for this mess," Eric replies. "This is bad. This is really bad. She's trying to protect us. If new Qadir come in, they'll just wipe us all out, start over."

"Why aren't there any sentries?"

"They're all on the others," Eric whispers, scanning his chat windows. "Two got outside."

Lucy cranes her eyes to see if Gabriel's breathing. He is. He's just taking a spell to recover. Though by the looks of that blow, he might not be moving any time soon. This Nafikh needs distracting, most basic rule of the game, and there's no sentry in sight to take care of it, just a bunch of loser servs hiding under their desks, and a hobbled Qadir.

No way, she warns herself, extinguishing the notion.

But if she makes an effort, maybe they won't put her on the sets. And then maybe, just maybe, she can still be bought out. *You are crazy,* she warns herself, but the idea's growing on her fast. She's got nothing to lose. Nothing. It's the sets or, at the rate things are going, getting wiped out by new Qadir.

The phone grows sweaty in her hand. She looks down at the blank face, willing it to ring. Then hurriedly switches off the ringer, so as not to spur the Nafikh into an even worse state.

Hansel flexes His hand, then shapes it into a tight fist, fixated on the injured Qadir. He bends, cocks His head. The First is motionless. Lucy wonders if he can see, if he's aware at all that the Nafikh is about to finish him off.

Hansel swivels around. He says something to the Second, His lips in a snarl. The Qadir shakes her head, her posture meek, slavish.

The phone jitters inside Lucy's hand. She looks down. It's a text. It reads: 3 Larkpond Lane.

Lucy's heart smashes her ribs. *Don't you dare. Don't you fucking dare move.* But she hands the phone backwards, feels Eric take it. Wipes her palms on her jeans. *Nothing to lose,* she thinks savagely. She takes a breath. Turns around. "He's going to kill the Qadir. I've got to distract."

There's no harm in putting an altruistic spin on her action, in case she makes it out.

Eric just looks up at her in shock, mouth agape. Yeah, well, it probably never crossed his mind to do something about the carnage out there. She walks the length of the room, conscious of everyone watching her. She comes to the doorway, steps out. She taps the floor with her boot. It isn't enough, Hansel's so fixated on the Qadir, bent over almost double, back muscles flexing, shifting.

She adjusts her face into the grin They prefer. She steps forward, plunking her heel down hard on the wooden floor.

He starts. Then His upper body slowly swings her way, still hinged at the hips.

For a second, her plan quakes and fritters, shredded by the swiveling head, the swirling pits of hell now fixed on her. In the corner of her swimming vision she sees the Qadir's inscrutable gaze.

Across the way, a door opens, and a sentry slips out. *About fucking time.* It is Sina, rifle cocked. *Please please please shoot.* But she doesn't. The Nafikh probably can't take any more doses. Their eyes meet: Sina nods, *Go for it.*

Lucy's mind drains but for high humming panic. She's moving forward as she intended, though every part of her body screams, *Run.* But you can't outrun Nafikh. They're like tigers. He's out of the cage. Lucy's face stretches so hard it hurts, her teeth gritted together.

She moves forward until He's so close she can feel His breaths blasting her skin, hot and wet.

She stops no more than a foot away, staring up, trying to keep her spine straight because They can't abide fear, They can't bear any reflection of Their own torment, why do They come here, *Why why why?*

"*Shanesh,*" He says. *What.* His voice is deep as the fire from which He emerged.

Lucy swallows, her mouth paper dry. "If you please," she says, then forces more strength into her voice: "I know where Dara-Lin is located."

At the mention of Her name, Hansel's whole body stiffens. He leans in, suspicion twisting His face grotesquely.

"*Gatareh el Dara-Lin,*" Sina calls out the translation, slowly approaching from behind. "*Gatareh el!*"

The silence is absolute. From the corner of her eye, Lucy can see the Qadir's enormous form, still as stone, watching.

The Nafikh seems to drink in the words, His throat moving hard once, twice.

Gatareh *must mean find,* Lucy supposes in some far-off place in her mind.

"*Kojeh?*" Hansel says abruptly.

"How?" Sina calls at once.

"I know where She was taken. I can take you there."

Sina translates as she speaks. The Nafikh takes deep, long breaths, apparently considering this. Inch by inch, He closes in on her, until the hot wetness of His breaths touches her face, and the heat pouring off His body makes her skin prickle with sweat. She can't bear to look into His eyes, but they're sucking at her like magnets. *Help me,* she begs Sina with her whole being, regretting her decision, what is she, stupid, no matter what the Qadirs planned for her it would be nothing like this hell, her bones crunching inside the massive fists, blood pouring out—

Shit shit shit because now she's crying, the tears popping out helplessly, she's just so tired is the problem, hasn't slept in days—and she can't take it—

He's right in her face, and she steps back, just one step, and in that instant glimpses Sina's drop-jawed, astonished expression: *Why does she look like that?*

The Nafikh's eyes roil darkness, sickening her insides. Then He grasps her chin, drags her close, pressing on her jaw like a dog's, forcing her mouth open wide.

His chest expands, cracking sound, sweat in glistening rivers, and she glimpses fiery white wisps trickling past His lips. Then the Nafikh plunges towards her, and His mouth clamps over hers. The last thing she remembers is screaming, but there's no sound.

Wake up wake up you have to wake up now Lucy.
Wake up Lucy.
Can you hear me?
You must wake up and thank the Nafikh.
Wake up Lucy.

HER TONGUE IS HEAVY and hot as baked potato inside her mouth, and her throat hurts so very much, she can't breathe or speak to the voices, she can't move. *I can't move!* she tries to let them know, but all that happens is her lips crack apart the slightest little bit, allowing in a wisp of cool air.

Huh-huh-huh-huh.
It's all right, Lucy. Lucy, look at me.
Huh-huh-huh-huh—

Herself, breathing hard and fast.

Look at me, Lucy.

Shapes, dark and light, motion. She blinks till the image clears: Gabriel, bent close. He tucks his hand under her head, lifts it.
   "Get up. He's waiting."

With his help she finds her way to her feet. Her mouth tastes burnt. Her chest feels weighted, strangely opaque, like it's wadded up with stuffing.

It's the Source.

She can't feel it. Or—just barely. A tiny winking spark.

She licks her lips, suddenly overwhelmed with craving for water. Her hand creeps to her chest. She feels different. She feels—solid. Rooted.

"You got a boost," Gabriel says in her ear. "You understand? You're one of us, now."

She blinks at him. She'd forgotten he was there.

A boost?

"*Ajhare-in,*" the deep voice intrudes.

"You are joyous," Gabriel translates. "Say *Anesh ajhari.*"

"*Anesh ajhari,*" Lucy says. She tries to make her face smile.

"Just be normal," Gabriel whispers.

Lucy's smile falters.

Hansel lifts His hand, languidly shapes a pointed finger that reaches out and touches her lightly on the forehead. "*Gatareh el Dara-Lin.*"

Gabriel maneuvers himself between them, causing the Nafikh's hand to drop away, and he speaks with pressing, cajoling insistence. It's all incomprehensible to Lucy other than the repeated mention of Dara-Lin. Hansel doesn't appear pleased with what He's hearing. He points at Lucy, shaking His head. Lucy sways in place, fascinated. She's never been so close to a Nafikh without the urge to hurl her guts up from anxiety. Without the Nafikh zeroing in on her, His intentions a blank, wild horror. He's just not looking at her that way, now. He's not looking at her at all; she's become invisible. She could hang out right at His side and He'd not harm her, because she's become important. She's the one who's going to keep Him safe, she realizes. She's special to Him.

Then all of a sudden the Nafikh is walking away, guided by Sina. An incalculable disappointment springs up inside her. She doesn't want Him to leave.

"Oh, no you don't," Gabriel blocks her passage. "You tell me you can make good on that promise. Look at me, Lucy."

She feels her feet pressed into the ground. Her heart drums steadily. The light inside is a shimmering coal, and when she draws her mind to it, she feels its heat reaching outwards. It doesn't hurt. It doesn't *hurt*. Her muscles twitch, she could just blow right up, crash through the ceiling and rocket into the sky—

"Whoa," Gabriel warns, shaking her by the shoulder.

She starts, staring at him in confusion. She fights to halt the wildness raging inside her. She could pummel him a thousand times and still have enough left over to spin like a top.

"This is adjustment. Normally you'd be monitored and helped along, but there's no time for any of that now. You feel that craze kicking around inside, you suck it up and focus, you hear me? He's insisting on coming with us and that you come along, too, so you *have* to hold it together!"

She doesn't know why Gabriel's so bent out of shape. Of course she should come along, if He wants her to. She cranes her neck to see where the Nafikh has gone. She should be with Him, because that's what He has requested.

"Oh, someone shoot me now," Gabriel mutters. "Lucy. Look at me. Tell me we've got a destination. Tell me you can make good on that promise."

"She can make good," a voice says.

Lucy turns her wobbly, addled head. It's Eric, holding up his phone in triumph. "It's north of Route 15, middle of nowhere. We're running down all the records now, but the property's in the name of an Elijah Lord, which has to be one of Elander's aliases. The aerials look right: the property's over twenty acres with a main house, barns, and two cottages inside a security fence. Very isolated, very expansive. Aside from the structures you're looking at forest."

"How'd you find it?"

"It was her," Eric points at Lucy. "She figured it out."

"Figured it out, or knew all along?"

Eric is taken aback. "No—she didn't know. I'm sure of it."

Gabriel looks Lucy up and down. "All right, then."

She wants to reply, but finds she still can't speak, instead a weird *nnngh* sound dribbles out of her mouth. She clamps her lips closed. Crushes her two hands into fists so they don't fly out and smash everything to pieces.

THEY'RE OUTSIDE IN A cold wind blowing off the river. It sweeps the empty lot, whirls snow clouds through the air. The snow prickles Lucy's cheeks. Every touch is a thousand points of fire. She stays close to Gabriel, hands clenched behind her back. She should make a break for it. She might. She feels like screaming. If she has to stand here a moment longer, she'll crack into a thousand boiling pieces and ignite the whole bloody lot of them.

Gabriel and the Second Qadir are having an argument. The Qadir's like a granite statue, all planes and jagged surfaces, with gray hair and gray eyes and skin the color of milk. She stays just inside the door track, as if it's a border she cannot cross. Lucy considers this, mystified. She imagines pushing her over the track, like shoving a vampire into the sun. She can't think what might happen.

She's trapped here, Lucy realizes, suddenly awash in sorrow, recalling the First Qadir gazing out the window.

He's almost dead, she heard. It's almost over.

She could just cry.

She becomes aware that she's breathing that way again, huh-huh-huh-huh. She shifts all her focus to stopping the noise. The argument unfolds in clipped, hard undertones, so that it doesn't carry to the rest of the sentries pacing by the idling vans. It's all in Nafikh, but Lucy got the gist earlier. Gabriel told the Q.C. Gate to go in without them, is the problem. It was a strategic decision: Q.C. is only a few hours away from Theo's hideout. But apparently, the Boston Gate will incur a huge debt, never mind the shame, and the Qadir's incensed.

"*Edjeh een!*" she snaps, and Lucy jumps. *Come here.* She obeys. Her legs feel like bombs on a timer.

"*Fahareh!*"

Lucy blinks, looks up. The Qadir's craggy face comes into focus.

"You did not deserve this gift."

I saved your life, Lucy could argue, but the Qadir's mood is too foul. "It was the Nafikh's decision."

"Huh," the Qadir sneers. "He gave you a boost, and now you adore Him. It is always the same. Look at where you are. Look at where you are going. You should try and speed up your adjustment."

Lucy flushes. Her weird longing to see the Nafikh falters, cracks a little. Along with it comes a pang of wistfulness, so acute she can't speak. A hole spreads open inside her. Dark, pitiless, devastating.

"She will be useless to you," the Qadir tells Gabriel. "Keep her on the side. Go."

She turns and strides away, the door clattering down behind her. Gabriel seizes Lucy by the arm, pulls her down the stairs. "You will not carry a weapon, you will not stray from the line, you will do exactly as you're told," he instructs. "Right now, the way you are, you're a liability, you're a shackle, you hear? You do anything wrong and you get us all killed. Answer me. Do you understand?"

"Yes."

Lucy's cheeks boil with shame. There are five other sentries waiting by the van, Sina included. They're a hulking mass of metal and leather and fierce stares. They're carrying machine guns, ammo belts, knives, all in addition to the dosing rifles. Lucy's the one who warned them about Theo's weapons stockpile, but all she got was some other sentry's dark woolen coat and boots; the boots are dead heavy with metal toes, and that much harder to walk in being a size too big.

"You will stay glued to me or Sina, one or the other. You keep away from the Nafikh. Do not engage Him. You act like He's not there, you hear?"

"Don't worry, I'm losing that sick feeling already," Lucy is glad to inform him. "I'll be fine on that count."

"You have no idea how fast it can come back up to wreck your day," he corrects her. "Takes an average of a week to get back to a healthier way of seeing things. And He's not looking good. He came out too soon, His pain isn't being managed, and can't be. What I need from you is to stuff those desires to get closer to Him, you understand?"

Lucy can't imagine actually wanting to be close to a Nafikh. She glares at Gabriel, conveying her disdain for this whole damn lecture.

"Jaysus," he snaps. "I will not hesitate, do you hear? I will not, Lucy Hennessey."

"You won't have cause," she says through gritted teeth.

"Oh, dammit," Sina says.

Hansel has climbed up on top of the first van. He's staring out over the weedy snowy lots towards the river. He leans forward, swaying a little, as if drawn towards the view.

"Get Him before He falls," Gabriel says. One of the sentries breaks away, lopes around the van and climbs onto the hood. The Nafikh turns, frowning. The sentry murmurs in Nafikh, making unhurried, graceful gestures. Finally, He climbs down. His thick blonde hair lifts in the breeze. The sunlight strikes His bare skin, which glitters brightly: He's covered in a fine coat of ice crystals formed by sweat. Strands of ice hang from His nostrils. His lips are bruised blue.

The sight provokes a lurch of worry. "Shouldn't we get Him some clothes?"

Gabriel shifts his gaze, looks sternly down his nose at her.

"Oh," she says. "O.K. Right. Why the fuck is it like this?" Lucy blurts.

"Why the fuck is anything like anything?"

It's pretty much the dumbest response she might have gotten, but uttered in that bland English accent, he somehow pulls it off. For a second, she's reminded of the crush she's always had on him. Then he gives her a shove, points, indicating her ride, the closest van.

"Not the limo?" Lucy asks, disappointed.

"I told you, you're staying away from Him. All right, let's do it," he calls out, turning. The other sentries swiftly move in one by one, grip his outstretched hand, then lope off to their designated vehicle. Lucy jams her own hands deep into her pockets, pretends not to see. She hasn't felt this way since she was a kid with her arms folded tight around her scrawny frame, white stork legs pressed together, last one picked for kickball. It's so fucking stupid, but it hurts.

LUCY'S RELEGATED TO THE back row. She twists on the bench, looking out across the river. The harbor islands in the distance look like a handful of pebbles flung towards the crooked peninsula of Hull. Somewhere along that shore is the little brown house, the barnacled boat, Eva sitting near her picture window, the TV blaring news about the terrorist attack in Boston. Phyllis will be there by now—no way Eva wouldn't call her—and they'll make Sean repeat his story of Lucy's frantic call, how he searched for the car, the GPS. She knows so intimately the scene of people banded together in a time of trauma, having witnessed it time and again, the murmuring, the food and drink, the buttressed, excited feeling of surviving.

She presses into the freezing window, tipping her head back till all that remains is the vast blue sky. Every shudder and bump jolts her forehead against the cold glass. The engine thuds steadily, and a cold wind blows through the vents. No one speaks. Time passes. She sees snow-covered fields, stands of trees, the occasional cluster of homes on a stretch of black road. The city's already a world away. She imagines people in these country houses also glued to their TVs, the truth of what's actually happening beyond anything they'd ever imagine. She wonders if any more Nafikh have blown, and if Theo knew what would happen, if he cares at all.

GABRIEL HUDDLES UP WITH his phone, getting more details from Eric on layout, distances between structures, possible numbers they might face, all of which he relays to Sina, leading to repeated changes in the plan. The plan continues to include Hansel potentially blowing them all to smithereens. A numbness, and a kind of wonder, gradually replaces Lucy's concern. She feels at her jeans pockets: no, right, the phone is in Bedrosian's car.

He wanted to buy her out: the memory wells up as if from weeks ago. Sentries can't be bought out, they're too important. *I'm important*, she thinks a little smugly, then comes back to the reality of the van careening along the highway, and where they're headed.

She dozes off for a time, curled up on the back seat.

About three quarters of the way to Eden, Gabriel gets word that Q.C. entered the compound way later than anticipated. They're taking fire and don't have enough manpower. They're retreating till Boston arrives.

"That sick bastard," Gabriel fumes. "Fast as you can," he barks at the driver, then gets on the phone again with Eric.

"The Q.C. Qadir's screwing ours over," Sina explains to Lucy.

"You can bet he'll still send a bill," Gabriel snaps.

"Yeah," Sina says, tilting her head back and closing her eyes.

Eric lets them know there's a storm rolling in that's going to dump up to ten inches, which they knew about already, but it's picked up speed. Gabriel snarls into the phone like it's Eric's fault, then hangs up. His eyes glaze over, staring into the middle distance. He hasn't shaved, and Lucy sees streaks of gray in his beard; she wonders how long sentries get to live, she's heard a century, at least.

I'll bury Sean, she realizes, dismayed. She always just assumed she'd be the one to die first.

Everyone did, doubtless.

"WHEN WE ARRIVE," HE says, "you jump and run, we stick together, you understand?"

She nods. The sentry's grim, earnest face floats in her vision, his lecture disembodied chatter outside the high hum of the engine. His name is Aaron. The name is familiar, but she can't place why. He has a fat, brown mole under his eye she's trying not to focus on. He keeps ramming information at her: "We'll come in twenty-five yards from the rear of the main house. We'll break off into four groups, one at the house, and the others at the outlying structures."

Aaron, she realizes at last. "Is Detective Bedrosian O.K.? Where is he?"

The interruption annoys him. "Pay attention. We might be taking fire, so you stay low and close. Do not run off on your own. Are we clear?"

She nods, wondering why he thinks she'd be so stupid as to run off on her own.

THE VAN ROLLS TO a stop. The door opens onto a swirling storm of white, and the sentries vanish into it. Lucy's boots are heavy as rocks. She gets pushed from behind. The lumbering boot catches on something, and she lurches forward into the air, her arms flung out in panic.

SNOW CLOGS HER MOUTH, clumps all over her face, she tries to see but can't make out anything except bright orange flashes illuminating the hulking darkness of the house looming ahead. Gunfire thuds all around. Which way is she supposed to go? She spins frantically on her belly, propelling herself with elbows and knees, but she can't see anyone else. She goes still, staring around in despair. Snow trickles freeze down her neck. The wool coat is sodden, heavy, and the cold's starting to seep in through her sweater. The vans are gone, obscured by the swirling white. She's alone in this huge empty space, by herself, they left her: she can't believe it, Oh my God, she's going to get shot— "Move it!" Gabriel barks in her ear. She feels herself lifted up, and she grabs at his coat. He lets her cling to him as they run, and she's so grateful, he's as big as the house, he's strong, she can hide in his lee. There's a sudden rat-tat of gunfire nearby, and she cries out, except there's no sound, just the wild rush of her own body plunging forward. She can't see, she's going to fall, then he reaches back, closes his hand around her arm, and yanks her through a doorway.

They're inside, they made it inside.

Wheezing, mouth agape, she scuttles close to Gabriel, pressing herself into his broad back. He's just inside the doorframe, firing. Her hands make their way up to her ears, she presses hard. There's the tromp of boots on the tile floor, bodies blundering by bringing gusts of cold and snow and wet.

She gets dragged onward with the wave of them, deeper into the house.

"Stay here," Gabriel says suddenly, and shoves her. Her knees rap stone: a curved bench beneath a narrow stained glass window, high up and conical, like you'd see in a church. An alcove. Theo always did like his medieval shit.

"You're in the way," Gabriel explains, and then he's gone.

She climbs onto the bench so as to be closer to the wall. Huddles up, arms tight around her knees. A soft round light high up on the ceiling illuminates her nightmare: long narrow tiled corridor, cream walls, the alcove where she's trapped, shaking. *You have to calm down,* a stern, rational part of herself commands. But she's plagued by panic: is Gabriel coming back, is she supposed to go find him at some point? He didn't tell her what to do.

The stone house echoes with the noise of gunfire, breaking glass, loud crashes, metal pings. She huddles tighter.

Her head is a metal song, there's nothing left but noise, no room for thoughts. Her body curls into itself until she's on her side, face pressed into her knees, hands jammed against her ears.

At last, gradually, the noise starts to die. The silence that fills in the gaps is gigantic. The gunfire's sporadic and more distant. She forces her bent legs to uncurl. Pain shoots through her muscles at this near impossible effort. When she sets foot on the floor, her legs buckle. She hangs onto the wall, listening.

Shouts, far away, barely audible.

She edges along, hugging the wall, trying not to make any noise. The shouting fades. No one was coming for her, she realizes, with a new rush of anxiety. But, maybe that's because it's not safe yet. She should go back.

At the end of the hallway is an oak door that opens onto a short staircase. She climbs. At the top, there's a living room, or what used to be one. The furniture's overturned, glass lies shattered all over the place. She steps around a toppled bookcase, the books fanned out across the floor. There's a pair of bare feet sticking out from behind the couch. She creeps forward. The guy isn't a sentry, nor one of the soldiers. She doesn't know who he is. Half his face is blown off. A gun lies in his slackened hand. She swallows, turning away. There's someone else a few feet away, all curled up. Barefoot. They must have been servs, living here with Theo. They came out in bare feet, against an army of sentries. Total morons.

Could've been me.

Because here she is at last, in that magical la-la land where they'd be freed from Service, tucked safe under Theo's paternal wing. Eden: she'd pictured columns, sweeping marble, something derivative of an ancient temple. The actuality is a lot different, but it still feels familiar, it has that heavy splendor that might befit a restored Nafikh in this realm, from the shining grand piano to the ornately framed oil paintings to the crystal chandelier she can just see hanging low over the formal dining table in the adjacent room.

Just hours ago, this house must have been filled with the anticipation of great things to come. The feeling of those precious days in Ayer balloons inside her, along with the bitterness she's nursed all this time for being shunted and rejected.

And yet, for what? This is the truth of it, this schmuck serv's curled-up rigid corpse, his hand over his face, like at the last second he finally grasped the reality of what he signed up for.

He was expendable. They all were, right from the start.

There's shooting far off, a dull series of pops. She recalls the aerial view they examined before leaving, trying to figure out where the sound might be coming from. The big barn, maybe, the one near the lake. She wonders how many more servs were already tucked away here, living the dream, full of smug pleasure at Theo's attention. Now getting picked off one by one.

She makes her way through the debris, passes into the dining room. Her boots crunch glass beneath the broken window. The gently falling snow blows in from the outside, melting into the carpet, floating across the furniture. In this untouched, splendid room, the weird whiteness layering everything, Lucy has the impression of sinking undersea, in the wreckage of the *Titanic*.

She stands there, not knowing what to do, watching the snow float in.

Becomes aware, gradually, of a faint reverberation beneath her feet. A motor, maybe? A generator?

"Lucy! Come on!"

She almost topples over from fright, but it's Sina, gesturing from a doorway. Lucy bangs her shins on the table leg, then skids a few feet on the carpet in her haste to reach Sina's side, breathless and grateful.

"Pull yourself together," Sina snaps, then turns on her heel and lopes off.

The criticism stings. The little pocket of solitude and reflection that she'd crept into suddenly tears open, drops her hard. An urge comes over her with the force of a tidal wave, to smash her fists into the wall, or into the back of Sina's sleek head more like it.

"Where are we going?" she asks through clenched teeth. "Where is everyone?"

"Clearing the rest of the buildings."

"You came back for me?"

"Yes. What's happening?"

It takes a moment for Lucy to understand the question isn't directed at her. There are some servs up ahead. They must be from Q.C. They're decked out in military gear. One of them steps forward, a block of a guy with a stiff square crop of blonde hair, a tattoo on the shaved scalp above his ear. His nametag reads A. Coutreaux. He says, "No change."

"Shit," Sina mutters. She shoulders by, and he spins and follows close behind. Their departure creates a sudden vacuum. Silence. The two other servs eye Lucy from the shadows, dead quiet, machine guns cocked on their hips. She feels their hostility like a sharp prickle across her skin, and it aggravates the turmoil in her limbs that she's trying so hard to suppress. She can't look at them, not directly. Just the boots, the cockily bent legs, the Victorian pattern wallpaper behind with its golden birds perched among fruit bushes.

"T'as un problème, toé?"

She lifts her eyes. It's the taller one that spoke. P. Lefevre, narrow chin jutted like an aggressive dog.

She says, "I don't know French."

The guys exchange a quick, suspicious look. She chooses this moment to walk on by. They follow. Their presence behind her is like two heavy weights. She can hear every little thing. Their breathing, which is tense, fast. The rustling clothes, the boots. Faint metal on metal, the weapons brushing a buckle or belt. The pungent smell of them, too, of sweat and oil, leaves a sour taste on the back of her tongue. It takes every ounce of will not to glance back.

It must be the boost giving her such awareness. This better be a passing phase, because living like this will be a bitch.

Sina and Coutreaux are in the kitchen, fixated on something going on outside. The wide-open doors creak on their hinges in the gusting wind. Snow blows in, dampening the breakfast table. Beyond the patio, about thirty feet from the house, Hansel stands in a slump, His outstretched arm propping Him against a giant old oak tree. There is something similar in their two forms, both so massive and still, snow settling silently onto them.

"What's He doing?" Lucy whispers.

"He was shot. He should leave, but He's still refusing. Dammit," Sina curses. She taps the mic on her headset. "Gabe, we can't wait any longer."

Her jaw works hard as she listens to the reply, staring at the slumped Nafikh.

"There is no time," she says flatly.

Pause.

"Negative," she says. "I'm forcing the blow."

She switches off her headset. "Coutreaux, move out. Now. She goes with you."

Coutreaux's pale blue eyes flash across Lucy, emotionless, like a computer reading her presence. "Acknowledged. Good luck."

"What are you doing?" Lucy demands. "What's going on?"

"If this one dies, we'll have even more of a shitstorm on our hands," Sina says. "Go with them."

The sentry's so cold and calm, not even looking in Lucy's direction.

"Come on," Coutreaux barks from the hall. "Hurry up!"

Lucy can't, though: she's riveted by Sina's methodical passage around the kitchen table and out the open doors. Her boots sink into the snowdrifts, making her gait choppy and labored.

"*Tajjakah!*" she shouts. "*Tajjakah! Eyaman-eh!*"

Hansel sways. The snow blows horizontal in the howling wind. He lifts a hand, touches His mouth uncertainly, then peers at His fingers.

Sina walks forward. "*TAJJAKAH! TAJJAKAH!*"

Hansel turns His head, and even at this distance, Lucy feels the sick lurch from looking upon the void of His eyes. Then, she senses the change in the Nafikh; it happens all at once, with the violence of a bursting dam.

"Get back!" Sina screams, running at her. "Back, back, back!"

A beat, another, and Hansel lifts Himself to His full height, arms thrust outward. A brilliant light breaks through the whirling snow, emanating from His form. Lucy cries out, the light sharp as splinters in her eyes. She runs blindly, slams into a wall, turns, runs. There's a weird, hollow thump inside her chest, and then everything goes black.

Then consciousness: *What?*

Fire, her mind informs the panicked, stunned self lying on the floor.

Fire!

Her eyes open to see the kitchen far down the hallway engulfed by flames pouring towards her, the heat searing her face.

Sina: she was coming from there, from where the fire roars. *She didn't make it. No way she could have.*

Lucy's limbs explode to life. She scrambles backwards, gets to her feet after a few stumbling attempts. Starts to run. Bursts into a huge room, a parlor with lounge chairs and books. It is bright as day in here, the room encircled by a dancing carousel of flames. She cries out, throwing her hands up over her face. Backs away, stumbles over something.

A body. One of the Canadian servs. The shorter one with the red freckles.

The second she touches him, she feels that awful weight of something dead. Unmoving. Now she registers the pool of blood beneath his head. The ceiling, she understands numbly, slowly turning her gaze upwards. This part of the ceiling collapsed.

Snow's falling on her face, into her mouth. She backs away into the corner. Feels the immense pressure of heat all around. Sweat pours into her eyes, blurring her vision. The flames light up the posh mahogany, green velvet, paintings in ponderous, gilded frames. The light is so brilliant that color's stripping out of everything, it's like looking at an overexposed photograph. *Jump out the window!* she cries to herself, but the fire is outside, too: it's in the snow. Or, it's displaced the snow. The snow is gone, it's just fire outside. *Not fire,* a distant part of herself corrects. *Nafikh-fire.* And it's everywhere inside, too, spreading slowly, almost languidly, through the crackling flames it has ignited.

There is nowhere to go. All ways blocked off. Her eyes stream tears, blinded by the brightness.

I'm going to die.

"Hey! You!"

She turns in place. Through the flames she catches sight of a shadowy figure. She blinks, rubbing her eyes. It's Coutreaux, far away across the room. His arm pumps direction, "That way! Jump!"

Her legs obey, dragging her in the direction he's indicating. A fiery obstacle lies across her path. She clambers over it, failing to jump. He's on her in a heartbeat, spinning her around as he tears her burning coat off one arm then the other, and tosses it aside. Then he shoves her along, towards an archway framed by burgundy drapes tied back with gold cords. Flames lazily snake their way up the material, creating a halo of light around them as they pass through. She wonders if it, the Nafikh-fire, can tell it's elsewhere, if it is alive in its own way, because it almost seems like it's tasting the drapes, encircling, dancing, and finally obliterating.

She blinks, trying to focus. Her eyes hurt awfully. But she can see where they are: a dead end.

They're at a dead end, and there's Lefevre, slamming his shoulder again and again into a metal door, his face worked up into a twisted knot of fear and rage.

"*Tasses-toé!* Let her do it!" Coutreaux hollers.

Do what?

"Open the door!" Coutreaux screams. "Open the fucking door!"

Lefevre steps aside, bubbles of spit on his gaping lips. Lucy stares uncomprehendingly at the door.

"*Quelque chose ne tourne pas rond avec celle-là!*" Lefevre rages.

"What's wrong with you?" Coutreaux shakes her, pushes her towards the door. "Is there something wrong?"

He peers into her face, like he might detect the flaw.

"I don't know," she says. "I don't understand."

"What the fuck!" he explodes, spit flying into her face. "Just open it! You're a goddam sentry! Open the fucking door!"

"*Dépêches-toé!*" Lefevre wails, his eyes wide on the approaching fire.

"Hurry up!" Coutreaux yells. He grabs her hand, forces it onto the door handle. "Come on!"

She grips the handle and pushes. Nothing happens. There is a gentle, rumbling thunder, followed by the musical tinkle of a thousands of pieces of glass shattering. She whips around to see the flames pouring in like a curling wave through the shattered windows, rolling upwards when they strike the floor. In front of this backdrop, the two servs gaze at her in horror. Then Coutreaux's face twists up into a mask of pure panicked rage:

"*OPEN THE FUCKING DOOR!*"

Lucy screams in response, a wordless protest hurling from her deepest insides. What the fuck does he mean, he's crazy, she hates him, she's going to die. She wrenches at the door handle, throwing her whole being into the act. She's jerked back by the force of her own gesture, the massive iron door swinging outwards, the bolt snapped clean in two with a distinct metallic crack.

She stares bewildered at the stone stairs leading down, the way dimly lit from below.

"Go, go, go!"

Coutreaux pushes her in. The three of them squeeze into the narrow space. Coutreaux heaves the door closed, plunging them into pitch dark.

Noise of breathing, rustling, metal knocks.

A light switches on, and Lucy blinks into the barrel of Coutreaux's weapon, above which is the bright circle of a torch light.

"What the hell is wrong with you?" he asks. "Are you *trying* to get us killed? Do you *want* to die?"

She takes a shaky breath. "I'm new," she says.

"What do you mean?"

"I just got boosted!" Lucy screams back at him. Her body a rigid frozen explosion. She could rip his head off, one-handed. She could smash his skull into the stone like a melon.

They're wide-eyed statues. She hears Coutreaux swallowing, notes the swift shove at Lefevre, silencing him. "O.K. That's O.K. That's fine. How about you get yourself under control, and we'll figure out what to do."

"*Mais qu'est ce qu'on fait là?*" Lefevre interrupts. His voice is pitchy with anxiety. "*C'est fou, çà! Ç'est pas notre problème!*"

"*On continue,*" Coutreaux shuts him up. "We go on with the mission," he says, for Lucy's benefit. He switches the channel on his earpiece. "Gabriel Sentry, come in. Gabriel Sentry."

There is a pause filled with the noise of their breathing and the steady oppressive crush of the compressed space. Then Coutreaux rapidly describes their situation. Listens. Repeats that yes, they have the sentry called Lucy. Yes, there should be more than one entrance. They will proceed with caution. If they locate the Nafikh they will wait for backup.

"Wait. I want to speak to Gabe," Lucy says.

Coutreaux removes his headset, hands it to her. Adjusts the mic for her, his eyes brushing hers, full of wariness, mistrust.

"Gabe, are you there?"

A crackle, hissing. The connection's bad. He says, "You O.K. with those two?"

"I think so. Are you coming?"

"We'll find you soon. Hang in there."

"Sure," Lucy says, her mouth suddenly filled with dust. "O.K."

Her eyes meet Coutreaux's in the glow from the mounted torch. She feels acutely the closeness of the stone walls, no going forward or back. She removes the headset, hands it over.

He says, "You all set?"

"*C'est terrible, ça,*" Lefevre mutters, pale with anxiety. He gestures at Lucy. "*Elle va toute fucker!*"

Lucy goes rigid, her muscles suddenly bunched, ready to explode. "You shut the hell up, you understand?"

Lefevre is amazed. "*Elle est folle!* You are crazy!" he adds, enunciating each word with his forefinger rolling at his temple.

Coutreaux takes one step, blocking her. "Settle down," he tells Lucy, lowering the machine gun a few inches, just enough to make his point. She meets his eyes dead-on. Weirdly, she's unafraid.

Because in her mind's eye: the single motion of plucking the weapon from his hands and crushing his skull with it. There's truth there, stark as her own feet rooted to the ground. Though she's not sure how, exactly. Just knows she can.

"*Ça suffit,*" Coutreaux says over his shoulder. Then, to Lucy, "Protocol is we team up, and we stick to it. You're the sentry, so you tell us what you want to do."

They regard one another in the shifting yellow light. She reads in his eyes a latent willingness to buck his precious protocol, if pushed a mite too far, even if it's a losing proposition.

She says, "The Nafikh is being held somewhere down below. We have to try and find Her."

"Then that's what we do," he nods. "*Enweille,*" he tells Lefevre.

They set forth down the stone stairs, Lucy in the rear. She falls back, filled with distaste at their stench of sweat. The space is suffocatingly close, the ceiling so low she has to hunch her shoulders. One step, then another, and in the oppressive close passage, she becomes aware that her knee is throbbing and swollen, her whole body's battered into a limping, trembling wreck. And yet, there's a tense readiness in her muscles, the knowing that if need be, she could smash her way through another iron door. And another.

It's the boost. What she's been through is about as bad as the worst Service—and she hasn't slept in what, two, three days now? And yet she's still going. Her hand unconsciously squeezes into a fist, recalling the door handle, the *crrack!* of snapped metal reverberating through her flesh. It was so easy.

She wouldn't mind trying that again.

The light from below brightens, and they arrive in an equally narrow tunnel lit with buzzing fluorescent bulbs hung at intervals on the hewn stone wall. The tunnel curves to the right, the way not visible. It's so quiet down here, one would never know the surface was ablaze with fire and violence. The ceiling drips moisture, increasing her acute sensation of the weight above them.

Coutreaux nods at the tunnel ahead. "Can you hear anything?"

Lucy shoulders by to get ahead. The heat coming off them sends prickles of discomfort across her back. She listens. Beyond the silence, there's a faint drumming shudder, steady and rhythmic, what she felt upstairs. There's something else, too. An odor, very acrid, singeing her tongue with bitter. She licks her lips.

"I hear some kind of motor."

"Like a generator?"

"Maybe," she says. "There's the smell of something burning, too."

There is a pause, the possibility sinking in that Nafikh-fire is making its way down the tunnel towards them.

"We can't wait here for backup," Coutreaux says at last. "No point. Move on."

"He should stay," Lucy interrupts, nodding at Lefevre. "Keep checking upstairs for the fire dying out. In case they don't find the other entrance."

"That leaves you and me against a Nafikh," Coutreaux shakes his head.

"We aren't against Her."

"Will She know the difference?"

"She should, with me here."

"But you don't know for sure."

"If She doesn't, it won't matter that we have one extra."

He rubs his jaw, and the gesture stabs her with recognition: Bedrosian, a thousand years ago, it feels like. "You make a good point. Lefevre, *reste là*."

Lefevre mutters something unhappy. He backs a few paces, takes up position at the foot of the stairs.

They keep moving forward, and soon Lefevre falls out of sight. The walls run with moisture; Lucy's throat tightens, she can't shake the immense weight of earth and rock above, all of which could bury them in an instant. She loathes the idea of continuing deeper into that dank, claustrophobic darkness.

She reminds herself that Theo wouldn't stand for a poorly made tunnel.

The thud of the generator gradually becomes audible to Coutreaux, as does the burning smell, which is so strong now it causes her to swallow repeatedly, her tongue thick with the acrid taste. Coutreaux twists in place, touching his nose, gesturing *What?* She mimes that she doesn't know. But it's not far now: she can feel the heat inside her flaring up, her whole body at the ready. The lights flicker on and off farther ahead, popping and buzzing as if they're about to bust. Her tension causes her to sweat profusely into her eyes, down her sides.

Coutreaux halts and points: up ahead on the left is a door, iron like the one above. Just beyond, Lucy is aghast to see a wall of earth. The tunnel dead-ends. There's no way out but back.

Coutreaux edges close, whispers, "If there's another exit, it's through there. My guess is there's got to be. Elander anticipated the possibility of being found. He was ready upstairs, he's got to be ready down here."

"So we should wait for Gabriel?" She reads a mounting frustration in his expression, so she says, "If you think we should go in, fine."

"That's your call."

He's really nervous, she can see it in the twitch in his jaw, the tautness around those sharp blue eyes. His whole body is a tight, hard effort not to let on.

"Let's go in," Lucy says. "I'll deal with Dara-Lin. You take care of whatever else is going on."

He looks around, as if someone might pop out to lend advice. Then he sucks in his breath, exhales hard. "O.K. Let's do it. If there's another exit, take Her out that way."

They look at each other and nod.

They move forward.

Lucy reaches out to touch the door's surface. It is warm. The thudding from within is loud and steady. Coutreaux edges around to the other side of the doorframe. Their eyes meet. He gives a slight nod. She seizes the door handle, wrenches it with one massive effort. The metal cracks, the noise ringing in her ears, and she swings the door wide. Instantly, Coutreaux steps into the doorway, gun cocked at his shoulder.

"Jesus," she hears him whisper.

She peeks around him, then edges by.

The smell in here is sickeningly sweet, like a thick perfume. Smoke clouds the air, stings her eyes so she can hardly see. The room is a mess of large metallic shapes, glass surfaces, white walls. It is huge, she can tell that much. She can hear trickling water, rustling noises, and now breaths, harsh and ragged. All beneath the steady hollow thumping.

At last, she registers what Coutreaux saw at once: up ahead a figure, seated in a chair. He isn't getting up, which seems odd. The breathing is coming from him.

"Is that you, Lucy?"

Her heart pounds hard, fear spiraling up inside. "Theo?"

"I didn't expect to see *you* again," he says, each syllable exhaled with a crackling, hissing noise.

She edges forward, Coutreaux at her side with the gun to his shoulder, turning this way and that. Her hands crush themselves into fists, ready to fight with all her strength. But Theo still doesn't get up. Every step she takes, she gains courage for the next, because he doesn't react. There's a glass domed case behind him. Inside, she makes out a huge, pale, muscled body. It is writhing steadily, sinuously, like a worm. Her eyes travel, searching, until she finds Dara-Lin's face.

Her breath catches: the Nafikh's expression is one of absolute terror, eyes popping wide, teeth bared like a dog.

The head turns, slightly, the Nafikh drawn to Her sentry. The despair seeping from Her is mind-numbing, it sucks the strength right out of Lucy's limbs. It's unbearable, unthinkable. The Nafikh mouths words that Lucy doesn't understand. But she feels their meaning in the deepest parts of her bones: *Help*.

"Well, well. You're different," Theo utters through gritted teeth.

She's been seeing him for the past several moments, but only now the full horror begins to seep in. His face is a purpled, hideously swollen parody of itself, pouring with sweat and, weirdly, smoke. A thick tube leads into his chest, the entry wound wrapped in bandages and surgical tape with a tidy precision that seems ridiculous given how the patient is actually faring. He looks dead. Like a bloated, discolored, seeping corpse, but he's not aware, she understands. He doesn't know he's on fire. The sweet stench is of his flesh burning from the inside out. The smoke slips languidly from beneath the bandages, from his ears, from his eyes, from under his nails, from his limp penis and his belly button. It seeps from his skin itself. More in some places than others, where pores have opened up into holes, their edges crimping, blackening.

He is the source of the tremendous heat, pumping in waves off the bloated body. He grips the chair arms with such ferocity his veins pop from his skin, and his neck is corded with strain.

"It hurts," he hisses. "I knew it would."

He seems to want to continue but can't. His dark eyes fix on her, the whites bloodshot, tears streaming down his purpled cheeks.

"Theo," Lucy says. It's a miracle she can speak at all. "I don't think it's working."

His mouth twists into a snarling grin. "You'd better run, Lucy."

He seems to be powering himself up for some kind of attack. But all he manages is to lean forward an inch or so, his whole body shaking so hard his hands slip off the chair arms. They clutch their way back, seize the wood again.

"When it's done," he hisses and spits, "I will be restored."

For a second, she believes him. She does. Maybe because he's so convinced. Because how can he possibly have been wrong, after all these years.

But he is.

We were never Nafikh.

The words pile up in her mouth unspoken. What's the sense in telling him? He's as good as dead. Her throat constricts—that she can feel that pathetic, daughterly sadness for him, even after all he's done, it's unbearable—

"Hey," Coutreaux barks. "Come here."

She drags her gaze away. He's over on the right side of the room, gun angled down at someone slumped on the floor against a lab bench, splayed legs ending in shiny black dress shoes.

It's a person, not a serv. Dark Indian guy with black hair and a long, bony body slack in a lab coat, gray suit underneath. His shirtsleeve is rolled up high. Lucy notes the needle on the floor beside him, next to some empty vials. She nudges his chin off his chest. His dark eyes look dulled, confused. "Who are you?" she demands.

His mouth moves, but all he emits is a strangled noise.

She pries at his hands, which are clutched as if in prayer at his chest, protecting something. His fingers loosen without much resistance. She extracts a tiny vial. She holds it up, squinting. Detects the wavering, silvery mist.

"You took some grabs?" she asks in amazement.

"It's my reward," the man whispers.

"For what? For helping him? What's your name?"

"Doctor Raminder Singh." He gazes at her sadly. "He said I could live forever."

"He lied. People can't absorb this," she holds up the vial. "How do I get the Nafikh out of there?"

"You can't."

"Why not?"

His shoulders lift a little. "It wasn't designed that way."

"So this was the plan?" Lucy says, pointing at Theo's smoldering form. "No? So what's gone wrong?"

His gaze travels sideways, trying to see, but the lab bench blocks his view. "The alien didn't respond to the sedatives. She is resisting. But I don't think it would have worked," he mumbles. "As soon as I realized, I told him, again and again. He wouldn't listen."

"Realized what?"

"The substance animating Her is not the same as the Source. It's similar, but not the same. I believe the Source is a derivative element, like a little tendril," he explains, his fingers opening and spreading, miming shoots.

Coutreaux loses his patience. "Go on, get up," he commands, prodding him with his boot. "Tell her what to do!"

Raminder Singh slumps, falls over. He lies at their feet in his slick suit and shiny shoes. His mouth hangs open, bloodshot eyes fixed on the nothing zone.

Lucy closes her hand around the vial, then tucks it into her jeans pocket. "Do you see an exit?"

Coutreaux points across the room. They round the lab bench. She sees the source of the trickling sound: a small, limpid pool, beyond it a path leading to another iron door, this one hinged into the rock face. They're in a cavern, which Theo remodeled into a lab. God knows how much time and money this whole setup consumed, never mind orchestrating kidnapping a Nafikh. No wonder Theo wouldn't listen to Singh, when it turned out to be all for naught.

She says, "Take him. I'll get the Nafikh."

"How?"

She turns back, bracing herself. The Nafikh has not broken Her terrible stare, and the feeling is of being bowled over by a tide, so potent Lucy's balance shifts, she sways like a drunk, overwhelmed by emotion. Dara-Lin stares and stares, pulling Lucy into the pit of Her misery. Her splendid, muscular body squirms against the torture being inflicted upon Her. She is helpless, buckled down tight with leather straps. Tubing protrudes from Her chest, held in place by bandages and tape soaked with blood. The tubing loops out of the chamber, delivering its yield directly into the bloated, smoking body outside.

"How?" Coutreaux repeats in a hiss. "It looks like She'll just bleed to death."

"You just get him out of here," Lucy snaps. "Get Gabriel."

He seems a little taken aback. Maybe relieved. Lucy returns to confront the bloated, stinking mess that is Theo. His face works away as soon as he glimpses her; an attempt at a smile.

"You got a boost," he rasps. "Aren't you special."

"Fuck you, Theo. How do I get Her out?"

He clamps his lips, grinning.

"Do you know what's going on, because of you? Do you know how many people got killed?"

"You think I give a shit about *people*?"

"Then what about Julian, or Ernesto? Jesus, how *could* you?"

A scratching sound carves its way into Lucy's hearing: the Nafikh's nails, clawing at the glass. The great, devouring eyes filled with pain.

"It's just like your dream, isn't it," Theo wheedles, and his body shakes a little with his effort to chuckle. "This should make you happy, Lucy."

Her most cherished dream: to stand tall over a Nafikh, watch It wail in terror. But it's nothing like she ever imagined. She's not happy. She's physically ill with grief, she can't bear the Nafikh's suffering. *Maybe it's the boost, all those crazy feelings,* she thinks desperately. She can't tell. All she knows is, she can't bear it.

"Did you do that to the arrivals?" Lucy blurts, pointing. "Is that what you did? Because that's hurting Her, Theo. You said it didn't hurt. You *swore!*"

His eyes swivel in confusion and alarm. "Of course not to them," he wheezes. "I'm not a monster."

Lucy drags her eyes away, plunges straight back into the Nafikh's silent yowl. Her huge black eyes are fringed with white lashes, the incongruity mesmerizing. They're like cosmic kids on a bungee jump, someone said once. They want to see what it feels like, to be scared to die.

Except now, it could really happen. It's the first time Lucy's witnessed any sign of self-consciousness in a Nafikh. All she's ever experienced with Them is detached, remote violence, need, curiosity. She's never seen Them in any kind of danger. This Nafikh conveys a terror that goes far beyond anything Lucy's ever felt. She's always been scared of dying, of course she has. But she's also always known it will come. Dara-Lin, She never once imagined it could truly happen. She never once conceived that sometimes, the bungee cord snaps.

The Nafikh's face contorts, mouth wrenched wide in a silent scream.

Or no: She *is* screaming, it's just muffled.

Lucy turns back. "Theo, just tell me how to get Her out!"

"You should stay with me," he suggests, quivering, leaking putrid smoke.

Well, that she didn't expect. He genuinely thinks he's making an appealing offer. He shakes and bobbles about in the chair, peering at her suggestively from under his burnt brows.

"You're awful," she whispers. "You're sick and crazy."

"Go to hell, Lucy," he retches. "She's dying. You'll be next."

She turns away, unable to stand looking at him any longer. The Nafikh is weakening. Her writhing is slower, more labored. *There is no way to save Her.*

She can't help it, she imagines bolting out the door, reporting the Nafikh died, she couldn't save Her. Who's to know what will happen? The other Nafikh freaking out about Dara-Lin could get bored with Their own distress, They could give up and leave. Things don't develop one from another with Them. There's no pattern, no predicting what Nafikh will do: it's rule number one. Why should Lucy help Her, when in any other circumstance, Dara-Lin could just as easily strangle her as feed her a strawberry?

They've terrorized her for years, and here she is, conflicted about getting the revenge she's always dreamed of. It's enough to make her scream laughing.

"What are you doing?" Theo cries, craning to look over his shoulder. "No!"

Her hands hover over the bewildering array of switches and lights on the chamber panel. She starts flipping switches. The Nafikh stiffens, mouth agape. Lucy's done something wrong, something worse. It's like the Nafikh is suffocating. Lucy can see blue tingeing the white cheeks, the lips.

Fuck!

She grips the edges of the clamped bubble, pulls. Pulls harder. Nothing happens. The Nafikh's eyes start to roll back, Her body arches upwards.

Lucy channels all her might into pulling. She can feel the veins in her head popping, and her vision starts to swim, darken. Then there is a faint yielding sensation in the metal. She pulls harder.

The chamber explodes open, the top flying through space to shatter on the floor.

The Nafikh's heat pours out like flames. Lucy seizes the leather restraints and rips them apart, one by one. Dara-Lin's arm swings out, smashing into Lucy's jaw, the blow so feeble that Lucy merely stumbles a little. The Nafikh tries to sit up, but Her body crumples, shaking. Her hands fumble at the tube protruding from Her chest.

"*Badel,*" Lucy cries, seizing the clawing hands. *Wait.* Dara-Lin does not resist, or maybe She isn't strong enough to. "If you pull it out, it could kill you! Do you understand?"

The Nafikh stops all movement, panting, staring up at her. She seems to be waiting. But Lucy doesn't have some alternative plan. She stares in mute dismay at the tube, the bandages seeping frothy blood.

"I don't know what to do," she whispers, her hands pulling back, hanging helplessly in the air. "I'm sorry."

The Nafikh stares at the ceiling. For a short time, there is only the sound of Her breaths, and of Theo gurgling and moaning, slumped in his chair.

Then Dara-Lin turns onto Her side, eases Herself into a sitting position. She gazes down at the monstrosity protruding from Her body. Her face is angular and hard-planed, like a perfect sculpture, the smooth skin streaked with pale rivulets of tears through smeared blood and sweat. Slowly, She lifts Her chin. Her eyes are huge pools of black, jarring contrast to the white skin and hair She chose for Her trip to Earth. Lucy cringes, backing away.

"*Aysha arranish,*" the Nafikh tells her. "*Alee.*"

Stunned, Lucy ceases all movement, the one word she knows drifting into her like a feather, settling, the final touch of it a searing hurt. How many times she said the same. How many times.

Dara-Lin looks down at Her chest, closes Her massive hand around the tube, and yanks.

Blood spurts forth, soaking the bandages. The tubing snakes and clatters on the stone floor. In one motion, Dara-Lin swings Herself off the chamber bed and stands up. She towers over Lucy, swaying in place, Her expression blank with surprise at Her continued weakness, then hardening with determination.

Theo falls out of his chair with a thump. He inches along the floor, a smoking heap of bloated meat, emitting soft moans.

Dara-Lin turns. She approaches Theo, peering down at him. He's positioned so Lucy can see his face, the slanted eyes so swollen they are slits seeping smoke, his mouth sagged open. He's already dead, she thinks, but then he moans again.

Dara-Lin bends down and grasps him by the neck. She lifts him into the air. His legs hang limp, dripping blood and piss.

"Angh," he moans.

The Nafikh's body tenses, all the muscles in Her back rippling in waves. Then She flings him aside. He whirls through the air, smashes into the wall with a crunch, and thumps to the floor.

Silence.

Lucy looks away, gulping bile.

"*Annyeh tajjak,*" the Nafikh pants.

"*Osh een,*" Lucy manages to say. *Not here.* "*Osh tajjak een.* Outside," she points at the ceiling.

This is received with tightened mouth, flared nostrils. The black eyes swirl with what Lucy reads as mounting rage. The mouth hangs open, saliva dripping down Her chin.

This, Lucy recognizes.

She stands taller, hardening herself. "Please, this way," she says firmly. She indicates the path beyond the shallow water.

The Nafikh approaches. Her hand lifts, and Lucy takes it, unconsciously mimicking the actions she has seen sentries perform during Service.

She leads Her through the shallow pool and onto the rocky path on the other side. The door stands open, Coutreaux already having gone this way. The tunnel ahead is pitch black, and she suffers a moment of panic, only to discover, utterly absurdly, a tidy row of flashlights on a nearby ledge. She takes one and lights it. They enter the tunnel, which is broader and higher, not man-made, but a twisting, turning passage over rock piles that requires some effort and climbing. She keeps checking on the Nafikh, whose labored breathing sounds awful. Blood streams out from the hole in Her chest, sweat forms a sheen across Her skin. Despite Her wounds, She carries on steadily, making Her way over the obstacles. The air grows colder, blowing hard and fresh and damp, and it tastes delicious, dizzying. At last, they emerge into a stand of trees. No wonder Gabriel and the rest didn't find this entrance. The farm lies in the distance across a snowy field, a cluster of buildings on fire. She catches sight of a lumpy shape steadily moving across the field in that direction: Coutreaux, with the doctor on his back.

The trees creak in the wind, shedding clouds of snow that sprinkle needles onto her upturned face.

"*Annyeh tajjak,*" the Nafikh whispers.

Every breath is massive, Her whole body lifting to support the effort.

"*Tajjakah,*" Lucy says. "*Aji, tajjakah.*"

Dara-Lin's eyes pass over her, barely seeing. She starts to lift Her arms, and Lucy turns and runs in the only direction that might save her, back down below.

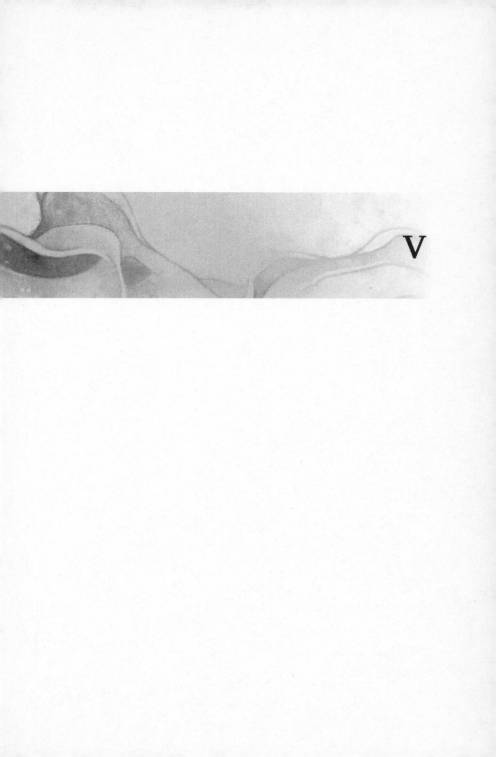

V

LUCY BECOMES AWARE FIRST of a soft ticking sound. Her eyes flutter, still closed. She feels herself gradually being dragged from the deep heaviness of sleep. There's the pull of a blanket against her legs. The ticking sound. Slowly, her eyes drag open, focus through the dim light. She's in a bed. The ticking is from a clock on the bedside table. It reads 12:17.

Memory flits up through the mud: someone bending over her, the prick of a needle. Go to sleep now. The noise of her own weeping, from exhaustion. Or, was there an argument? She thinks there might have been. Gabriel was there.

The events come back slowly, in pieces. The roaring flames, the walls tearing apart like paper. The dark, damp tunnel, and what lay behind the iron door.

She went back into the lab and waited there. She sat for ages against the rock wall hugging her knees, staring at a spot between her boots so as not to look at Theo's bloated corpse. Then Gabriel came.

What did they fight about?

She sits up slowly, brings her bare feet to the floor. Someone must have removed her boots and socks. Or maybe she did. Her clothes feel grimy, damp with sweat. She's sore all over, especially her right side. She pushes up her shirt, finds her skin dark with bruises, as if she was kicked around by a Nafikh.

But it wasn't one of Them. It was Gabriel. Flashes of herself screaming, beating on him. They were in the lab down below. Where he found her.

After that, everything goes black, and now this.

She looks around. Plywood walls, bare wood door, like an unfinished project. It's one of those rooms in the warehouse. She stands up with some effort, makes her way around the bed to the rectangular cutout overlooking the Gate. She's one level up. All is quiet, the space dim as a tomb. A sentry across the way sits on a scaffold, smoking. Some towels hang from the rail next to him. Murmurs carry from here and there, someone coughs. She can see Eric's office down to the right. The lights are on.

She backs away, sinks onto the bed, numbed by the possibility that this is where she'll have to live from now on. It can't be. She's going to wake up and discover herself in bed at home, and Eva will be downstairs with the radio blaring, whipping up omelets. She was supposed to be bought out. It was supposed to be over.

It's not real. It can't be real.

But it is. She's here, at the Gate, and she's been boosted. There's a strange, heavy potency deep in her body, as if she could kick down the wall with one blow. It's all she can do not to give in, not to rage against the walls, the shitty metal bedframe, the bare floor.

She wonders if Bedrosian's gotten his money back. He's probably leafing through Alaskan cruise brochures, and meanwhile, she's stuck in this box of a room, staring down the bleak reality of her future.

He'd better still do Eva's loan like he promised.

A memory comes floating up out of the mess in her head. She digs inside her pocket, finds it. The tiny ampule, amazingly, is unbroken, filled with shimmering mist, sparks glinting within.

She balances it on her palm: it weighs nothing. She wonders if it's the last one, or if a larger stash was found. Probably not. There was something about the way the doctor was holding it, like it was the most precious thing in the world.

The last of Theo's grabs, the last spark of the last arrival to end up in his hands.

Not necessarily him.

But it's so small, so fragile and weightless, calling up his slender shivering frame, his feet going blue. Her throat thickens up inside. It's over now. It's all over, and she just needs to get the hell out of this claustrophobic room, find out what she's meant to do next.

She tucks the ampule back into her pocket. She listens at the door, nervous of stepping out, running into someone. There are voices, but not close. Murmurs, footsteps, the scrape of chair legs. She turns the doorknob, trying to be as quiet as possible. Pulls it open just a crack. The corridor is empty. Gray light filters in through the tall windows, and she stares up at the sky with a feeling of amazement. She believed, in those last moments, that she was going to die: she ran so hard, plunging over the rocky terrain towards the black hole of the tunnel. She unconsciously reaches for her shoulder, recalling how she slammed into the rock wall, the flashlight lost, the way pitch black. How the fire rolled in behind her.

And now, the ordinary gray sky through dirty windowpanes, the silence and the calm.

"Hey," someone says, and she starts.

A sentry's leaning in a doorway down the hall, arms crossed. Lucy approaches, recognizing her from past Services. Em, her name is. She's dark black with close-cropped hair, bright green eyes. A ragged AC/DC tee shirt hangs over her sweatpants. An image comes: Good Harbor Beach, the moon hanging low over the bay. Lucy on her knees, Em guiding the Nafikh away across the sand.

"You're Lucy," Em states.

"Yes." Lucy's voice comes out a dry crackle. She tries to swallow spit, clears her throat. "I know you. You're Em."

"Yeah, that's right." Em lifts her chin, eyeing her. "Look. Even if you got Dara-Lin out, there's a lot here that are pissed you got a boost after all you did. And that you came back, but Sina didn't. You should know that, up front."

Lucy flinches at this speech, delivered like something set down hard between them. She curbs the urge to spit out some retort. They have a right to be angry. She was supposed to be dumped on the sets, not be here with them. She says, "I understand."

Em acknowledges this with a nod, closing the topic. "How'd you end up working for a prick like Theo Elander, anyway?"

"Who isn't a prick, that servs get to work for?"

"Fair enough. Is it true you grew up with people?"

"Yes."

"That is some crazy shit."

"Yeah."

"All right, then," Em says, when Lucy offers up nothing more. "You should get cleaned up. Come on."

Em heads off down the corridor, giving Lucy no choice but to follow. She hears music, the slap of cards, low laughs coming from the open doors ahead. She's conscious of other sentries watching her go by, and she holds herself tall, nodding casual greeting and ignoring the bland hostility in their expressions. Maybe she deserves some of it, fine. But she can't help resenting that her rescue of Dara-Lin seems to have no value.

They come to the shower room. Six stalls in a row, sinks opposite, bathroom stalls adjoining. Gray tile walls, unframed mirrors. Em asks her size and digs around in a closet. She comes up with a change of clothes, along with a folded towel and a bottle of combo soap and shampoo.

Lucy takes what's offered, saying thank you. Em leaves without reply. The shower is a long, slow tamping down of hurt and anger, her head bent under the stream, hands splayed on the tile wall. *It is how it is,* she finds herself thinking, over and over. It's a serv truism she always found pitiful and cowardly, but it's coming in handy right now, as a means of tolerating the magnitude of where she has landed.

She is going to be here for a long, long time. Way longer than she can grasp, yet. She needs to lay low, take stock, not get on anyone's nerves.

She dries off and changes into the tee shirt and sweats Em gave her. They don't fit too badly. She wipes the steam off the mirror. There's something different in the reflection staring back. It's unsettling, subtle. She turns this way and that. She looks harder, is the only way she can describe it, even in her face. Hard, and strong.

She pictures herself arriving at the house, Eva coming to greet her. *She'll see something's different right away.* What the hell is she going to say, now? That she got a new job? She'll be canceling visits last-minute and missing holidays, the same as she always did, and they'll assume the worst.

The door opens and someone comes in. A serv, a guy. "Hey," he says, a little embarrassed.

"Hey," she replies.

He ducks into the bathroom area. She gathers up her towel and dirty clothes and steps out. Gabriel is a little way down the hall, in conversation with Em. He sees her. "How're you feeling?" he asks.

"O.K."

Em nudges him goodbye, enters her room and closes the door. Gabriel comes up to her. "She told me what she said. Everyone's still pretty raw, Lucy. It's only been a few days."

"A few days—?"

"You've been out since Saturday night. It's Tuesday. I kept you dosed," he explains, noting her confusion. "You weren't in any shape to ride out adjustment. Sorry about that, by the way," he gestures.

She realizes she's holding her injured side, drops her hand. Three days lying there, for anyone to see. Theo Elander's cohort, the one that grew up with people. "What happened, anyway?"

"By the time I got to you, you weren't very reasonable, is all. It was the boost. Too much, too fast. You went a little wacko."

"I don't remember."

"It's normal."

She hesitates. "If everyone's so pissed—the Qadir were going to stick me on the sets, before. What will they do to me now?"

"Nothing. Unless you refuse to do your duty and cock things up for the rest of us, you're here to stay."

"Just like that?"

"The Gate can't let a sentry go to waste, even in good times. As things stand, we lost Sina, and we've got five out due to injuries. That means everyone on back-to-backs till the end of the season, yourself included."

"No wonder they hate me."

"Yeah. It also means you're bunking here for now. We'll set you up in one of the rooms in town when things get back to normal. After that you'll be on rotation. Come on, Eric's waiting."

A room in town: *Thank you, thank you.*

She falls into step. "I'm sorry about Sina."

He stiffens a little, shakes his head like it's not something to discuss. She feels like a fool for bringing it up. She didn't even know Sina, she's got no right. Sina came back for her, and Lucy felt moved by that, but after all, she was just doing her duty.

She clutches the lump of her dirty clothes and wet towel tight to her chest, wondering how she's supposed to fit into this place where she isn't wanted and doesn't belong. Then again, she's never really belonged anywhere, she reminds herself, the voice in her head harsh, drumming at her. Julian said as much, all those years ago. The thought of him brings a sharp lurch of hurt. And Ernesto. They'd fall over laughing to see this, of all things, Lucy-goosie a sentry.

At least Gabriel doesn't seem to share everyone else's feelings towards her. Or, he's just being more professional, is all.

"Drop all that here," he says, pointing to an industrial-sized hamper at the end of the hall.

She obeys. "Will I get my clothes back?"

"Yeah."

She ignores his amusement. Those jeans and the gray sweater are her favorites, and right now, they feel like all she's got. He leads her through an empty room to a landing on the scaffolding, points her down the narrow metal stairs. They come to the main floor. The Gate's iron walls have a dull, mottled shine. The floor all around the sealed exit is charred, and there is a faint burnt smell hanging in the air.

"It's so quiet," she says.

"There've been no Nafikh since Dara-Lin blew," he replies, coming to her side. "They all took off the minute She was out. The blows set off a few more fires, but since then, it's been dead. Which is a good thing, as we're still reeling."

His words fill her with shame she can't help. "I really didn't know anything about Theo's plans, Gabe. I swear."

He softens a little, looking at her. "It'll just take time. Keep your head down, and don't mouth off."

"I won't."

He leads her to Eric's office across the way. The door stands open. Most of the desks are unoccupied. Eric waves them over, and they sit down. He proceeds to ask Lucy about every detail of the mission, from when she first fell out of the van to the parts she can't remember, when Gabriel found her. He types as she talks. Every sentry has to file a report when there's an incident, he explains.

Incident: now there's a joke.

He pushes his glasses up his nose. "Let's go back over the part where you found Dara-Lin."

She's hungry, and she's getting frustrated with his need for repetition. Gabriel's chewing on a pen, chair tilted back against the wall. "This is important," he reminds her. "Keep going," he tells Eric, who obediently squints at the screen.

He says, "You told the soldier Coutreaux to go on without you."

"Yes, like I already said."

"To take the dead doctor out."

"I didn't know he was dead. I thought he might make it, if he got some help."

"And you took it upon yourself to remain on your own, with the Nafikh."

"I didn't take anything upon myself. I told you, I had no fucking idea what I was doing."

There is a pause. Eric twists a little in his chair to glance questioningly at Gabriel, who says, "Yeah, fix it up."

Eric looks a little relieved. "I can't leave that in," he tells Lucy.

"Why?"

"As soon as the First fritzes, there'll be a new Qadir coming. The Second will be raked over the coals. The last thing she needs is to be accused of sending in a sentry that, quote, had no fucking idea what I was doing, unquote."

He stares at her with his magnified, worried eyes, waiting. She recalls the Second bowing before Hansel, unable to lift a finger lest she be killed, condemning to death everyone under her care. That a new Qadir can waltz in and put her under threat all over again brings an unexpected burst of loyalty.

She says, "I took it upon myself because I knew I'd have no trouble extricating the Nafikh on my own, which I then proceeded to do."

"That sounds good," Gabriel says, chewing on the pen.

Eric starts typing.

AFTER ERIC'S GONE OFF to deliver the report, Gabriel brings her upstairs to the north side of the building, where there's a kitchen and a dining room consisting of four long tables and benches in rows. A couple of servs are tasked with keeping the kitchen stocked, he explains, and if she wants something special she'll have to dig up the funds to get it, because what she sees is what she gets. It pretty much looks like her own kitchen, is her reply, and she's got no need of anything fancy. He helps her get a sandwich together, make a pot of coffee.

Lucy sets her tray down and slides onto the bench. There are two other sentries at another table, minding their business. It's late afternoon. The view from up here is beautiful: the river is dark and choppy under a sky swept with white fronds. A gray tanker pulled by a tugboat moves ponderously towards Boston Harbor in the distance. She's got to call Eva, let her know she's O.K. The idea that they're fearing her dead while she sits here with a sandwich, it twists all sorts of anxiety and sorrow up in a knot that might choke her. But she has no phone, and nothing yet to say that will make sense.

Gabriel drags the bench out, sits down across from her with a mug of coffee. He talks while she eats. The Second won't send for Lucy for a while, he tells her. She's attending the First while he fritzes. He's been hanging on by a thread, for all their sakes, eking out one more breath at a time so they have a chance to clean up the mess. When the new Qadir arrives, the system's got to be tight and orderly so it's just a matter of pressing the newbie in the right direction. What they desperately need right now is sentries. Normally, they'd borrow some from Montreal or Q.C., but they're already too deep in debt. They'll scrape through as they are, cross their fingers for a boost or two, and regroup over summer. Spring, summer, and fall are when the Gate makes money for the upcoming season, he explains. "Don't think we lie around doing nothing when the season's over," he warns.

She sets down her sandwich, only a few bites in, but her stomach's churning queasily. "What do you do, then?"

"There's the car rental, the imports, and a few other businesses in town you'll learn about. If need be, we put ourselves up for loan, too, because that's quick solid income. This year, obviously, none of that. You'll also get assigned to some bunks. You make sure they stay running smoothly and the cuts come in on time. In general, you get one day off a week, and one week's vacation a year, but that's contingent on numbers in the ranks, whether we're in the black, and so on. What's wrong?"

Lucy fumbles for words. "I just—I guess I thought you all had it easier."

"We do. We don't go hungry, we hardly get punched around. We never get violated. Should I go on?"

She flushes. "I didn't mean it that way. I didn't realize what you do, is all."

"I know," he says, more patiently. "This side of the fence is a whole other world, Lucy. You have to see things differently," he taps his temple, looking at her from under his brows. "We've got only one job, and it's to prevent the shit from hitting the fan the way it just did. To keep all of us safe, and to keep people safe, too. How do we accomplish this? Money. The happier we can keep the Nafikh, the easier things go. It's that simple. The primary focus, always, is to shore up for the season. You have days off, but sometimes you won't get any, you understand? You also have to learn Nafikh, by the way. One hundred percent fluency. Eric will teach you. A couple of hours a day at least."

Lucy crumples her napkin, puts it on her empty plate. There's a tightness in her throat, like she's suffocating.

"Hey," he says. "It's a lot to take in. I know that."

A lot to take in? She could just scream. *I was getting bought out!* He just has no clue. She was headed home, she was meant to be lighting fires on the beach, baking clams with Eva over a bottle of sherry. She bites the inside of her lip, hard, willing herself back from the brink. The last thing she needs is to be labeled a pathetic whiner.

It is how it fucking is.

"How did you get boosted?" she asks. "Did you angle for it, or did it just happen?"

"I was almost at quota," he says, holding up three fingers. "It's the biggest irony. You have to be so good to get through, but then They take notice, and want to keep you on, right? You can't win. First few weeks after adjustment, I wanted to end it."

"Really?"

"The point is, every one of us has been there, you hear me? Then you wake up, you realize you have a job to do. Your mates are counting on you," he nods at the sentries across the room, "and so are the Qadir, and the servs you left behind out there when you got a boost. So you step up. Because you have to."

"O.K.," she says, unable to come up with anything more. Her mind is locking up around the image of herself still here tomorrow, the day after. That other sentries might count on her, or count her in at all.

He swills the last of his coffee. "You done with that?" he gestures at her half-eaten sandwich. He sweeps it up along with his mug, swings his legs over the bench, heads off into the kitchen. She can see him through the doorway working at the sink. He's giving her some space, she understands, because he takes an inordinate amount of time washing the few items, then drying them with a striped towel. A kind of puzzlement settles over her, watching him shake out the towel and drape it over the rack. Because this also is going to be part of her new life, this ordinary eating and cleaning and tidying up.

Along with all that is still unimaginable: being present at the Gate when the fire explodes inside. The Nafikh pouring forth into this world, screaming. And everything else.

Gabriel returns and takes his seat. "You holding up O.K.?"

"I guess. Yeah."

He cracks his knuckles, waiting.

"I have a question," she confesses. "When I was down there, trying to get Her out—it was really hard. She almost died. She—She was in so much pain."

He looks at her sideways. "Am I hearing what I'm hearing?"

"I felt bad for Her."

"It's the boost. Residual. It'll go, trust me."

Lucy looks away, chewing on her lip.

"What?"

"It's more than that. I can't stop thinking—it's like *She* cared, in some way."

He sits back, arms folded. "How so?"

"What happened was, I almost killed Her. Because I'd turned off the oxygen or something. So when I broke the glass and She got out—I was scared. I thought She'd hurt me. She saw it," Lucy insists, her voice shaking. "She *saw* I was scared. She said *Alee.*"

To her shame, her eyes suddenly bloom with tears that tumble helplessly down her cheeks. She bends her head, wiping them. Big drops fall on her legs.

"I'm sorry," she says. "I didn't mean to—I don't know what's wrong with me."

"It's the boost," Gabriel repeats patiently.

"But it can't be just that."

"You're also adjusting to how They treat you now. But Lucy, don't forget, They don't feel. They don't care. She said it, but it was just a word. A reaction to your action."

"So it meant nothing."

"In my experience, yes, it meant nothing. Yeah, you hear stories now and then, but they're bullshit. Trust me. You know it from the Stayers. They're here months. They look just like people, you wouldn't believe it. They're fucking creepy, how much They blend right in. But, when you look," he points two fingers at his eyes, shaking his head. "Same old shit. Nothing there. There's just nothing there."

Lucy slips her hands under her thighs, staring down. "It felt so real."

"They treat sentries differently. It's a big, big change from what you're used to. But any regard They seem to have for us, it's just because we're useful, see? They boost us for that reason. So if She said something, or acted one way or another, it was to maintain your usefulness. Maybe you were cracking. So She says *Alee*, to make sure you don't, so you continue to be useful. Understand?"

"But They *are* able to care. Look what They did to save Dara-Lin."

He twists his face, thinking. "O.K. How about this. Did you know that some trees can emit pheromones into the air, warning other trees about a threat, such as caterpillars?"

"Seriously?"

"Would you call the tree scared?"

Lucy shakes her head. "She was absolutely terrified."

"All right, then. An animal in a trap."

"Maybe," she concedes, deflated by his confidence. "So you don't think She understood, the way we do, what it means to die?"

"The question is, do I give a shit," he corrects, "and I don't, and soon you won't, either. You have an apartment, right?"

The abrupt change in subject takes her off guard. "Yes, in Somerville."

"You'll need to break that lease—unless you have the funds to keep it? Didn't think so. Get out of here, do what you have to do. If Nafikh visit, it'll be better you're not around anyway. Come back tomorrow. And Lucy, there's one other thing," he says, getting to his feet.

She looks up. "What?"

"Everyone here's heard you have ties out there. People, a family."

The stiffness in his tone alerts her. "It's not an issue, I swear."

"He kept calling back, you know. The one who tracked down the GPS."

Lucy is startled. "Sean? So they know I'm O.K.?"

"Eric didn't answer," Gabriel frowns, as if this should have been obvious. "He had to disconnect, get a new number. Look, you're not the first to cross the line, but this goes over and beyond having a real-person acquaintance you chat with at the market, you understand? I'm taking your word, those people, they don't know about us, and won't find out."

"They won't."

He waits, examining her for signs she's lying. Some tension in him settles. "You need to understand, for most of us, this is it," he draws a circle in the air, encompassing the room and the spaces beyond. "It's all there is. So don't go on about all that, even if you're asked, is my advice."

"I never do," she says.

"Good, then."

She gets up as he rounds the table. He puts out his hand, and she almost shakes it, then remembers, responds with the brief, strong grip she witnessed the others make.

"See you soon," he says, and strides away.

LUCY RIDES THE 111 bus with a box on her knees containing all the stuff she owns in the world: the old quilt, some pictures, the album, the laptop, the clothes that might be suitable for her new life. She left everything else for the super to find; she can just imagine his bug-eyed amazement at the slinky wardrobe she maintained for Service. The bus is crowded as it's deep into rush hour, and she holds the box tight, scrunched up against the window. Her head's full of the imploring, weepy messages Eva left on the machine, so many that the tape filled up. Lucy listened to them all, each one building on the jagged lump of guilt sitting heavy in her chest. For a time, she sat cross-legged on the floor, smoking, staring through the haze. At last, she called Eric for Bedrosian's address, then locked up and left. There are the utilities that still need to be canceled, but she can do that online, later tonight.

She gets off the bus, lugs her box uphill into the residential part of Charlestown. She wishes she'd checked the map with more care because she has to turn way too many times, unable to remember the route she plotted before leaving. By the time she figures it out, she's sweating under the heavy wool coat, and she's dragged off the charcoal-gray hat and finger gloves, clothes she found strewn on her bed before she left the Gate.

She knows she's in the right spot when she sees Bedrosian's big old sedan parked in a driveway behind a yellow Mini Cooper. She peers through the passenger-side window, sees her phone on the floormat. The door isn't locked, so she gets the phone, dumps it in the box, then picks her way up the icy sidewalk. As she climbs the steps, a young man emerges from the building. He's wheeling a road bike. He pushes open the door, grinning thanks when Lucy holds it wide for him. He flips the bike out, lifts it with one hand, jumps down the stairs with a wave. His bright energy saps her.

She checks the buzzers. He's in 5C, top floor. She walks into the dark hallway. There's no elevator. She debates leaving the box, then sighs, starts climbing. Each landing is decorated with a little bench, or a painting, or a potted plant thriving on sun streaming through the stairwell windows, the striped shadow of the fire escape railing spread across the wood floors. It is a homey, peaceful atmosphere. She imagines Bedrosian coming home every night, a big bear shambling up the steps, his head full of the horrors of his life, corpses, blood, firearms. Servs murdering serv children.

On the top landing, there's a wooden chair with the latest issue of *National Geographic* and a dead spider plant. She knocks. After a minute or so, she hears footsteps, then Bedrosian demands who it is. She answers. He unlocks the door. He looks like shit. He's in a dressing gown open over an undershirt and sweatpants, unshaven, one eye bruised and swollen.

"You made it," he says. It sounds like an accusation.

"I guess I did."

He looks her up and down, narrowing his good eye in suspicion. "You got a boost?"

She nods.

He stands aside to let her in. Ahead lies a long corridor with light wood floors. She goes forward, comes to a wide expanse of oversized leather chairs and couch, mahogany furniture, plasma TV on the wall, glass coffee table. To the right is a kitchen that's all that and more, stainless steel, granite, tile.

"Wow," she says. "Aren't you domestic."

"How'd you swing a boost?"

"It just happened."

"The money came back yesterday, with no explanation. I thought you were dead."

The way he sounds about that, she feels badly. "I'm sorry. I guess I just assumed they'd tell you."

"Huh. They don't tell me anything. What's that?" he nods at the box.

"Just some stuff from my place. I have to go back to the Gate tomorrow. So much for getting bought out."

"Yeah, well, things could have gone a whole lot worse."

Lucy could say a thing or two about that, but given his miserable condition, holds her tongue. He winces as he settles into one of the armchairs, closing his eyes briefly in silent negotiation with his pains. The side table is strewn with tissues, dirty cups, a crusty plate with what looks like the remains of a spinach dumpling on it, probably some Armenian thing. The air smells of stale sweat.

"What'd they do to you, anyway?" she asks.

"Fucked me up. They like to do that every once in a while, keep me in my place."

"That sucks."

"You're telling me."

She sets down the box. There's nowhere to sit. The couch is buried under a rumpled load of laundry, mostly bedding. The other armchair's piled with books. He gestures impatiently for her to move stuff, but she finds a spot on the floor instead, her back against the wall. He asks what happened, and the story comes out haltingly, in fragments elicited by his questions. She tells him about Eden, what Theo did to himself, and how she got Dara-Lin out. She skips over the details of waking up at the Gate and how it's left her feeling, because it's too raw, and she'd never find the right words, anyway. "And here I am," she shrugs, winding down. "I have to go back in less than twenty-four hours. It's unreal."

"You call home yet?"

She shakes her head. In response to his surprised look, she leans over, rummages in the box for the charger she packed at the apartment. He watches as she plugs in her cell phone near his chair, waits for it to kick to life. As she expected, voice mail is full, all calls from home. She hands the phone over.

He listens a few minutes, then hands it back. "Seems to me, you need to call your mother."

"And say what?" She leaves the phone to charge, returns to her spot on the floor. "It's been days. They think I'm dead. I came here because I wanted you to help with a story. But—"

"But what?"

"I'm just so fucking tired of it." She bends over her crossed legs, pushes her hands through her hair, pressing against her temples. "It's just too much."

"Can't say I know how it feels," he admits. "You'll adjust."

Adjust. She could scream. *Maybe it's the boost,* she wonders, but it isn't. This is the same old shit she's been facing for years. The lies. The apologies. Never measuring up. "I dunnow, I keep thinking, maybe it's better like this. Just let them think I'm dead."

He cocks an eyebrow. "You're kidding."

"You did the loan, right?"

"Went through yesterday. This is fucked up, Lucy. Have you considered what it'll do to her? Jesus, you know how *I* felt when I thought you were dead?"

Lucy's momentarily tongue-tied. How he felt. "I'm just trying to figure out the right thing to do."

"Huh. Well, that isn't it."

"You don't understand," she retorts. "I told them things were changing, and instead it'll just be worse. Sentries get hardly any time off, even in summer. It'll be the same old,

'Sorry, Ma, I can't come after all.' 'Sorry, Ma, I meant to call, but work got in the way.' All I do is disappoint her, all the time."

"So what? That's what mothers are for."

"The point is," she says, gritting her teeth at his weak joke, "it was supposed to be finished. I wanted to go back to school—make up for everything—" The words catch on themselves, and she digs her fingernails into her palms hard. "I thought I could finally show them I'm not—a *fake*."

He leans forward, elbows on his knees. "Their whole world is a fake, you want to talk that way. You're the one living in reality. You're the one protecting them from it, actually, especially now. Did you think of that?"

"Fuck it," she snaps. "Just forget it."

She stares hard across the floor, clenched around herself like a fist. It's dusty. There's a can under the couch. She's got a wicked headache coming on. It's all too much, and every time there's a moment where she thinks she can sort it out, instead it's like she's getting slowly crushed under a ton of concrete.

She hears him mutter in discomfort as he gets up. He drags an ottoman over, sits down in front of her. He leans forward, pushes her hair out of her face, tucks it behind her ear. She shakes her head a little, and the hair falls back over her eyes.

He says, "You need to pull yourself together. You need to think about your mother."

Ain't no serv ever had a ma, the words float up from the past. She tightens her arms around her knees. She watches through her hair his fingers lightly drumming his leg as he waits. There's the smell of his sweaty robe and dried blood and the noise of his labored breathing, likely due to the ribs Sina cracked. And now Sina's gone, and so much has happened, and here she is huddled up under Bedrosian's stare.

She peeks up, and the pity in his sad-dog eyes makes her want to cry, and that makes her want to smack him. She straightens a little, tucks her fists between her knees. "Fine," she says.

"O.K.," he says slowly, waiting for more.

"I need a better story. I don't want them thinking all that stuff anymore."

He shrugs assent. "That's no problem."

"And you have to be the one to tell them, in person, so they can't possibly think I'm making it up."

"Don't worry. I'm a very good liar, better than you, even."

She rolls her eyes. "You're sure you did the loan? Because I don't get paid much, I don't think."

He lifts his hands, as in, enough already. "I did the loan." There is a pause.

"Come on, get up," he reaches out and gives her knee a shake. "And be nice. You can kill me with your pinkie now."

This is somewhat true. She manages a small smile. "Don't you forget it."

"I'll take a shower, then we go," he says.

HE PUSHES OPEN THE glass entrance doors, steps aside to let her out. It's dusk, and the ice in the trees glitters like crystals in the failing light. She still has the ampule in her pocket, she realizes as they walk around to the car. She can't feel it there, it's so tiny, but she's aware of its presence in the darkness of her pocket, that near invisible point of light.

They buckle and he switches on the engine, flooding the cabin with noise and the faint scent of gas. The radio's on a news station, low murmur of voices. She props herself up a little to dig around in her pocket. Carefully withdraws the ampule and unfolds her hand over the console, so he can see.

"I found it at Eden," she whispers. "It's part of a grab."

His eyes lift to meet hers. In them she sees the biggest sadness, like all the world is coming apart. "What're you going to do with it?" he says.

Lucy's fingers slowly close back around the ampule. She leans back. The slice of fire within now burning a hole, it feels like, right through her flesh and bone. She stares out the window at the darkening street. "Maybe sometime, during a Service, if there's someone who needs it," she says.

"There's always someone."

"Yes," she agrees.

He reverses out of the driveway. The car rolls down the hill, the city a splendid silhouette against the orange sky. Lucy turns up the radio a little. It's going to snow again tonight, with more expected on the coast. It's good she'll be home to shovel. Lucy carefully places the ampule in the empty cup holder, drawing a worried glance from Bedrosian, but it merely rolls around a little. She flips open her barely charged phone and dials Eva, leans back and closes her eyes. She counts the rings, imagining Eva getting up from her chair and making her way down the hall to the telephone stand, the cats rushing around her ankles as she walks.